THE
SPECTER
IS BORN

THE
SPECTER
IS BORN

A.J. SMELTZER

NEXT CENTURY
PUBLISHING

Specter is Born

Published by Rebel Press
Austin, TX
www.RebelPress.com

ISBN: 978-1-68102-390-8

Printed in the United States of America

CONTENTS

THE
SPECTER
IS BORN

CHAPTER 1

Monday, July 20

"Ah, yes, my dear." Dr. Jacobs squinted a bit and moved very close to the name tag just above the waitress's left breast. "Forgive an old man with failing eyes … Gladys."

"Somehow I don't think your eyes are failing quite that much," she responded, smiling. "What can I get for you?"

Dr. Jacobs finally pulled his face back from her breasts, but that smile never wavered in the slightest. "This is a pub, so let us start with a good dark ale. Something with as full a body as … say you, perhaps?"

Gladys shifted the menu to her right hand and held out her left. "You're cute, but I'm married. One dark ale, coming up."

It was then that he noticed a woman standing just inside the entrance watching him intently with a broad grin on her face. She was absolutely gorgeous, and his jaw dropped a bit when their gazes met. Her eyes were deep and dark—smoky would be a more apt description—and tearing his eyes away from hers would have been nearly impossible were it not for her taut, fit physique. After he scanned her up and down, he met her gaze once again and was transfixed. He reached up before Gladys left the table and caught her gently by the wrist.

After stammering for a moment he finally managed to say, "Hold on just a moment, my dear. I believe the young lady I'm here to meet has just arrived. Can you play something sultry and seductive on the jukebox for me? I'll need all the ambiance this place has to offer if I'm to have any chance with this one."

Gladys turned and caught sight of the woman watching them, and even her pulse quickened a bit at how simply captivating she was. After a few moments and a deep breath, she motioned to the empty chair and asked, "Are you here to meet with this, um, gentleman?"

Dr. Stacey Poole nodded while still maintaining that grin. As she approached the table, she wagged her finger disapprovingly toward Dr. Jacobs. "You're not giving this nice young woman grief, are you, Dr. Jacobs? You should be ashamed of yourself." She then slid out the chair opposite him and sat with the grace of a ballerina.

With his mouth still agape, he nodded slowly for a second before realizing how he must look. Quickly he pulled his hand away from the waitress's wrist and shook his head vehemently. "Of course not! I was just being friendly. And may I say you are far more stunning than that old bastard Professor Hadley described. Dr. Poole, I presume?"

With that, he flashed what he believed was his most handsome smile and extended his hand across the table. Dr. Poole, still with that same grin on her face, gently shook his hand and then, for the first time since he noticed her, she released him from her gaze as she spoke to Gladys.

"Good afternoon, miss. May I have a cup of green tea please?"

Gladys pulled a rolled napkin that contained silverware from her apron and leaned close to Dr. Poole as she set it down. Adopting a conspiratorial whisper, but still speaking loudly enough to make it clear she wanted him to hear her, she said, "Be careful with this one; he's quite the charmer."

Dr. Poole shifted her smoky gaze back to Dr. Jacobs and nodded. "Yes, so I see. Perhaps he forgets that he's nearly old enough to be our grandfather. Dementia does tend to show the first signs of onset at about his age."

Gladys giggled quietly and promised, "I'll be right back with your drinks."

After several seconds of silence, Dr. Poole raised her eyebrows slightly and said, "Please let me know when you're done undressing me with your eyes. I have a fairly busy afternoon planned."

Dr. Jacobs blinked quickly a few times and said, "Forgive an old man, but I wasn't always this old, and while the fire needs to be kindled with a little more vigor now, it does still burn. You must be used to reactions such as this from men. After all, with beauty such as yours, even gay men would be forced to reevaluate their sexual nature. So would straight women, for that matter."

Dr. Poole had dealt with similar situations and discussions all of her adult life and most of her adolescent life as well.

"I thank you for such a compliment, Dr. Jacobs. But remember that you accepted my offer to look after your practice for you based solely on my mind … not my looks."

"Quite right you are, Dr. Poole, and I should be ashamed of my blatant chauvinism." He then leaned a bit closer and lowered his voice. "I just found that as I reached my sixties, I'm able to get away with flirtations that would have gotten me slapped twenty years ago. It's very difficult not to take advantage of that."

"I believe Professor Hadley mentioned that twenty years ago you were still married, but I'm not judging, Dr. Jacobs. I'm sure Gladys would agree with me that your obvious flirtations come off as flattering and cute as opposed to creepy. But now that the introductions are done, may we discuss business?"

Dr. Jacobs instantly adopted a more stately posture and demeanor. "Twenty years ago I was an inmate, and that soulless harpy that used to call herself Mrs. Jacobs was draining the life out of me on a daily basis. But you're quite right; let's get down to business. As we covered by correspondence and phone, I'll be on sabbatical for the next year. You'll be taking over my clientele and managing my therapists. I left a folder on my desk outlining some of the basics on how I run my business. Consider them guidelines; by no means should you feel obligated to operate exactly as I do. I read your doctoral thesis, and some of the concepts that you laid out are very intriguing, to say the least. I found it to be worthy of the word *revolutionary*, in fact—and I'm aware of others who share that opinion. You're going to make great strides in the psychological field, and I'm honored that you'll be getting your start with that in my practice."

"Thank you, doctor. Most of what's contained in my thesis is really little more than refining and tweaking many of the existing techniques. *Revolutionary* may be quite a stretch, but I'm flattered nonetheless."

"Oh, I must disagree! The concepts that you defined concerning criminal psychology were …"

Just then Gladys returned with the drinks, "Is there anything else I can do for you?"

Dr. Jacobs instantly flashed that flirty smile and said, "Well, now that you mention it …"

"Dr. Jacobs, please stay on point," Dr. Poole interjected. "I'm sure you'll have plenty of time after our business meeting to get turned down by our lovely waitress."

Dr. Jacobs scowled slightly and mumbled, "There's nothing wrong with a healthy libido … especially at my age."

"Thank you, Gladys, I think we're all set for now. Before I leave, I'll give you my number. If this letch hassles you further, just call me. I'm trained in martial arts." Gladys laughed and nodded as she left the table.

"You probably are, aren't you?" Dr. Jacobs asked with sincerity.

As Dr. Poole finished a sip of her tea and set the cup back onto its saucer, she nodded. "I was a full black belt in both Muay Thai and Brazilian Jujitsu by the age of seventeen."

"You were also more than halfway to your first college degree by the age of seventeen, but that does explain the athletic physique. Brains and body ... I bet you put more than a few college boys in their place, didn't you?"

Dr. Poole let a mischievous grin touch her lips for a moment before saying, "Back to business now?"

Dr. Jacobs sighed and continued, "Essentially, everything you need to know is in that folder on my ... I suppose it's your desk now. Just a couple of things I need to go over before you get there. My staff are the therapists, and we're the psychiatrists. With that said, it's actually Rebecca that runs things. She's my receptionist, but she keeps everyone in line and handles all of the appointments and scheduling. Without her, that place would have folded years ago. Any questions I failed to cover, she'll either have the answer for you or she'll be able to get the answer for you.

"The therapists are all quite good. I'm hoping that some of them continue their education and become psychiatrists, themselves. I'm told that you'll be meeting them all today after their sessions. I believe Rebecca mentioned a four o'clock meeting? Anyway, I have six therapists and, as I told you, they're all top-notch. The one you'll have the most challenging time with will be Quinton, or Quinn, as he prefers to be called. If you think I'm a letch, wait until you meet him."

Dr. Jacobs pulled a heavy key ring from his jacket pocket and slid the keys across the table. "Those open every door, cabinet and desk in the building. Should you lose them, Rebecca can have the locksmith called in and all of the locks changed on everything in less than twenty-four hours."

As Dr. Poole slid the keys into her clutch she raised her eyebrows. "Does this mean that you've lost your keys before?"

Dr. Jacobs nodded, "Three times. Each time I heard about it from Rebecca for at least a month before she let it drop. Actually, aside from the clients' files, there really isn't much of value in the entire building. We don't keep any meds on site, and all of our clients are billed for their time, so payments are neither required nor accepted at the front desk. The best advice I can give you is to carry only three keys on you and leave the rest in the desk in the office. You'll need the employee entrance key, the office key and the key to the desk. They're all marked."

"You said Rebecca can answer any questions I may have. Does that mean you'll be unreachable while on sabbatical?"

"I'm afraid it does. Hadley and I will be off the grid."

"You know, the professor was quite evasive about this sabbatical when I asked him what you two were going to be doing. You're not going to do something that'll get you jailed, are you?"

Dr. Jacobs thought about it for a moment then flashed a boyish grin as he replied, "Actually, I can't state for certainty that anything I may or may not do will be completely legal. What I can say is that neither the destination nor the goal of our sabbatical will be cause for law enforcement to stuff us in a cage. Any extracurricular activity, however … I suppose that depends on the laws of the lands we'll be traveling in and just how attractive the women are."

"So you're going to be evasive as well? Come on, what could be so clandestine about two elderly gentlemen on sabbatical?"

"Elderly? Careful, little missy. Martial arts or no, I can still drag you across my knee for a good paddling. That's how we dealt with youthful impertinence back in the day, you know. None of this coddling nonsense that's so popular today. Besides, despite both of us being in our mid-sixties, neither of us is what I'd call fragile. And though individually neither of us can match your incredible IQ, we're not idiots, either. We can take care of ourselves. As for why Hadley was evasive, I'm sure it would be frowned upon by the University of Michigan if word got out that one of their prestigious professors was off on an alien hunt."

A genuine look of shock captured Dr. Poole's face. "An alien hunt? You mean … actual aliens? The kind from outer space?"

"Well, we won't actually be hunting the aliens themselves. At least not in the flesh. Or, not in whatever passes for alien flesh. Perhaps I should begin at the beginning."

Dr. Poole nodded slowly. "Yes, perhaps you should."

"Without droning on in detail, I'll cover the highlights of our upcoming trip. We're off to Mali, West Africa where we'll be studying the Dogon people. They're believed to be of Egyptian descent, and their lore dates back to approximately 3200 B.C. Back in the '30s, a couple of anthropologists began studying this tribe and eventually published the findings of their time with the Dogon. Most of it is, as you'd expect when reading a study of primitive tribesmen, except for the creation story of the Dogon. Their lore stated that the star we today call Sirius A is accompanied by a smaller companion star. Of course, at that time the technology didn't exist to be able to verify whether this star existed or not. It wasn't until the early '70s that scientists actually did verify that, indeed, Sirius did have a companion star. We call it Sirius B now. The Dogon gave details concerning the orbital path and density of this star, but suffice it to say that what the anthropologists published later turned out to be quite accurate."

"Alright, you have my full attention now. How did a primitive West African tribe have information about a star that modern science didn't know existed? Actually … never mind that. When it was discovered by modern science and verified that the Dogon lore was accurate, the scientific community should have exploded with further studies. Why is it that I never heard of any of this before?"

"Your course of study has been in the fields of medicine and psychology. It isn't surprising at all that you've never heard of this before. The Dogon claim that their ancestors received this knowledge directly from the inhabitants of a planet that orbits that star. In short, from alien visitors to earth. So in answer to your question, scientists in the '70s who gave serious credence to alien visitors would have been ostracized; their credibility would have been destroyed. And as you well know, in the world of science, credibility is a valuable commodity. The whole thing was swept aside and tagged as an anomaly. It was considered to be mere coincidence that the Dogon's claims that another star orbited Sirius were validated.

"Anyway, Hadley and I are off to do our own study of the Dogon. Officially it's going to be a psychological study. Unofficially, we're essentially going to be alien hunting. It should be quite the adventure, don't you think?"

"I think I'll be very interested in reading your final publication, but I'll be even more interested in reading your personal notes. Promise that upon your return I'm granted full access?"

"Absolutely. I look forward to your opinion on our study. Hadley's been pushing for this trip for quite some time actually. I just never had the opportunity to tear myself from my practice long enough to make it happen. That is, until now. When Hadley told me that you'd finished your internships and expressed interest in coming to the Colorado area, I jumped at the opportunity that was presented. It's a win-win in my opinion. You get practical experience heading up an established practice, and I get one of the brightest psychiatrists in our field to take over for me so I can go act like I'm young again."

"I'm honored that you're allowing me to head up your practice, doctor. Speaking of which," she glanced down at her watch. "I really should be getting on with it. I'd like to have an hour or so to go over the notes you left before I meet with the therapists." With that, she stood and extended her hand.

Dr. Jacobs remained seated but firmly grasped her hand. "Take good care of my practice while I'm away. Don't forget, you were warned about Quinn. He'll take one look at you and decide it's hunting season and you're the prize buck he'll be hanging on his den wall."

"Thank you for the warning, but as you said earlier … I can handle myself."

"Of that I've no doubt. Now, where is Gladys? My glass is nearing the bottom, and my thirst is not nearly sated. Gladys? I'd like a refill and perhaps a shot of tequila! Better yet, make it a double shot! After all, I'm on sabbatical."

Dr. Poole smiled and shook her head then turned to leave the pub. Dr. Jacobs leered after her until she was out the door. Finally, he muttered to himself, "If only I were thirty years younger."

*****

Dr. Poole followed her GPS navigation unit to the office building she'd be working in for the upcoming year and found the employee parking lot. She carefully scanned and memorized the other vehicles parked there—a game she started playing with herself when she was still a teen. The model, make, year, and possibly most importantly, the condition of one's choice of transport speaks volumes about an individual's personality. She tagged the bright red Porsche as belonging to Quinn. She'd know after meeting him. The late model black Chevy Blazer with oversized tires and lift kit must belong to Rebecca. It's certainly a vehicle that says its owner is in control. The fact that it was over thirty years old yet remarkably maintained helped confirm her conclusion.

After looking at the employee entrance for a few moments, she decided to get her first impression of the building by seeing it as the clientele do. She walked around to the front and pushed open the main doors. The entrance and lobby were all done in quiet earth tones with soft but adequate lighting. Potted plants and plush dark brown leather chairs and sofas occupied the waiting area. The end tables held a wide variety of magazines, but in all it appeared to be quite comfortable and soothing.

As she was taking in the scene, a subdued yet powerful female voice from off to her right asked, "Hello, are you here to set up an appointment?"

Dr. Poole slowly turned to face the voice as she was completing her assessment of the lobby and smiled. "I suppose I might be."

She approached the long, curved counter that served as the reception desk and reached over it to extend her hand. "I'm Dr. Poole; I believe you're expecting me?"

The petite redhead behind the counter beamed broadly and slowly extended her hand so they could shake. "Oh, Dr. Poole! It's an honor to meet you; I've heard a lot about you. I'm Rebecca Mann. You can call me Rebecca. I'm the receptionist. I also make certain that the office supplies are stocked, but my main role in this company is as the babysitter."

"Babysitter? I wasn't aware that Dr. Jacobs accepted children as his clientele."

Rebecca frowned slightly and shook her head. "No, we don't. Watching children would be much easier than making sure our therapists don't get out of hand. Actually, compared to Dr. Jacobs, I suppose even our therapists aren't that bad."

Dr. Poole smiled and leaned closer. "I just left a meeting with Dr. Jacobs. Believe me, I know exactly what you mean. There are no clients waiting to be seen. Is this a slow day?"

"Oh, no; we knew you'd be arriving this afternoon so we have no appointments scheduled after four o'clock. Our last few appointments just went back a few minutes before you arrived. We have a full hour before you meet with the therapists for introductions, and I slated an hour so you can go over any changes to procedure that you'll be making."

"Alright, but I'm the new kid on the block. I won't be making any changes to the way things are done around here. It's still his business, and it'll be run his way while he's gone, so the introductions shouldn't take very long. Maybe they'll be happy to leave a bit early since there won't be any more appointments for the day. Can you show me around a bit?"

"I'd be happy to." She stepped down from the raised platform behind the counter and motioned for Dr. Poole to follow her toward a heavy wooden door. At five foot three, Dr. Poole was considered to be of slightly below average height, but if Rebecca stood even five feet tall it would have been due to thick-soled shoes. With a body weight that wouldn't have approached a hundred pounds even if she were fully clothed and soaking wet, tiny would best describe her stature. Yet she walked with the posture and gait of a drill sergeant about to address the trainees.

As Dr. Poole approached the door she stopped Rebecca and asked, "I don't suppose that black Chevy Blazer in the employee lot belongs to you, does it?"

Rebecca's eyes lit up. "Yes, that's my baby! How did you know? Did Dr. Jacobs make some corny joke about me struggling to reach the pedals or needing a ladder to climb in or something?"

"No, he didn't say anything. It's a little game I play. After looking at all of the vehicles in the employee parking lot, when I meet the employees I try to match them to what they drive. The Blazer just seemed like a good fit for your personality and mannerisms."

"That Blazer is over thirty years old and runs like a dream. Don't get me wrong. I've put a lot of money into keeping her in peak condition. But compared to the pieces of junk they're selling today, what money I spent on her is nothing. Also, it's from a time when people drove cars, not the other way around. I don't want a damn car that talks to me or applies the brakes when I don't want the brakes applied. Cars today are just rolling computers, and I guarantee you, within one generation, nobody will be able to drive worth a shit because of it. They'll expect the car to do everything for them while they just sit behind the wheel trying to look good. Give me a powerful V-8 with four-wheel drive that responds to my touch and get the hell out of my way. That's how I feel, anyway."

"I actually agree with you. I drive a twelve-year-old Subaru Outback. Maybe one of these weekends we'll have to get out of the city and you can show me some of the countryside. I don't have the ground clearance to go where your Blazer can, but as long as we stay out of the really deep stuff, I should be able to keep up."

With a broad smile Rebecca said, "It's a date! There are some beautiful areas not far from here. I'd be happy to take you sometime. Just let me know when you'll be free."

"Alright, just give me a few weeks to get settled in and up to speed."

"You're okay, Dr. Poole. I think we're going to get along just fine." With that, Rebecca opened the heavy wooden door and led Dr. Poole along a hallway.

Rebecca spoke in a hushed tone as she motioned toward the doorways on either side of the hall, "These are the therapy rooms. Your office is upstairs. Follow me, please."

Once they climbed the single flight of steps at the end of the hallway, they came to an open area with a much smaller waiting room. "Your new office is through that door. These seats are for the few cases that Dr. Jacobs personally handles. That door leads to where we keep the office and restroom supplies, so if you run out of staples or paper clips or anything, that's where you restock. Did Dr. Jacobs remember to give you his keys?"

Dr. Poole pulled the keys from her clutch and nodded as she found the one that opened the office door. The office was tastefully decorated, conservative in its style but very roomy. Behind the desk was a picture window that allowed the morning light to shine directly in. There were thick vertical blinds in place to temper the glare of the sun but at this time in the afternoon, the window was on the shaded side of the building. On each side of the window stood large filing cabinets. The wall on the left was entirely covered by a well-stocked bookcase. Most of the books were medical and psychological tomes, but Dr. Poole caught sight of a few shelves that contained works of fiction by popular contemporary authors. A large padded leather sofa and straight-backed chair completed the furnishings. The wall on the right had two doors in it, both bracketed by small potted trees with a water cooler sitting directly in between.

Rebecca was already explaining how harsh the morning sun was while she pulled a file folder off the desk. "Dr. Jacobs left this for you. He had me compile most of it, but there are a few papers in here that he personally left for you. My guess is that they contain information about the handful of clients he personally tends to. The first door leads to a lavatory, and the other leads to the archives where former clientele files are kept. Our current client documents are stored in the filing cabinets here in the office. The computer is one of the latest models and, as you can plainly see, it's one of the few things in this room that's from the twenty-first century. The login information is also in that folder for you."

Dr. Poole accepted the folder and eased herself into Dr. Jacobs' plush office chair.

"If there's nothing else right now, I have a few things I need to tend to before our four o'clock meeting."

"What of security? Should a client become agitated, how is that handled here?"

"There's a panic button just under the edge of the desk directly in front of you that sends a signal to my counter as well as to my cell phone. Then I come up here and determine whether police or an ambulance is required. To be honest, our clientele are carefully screened and pretty tame. Dr. Jacobs has used that buzzer only once due to a female client who had mixed some unauthorized medications and was having a reaction to them. The ambulance was summoned and she was off to the ER within ten minutes. As for the security in the building, there's a standard alarm with a keypad at the employee entrance as well as a second keypad over here by the door. The doors and windows are hardwired, and there are motion sensors placed in the hallways. If you're working late at night, you can set the alarm to disregard the motion sensors so you can move freely about the building while still keeping the doors and windows active. Those codes are also in that folder."

"Well, Rebecca, I believe that about covers it then. I'll review the folder and start to get myself acquainted with the client files.

When it comes time to meet with the therapists, will you come get me please?"

"Of course. We have a small break room off the main hall downstairs. That's where we'll gather. Would you like to be there as the therapists come in or do you want to make an entrance?"

After a moment she smiled and said, "I have been warned by Dr. Jacobs about Quinn, so I think I'd like to be there as they file in. I'd like to see how they walk, how they carry themselves, how they choose where they'll sit. It'll give great insight into each one's personality. They're probably not used to dealing with a psychiatrist that's so young, so if I can gauge their reactions individually as they see me, that'll also help."

"Dr. Poole, nobody is used to dealing with a psychiatrist as young as you are, and Dr. Jacobs was most definitely *not* exaggerating about Quinn. Even after I nearly dislocated one of his fingers, he still hits on me incessantly. He's worse than a dog in heat. As beautiful as you are, you're going to have your hands full with him. If you'd like, I can issue a few stern warnings concerning his behavior before he gets to this meeting."

"No, I'd like an unadulterated reaction from them all. If I'm going to be making determinations of clients' medications and courses of treatment based on the notes of their sessions, I need to learn what makes each of them tick."

"Yeah, I think we're going to get along just fine, Dr. Poole. I'll come get you a few minutes before the meeting."

She had reviewed the information left by Rebecca and Dr. Jacobs and had already gone through three of the client files when there was a knock on the office door.

"Yes?"

The door opened a crack and Rebecca peeked inside. "The children will be done with their sessions in five minutes; are you ready?"

Dr. Poole returned the file she was reviewing back to the cabinet and moved around to the front of the desk. After smoothing out her form-hugging dress slacks and adjusting her blouse she asked, "How do I look?"

Rebecca smiled and replied, "Like a fashion model for business weekly. Let's go."

Rebecca had moved the chairs and tables in the break room so that they all faced the back wall directly opposite the sink, counter and refrigerator. Dr. Poole positioned herself in a relaxed stance, leaning against the wall with her legs crossed and her hands loosely clasped in front of her. She then nodded to Rebecca who made her rounds to gather the therapists.

As they filed in, Dr. Poole made a quick study of each facial expression and the body language they displayed as they chose their seats. The last one in through the door caught sight of her and froze in his tracks.

"Oh, my God, I'm in love," he said as he stood staring at her.

The other five therapists rolled their eyes and a few made comments like, "grow up" or "shut up and sit down."

Dr. Poole showed absolutely no reaction to the comments and gave them all time to choose their seats and get settled. As expected, Rebecca remained standing by the door, behind the therapists. She stood with her arms folded, eyes scanning back and forth as though she were a mother waiting for her children to become unruly.

Once everyone was in place and quiet, Dr. Poole made a point of silently making eye contact with every therapist individually. She noted the posture of each and how each was dressed as well as the level of makeup the two female therapists wore and the way all of them had their hair done. For the therapists, this few moments of silence was taken as an indication of the changing of the guard. Out with the old, in with the new. Dr. Poole hadn't meant for it to be taken this way, however. She was just sizing up who she'd be working with and forming mental profiles of each one's personality.

When she was done she pulled herself up from her relaxed stance against the wall and unclasped her hands. "As you're already aware, I'm Dr. Stacey Poole and for the next year I'll be taking over for Dr. Jacobs. I'm not going to be making any changes to the way anything is done here so as far as you're all concerned, this practice will continue as though Dr. Jacobs were still the one sitting at his desk. Do any of you have any questions or concerns for me before we continue?"

"Yes," an attractive black woman leaned forward slightly as she spoke. "How old are you, if you don't mind me asking?"

Dr. Poole was careful to keep her face expressionless as she responded. "I just turned thirty-one last month. Are you concerned that my age may hinder my ability to properly do my job?"

"No! Not at all. We ... well, most of us I'm sure, have heard of you and knew that you'd completed your studies at an early age. I was just curious, that's all."

"I don't know if I consider it flattering or scary that my reputation is preceding me here. If it's any consolation, I could have completed my internships two years ago and become a licensed psychiatrist at that time but there were still a few courses of study only loosely related to the psychological field that I wanted to complete first. I wanted to be in my thirties before becoming a practicing psychiatrist simply due to the fact that I was afraid I wouldn't be taken seriously if I were still in my twenties. I suppose this is as good a time as any to offer you my resume, as it were. I'm a fully licensed medical doctor and I hold Ph.D.'s in Criminal and Clinical Psychology as well as Master's Degree in Criminology, anthropology and forensics. If any of you have any concerns about my qualifications, now would be the time to bring them up."

The faces that she scanned plainly showed how impressed they were by her list of degrees, and nobody raised any concerns.

"Does anyone else have any questions about my education or background?"

At the back of the small gathering, one man had leaned back in his chair with his legs stretched out in front of him and crossed at the ankles in a completely relaxed pose. "I have a question, if you don't mind."

She knew this had to be Quinn, the same one that made the comment about being in love when he entered the room. Still careful about maintaining a completely neutral expression, she nodded and asked, "Yes?"

"I'm aware that you're new to the Denver area and was wondering if you'd accompany me this evening for dinner, drinks and a tour of our lovely city."

She waited just long enough to see the reactions of the other therapists before responding. Again, there were eye rolls and shaking heads but no one spoke.

"Would you mind standing up for me, please?"

The man smiled and casually rose to his feet.

"Would you slowly turn around for me, please?"

He did as he was asked and when he was once again facing her he stopped. That confident smile held firm on his lips.

She took a few steps to get closer to him and when she was only a couple of feet away she stopped and took the time to slowly scan his physical form from head to foot. He had to have been in his late thirties. He was dressed in a tan sports jacket, white dress shirt with dark brown slacks and dress shoes. His tie was patterned and contained conservative hues of yellow and black. He was definitely handsome, and he knew it.

She reached up and adjusted his tie slightly as she slowly began to speak. "Now, what would the blonde whose bed you woke up in this morning say if she knew you were hitting on me right now?"

His confident smile disappeared. "What? How could you ... ?"

She slid her hand from his tie to his sports jacket and plucked a strand of long blonde hair. As she held it up she explained, "This is how I knew she was blonde. As for the part about waking up in her bed, you still have a lingering scent of lavender in your hair. Not what I'd consider a normal shampoo for one who is as obviously manly as you are. Your shirt and tie have fold creases in them meaning that you didn't get them from a closet, but more likely from an overnight bag. One I'm guessing you keep in your bright shiny red Porsche for those times when you happen to find some bimbo that has a bra cup size that more than likely matched her high school grades. I could continue, but I see from the expression on your face that won't be necessary. No, I'll pass on your very gracious offer because I really don't think I'm your type. But thank you all the same."

As she returned back to her position in front of the therapists and turned to face them, they were all grinning from ear to ear, none more broadly than Rebecca. She gave them all a moment to enjoy the minor level of shame she'd just inflicted on Quinn before speaking.

"Now, all of you know my name and apparently have a fair amount of information about me. I'd like to get to know all of you a bit better."

She then quickly looked at Quinn who had just sat back down before adding, "In a purely professional manner, of course."

She chose the attractive black woman who asked her age earlier and said, "Let's start with you. Your name's Regina, I believe. You're the one that drives that blue Dodge Dart, right?"

Regina nodded and opened her mouth to ask how she knew, but then closed it again and simply acknowledged, "You're good."

"Thank you," she then looked at the pudgy gentleman in his fifties sitting across the aisle from Regina. "You must be Anthony … do you prefer to be called Anthony or Tony?"

"Tony, if it's all the same to you, ma'am."

"Very well, Tony. The first thing you should know is while at work I prefer to be called Dr. Poole or simply Doctor. Never call me ma'am. Second, I would have to say that white Equinox is yours, right?"

Tony raised his eyebrows and nodded. "It is; I chose it because it had enough room for the grandkids and still got decent mileage."

On it went until she got back to Quinn. When she looked at him, she smiled. He had remained silent after their initial encounter and his swagger was definitely gone. He was no longer sitting with his legs relaxed in front of him. Instead, he was sitting upright and paying attention to what she was saying as opposed to how her hips moved when she walked. The confident smile was gone as well. In its place was an expression of admiration.

"I'd like to apologize to you, Quinn. What I did wasn't exactly considered fair play. I met with Dr. Jacobs before arriving here today, and he gave me warnings about you, specifically. I was just trying to get you to see me as a fellow professional that you could work with as opposed to a piece of ass to be conquered. No hard feelings?"

Quinn lifted his chin slightly and just the hint of a smile returned to his lips. "Mission accomplished and message received. I was out of line, and you put me back in my place with style."

He then looked down toward the floor for a moment before looking back up at her. "I'll probably still hit on you though. It's just in my nature. Eagles got to fly, fish got to swim and I just got to be me. Don't take it the wrong way when it happens, okay?"

She nodded and replied, "Understood. But don't you take it the wrong way the next time I'm forced to set you straight again, okay?"

"Deal…now, about that dinner."

Dr. Poole cut him off immediately. "On that note, unless someone has something else, I think this meeting is over. Since it's a Monday, you guys get out of here early and enjoy the rest of your evening off. I'll see you tomorrow. I look forward to the time I'll be working with you. I think it's going to be a very good year."

In turn, each of them approached her and shook her hand and welcomed her. Even Quinn displayed professionalism, though his eyes did tend to wander from her eyes to her body and then back again.

When Rebecca was the only one left in the room, Stacey approached her and asked, "Do you think that went alright?"

"I think you did great. Now, I know you shot down Quinn's offer of dinner, but if you'd like to grab a bite to eat, I know the best places in town."

"I appreciate the offer, but I'll be here late going over the files. I have a lot to do before I can get comfortable here."

"Then you should try the takeout place just up the road. They have incredible grinders. When I leave, I'll lock up and set the alarm for the windows and doors only. Don't forget to reset it to full protection when you leave later."

"Thank you again. Dr. Jacobs said you kept things running here. I'll be leaning on you a great deal over the next year. Have a good night, Rebecca."

Once back in her new office, she pulled out a stack of files and flipped open the first one. "Now for the homework."

CHAPTER 2

———•———

Thursday, July 23

"Alright everyone, look sharp! King Midas is entering the crime scene."

"Billings, I told you to stop calling me that."

"Yes, sir, sorry, sir."

"Is the ME done with his initial examination?"

"Yes, sir, the assistant took some photos while the ME checked the body. Forensics is enroute, and they'll begin bagging and tagging the physical evidence as soon as you've had your look around. The victim is in the sitting room right through there."

Michael Cassidy took another sip of his coffee and rubbed his eyes. He then turned to his partner and asked, "It's 7:30 in the morning. How come dead bodies are only found very early in the morning or very late at night? Why can't someone find a corpse at two in the afternoon?"

"I don't know … quite inconsiderate if you ask me. Hey, I know! When the media gets here I'll have them broadcast to the city that from now on, any reports of dead bodies are to be made only between noon and five on weekdays."

As Cassidy yawned he shook his head. "It's far too early to be a smart ass. I don't know why the captain partnered me with you. I hate morning people; you all piss me off."

Jeremy pulled out his notepad and flipped it open. He took a pen from his breast pocket and scanned down the sheet for a moment before making a check mark. As he did this he muttered, "Piss off Cassidy. Alright, first order of business for the day is complete."

Cassidy sighed then turned back to the uniformed officer that he spoke with when he first arrived. "Who found the body? Was it someone else that lived here?"

Officer Billings pulled out his own notebook and flipped a couple of pages. "No, Susan Monroe discovered the body … employed by the deceased as a housekeeper. She works Mondays and Thursdays and generally arrives between six and seven a.m. She told us that when she got here the door was unlocked, which was unusual. When she looked into the sitting room and saw the blood, she stopped and didn't enter. She could make out the slumped form of a person sitting in the chair facing away from her and immediately went out to the porch and called 911 from her cell phone. Nobody entered the room until we arrived. I was the first one in the room. I made a cursory visual inspection while my partner cleared the house. Then we called the medical examiner and sent for you two."

"Good, at least she didn't touch anything in the room. Other than you and the ME, who else entered the room?"

"Just the ME's assistant. They determined the time of death and a preliminary cause of death, then they went back out to the van to wait for you to arrive."

"So we're going to be looking at a nearly pristine crime scene?"

"Yes, sir. I have officers knocking on the neighbors' doors right now; by the time you're done in there, we should start getting reports back about any disturbance they might have heard last night. According to the ME, the vic was murdered at 6:03 yesterday evening."

Both Jeremy and Michael raised their eyebrows and looked at Officer Billings in obvious surprise.

Billings smiled as he continued, "There's an open-faced clock on the stand next to the chair. The blood spray from the head wound was fairly even across the face of the clock, except where the hands were. That indicates that the killing blow was struck at 6:03, and since they determined she'd been dead for approximately twelve hours, that leaves us with an exact time of death."

The detectives looked back and forth at each other then back to Officer Billings before Jeremy Kidd spoke. "Just a few things before we go in there. First, she was a human being and deserves enough respect to be called a victim instead of a vic. Second, good job securing the crime scene and making sure we arrived long before the media. Third, what's the ID on the *victim*?"

Billings flushed slightly as he flipped a few pages in his notebook. "Sorry about that. The victim is one Sarah Connelly. She was the widow of the late Senator Connelly."

"Ah, shit!" both detectives muttered in unison.

"Thanks, Billings; let us know when your men get back from canvassing the neighbors. Is Ms. Monroe still around here somewhere?"

"She's outside with another officer."

"Have her wait; when we're done in here, we'd like to talk to her."

With the obvious professional portion of this conversation over, Billings poked his head out the front door and got the attention of the officer that was babysitting Ms. Monroe. "Butch and Sundance want to talk to her in a bit, so make her comfortable."

Both Michael Cassidy and Jeremy Kidd shook their heads and sighed but said nothing. What could they say? The coincidence of their last names was nothing they could argue with. They were convinced that their captain partnered them up together just because he had a warped sense of humor.

They moved to the open archway that separated the sitting room from the rest of the house. They could see the back of the chair that contained the body of the victim. It was slightly angled toward a massive brick fireplace. To the left of the chair was the side table that held the open-faced clock. There was also a linen napkin with a used tea bag on the table as well as a paperback novel. Across from the chair was a low coffee table that held a couple of magazines and a small flower arrangement. On the other side of the coffee table was a loveseat upholstered to match the chair.

They each reached into the bag Detective Kidd was carrying and pulled out plastic shoe covers. After slipping them over their dress shoes, they donned latex gloves. Once inside the room, they noticed a five iron lying on the carpeted floor off to the left, and noted that the end of it was heavily covered in dried blood.

The ceiling lights were on in spite of the fact that the morning sun was shining directly through the four by eight window on the wall behind the loveseat. Jeremy turned a bit to talk over his shoulder. "Billings, did any of you turn on this light or was it that way when Ms. Monroe arrived?"

"None of us turned on the light, I'll have to check with the cleaning lady to see if she did."

"Never mind, we'll cover that when we question her." He jotted a reminder into his notepad.

Billings called back into the room, "By the way, the forensic guys are here."

From outside the open front door they heard a woman yell, "Forensic team, you male chauvinist. We're not all guys."

Cassidy yelled out, "Can you give us just a few minutes, Robin? We'll be out of your way in a bit."

The same female voice yelled back, "Take your time, we're still getting our equipment together."

They skirted the majority of the blood splatter and moved to get a better look at Mrs. Connelly. As they did this they began quietly talking. Some of it was to each other; some of it was for their own benefit. The whole time, they were furiously jotting down notes in their own respective notepads.

"Five iron, likely murder weapon," one said as he wrote. "Oh, and left-handed at that."

"Saucer in lap near left hand, teacup on floor near dark stain on carpet … "

"Apparel … tan house slippers, brown slacks, beige buttoned blouse … "

"Cassidy, take a look at this. Tell me if you see something wrong with this blouse."

Cassidy edged in next to Kidd then moved closer to the victim. "It looks like it's buttoned wrong."

Detective Kidd used his ink pen to move the collar of the blouse slightly. "That's what I thought. Yep, this button is in the wrong hole." As he continued to open the collar further he said, "No bra."

"The slacks don't look to have been disturbed," Cassidy offered. "If there was a sexual fetish involved in this, it has to be one I don't know about yet."

Kidd smiled and retorted, "*Yet* being the operative word there."

Both of them made notes and moved about the room, but there really wasn't much else that caught their attention. The blood splatter looked like it matched the wound, though forensics would verify or counter that later. The only visible wound was a single blow to the left side of her head that caused a large skull fracture, presumably the cause of death. Also, the blood spray that landed on the face of the clock clearly indicated that the hands were set at 6:03 when the blow was delivered. They had rarely seen a crime scene that so definitely told them exactly what happened and when. All they had to do now was figure out who and why. The only curious anomaly was the blouse being improperly buttoned. Even the fact that she wasn't wearing a bra could be seen as potentially common behavior by the victim. It was early evening; she had on house slippers and was drinking a cup of tea. She could have taken off the bra earlier before settling down for the evening.

After a few more minutes of looking, they both left the sitting room and went back to the front door. Cassidy asked, "Monroe or rest of the house?"

Kidd glanced out at Ms. Monroe for a moment and said, "I'll question her; you do the walk-through."

For the first time that morning, Cassidy smiled. "It wouldn't be because she's in her late twenties and attractive, would it?"

"Well, you are a married man. I'm just looking out for the sanctity of that marriage, my friend."

"My wife thanks you for that, I'm sure."

With that, Cassidy made his way past Billings to go check out the rest of the house while Kidd went outside to question Ms. Monroe.

"Hello, Ms. Monroe. My name's Detective Kidd. I need to ask you a few questions but don't worry, it's just routine and shouldn't take very long at all."

"Sue, please call me Sue." She was obviously somewhat shaken, but no more than anyone would expect after finding their employer bludgeoned to death.

"What time did you arrive?"

"I got here about 6:15. I start anytime between 6:00 and 7:00 a.m."

"Isn't that a little early for housecleaning?"

"Mrs. Connelly was an early riser. Sometimes she was already at the gym before I'd get here."

"The officer said that the front door was unlocked when you arrived today."

"Yes, and even when Mrs. Connelly was home, the door was locked. I'd never arrived and seen it unlocked before today. Also, the alarm was off, so I knew she was home. That's the only time it's ever off."

"How long have you been working for Mrs. Connelly?"

"Three years now. I have a few people that I clean for, and Mrs. Connelly was my Monday and Thursday morning customer. I'd come in and clean what needed to be cleaned and was generally done by noon. By one o'clock I'd already be at the house of my afternoon customer. Cleaning here was easy because Mrs. Connelly was a very tidy lady."

"You didn't go anywhere else in the house once you noticed the body?"

"No, straight back to the porch to call 911."

"Would you be able to tell me if something in the house were out of place?"

"Of course. As I said, Mrs. Connelly was a very tidy lady."

Kidd led Ms. Monroe back into the house and used his body to shield her from the crime scene. "You don't have to spend a lot of time here, but if you could just look into each room and let me know if anything seems out of place? Also, was that light on when you arrived?"

"Yes, it was. Is that important?"

"It's a murder investigation, Sue. Everything is important."

She nodded and began leading him through the house. Eventually, they caught up with Cassidy who was standing in the doorway to the main bathroom scratching his head.

"Ms. Monroe, this is Detective Cassidy and that's his perplexed look."

"Pleased to meet you, Detective Cassidy; call me Sue."

Cassidy just grunted and nodded before asking, "Does anyone else live here?"

"No, since her husband died, it's just been Mrs. Connelly. She had a boyfriend for a while but they broke up last year. I'm not sure if she'd started seeing anyone else recently."

Kidd turned to Ms. Monroe and asked, "Can you give me the name of the ex?"

Sue thought about it for a moment and offered haltingly, "Richard … Rick, maybe. I think his last name was Blake."

After Kidd jotted down the name he stared at Cassidy until he finally asked, "What's up?"

"The toilet seat. That's literally what's up. If it's only a woman that lives here, why would the toilet seat be up?"

Ms. Monroe said, "Yesterday was golf day for Mrs. Connelly and her son. After golf they'd come back here. Whichever one drove, the other would leave their car here. Maybe he used the toilet. He does tend to drink a bit at the clubhouse after they play. At least that's what Mrs. Connelly would tell me, anyway."

Cassidy nodded and asked, "Can you tell me her son's name and where we might find him?"

"Oh, he couldn't have done this. Sure, he's spoiled rotten and he'd been sponging off her for years, but he's harmless. He'd never be able to do anything like … well, like that."

Never one for being politically correct, Cassidy said, "The last person known to see her alive and also a leech? Yes, we definitely need to have a little chat with him."

Ms. Monroe raised her eyebrows at the same time as Detective Kidd closed his eyes and shook his head. Cassidy ignored both of them. "Name and address, please?"

Ms. Monroe sighed and replied, "Dean Connelly. I'll have to look up his address in Mrs. Connelly's address book."

Once the detectives had the address they made their way back to their car while comparing notes. Nothing else in the house seemed out of place. There was a freshly rinsed rocks glass sitting in the kitchen drainer which indicated that someone else was in the house that the victim knew well … at least well enough to have a drink with. They found jewelry left untouched in her room and a locked safe. They'd have to have someone come down to open the safe, but they didn't expect to find anything missing from that either. Generally, if someone were going to rob a safe after committing murder, they wouldn't take the time to close it again. The only other items of interest in the house were the two sets of golf clubs. A set that appeared to belong to a woman was found in the garage, and a man's set of left-handed clubs was found in a back bedroom. That set was missing its five iron.

One of the uniformed officers called out to them while they were catching up with each other concerning the details of the case and said, "Detectives, nobody heard any arguing yesterday evening around the time of the murder. Not surprising given the neighborhood. The houses aren't exactly on top of each other. But we did talk to someone who heard tires squealing and saw the victim's son speeding away from the house. The person wasn't certain of the exact time but said it had to be somewhere close to 6:00 p.m."

"Did the witness say he actually saw Dean Connelly or did he just see his car?"

"According to the witness, Connelly drives a two-year-old Ford Mustang convertible that he got for his twenty-first birthday. It was his car, and he was driving. The top was down, and the witness got a clear look as he sped by."

*****

A thin, dark-haired man raced up the road on a mountain bike. As he neared the crime scene tape barrier, he hit the brakes hard and put down the kickstand. He was breathing heavily and sweating profusely as he moved right up to the yellow tape. There were five others standing near the tape talking with each other.

One of the women standing there addressed the young man as he approached the tape, "Did you know Mrs. Connelly?"

The young man glanced at her as he pulled out a digital camera. Between panting breaths he asked, "No. Is that who the victim is?"

The woman nodded. "I'm one of her neighbors. My name's Tabatha Andrews." She reached out a hand to the young man.

He smiled broadly and introduced himself as he shook her hand, "Travis Parker. Very pleased to meet you."

"I don't recognize you from the neighborhood. Do you live around here?"

"No. Well, sort of. I live several blocks away right now. I'm staying with a friend of mine and helping him remodel his home. Next month I'll be going back to campus to live in the dorms. I attend Denver University."

She appeared quite interested and asked, "What do you study there?"

"I'm studying law. I hope to be an attorney someday. That's part of the reason I'm here. I heard on the police scanner about the homicide and really had to rush to get down here. Getting to witness an actual crime scene investigation firsthand is quite rare. Especially one that Butch and Sundance are investigating."

"Butch and Sundance?"

He pointed to where the two detectives were speaking with a uniformed officer as he answered, "Those two. Of course Butch and Sundance aren't their real names. Their real names are Michael Cassidy and Jeremy Kidd. Because of the last names, the other officers started calling them Butch and Sundance. They're kind of heroes of mine. I've followed their careers for some time now, and they're the best there is. I feel bad for the person who committed this crime because once those two start hunting, it usually doesn't take them long to find their man." He aimed his digital camera and began taking photos.

As he was speaking, a few other curious onlookers were listening to him as well. One of them nudged the woman and asked her a few questions. She turned to Travis Parker and said, "It was a pleasure meeting you, Mr. Parker. Good luck with your studies. If I ever need a lawyer, maybe I'll look you up."

While he was still aiming and shooting photos he replied, "Thank you. It won't be for several more years, I'm afraid. It takes quite some time to complete the education. Then there's the bar exam. But please remember the name. Eventually I'll make it and when I do, I'll need all of the clients I can get so that I'll be able to pay off my student loans!"

"Travis Parker, I'll remember the name. I have to start getting ready for work now. Bye."

Without looking he nodded and said, "Bye now." He shot a few photos of the detectives as they drove away. He then turned to begin shooting photos of the house and the forensic team as they moved back and forth from their van to the house.

While he was moving around outside the crime tape seeking better shot angles for his photos, he noticed a cameraman checking his equipment while a very attractive woman was trying desperately to get the attention of one of the uniformed officers. He turned his camera and shot a few pictures of the reporter as she spoke to the officer, then he realized that his memory card was nearly full. He had just made it back to his mountain bike when he heard the cameraman say, "Alright, go."

"Good morning. I'm Angela Baker and we're here at the scene of a brutal homicide that occurred sometime yesterday evening. The victim of this horrific crime was Mrs. Sarah Connelly, widow to the late Colorado State Senator … "

Travis Parker couldn't make out any more of what she had been saying as he was furiously pedaling as fast as he could to get back and upload the photos from his camera onto his laptop. As he rode away from the crime scene, he muttered excitedly to himself, "Butch and Sundance. King Midas, himself! This is going to be so exciting. I hope these pictures turned out well."

*****

As the detectives left the crime scene on their way to Dean Connelly's house, Kidd said, "Let's hope that this is really as easy as it seems. The late Senator's widow, murdered in her home … you know the captain is going to want this resolved before the media frenzy has a chance to explode."

As they mentioned the words 'media frenzy,' they passed the first news van heading toward Sarah Connelly's home.

"Right, let's hope the son did it, and he's so overcome with grief that he confesses the instant we get there."

They arrived at Dean's house just after nine in the morning. By now Cassidy was starting to wake up and the bags under his eyes were beginning to disappear. After double-checking the address, they looked around the area to make sure neighbors or passersby weren't scrutinizing them. Then they cautiously approached the front door side by side with their hands on the butts of their service pistols.

After listening at the door for a few moments and hearing nothing, Cassidy moved to a large window and peered inside while Kidd went back to the driveway to inspect the Mustang. The top was up and the doors were locked, but instead of being in the garage, it was parked crooked in the driveway with one tire on the grass.

Through the window, Cassidy could see several empty beer bottles on a large coffee table and a crumpled blanket half on the couch. There was no sign of movement though.

They went back to the front door and Cassidy knocked loudly. After a few moments of not hearing anything, he knocked louder. From somewhere inside they heard a man's voice yell, "What the hell? Go away!"

Cassidy knocked again and said, "Mr. Connelly, it's the police. Something's happened to your mother, and we need to speak with you!"

They heard a loud thud then some scuffling as someone came toward the door. The door flung open and a man wearing only boxer shorts stood before them. "Mom? What happened? Is she alright?"

His hair was greasy and disheveled and his eyes were bloodshot. They could smell a strong odor of stale beer as he spoke, and his face was puffy. He was either badly hung over or still drunk.

"I'm Detective Cassidy and this is Detective Kidd." Both of them quickly flashed their credentials. "May we come in?"

"Uh … yeah. I guess so. What happened to my mom?" He stepped back from the door so the detectives could enter then closed the door behind them.

Once inside, Detective Kidd did the talking while Cassidy observed Dean's body language and expression.

"Please sit down, Mr. Connelly."

He shook his head. "Just tell me what happened to my mother. Was she in an accident or something? Is she alright?"

"Sir, Mrs. Connelly is dead."

At that instant several expressions flashed across Dean's face. Shock, bewilderment and disbelief were immediate. Then his eyes began to tear up and pain took over as his body began to quiver. He took a couple of steps toward the couch but stumbled and fell against the coffee table, splitting open his shin and knocking beer bottles onto the floor.

Detective Kidd reached out and helped him to the couch before he fell to the floor then stood back to observe. After a full thirty seconds, Mr. Connelly composed himself well enough to hoarsely ask, "How?"

Still employing a soft, sympathetic tone, Detective Kidd replied, "She was murdered in her home yesterday evening."

"No, that can't be. Everybody loved her. Nobody would want her dead. You must have the wrong person; it can't be my mother!"

Now it was Cassidy's turn, and he sternly ordered, "We need you to get dressed and come with us. We have some questions concerning your whereabouts last evening."

This was a routine they had used several times before, and Detective Kidd turned on Cassidy. "Hey, the poor guy just lost his mother. Try using a little tact for once in your life."

Cassidy made a sound of disgust and exploded, "To hell with tact! He was the last person to see her alive."

He then glared at Dean and commanded, "Clothes! Now! Let's go."

"Forgive my partner, he's not much of a morning person." Kidd then reached out his hand in an offer to help Dean to his feet. "Let's get you cleaned up and see about that cut on your shin. Then you can come to the station and, maybe with your help, we can figure out what happened last night."

"Yeah, why don't you take him out for breakfast while you're at it? This bleeding heart shit is killing me." Cassidy then stormed out of the living room toward the kitchen.

Dean was bewildered but he latched onto Kidd as someone who'd protect him from the mean detective. "Alright, I have some bandages in the bathroom, I think."

Jeremy helped him to his feet and steadied him as they went to get him cleaned up. Kidd quickly scanned the bathroom but saw no obvious signs that anyone had washed off blood in there recently. He picked up a washcloth from the edge of the sink and ran cold water on it. He handed it to Dean and told him to put pressure on the cut on his shin. In the medicine cabinet he found bandages and Neosporin. The few pill bottles he saw were just over-the-counter stuff ... aspirin, cold and flu medicine, Tylenol ... nothing prescription. After getting the leg bandaged, he helped Dean to his room and watched as he put on pants and a shirt. After slipping on a pair of sandals, Dean looked up at the detective.

Kidd yelled out, "Cassidy, are you done being an asshole yet? Dean's ready to come talk with us."

From somewhere else in the house they heard, "Sure, he won't be bleeding all over our car, will he? If so, you're cleaning it up."

Kidd smiled and helped Dean to his feet. "He's not so bad once it gets closer to afternoon."

On the drive to the station, they asked Dean questions and he spent most of the trip crying. Not much of what he said made any sense, and what little they could make out let them know that an immediate confession wasn't going to happen. He kept repeating, "I should have stayed with her. If I hadn't left, she'd still be alive."

At the station, they led him to a small room that had a hard wood table, four plastic chairs and a wall-mounted camera high in one corner. The room was brightly lit and painted white. There was absolutely nothing else in the room—nothing hanging on any of the walls, and nothing on the table. Detective Kidd remarked as he left, "I'll be back in a few minutes; try to make yourself comfortable. Do you need anything to drink?"

"Can I have some water, please? My mouth is dry."

"Of course, I'll have someone bring it to you." With that he closed the door.

Once well away from the room, Kidd asked Cassidy, "Well? What do you think?"

"I have to admit, the reaction seemed absolutely genuine. The kitchen was clean, no dried blood on any towels or anything. If he did this, he either covered his tracks well or cleaned up somewhere else."

"Yep, no signs of him washing off blood in the bathroom. I agree about his reaction; in fact, I think he's still in shock."

"He's either one hell of an actor or he's innocent."

"Let's let him sit a while. Maybe an hour. I'd like to get a good recording of him before we start questioning him."

"Agreed. Since I was the one playing the asshole, you question him without me in the room. He responds better to you, and I don't think strong-arming him is the best tactic. I'm going to head over and talk with the tech guys and see what they gathered. They should be done processing the room soon."

"You sure you were playing at being the asshole?"

"Hey, screw you! I'm a damned nice guy."

"Yeah, so I see."

*****

Cassidy headed over to a large building adjacent to the police station where forensic evidence is processed. He jogged up the wide cement stairway on the front of the building, past the first-floor parking garage, and swung open the double doors that led into a small room. He addressed the officer sitting behind the bulletproof window.

"Hey, Grant, how's it going?"

"Butch! It's been a while. What can I do for you?"

"For starters, stop calling me Butch. My name is Michael and my partner's name is Jeremy. Your guys processed a homicide this morning; I was wondering if I could go back and talk with the techs. I know it's pretty early to expect any findings yet. I just want to get some impressions from them. We have a guy in for questioning who looks good for it on the surface, but his reactions don't match those of someone who murdered his own mother last night. I'm just trying to get some sense of direction to take with this guy."

"Sure thing, Butch, I'll buzz you back."

Cassidy opened his mouth then decided against saying anything and just sighed. Once through the security door, he made his way to the lab on a route he'd taken many times before. As he moved from one hallway to another, everyone he passed greeted him like an old friend.

As he pushed open the doors to the lab and entered, he heard a female voice say, "I win. Pay up, bitches!"

Three guys in white jumpsuits all crossed the lab, and each one in turn dropped a ten-dollar bill into the woman's hand as she chuckled.

"Come on in, detective, and thank you for dinner tonight. My kids and I greatly appreciate it."

Cassidy looked at his watch. "It's 11:45 a.m. Let me guess, you said I'd be here before noon?"

"Yep! Larry, Darryl and Darryl all guessed times later this afternoon."

Cassidy nodded and continued, "Well, when the widow of a former senator is murdered in her home, it's probably best if nobody catches you wasting time on the case."

"Wait," one of the techs said. "Nobody told me that the victim was the wife of a senator. Give me my ten back, that's bullshit. And why do you keep calling us Larry, Darryl and Darryl?"

"Tough shit, a bet's a bet. Guess next time you'll pay more attention to the officers who're talking around you. And don't worry about it, Darryl. It was obviously before your time."

Cassidy was smiling by this point. "Robin, you're rotten to the core. Maybe that's why I like you so much."

"Careful, Midas, you're a married man. People might start to talk."

One of the other lab guys turned with a puzzled look on his face and asked, "Midas?"

Robin swiveled around in her chair and explained, "Yeah, newbie. As in King Midas. You know … the guy who turned everything he touched into gold? This is Detective Michael Cassidy. Youngest man in Colorado to make detective and solves every case that lands in his lap. Everything he touches turns to gold."

"Aw, knock it off, Robin. I just follow the evidence. Eventually that leads to someone who's guilty. It's really not all that tough."

"Still, your legend precedes you, your highness. But, I'm afraid I can't tell you very much at the moment. We just got back from the crime scene. If you come back tomorrow, we'll have all the info you need. In the meantime, Old Doc Brown's had the corpse in autopsy since about 8:30. Hell, he may even be done with the autopsy by now."

"Come on, Robin. You must have something to tell me."

"Only that there's one set of prints on the golf club and that the blood type from the club head is O negative. We haven't gotten anything to match the prints or blood with yet, so there's not much else to tell you."

"At least now I know there's going to be a print to match. I was kind of hoping that there'd have been two sets though."

"Oh? Why's that?"

"Because that poor guy that Kidd's questioning struck me as innocent. I'm guessing the club is his. We found two sets at the house; hers were in the garage and still had the five iron. A man's set of clubs was found in a back bedroom, and that's the set the five iron came from."

"Is he left-handed? Because the club is."

"I still have to verify that, but I assume so."

"Well, like I told you … come back tomorrow and we'll have more information for you then."

With that he left the building and drove over to the coroner's office. He found the medical examiner in the hallway when he was on his way toward the autopsy room, and the look on that man's face made him stop dead in his tracks.

"I've seen that look before. What's the bad news?"

"Follow me," said the ME.

Once in his office, he shook his head as he spoke. "You know, at first this seemed like a straightforward case. Time of death was confirmed by that clock. The body was as one would expect to find it considering the wound that had been inflicted. But once we got the body back here and began a closer examination, more questions than answers began to arise."

"Oh, shit, what questions?"

"You saw the body before we moved it. It looked as though it hadn't been tampered with. But someone removed her bra after she was killed."

"Wait, how do you know that she was wearing a bra when she was killed?"

"Because when it was removed, the clasp left abrasions on her back. Someone cut the bra and straps and pulled it up from under her shirt. But that wasn't the most puzzling thing that we found. Each of her baby toes had been removed."

Cassidy couldn't hide his surprise. "Doc, she was wearing slippers."

"I know, someone removed the slippers after she was killed and cut off the outermost digit of each foot. Then they put the slippers back on her."

"Can you tell me what was used to cut off the toes?"

"I can give you some ideas but I can't tell you exactly which tool was used. It would have been something like hedge shears or bolt cutters. But they'd have to be VERY sharp. The cuts were clean and precise. The tissue around the wounds didn't show signs of being crushed. I suppose ... "

"What?"

"Well, I only mention this because from time to time I enjoy a fine cigar. I suppose a good cigar cutter could have been used. They're sharp enough to amputate a digit."

"Was there anything else unusual about the body?"

"Nope. The cause of death was the five iron to the side of her head. She didn't have a clue that it was coming, either. The bra and toes were post mortem. Other than that, the body was left exactly where it was when she expired."

"Was her blood type O negative?"

"Yes, it was."

Sounding disappointed, Cassidy said, "Thanks, doc. How long before we get your official report?"

"I'll write it up this afternoon. It'll be at the station first thing in the morning."

*****

When Cassidy got back to the station, he found Kidd at his desk. He was just hanging up the phone.

"How'd things go with Dean?"

"I tell you, if it weren't for the eyewitness verifying that he left the crime scene at about the time of the crime, I wouldn't think he was involved. He gave no indications of lying and genuinely seemed shocked that his mother had been murdered. I had one of the officers drop him back off at his house. Nothing in his behavior said I should hold him. Did you find out anything from the lab or the doc?"

"No … and yes."

"Cryptic, are you going to elaborate or just leave me hanging in the wind?"

"The lab let me know that I'm becoming too predictable. They're actually placing bets on when I'll arrive. Robin won, by the way."

"No surprise there; she could probably be a detective if she wanted. She's really sharp."

"They still have to process the evidence. All they could confirm was that there was only a single set of prints on the five iron and that the blood on the club head was type O negative. Same as our victim. Hey, was Dean left-handed?"

"Yeah, when he signed the paper for his prints, I noticed he was left-handed."

"I'm pretty sure the lab will confirm that the prints on the five iron were his, but I'm also pretty sure the five iron was his, so that tells us nothing."

"What about the doc?"

"That's where things get strange."

"How strange?"

"Very. Apparently she was wearing a bra when she was killed, and the killer took the time to cut it off her. That's strange, but still not 'very' yet. The 'very' came when the doc told me that each of her baby toes were cut off."

"What? Amputated? You mean they'd been cut off by the killer or she didn't have those toes because they'd been amputated at some point in the past?"

"Post mortem. The killer cut them off then replaced the slippers."

"I really doubt Dean could have done that. He looked like he was going to throw up when I explained that her head had been caved in by a golf club."

"If it wasn't him, then who else could have done it?"

"Ms. Monroe told us she broke up with her boyfriend about a year ago. Maybe there was some animosity left over. We'll have to check him out."

"Alright, but did Dean tell you what he did after leaving his mother's house?"

"He went out and got blasted. I just got off the phone with the bar. He started a tab at 7:30 p.m. and kept using it until he paid it off at 1:20 a.m. The owner was there until 10:00 p.m. and since Dean is a regular, the owner remembered him. He said Dean was partying and having a great time like he didn't have a care in the world."

"What about before she was murdered?"

"He admitted that they were arguing. It was about money. She was going to cut him off from his trust fund until he got a job and started to act more responsibly."

"Too bad we don't have any witnesses to the argument."

"We do; the argument started at the golf course and continued into the clubhouse."

"Let me guess; you spoke with someone from the golf course?"

"Jeanie, and she sounds incredible. Raspy, sultry voice … what a turn on."

"Down, boy. I suppose you want to go interview her now?"

"Actually," Kidd held up the keys, "I was just getting ready to head over there. Want to tag along and see what married life is making you miss out on?"

"Sure, stud. I'd love to watch you get shot down by Miss Raspy and Sultry."

*****

As they entered the clubhouse a very attractive, tall, thin brunette in a waitress outfit approached them. Her bare legs were well toned, and she had just a slight wiggle as she walked. Kidd nudged Cassidy in the ribs. "That must be her."

"Hey, guys, just the two of you? Would you like menus?"

Cassidy nudged Kidd back in the ribs and said, "I don't hear raspy and sultry."

Kidd ignored him and flashed his credentials. "I'm Detective Kidd, and the idiot next to me is Detective Cassidy. I spoke with Jeanie on the phone a little while ago, and she told me I could find her here?"

"Yep, that's Jeanie behind the bar."

Cassidy smiled broadly as his eyes followed to where she was pointing. Jeanie looked like she was in her mid-sixties and probably passed 250 pounds several decades earlier without ever looking back. "Go get her, stud."

Kidd shot him a dirty look as the waitress remarked, "Ah, you drew a picture in your head from her voice."

Cassidy said, "Yes, he did. But while the voice was hers, the picture was yours."

As the two of them were laughing, Kidd walked away toward the bar.

"Jeanie? I'm Detective Kidd. We spoke on the phone."

"Well, color me pleasantly surprised. Looking good, detective. You must work out."

Cassidy strolled up just then and said, "Yeah, he's up to fifty pounds on the bench press. Another year and he'll be able to do a push up."

Ignoring Cassidy, Kidd went on, "Thank you, ma'am, but we're here to find out what you can tell us about the argument Dean and Sarah Connelly had while they were here yesterday."

"They're regulars here. During summer, every Wednesday that it isn't raining, they have a reserved tee time for 2:30 p.m. After their round, they come in here and have dinner. She has a Vodka and Squirt and he has two or three beers. Once she's finished her drink, he slams what's left of his, then they're off until the next Wednesday. Yesterday was no different, except for the argument. She was trying to keep it down so the other patrons wouldn't stare at them. He didn't care who heard. From what I caught, it was about money. She had the money, he wanted the money, and the spout was about to be turned off. Not just turned down to a trickle, mind you. She was cutting him off. But once she finished her drink, he slammed the rest of his, and they left together."

"How heated was the argument?"

"I'd say heated enough that I was considering asking them to leave … but not heated enough to call you boys in."

She leaned closer to them across the bar and opined in a quieter tone, "You ask me, I'm pretty sure that little filly could have whooped his whiny ass up one side of the parking lot and down the other. He wasn't exactly the manly sort."

"Thank you. Oh, one more thing. Can you tell me about what time they left?"

"Why certainly, dear." She reached below the bar and pulled out a slip of paper. "I pulled this from yesterday's receipts after we spoke on the phone. She paid this just before she left. It's a photocopy so you can keep this one. The time and date are stamped at the top. Yesterday at 4:47 p.m." She handed the receipt copy to Kidd and offered with a smile, "On the back is my personal number if you have any further needs you'd like help with."

"Thank you, I appreciate that."

"Anytime, handsome. Anytime at all."

As they left the clubhouse, Cassidy began to open his mouth but before he could make even a sound, Kidd said, "Not one goddamned word or I will shoot you."

Cassidy laughed but didn't utter a single word.

On the ride back to the station they were discussing Dean's behavior. Both of them were sure that he wasn't the type that could have committed this murder. Yet both of them had seen murders committed in the past by people that they wouldn't have believed to be capable of it. They agreed that they needed to get a psych evaluation on record for Dean Connelly. They'd become pretty good at judging people's character, but they weren't professionals.

Right now, the evidence was leaning toward Dean's guilt, but his reactions and characteristics were screaming that he was innocent.

CHAPTER 3

---·—·—·---

Friday, July 24

"Hey, Cassidy, did you see the news last night?"

"Yeah, I saw."

"When I got here this morning the captain almost met me at the door. We were right; he wants this solved and gone as of yesterday."

"Right, because homicides are as simple to solve as crossword puzzles."

"Word seek."

"What?"

"The puzzles … aw, hell, what does it matter? Here's the report from the ME. But there's nothing in it that you didn't tell me yesterday. Also, I cleared the ex-boyfriend. I found out that he's currently living in Miami. I called his place of employment and his boss verified that he showed up to work every day this week."

"Wonderful, back down to one suspect again. Have you talked with forensics yet?"

"I only got here fifteen minutes before you did and just told you that I reviewed the medical examiner's report and was on the phone with the ex's boss. You know, for a homicide detective, you sure miss a lot of obvious things."

"Pardon me, crab ass. Let's go to the lab; they said they'd have more information for us first thing in the morning."

"Crab ass? You're the miserable son of a bitch to deal with in the mornings. Yesterday you were pissed because I was happy, and today you're pissed because I'm not."

From a desk not too far away, one of the other officers interrupted them. "Hey! Some of us are trying to get some work done here. Could you two continue your lovers' quarrel somewhere else?"

In unison they both responded, "Fuck you!"

The other officer shook his head and replied, "Real mature. You know, my wife said there's a new psychiatrist downtown. Just took over Jacobs' practice. Would you like me to schedule you two an appointment? You sound like you need it."

Cassidy responded, "Not nearly as much as your wife obviously does."

"The only reason my wife goes there is because she has to listen to me bitch about working with you two morons. I thought you were on your way to the lab … why are you still here making me wish I'd taken a sick day?"

*****

Robin was peering into a microscope when they entered the lab. Without looking up she asked, "Hey, boys. Here to get filled in on our findings?"

Kidd looked at Cassidy and asked, "How does she do that?"

Before Cassidy could answer, Robin offered, "Just one of the many mysteries of the cosmos. One you two aren't meant to solve."

She then pulled back from the microscope and jotted a few notes on a clipboard. "Alright, it's a busy day and I can't have you clowns distracting my minions; let's get down to it. The killer swung the club with a left-handed motion, very hard. The blood splatter at the crime scene along with the wound on the left side of the victim's head confirms this. The killer was behind the victim, and according to the evidence we have, she had no idea the blow was about to be struck. The blood, hair and tissue from the club head are a match for our victim. No big surprise there.

"The fingerprints from the shaft match the victim's son, one Dean Connelly. The rocks glass that was left in the kitchen drainer hadn't been rinsed very well, and we managed to pull a print from it that belongs to Dean Connelly, as well. We found several sets of other prints in the room where the murder took place, so obviously nobody bothered wiping down the crime scene. The housekeeper's prints are on file with the state due to her occupation, so once we eliminated her prints, the victim's, and Dean's, that left us with four unidentified sets. Those were found in various places within the room, but none were found near where the body was. In short, I don't think those are going to help you a bit since none of them were on the murder weapon. The only prints on the buttons of her blouse belonged to the victim, and you can't pull prints from fuzzy slippers, so those were useless. Before you ask, yes you can button a blouse without leaving any prints at all. So the fact that Dean's prints weren't on any of the buttons is meaningless.

"The only prints on the safe belonged to the deceased as well. So if someone's going out there to pop that sucker open for you, my bet is that it'll be full of whatever she put in it and nothing will be missing. The only thing that may eventually help you is that we did pull some foreign fibers and a few hair samples from her clothing that match neither mom nor son. If you bring us something to compare those with, we can press forward; but as for now, you got all you're going to get without giving us something new to work with."

Both of the detectives were scribbling in their notepads during the entire briefing. Finally Kidd asked, "Did you even take a breath during all of that? You know what … never mind. So what you're telling us is that, at least so far, the forensic evidence still says Dean is our best bet."

"Unless someone else, who was wearing gloves, walked into the house undetected immediately after Dean left the scene, made his way to the back bedroom, grabbed the golf club and snuck up behind her without her knowing about it … it's looking like Dean is still your guy."

"Okay, thanks, Robin. Those foreign fibers and hair samples probably won't lead anywhere, either. They went golfing and had drinks in the clubhouse before the murder. They were probably picked up there. But if we come up with anyone else, we'll get you some samples for comparison."

"Okay, boys. As I told you, it's a very busy day so go find somewhere else to be, please."

Cassidy turned to Kidd and said, "I'm getting the impression that nobody wants us around today."

*****

As soon as they were back out on the street Cassidy said, "I hate to say this but … "

Kidd cut him off in midsentence. "We need to get a search warrant for Dean Connelly's home."

"Exactly. I know the guy seems like he was being genuine with us and really doesn't strike me as the type that would cave in his mother's skull, but we have absolutely nothing that points to anyone else committing this crime."

"I know. I was hoping that the contents of that safe might bring another person of interest into play though."

"When's that supposed to be opened up?"

Kidd pulled out his notepad and flipped back and forth through several pages then looked at his watch. "Actually, he should be there working on it now."

"Who's on site with him?"

"I think it's supposed to be Billings."

They stopped for a moment and just stared at each other. Finally, Cassidy spoke. "Alright. Last chance we give him. We find out what's in that safe, and if it doesn't point to anybody new, we ask the judge to sign off on a search warrant."

"Nah, let's save some time; I'll call for the warrant now."

"By the way, you spoke with the captain this morning, right?"

"Yeah, why?"

"I'm sure he's withholding the information about the toes from the media; is he withholding the missing bra as well?"

"Yes, as far as the media's concerned, this is just a straightforward homicide."

"You know the media's still covering the house, right?"

"Yep, I was just planning on using the standard 'This is still an ongoing investigation, so we can't divulge any information at this time' bit."

"Works for me; let's go."

*****

When they arrived at the house, the reporters were milling around out on the front lawn. It reminded Kidd of vultures circling over a potential meal and Cassidy, of a feeding frenzy for a group of sharks that smelled blood in the water. They both knew the media played its role in things but still considered them a necessary evil. They had even used the media a few times to flush out a suspect in hiding, so they had their uses; but in this particular instance, they were simply a nuisance.

As they parked in front of the Connelly residence, the swarm shifted toward their car.

Cassidy remained silent and Kidd recited his practiced statement as they wove their way past microphones and cameras. When they reached the door, Kidd turned back to the reporters and said, "Please! As we stated, this is an ongoing investigation. When we've reached any conclusions, you'll be notified."

With that they ducked into the house and both took a deep breath. Officer Billings greeted them as they entered. "Good morning! Beautiful day today. They say we're going to hit the mid-eighties this afternoon."

Kidd and Cassidy looked back and forth at each other for a moment then turned back to Billings. Cassidy spoke this time. "I didn't see any vehicles that belong to the locksmith outside; when's he getting here?"

Billings maintained that cheerful smile and said, "She ... she finished with the safe twenty minutes ago. I thought you got our message. Isn't that why you're here now?"

"We weren't at the office," Kidd replied. "We just came straight from the lab."

"Oh, well, my guys just organized the contents. There wasn't much inside, but it's still here if you want to take a look before we turn it in as evidence. It's all in the kitchen."

Spread out on the kitchen table were stacks of documents and a pile of cash.

Cassidy whistled as he saw it and asked, "How much?"

Billings answered, "The cash? $8,250, mostly in fifties and hundreds."

Kidd said, "Must be nice to be able to just have that kind of money on hand. I wonder what she'd need that much at the house for?"

Cassidy was shaking his head as he replied, "No idea. Who can say why rich people do what they do? Maybe she'd just spread it across her bed and roll around in it from time to time."

"What about the rest of the paperwork?"

Billings stepped up and pointed to identify each stack, "These are insurance documents. These are personal documents— correspondence and letters and such. These are the legal documents, including titles and a will."

"Insurance—life insurance too?"

"Yes, sir, half a million. Dean is the sole beneficiary."

"Did you get a chance to review the will?"

"Yes, sir, I have a guy checking with her lawyer to make sure it's the same as the one on file. If it is, it looks like the bulk of the estate will also go to Dean."

Kidd sighed, "Is there anything that looks like it might give cause for anyone else … I mean anybody on the planet other than Dean … to want her dead?"

Billings shook his head. "We haven't read everything yet, but so far, no. Nothing."

Cassidy and Kidd stared at each other for a full ten seconds before they broke eye contact and looked down at the floor. Then Cassidy's cell phone rang.

"Captain? Cassidy here. Yes, sir … right. What about our search warrant? Yes, sir. Who's got it? Yes, sir, we'll meet him there."

Kidd anticipated the other end of the conversation and asked when Cassidy hung up, "They signed off on that search warrant already?"

Cassidy nodded. "The warrant will be there waiting for us."

Once in the car, Kidd finally said what both had been thinking all morning. "Maybe he played us, Mike. It is possible, you know."

"I know. I just hate to think that little weasel was able to convince both of us that he was innocent if he really did this."

"He could be a sociopath. Having no conscience would explain a lot."

"I guess we'll have to let the shrinks figure that out. Let's go get this over with."

*****

The media was swarming over Dean's house in even greater numbers than at the murder scene. It was the biggest news in the city and probably in the entire state. Even the nationwide media was giving it serious attention. It was so bad that the detectives met the officer who had the warrant a full two blocks away. A team of six officers plus Cassidy and Kidd were ready to execute the search as they rolled up to Dean's house in a convoy.

In stony silence, they pushed their way past reporters and cameras and banged on the front door. "Dean Connelly, this is Detective Kidd. Please open the door."

A few seconds later, the door slowly swung open a bit and bright strobes exploded as camera shutters clicked. Dean squinted and moved back quickly from the door. Kidd led the way into the residence but waited until the rest of the team was inside and the door was securely closed before he pulled the warrant from his pocket.

"Dean Connelly, I'm sorry that I have to inform you we have a warrant to search this property for any evidence related to the murder of your mother, Sarah Connelly. Please have a seat, and we'll try to make this as painless as possible."

Connelly plopped down on the couch, then after a few seconds he put his head in his hands and quietly began to sob. The image was heartrending, and Kidd looked away instantly. Cassidy, however, was quickly losing what sympathy he had for Dean. The evidence they'd collected so far pointed toward his guilt and didn't leave any room at all for anyone else to even be considered. Cassidy was reading body language and studying him for any hint that he was being played as a fool. He eventually turned away and went to the far bedroom to begin the search.

With eight officers performing a search of a three-bedroom, 1,800-square-foot residence, it didn't take very long. Within twenty minutes a uniformed officer called out for Cassidy and Kidd.

They met in the hallway and looked as the uniformed officer moved aside. "It was under a few boxes and a bowling bag."

Cassidy stared for a few moments before his face turned red and his fists clinched. Quietly he said, "That son of a bitch." Then he tensed even more and raised his voice. "You son of a bitch!"

Kidd caught him as he turned to storm toward the living room where Dean was.

"Hey! We got played, but now we got him. Calm down and don't give him and his lawyer a reason to get him off. Professionalism. Remember, the media is right outside the front door."

Cassidy stopped and took a few deep breaths. Finally, he turned to the officer who discovered it and ordered, "Document it. Document the hell out of it. Photos, measurements, the works. I want this son of a bitch put away in a hole where he'll never get out."

The officer set down a ruler and began taking photos of the wadded black bra. After getting as many angles as was possible in the small closet, with gloved hands he slowly lifted the bra for inspection. All could see that the straps and front of the bra had been cut.

Kidd moved closer to the bra that was being held by the officer and questioned, "Is that dried blood?"

"I can't be positive, but if I had to guess I'd say yes."

"Bag it."

Cassidy, who was shaking slightly with rage, finally asked, "Can I cuff that bastard now?"

Kidd nodded and stood. "By the book, though, by the book."

Cassidy approached Dean and said, "On your feet and face away from me. Spread your legs apart and put both hands on that wall. Do you have any sharp objects in your pockets or weapons on your person?"

Dean Connelly was dumbstruck but followed the instructions. "No," he finally said.

Cassidy patted him down to verify. He pulled Dean's wallet from the back pocket of his jeans and handed it to Kidd who was standing just behind him. Cassidy couldn't help but grin as he pulled his cuffs. "Dean Connelly, you are being placed under arrest for the murder of your mother, Sarah Connelly."

After securing Dean, even though the rights are now signed for at the station, Cassidy recited the Miranda Rights to Connelly. Before he made it to the front door, Kidd put a hand on Cassidy's shoulder, making him stop. Kidd then moved in front of Dean and faced him. "Would you like a hat to make it easier to hide your face from the media?"

Before Dean could answer, Cassidy asked, "Seriously?"

Kidd ignored him and stared intently at Dean. Finally, Dean, who was beginning to tear up again, shook his head and exclaimed, "I'm innocent! And I want the whole world to know that."

As the detectives led Dean out the front door, camera flashes exploded, motion cameras lit up and all the reporters began talking at the same time to their respective cameramen. A handful of them rushed forward with microphones, and a barrage of questions were fired at the trio.

None of the officers responded to any of the questions or even spoke. Kidd was in front clearing a path to their unmarked car. In the midst of all of that chaos, Dean Connelly raised his chin defiantly and proclaimed, "I'm innocent! All of you remember these words. I am innocent!"

*****

Once back at the station, they booked Dean Connelly and put him back in that same little white room where Kidd had questioned him only the day before. They left him alone for half an hour, then both Cassidy and Kidd entered with a legal pad and some ink pens. Before they could say or do anything, Dean Connelly shook his head. "This time I want my lawyer."

Kidd and Cassidy looked at each other for a moment before Kidd turned back to Dean and spoke with a nod, "That's the first intelligent thing you've said to us in two days."

They then left the room.

The lead story on the evening news was, "Wife of late senator, Walter Connelly, was slain by her own son." The media had already convicted him. Now it was up to the legal system to catch up to them.

CHAPTER 4

Monday, July 27

"Dr. Poole, what do you think about the arrest Friday?"

Dr. Stacey Poole raised her eyebrows and asked, "What are you talking about, Rebecca? Who got arrested and for what?"

Rebecca, obviously surprised, inquired, "Have you been under a rock for the last three days? Sarah Connelly's son was arrested for her murder Friday."

Dr. Poole slowly shook her head, "Who's Sarah Connelly?"

Rebecca threw up her hands and said, "It's been all over the news! Sarah Connelly was married to Colorado State Senator Walter Connelly. Her body was found Thursday morning by her housekeeper. Friday afternoon they arrested her son, Dean Connelly, for her murder."

"Oh, well, I guess that's a good thing then. At least the city won't have to worry about a murderer being on the loose."

"I don't believe you! This is only the biggest news story in the state—maybe even the country—right now. Haven't you seen it on TV? Or even heard about it on the radio while you were driving? It's all over every station. The evidence is supposed to be overwhelming."

"I have satellite radio, and I don't watch TV very often."

Just then the phone at Rebecca's desk rang. As she was picking up the receiver, she was shaking her head. "Jacobs Psychiatric Center, how can I help you? Yes? No, I'm sorry. Dr. Jacobs is out of the country at this time. Dr. Poole is the acting psychiatrist handling things right now. Really? Hold on, she's right here."

She handed the receiver to Dr. Poole and leaned back in her chair, staring intently.

"Hello? This is Dr. Poole. To whom am I speaking, please?"

After a lengthy pause she replied, "Yes, I'm qualified. Hold on a moment please; let me check my schedule."

She put her hand over the receiver and looked at Rebecca.

Rebecca flipped open a book behind the counter and after a few seconds responded, "Your last appointment today is scheduled to be done by 2:00 p.m."

Dr. Poole mouthed a thank you then removed her hand from the receiver. "Would today work for you? I'm available anytime after 2:00. Alright, I'll be there by 2:30. Yes … thank you, sir. I'll see you then."

Rebecca was nearly jumping out of her seat. As she replaced the receiver she questioned, "So? Do they want you to analyze Dean Connelly?"

Dr. Poole nodded and affirmed, "I have to be at the city jail at 2:30. Would you please mark down my appointment for me?"

"Yet again, I can't believe you! You're going to be all over the national news after this, and you're acting like it's just another appointment. Don't you understand how big … how absolutely huge this is?"

"Really, it's just a psych evaluation. The Assistant District Attorney expects the defense to pull in some expert to say that Mr. Connelly was temporarily insane at the time of the attack. They just want to preempt the defense by having me do an evaluation first."

"Unbelievable! The biggest news story out there right now, and you don't even care. It's just another day at the office for you."

Dr. Poole shrugged and said, "It's my job."

Just then the first client of the morning walked into the reception area. Dr. Poole smiled at Rebecca as she turned to head to her office.

At five minutes after two, Dr. Poole came down from her office with her keys and briefcase in hand. There in the hallway near the break room, all of the therapists were lined up, with Rebecca right up front.

Dr. Poole stopped for a moment and asked, "Is something wrong?"

Rebecca reached up and used her fingers to fix some of her hair that was out of place, "We're here to offer you good luck and to make sure you look your best for the media."

Dr. Poole looked at each of the therapists one by one, then turned back to Rebecca. "Thank you, but as I told you this morning …"

"We know—it's just another psych evaluation to you. We get it. But this practice is going to be put in the national spotlight because of this!"

Dr. Poole sighed and said, "I understand. Really, I do. And I hope this practice is shown in a favorable light because of it. Dr. Jacobs could expand this practice if that's the case. And I thank all of you for your support. Now, don't you have any clients to tend to?"

All of them muttered their wishes of good luck then disappeared behind their respective doors. All except Quinn. He paused long enough for Dr. Poole to ask if he needed anything.

Quinn smiled and replied, "Absolutely. If you refuse to join me for drinks this evening, it'll be a cold shower that I need. If you say yes, then after I make you breakfast tomorrow morning, we'll both need a hot shower."

Dr. Poole stood quietly for a moment. She then flashed a smile and sexy wink as she slowly walked up to him and grabbed him by his necktie. As she pulled his head down closer to hers, she moved to whisper in his ear. She took the time to allow a slow warm breath to gently wash over his earlobe before saying, "I hope your water is ice cold, Quinn." She then released him and pointed to his office door.

Quinn sighed and gently touched his ear. "You're warming up to me, doctor. I can tell. It's just a matter of time."

Rebecca made a sound that indicated her disgust before she spoke. "You're worse than a hormonally charged teenager. You should be ashamed of your behavior."

Quinn flashed a mischievous grin as he reached for his door. Then he paused for a few more seconds, staring at both of them.

Rebecca couldn't help herself any longer. "What are you doing, Quinn?"

Without hesitation he responded, "Imagining our threesome."

Rebecca took two quick steps toward him with her fists clenched. He wasted no time shooting into his office and quickly closing the door behind himself.

Rebecca turned to look at Dr. Poole and noticed that she was smiling. "You can't possibly find that pervert charming?"

"He has his moments. I have to admit, the interaction is fun sometimes."

Rebecca shook her head then took the time to adjust Dr. Poole's blouse and after a moment nodded her approval. "Gorgeous as usual. Go get 'em, doctor, and make us look good."

Dr. Poole rolled her eyes and adjusted her briefcase as she flipped the keys until she had the one to her Outback ready. "If I'm not back before we close for the day, don't forget to lock up."

Rebecca cocked her head in disbelief. "Really? You think I'd forget? Get out of here; you're going to be late."

When she arrived at the city jail, she saw three news crews prerecording broadcasts and another group of reporters gathered around an area of the parking lot that was set up like a tailgate party for a Denver football game. As soon as she parked and locked her car, a perky blonde rushed over to her with her cameraman in tow.

"You're Dr. Stacey Poole, right? A source inside the jail said you'd be here to evaluate Dean Connelly. Can you tell our viewers what's involved in an evaluation of this type?"

Dr. Poole smiled and replied, "I'm sorry, I can't discuss anything with you at this time. If you don't mind, I really need to get inside before I'm late."

The other reporters were all scrambling to gather their recording devices and join in on the questioning as Dr. Poole nodded courteously to all of them then calmly walked up to the entrance. Pictures were taken, and reporters were lining up to add this little tidbit to their reports. But aside from that first question, none got in her way or bothered her as she went inside.

After being searched, Dr. Poole was led through two sets of electronically locked doors and into a stark cinderblock room. There were no mirrors, no windows and the only door was the one she now stood in. Inside was a large wooden table that was securely bolted to the floor in the center of the room. Seated on the opposite side of the table was Dean Connelly. He was wearing leg shackles, and his wrists were cuffed to large metal loops that were bolted to the tabletop.

Dr. Poole turned to the guard to inquire, "Are the shackles absolutely necessary? I'm here to perform a psychological evaluation, and having the subject as relaxed and as comfortable as possible is key to getting reliable results."

"Sorry, doctor, keeping you safe is my sole responsibility here. You'll have to make do with him being secured for your evaluation. Also, you will be expected to remain on your side of the table and out of his reach for the entire time that you're in this room."

Dr. Poole sighed and hesitated as she studied the face of the guard. After a few moments she relented and waved her hand dismissively. "Fine, I'll do the best I can. You may leave now."

The guard nodded and stepped back out of the doorway. "I'll be just outside the door. If you get into trouble, yell and I'll come right in."

Dr. Poole, who had already started to take her seat across from Mr. Connelly, now turned to face the guard again. "Are you telling me that you'll be able to overhear what's being said in here?"

The guard looked a bit surprised and shook his head quickly. "No, ma'am … "

"Don't call me ma'am. Do I look old enough to be a ma'am to you? You'll refer to me as Dr. Poole or as doctor. Now please answer the question."

The guard hesitated before stuttering a bit, "N-n-no, doctor. Sorry, no, Dr. Poole. If you speak in normal tones, nobody can hear you. But if you yell, since I'll be just on the other side of that door, I will be able to hear that."

Dr. Poole thought about this for a moment and nodded as she waved her hand again. "Alright, close the door tightly, please."

The guard looked relieved to be excused and actually appeared to Dean to have been quite intimidated by this petite young woman. The fact that she could intimidate a large, armed guard impressed him greatly.

Once the door was securely closed, she waited a few moments then moved closer to the door before speaking in a normal tone. "It's my impression that you're actually a closet homosexual who's overcompensating for a lack of self-esteem and a substandard penis size by carrying a gun and spending all of your spare time working out in a gym." She then took a step forward and opened the door.

The guard turned to face her and raised his eyebrows. "Is something wrong, doctor?"

She smiled and replied, "Just making sure that I wasn't locked in. Thank you."

She closed the door and turned to face Mr. Connelly with the smile still intact. "Hello, Mr. Connelly. My name's Dr. Stacey Poole. Please call me doctor or Dr. Poole."

Dean nodded quickly but remained silent. He didn't know whether to laugh or cry, so he just sat there stone-faced awaiting her instructions.

She asked as she took her seat, "Do you know why I'm here, Mr. Connelly?"

"Yes, Graves explained it to me. You're here to determine whether I'm nuts or sane."

"Graves?"

"He's my lawyer."

"Oh, I see. Well, in layman's terms, I suppose that's correct. I'm here to perform a psychological evaluation. Part of that evaluation is to determine whether you understand the difference between right and wrong and legal and illegal. Also, whether you understand that there are consequences for actions and the ramifications of those consequences. I'm also going to determine whether you possess the traits and tendencies necessary to have carried out the act that you stand accused of."

"I understand."

"Excellent, now I know this may be difficult given the circumstances, but please try to make yourself as comfortable as possible. I'm just going to ask you some questions, and all I need is for you to answer those questions as honestly as possible. Shall we begin?"

Dean nodded and shifted in his chair. He was having a difficult time pulling his eyes away from hers. She was beautiful … there was no doubt about that, but he'd been around beautiful women his entire life. This wasn't just about her beauty. There was something about her eyes that held him captive more surely than any chains could have. He began to relax and allowed himself to get lost in her gaze.

"I'm ready," he finally said.

Dr. Poole smiled and opened her briefcase. "This won't hurt a bit, I promise."

The evaluation took just over two hours. She thanked Dean for his cooperation and gathered her notes. She opened the door to find the same guard standing in exactly the same position as when she'd begun her evaluation. With the door still open so Dean could hear her, she told the guard, "I'm unsure of your protocol in regards to my report, but I'm prepared to make a verbal assessment at this time. If a written assessment is required, I'll have it ready first thing in the morning. Now please unchain that poor man and see that he's made comfortable."

The guard glanced quickly at Mr. Connelly then back to her. "Yes, ma'am … I'm sorry, yes, Dr. Poole. I will as soon as I get you through the security doors. I believe the ADA is waiting for you. He'll let you know how to present your findings."

"Very well, lead on. But if I find out that you left him chained to that table any longer than it takes for me to leave this area, I will be back and you'll be the one chained up while I evaluate your fitness to continue your job. Am I understood?"

"Clearly, Dr. Poole. I'll see to him immediately after you leave."

She turned to look back at Dean once more and pleasantly said, "It was a pleasure spending this time with you, sir."

Dean was only able to smile as he gazed into her eyes once more.

She then turned and moved to the electronic door and waited for the guard to signal for it to be opened. Once out of the secure area, she was met by a tall, thin, dark-haired man wearing a suit that must have cost at least $2,000. He was clean-shaven even though it was nearly five in the afternoon, and she figured that he must shave at least twice a day. Possibly more. As he smiled she saw that his teeth had been recently whitened, and she concluded that it was for the benefit of the press. This was one of those cases that would potentially either make or break a career. Her first impression of him, while physically appealing, produced the distinct mental image of a snake silently waiting for his prey to get close enough so that it could attack without putting forth much effort.

As he reached out his hand, he said, "Dr. Poole, I'm Assistant District Attorney Robert Harrison, and I must say that it is truly an honor to meet you. The department shrink here told me that you are somewhat of a rock star in the psychological field."

As she shook his cold, clammy hand, she forced a smile to her lips. "I think a rock star is a bit of an exaggeration and, if you don't mind me asking, if this department has a psychologist on staff, why was I called in to perform this evaluation?"

"It was a political move, actually. We assume that his defense attorney will try to use the temporary insanity defense. It looks better to a jury if we have an outside expert, like you, perform the evaluation as opposed to a psychologist that regularly works for the department. Besides, by us having you do this evaluation, it prevents the defense attorney from hiring you to do it."

The inference was clear and Dr. Poole cocked her head slightly as she spoke. "Just so you know, regardless of who hires me, my assessment would remain the same. I'm not being rented by the highest bidder here."

The smile wavered for a moment, but only for a moment. "No, I believe you misunderstand. Of course your assessment will stand. It certainly wasn't my intention to attempt to sway you in any way."

Dr. Poole nodded slowly and said, "I see. So who am I to submit my assessment to?"

"That would be me. Of course the official assessment needs to be in writing, but I don't suppose you'd be so kind as to give me a verbal overview of your findings now, would you?"

Though she had been prepared to do just that, because she felt an instant dislike for this man, she responded instead, "No, I don't suppose that I would be so kind. I think it would be best if I proceed officially, don't you? I mean, this is a high profile case, is it not? I wouldn't want to be accused of breaking protocol."

His disappointment was obvious, but that ever-present toothy smile remained in place. "Of course, I understand, and you are quite right. Then when may I expect the written evaluation?"

"I'll deliver it to your office first thing in the morning. What time do you get in?"

"I'll be at the office at 8:00 a.m. sharp."

"Very well, until then." She then began to walk around him toward the exit.

"It was a pleasure meeting you, Dr. Poole."

Without looking back she replied, "You as well."

When she arrived back at the office, as she expected, Rebecca's Blazer was still in the parking lot. Before she could exit her Outback, the employee entrance door flung open and Rebecca stood holding it for her. "Well? How did it go? Was the media there? Are you going to be on TV? Was he a monster? Was he gross? Spill it! What was he like?"

"Rebecca, I have to type up my assessment and submit it to the ADA at 8:00 a.m. It really wouldn't be proper for me to give you a preview, now would it?"

"Assessment? Hell, no! I don't want to know his psychological profile, at least not yet. I just want to know if you thought he was a nice guy or an evil killer."

"I think that's called an assessment, though in the most base of terms. Let's go inside."

Once they were both in her office, Dr. Poole said, "Okay, woman to woman, he looked like a scared kid to me. I don't know what killers are supposed to look like, but if you saw him on the street, killer wouldn't be your first impression of him. Now, if you say a word of this to anyone, I will be forced to suspend you without pay or worse."

Rebecca was grinning from ear to ear and, though she was two years older than Dr. Poole, she reminded Stacey of a teenager who had just been told she'd be getting a fancy sports car for her birthday. The excitement was palpable. "Details woman! Details. You know I won't say anything. I deal with confidential information for a living."

Dr. Poole sighed and said, "Alright. First of all, have you ever met ADA Robert Harrison?"

"No, but I've seen him on TV before. Very handsome."

"Yeah, if you're only considering looks, I suppose some women might find him attractive."

Rebecca adopted a conspiratorial expression and leaned closer. "You don't like him."

"No, I don't. Take away the fancy suit and bleached teeth and all you're left with is a self-serving slimeball who'll crush anyone he can't use on his way up the political ladder."

Rebecca rubbed her hands together and smiled broadly. "Juicy! Go on. What's the killer like?"

"Does the phrase 'innocent until proven guilty' mean anything to you?"

Rebecca sighed, "Okay, what's the *suspect* like?"

"The *suspect* was like any other privileged rich kid, and believe me I saw my share of those in college. He grew up never knowing what adversity was and oblivious to anyone else's needs except his own. But he's a mama's boy, and I'm convinced that he's innocent. He spent his life being coddled by his mother. There's no way he would ever dream of killing her."

Rebecca took a deep breath as her smile faded. "Are you telling me that you think they have the wrong guy?"

"Yes, I am."

Rebecca's eyes grew wide and she sat silently for a few moments. "Are you sure?"

"I'd stake my reputation on it. What's with the sudden fear?"

Rebecca looked her directly in her eyes and said, "If you're right, that means there's a cold-blooded killer out there somewhere in this city, and nobody is safe."

Dr. Poole smiled warmly. "Rebecca, nobody is safe at any time. Safety is an illusion. But if it's any consolation to you, there are several million people in this city and the odds that you'll be targeted by whomever it was that actually did commit this murder is miniscule, at best."

"What about Dean Connelly? If he didn't kill her, then an innocent man is about to go to jail for a very long time."

"Innocent people go to jail for a very long time quite often in this country. That's why I studied medicine and psychology instead of law. The system is broken and has been since its inception. Either way, I just have to turn in my assessment and let others do battle over his freedom."

"I like you, Stacey. I really do. But don't you think that's just a little bit cold?"

"No, not cold, just realistic. Look, if he's convicted, I'll do whatever I can to assist with the appeal; but his fate isn't in my hands. They must have a fair amount of evidence or he wouldn't be in jail right now."

"I know, but a few minutes ago I was convinced he was a killer. Now, since you're convinced he isn't, I guess I'm just confused."

"Whether he's guilty or not, does it really change your life either way?"

"Well, I suppose not."

"Then relax. Let me give you some professional advice, if I may. Learn to prioritize. If something happens that personally affects you, then figure out how to deal with it. When something happens to someone that you don't know and it doesn't personally affect you, learn to relax and keep your focus on those things that do."

Rebecca smiled and said, "You're right; I just got caught up in the media hype surrounding this. I never met the Connellys. I don't live in their world and in the end, as far as I'm concerned, whatever happens to him doesn't actually affect me at all. I'm sorry, Stacey; I just got wrapped up in the drama."

"You have nothing to be sorry about. The media is designed to suck in everyone. They grab hold of a story and bombard people with it until it feels to everyone like it's a part of their lives too. That's why I don't watch the news."

After a few moments of sitting silently, Rebecca stood and nodded. "You have guts, girl. Everyone has this man convicted already. If you're going to submit an assessment that says he's not capable of such acts, you're going to have some seriously pissed off people on your hands."

Dr. Poole sat back and smiled. "As I told Dr. Jacobs before he left for his sabbatical, I can handle myself."

Rebecca started laughing and said, "I'm quite sure you can. Well, I'll stand by you. I trust your professional assessment."

"Thanks, now get the hell out of here. Go enjoy your evening. I have to get this typed up."

"Good night, Stacey."

"Good night, Rebecca."

*****

On the evening news, an attractive woman wearing conservative business attire and holding a microphone was shown in the parking lot of the county jail. In the background, a blurry image of Dr. Poole getting out of her twelve-year-old Subaru could be seen. As a reporter from another station moved to intercept Dr. Poole, the cameraman began running with the attractive woman struggling to stay just ahead of him. Her high-heeled shoes were hindering her greatly. She held up the microphone just in time to hear Dr. Poole explain that she wouldn't be able to give them any information. As she smiled and prepared to walk away, the cameraman zoomed in tight on her face and the image froze in place.

The voice of a female newscaster could be heard while the still image of Dr. Poole's smiling face remained on the screen. "According to our sources in the legal department, Assistant District Attorney Harrison initially sought to contact Dr. Jacobs of the Jacobs Psychiatric Center to perform the prosecution's psychological evaluation on Dean Connelly, but he recently left the country on a year-long sabbatical to Africa,. While he's away, Dr. Stacey Poole is acting in his stead as head of the facility. The Center's reputation is impeccable, so it's little wonder that Mr. Harrison reached out to them for such an important evaluation."

A male newscaster's voice jumped in. "That's right, Darlene, the reputation of Dr. Jacobs' center is incredible. In fact, I recall several defense attorneys using Dr. Jacobs to testify about the mental health of their clients over the past several years. Apparently Mr. Harrison has decided to get the jump on the defense in this case and hire the acting head of the Center before they could."

"Yes, that's exactly correct. I'm quite certain, after interviewing Mr. Harrison on several occasions myself, that the fact that Dr. Stacey Poole is young, intelligent and very attractive can't be lost on the assistant district attorney either."

The camera then switched to show the pair of newscasters sitting behind a wide counter. The still image of Dr. Poole remained on a screen behind them. "You're certainly right about her being attractive. She does seem quite young though, especially for a psychiatrist. How is it that Dr. Jacobs chose her as his replacement while he's away?"

"That's actually an interesting sideline. Dr. Jacobs went on sabbatical with University of Michigan's Professor of Psychology, Dr. Hadley. The two have been close friends for most of their professional careers. I've learned that Professor Hadley taught Dr. Poole in Michigan and recommended her to Dr. Jacobs. She's extremely brilliant, earning her degrees in a fraction of the time that it normally takes to complete such in-depth studies. Her doctoral thesis for psychology is still being studied in great detail. In the psychological community, some of the approaches that she outlined for this thesis are supposed to change the face of mental health in this nation. Quite possibly around the globe."

"The evaluation that she performed on murder suspect Dean Connelly is supposed to be submitted to the attorneys tomorrow morning. It will be quite interesting to see what her findings were based on the time that she spent with him."

"It certainly will. Now with this week's weather, we send you to … "

CHAPTER 5

Tuesday, July 28

"What the hell is this?"

"Calm down, Cassidy. Most of what's in there is unimportant. What is important is that she verified that Dean Connelly is aware of the difference between right and wrong, does know what's legal and illegal and is aware of, as well as understands, consequences for actions."

"She spent two hours with this dirt bag and believes that he's, and I quote, 'incapable of committing a violent homicide'? What kind of shrink is she?"

"Actually, from all of the checking I've done, she's considered one of the rising stars in the field. She's brilliant. I don't just mean as a psychiatrist, I mean literally brilliant."

"Brilliant, as in … "

"Brilliant as in her I.Q. makes yours and mine look pathetic. She got her first college degree by the same age most are graduating high school. She became a medical doctor by the age of twenty-three and holds two Ph.D.'s in psychological studies. She's quite literally a genius."

"Well after reading this assessment, I'd have to disagree."

Kidd finally broke into the conversation between Cassidy and ADA Harrison. "Mike, he had us fooled on the first day too. Actually, he had us fooled most of the second day as well."

"But she's supposed to be an expert. Hell, according to you, she's supposed to be an expert that's also a genius."

"As I said, relax. With the physical evidence that we have against him, even if it goes to trial, it's a slam dunk. This is very nearly the perfect case. No attorney would dare allow this to go to a jury without the possibility of an insanity defense. We got him, and there's nothing anybody can do to prevent his conviction. Not even this assessment has enough weight to counter the physical evidence."

"If you say so, but I'm still not happy about this."

"Look, Cassidy, this is going to end with a plea bargain. We'll offer a reduced prison stay in exchange for a guilty plea, and he'll go away for the next ten years. Take my word for it; this will all be done by Friday. Then we submit the plea agreement, and it gets finalized sometime next week."

"Yeah, yeah. But … "

At that moment ADA Harrison's cell phone rang. "Hold on a moment, guys, I need to get this."

He hit a button on the phone and answered, "This is Harrison. Uh huh. Alright. Umm … "

Harrison checked his watch and nodded as he said, "One hour at my office. And he agrees to this? Will he be willing to sign a confession? Alright, it doesn't matter. He'll still have to stand before a judge and admit that he's guilty. Second degree, that's right. We'll hash that out in my office. Alright, Graves, I'll see you then."

He hung up the phone and turned back to Cassidy. "That was Connelly's attorney. As I told you, he received a copy of this very assessment today and spoke with his client. He explained the amount of evidence stacked against him and told him that if it goes to trial he's nearly certain to get a guilty verdict and sentencing will be harsh. He's agreed to plead guilty for reduced prison time. I'm going to offer ten years and with good behavior he'll probably get out in six or seven. We're going to work out the details in an hour."

"That's sad, Harrison. Six or seven years for a human life."

"It's a win-win. The State of Colorado gets this case solved quickly and efficiently. The taxpayers don't have to foot the bill for a lengthy trial, and the media gets their headlines. You guys did an awesome job on this, and you both should be proud of yourselves."

Kidd hit Cassidy in the shoulder. "Hey, have you ever had a case that was solved this quickly?"

Cassidy shook his head and said, "No." But you could hear the pouting in his voice.

"Quit acting like a damned baby. This was the easiest case we ever had."

"I still want to talk to this lady and ask her what the hell she was thinking. Did she know about the evidence in this case?"

Harrison thought about that for a moment and replied, "If she hasn't watched the news, she may well not have known."

Cassidy looked up and a smile came to his face. "Then if she didn't know about the evidence, I guess she's no smarter than we are after all."

"I have to get back to my office to meet with Graves. It's Tuesday morning; if we can get this hammered out before lunch, we might be able to get in front of a judge as early as Thursday."

As he started to walk away he stopped short and turned to face them again. "Remember, no mention of the toes to the media. That was one of the things that Graves specifically said on the phone. It's bad enough a senator's widow was murdered; we don't need it getting out that she was mutilated afterward."

Cassidy remained silent but Kidd nodded and explained, "The captain already knows. It'll stay in our files alone."

"Good, I'll give you guys a call when we go before the judge. I'm sure you'd both like to be there."

"Damn right we would," Cassidy said.

*****

In the prison Graves was just getting ready to leave Connelly and make his way to Harrison's office. "I'm terribly sorry, but I'd be investigated for disbarment if I put you in front of a jury with this level of evidence stacked against you. I think I can get him down to ten years, and if you're a good boy while you're in, you'll be back out on the street by the time you're thirty. You'll have plenty of life left to lead."

"It just feels like I've been bent over without lube. I'm innocent, and I'm going to have to spend the next ten years in prison. This system is fucked."

"It's a gift given the circumstances. If I thought there was more than a snowball's chance in hell of even getting a hung jury, I'd push for a trial. I've just seen too many people convicted on far less evidence. Also remember, the sentence will probably be ten years, time served will most likely be six or seven."

Dean lowered his head and asked, "If it goes to trial and I lose, how much time would I be looking at?"

"For a crime of this nature, twenty years would be a guarantee. Quite possibly more."

Dean began to sob and through the tears he said, "Do it."

Graves gathered his papers and banged on the door. When the guard opened it, he tossed over his shoulder, "This is a smart move, Dean. Trust me."

CHAPTER 6

***

Thursday, July 30

The judge banged his gavel and demanded order. "Ladies and gentlemen, and especially those from the media, I will have it quiet in this courtroom or I will begin citing people for contempt." After a few moments, you could hear a pin drop. "That's better. Now, I'm aware that an agreement has been reached between the state and the defendant, is that correct?"

Harrison stood and said, "Yes, your honor."

The judge sat silently as he read the documents in front of him for the third time that morning. "Dean Connelly, please rise."

Once Dean and his attorney were standing, the judge asked, "Do you understand the charges that you're pleading guilty to?"

Dean Connelly answered, "Yes, sir."

"Make your statement, Mr. Connelly."

Dean took a deep breath and closed his eyes. "I'm pleading guilty to the willful murder of my mother, Sarah Connelly. I do so of my own free will and was not coerced in any way."

"The court has no issue with this plea and is ready to hand down the sentence agreed upon by both the prosecutor and defense attorney. Dean Connelly, you will be placed in the custody of the Colorado State Penitentiary for a term not to exceed ten years. Parole eligibility will be offered after a term of no less than five years."

As the gavel came down, Dean lowered his head and fought hard to hide the tears.

Dr. Poole and Rebecca sat silently while waiting for the media to clear the courtroom. Once the majority of them were gone, they stood and prepared to make their own way out into the hall when they heard a man say, "Doctor, I wondered if you would be here."

They turned and saw ADA Harrison weaving his way toward them. "Dr. Poole, so nice to see you again. And who is this lovely young lady with you?"

Stacey turned and said, "Rebecca, meet ADA Robert Harrison …"

Before she could introduce Rebecca, she was cut off.

"Hello, my name's Rebecca Mann, and it is a great pleasure to meet you, sir."

Harrison took Rebecca's outstretched hand, but instead of shaking it, he bent at the waist and gently kissed the back of it. "The pleasure is all mine."

"Oh, my," Rebecca replied as she began to blush.

Stacey just shook her head. Finally, she spoke to Harrison. "I hope you're happy with yourself. You just sent an innocent man to prison."

"That isn't what he just said. Didn't you hear? He admitted that he murdered his mother in front of this court and the media that was present."

"It was a two-day investigation. Nobody else was even looked at. Someday evidence will surface that exonerates Mr. Connelly. Tell me, attorney. When that happens, will you then be placed in prison for the same amount of time as Connelly is?"

"You know full well that isn't how the system works."

"That's a shame; it certainly should work that way. If it did, I'm quite certain there'd be far fewer innocent people behind bars right now."

"Is this her?" Cassidy was making his way toward their little group with Kidd trying to keep up. "Is this the woman that, after two hours, decided that all of our evidence was worthless and Connelly was innocent?"

Kidd was tugging at Cassidy's jacket. "This isn't the place, Cassidy. Not here, the judge will throw your sorry ass in jail."

Cassidy's face was flushed but he paused for a moment before saying, "I'd like to have a word with you outside, if you don't mind."

Dr. Poole nodded and replied, "I suppose I have a few minutes to waste."

Once outside in the hall and after the members of the media were out of sight, Cassidy stepped up to Dr. Poole and said, "That little bastard played us for two days until we found his mother's bloody bra in his hall closet under a bowling bag. If he was innocent, how do you propose it got there?"

"It was obviously placed there by whoever killed Mrs. Connelly. That is, unless you put it there to set him up."

Cassidy clenched his fist and drew back as though he were going to punch Dr. Poole. Kidd reacted instantly and grabbed him before he could swing. He then got between Dr. Poole and Cassidy and used his body to shield Dr. Poole.

In seeing that reaction, Rebecca immediately stepped back and raised her hands defensively. But Dr. Poole remained still, calm and collected as she spoke. "We haven't met yet. I'm Dr. Stacey Poole. You must be Detective Jeremy Kidd, and that would make your hotheaded friend there Detective Michael Cassidy. This is my receptionist, Rebecca Mann."

Kidd was still holding Cassidy back as he said, "We know who you are. Cassidy! Pull yourself together; she's a woman, for God's sake, and we're right outside a courtroom."

Cassidy stepped back from Kidd then made a focused effort to get himself under control. "Sorry."

"Christ, Cassidy! You're damn lucky that none of the media was still in this hallway. I apologize Dr. Poole, Ms. Mann. My partner is still a little sore because Dean had us believing he was innocent, and neither of us is used to a suspect being able to play us like that."

"I understand completely, but you weren't being played. Dean Connelly doesn't have the personality type that would allow for him to commit such a bloody murder. He has a weak stomach and wouldn't have been able to see that much blood without becoming physically ill. However, what's done is done. But mark my words, gentlemen. The truth eventually finds its way to the surface and when it does, I'm quite certain that Dean Connelly will be found to have been innocent of this crime."

Cassidy was still red faced but had taken a few deep breaths and calmed himself, somewhat. "I followed the evidence, and it led to him. The evidence is the truth, and I stand by my actions."

"I see. Let's say that you were out camping. You put your cooler full of meat on the picnic table. Then you go for a walk. When you return to the campsite you see that the cooler's lid had been pulled open and all of the meat had been taken. All around the campsite you see footprints from a rabbit. There are no other prints, and when you look around you see no other animals. All of the evidence says that rabbit hopped up on the picnic table and took the meat from the cooler. Are you going to grab a shotgun and hunt down that rabbit for stealing the meat?"

"Of course not; that's ridiculous!"

"So you'd take the time to observe the scene, maybe test a few theories? If you do that, you might be able to figure out that a vulture landed on the picnic table and looted your cooler full of meat. Just because there's evidence in place that points in one direction doesn't mean that's the only direction that exists. Gentlemen, you just put the rabbit in prison and somewhere there's a vulture circling its next meal."

Kidd raised an eyebrow and appeared to be considering what she said but Cassidy and Harrison were shaking their heads as Cassidy began to speak. "There was no vulture in that house swinging a golf club upside Mrs. Connelly's head."

"There certainly wasn't a rabbit in that house swinging the golf club. Yet that's who you chose to arrest."

"This is absurd, let me tell you something … "

Dr. Poole cut him off as she looked at her watch. "Well, gentlemen, it was interesting meeting you both. Mr. Harrison, remember what I said here. Rebecca, we should really be getting back to work now. Have a good day, gentlemen."

With that she turned and walked away without giving any of them a chance to speak. Rebecca stood for a moment looking back and forth from the ADA and the detectives to Dr. Poole who was growing more distant by the second. Finally, she sighed and waved at them as she called out, "Dr. Poole, I drove. I have the keys. Hey, wait up."

As soon as they were both out of sight Cassidy exploded, "That woman is infuriating! Who does she think she is, anyway? To hell with the evidence, to hell with the fact that he pled guilty, to hell with the fact that there was absolutely no other suspect. He's innocent. My ass he is."

Kidd was staring down the hall in the direction of their departure as he said, "Yeah, I like her, too. A lot. She's gorgeous. Rebecca wasn't bad either."

Cassidy slugged him in the shoulder. "Knock it off. She's the enemy here. Let's not forget that."

"Oh, come on, the case is over and he's on his way to prison. Besides, do you and your wife always agree on everything?"

"Of course we do! It's called being married."

"You're so full of shit. Come on, let's go before the captain thinks we took the rest of the day off. Mr. Harrison, you were absolutely correct. This was resolved very quickly and painlessly. We'll talk with you later."

Harrison nodded, "Have a good one gentlemen; I have to go, too. I have a few interviews lined up with the media."

*****

As Dr. Poole rounded a corner in the hallway of the courthouse, she nearly ran into a reporter who was doing a monologue for her cameraman. "I'm so sorry, excuse me."

Rebecca came barreling around the corner and ran full on into Dr. Poole's back. "Damn! First you take off without giving me any warning, then you stop cold right after turning a corner." She then saw the reporter holding a microphone and a man aiming a camera directly at her.

"Oh, my. Please tell me you're not filming this."

From behind the camera she could see the man smile. The camera never wavered from the two of them.

"You're Dr. Stacey Poole. You're the psychiatrist Mr. Harrison had perform Dean Connelly's evaluation. Would you mind answering a few questions for us? Our viewers would love to hear about your encounter with the killer."

Dr. Poole replied, "I didn't have an encounter with Mrs. Connelly's killer. I did, however, perform a psychological evaluation of her grieving son."

"So it's your contention that, in spite of the guilty plea, Mr. Connelly is actually innocent? Can you tell us why you believe this?"

"During the course of my evaluation he failed to meet any of the criteria that could define him as a potential violent offender. In layman's terms, he simply doesn't have it within his nature to consider committing such an act, let alone actually commit a brutal, violent murder against his own mother."

"I see," the reporter cheerfully said. "If that's true, Dr. Poole, how do you explain his plea bargain and the statement of guilt that he made before the judge only minutes ago?"

"It's quite simple. In cases such as this, our justice system doesn't properly work. It's designed to avoid trials and encourage plea bargains. A suspect is told that if he utilizes his right to a trial by his peers, he stands a good chance of being found guilty. When that happens, the judge issues a very harsh sentence. So the defense attorney weighs the odds as he sees them. If he determines that the odds are against winning a trial, he recommends that the suspect plead guilty to the crime that he's accused of.

"In order to get the suspect to voluntarily plead guilty to a crime that he didn't actually commit, the prosecutor offers him less jail time than the standard sentence would normally warrant. So, what you see here is a son who's had less than a week to grieve the death of his mother making the biggest decision of his life. He can either gamble with his life and elect to go to trial, where the man charged with defending him says he has no chance of winning, and face decades of incarceration … or he can accept a deal that the attorneys worked out with each other and be guaranteed to spend much less time in jail.

"Either way, an innocent man ends up behind bars. The prosecuting attorney looks great in front of you, the media. The defense attorney looks incredibly intelligent for preventing his client from spending decades in prison. The courts are spared the time and cost of a trial. You get your headlines and story for your viewers. Detective Cassidy comes off looking like a genius for closing a murder case in a matter of days. And the only losers are the victim of the crime and the innocent man wasting years of his life in prison when he doesn't deserve such a punishment."

"Dr. Poole, that is a very cynical assessment of our legal system. You make it sound like everyone involved is out to railroad people into going to jail."

Dr. Poole shook her head and said, "Not everyone. It all begins with the investigation into the murder. Once the lead investigator is convinced someone is guilty, everyone else in the system that plays a role after the investigation is complete simply falls in line with that assumption. In this case, had a proper investigation been performed, Mr. Connelly wouldn't be sitting in a jail cell right now. As far as making it seem like our legal system is out to railroad everyone into going to jail ... we lead the world in incarcerated citizens. That alone stands as pretty damning evidence against our legal system."

"Dr. Poole, if Mr. Connelly is innocent, how do you explain the brassiere which was covered in his mother's blood being found in his home?"

"After doing a full psychological evaluation on Mr. Connelly, I reached the conclusion that he possesses no sexual fetish tendencies toward his mother and is suffering from no mental illness nor defect. Had he been capable of killing his mother and then actually committed the act, it is my contention that removing her bra from her lifeless body would never have occurred to him. There quite simply would have been absolutely no reason for him to do so. I also found him to be an intelligent individual. Intelligent individuals who are not suffering from mental illness certainly wouldn't take that damning piece of evidence to their home and keep it. Therefore, the only way that I can explain her bloodied bra being found in his home is that someone placed it there in an attempt to shift guilt toward Mr. Connelly."

"Doctor, are you saying Detective Cassidy planted evidence just to close this case?"

"Not at all. I'm not blaming anyone specifically. I'm stating that someone removed Mrs. Connelly's bra from her corpse. I'm stating that someone took that bra to Mr. Connelly's home and left it there ... undoubtedly to make Mr. Connelly appear to be guilty of committing this crime. In my mind, it was a rather amateurish attempt to frame him, and I'm quite disappointed that Detective Cassidy couldn't see it the way that I do."

"But, doctor, who would want to kill Mrs. Connelly and frame her son for committing her murder?"

Dr. Poole shrugged. "I have no idea, though there are some theories that come to mind."

"Please, Dr. Poole. Share one of those theories with our viewers."

"Alright. Just to show that there are other possibilities that weren't even looked into, I will. During my evaluation of Mr. Connelly, it came to my attention that he was quite the womanizer. He would spend much of his time in clubs and bars and managed to accumulate a fair number of sexual partners over the years. I'm fairly sure, simply based on the law of averages, that not all of those young women were single while conducting their affairs with Mr. Connelly. Jealousy can be a very strong motive. Should a husband or boyfriend to one of those women have found out about such an affair, I could see an act such as this being committed for revenge. What better way to make Mr. Connelly suffer than by killing his mother and framing him for the murder?"

"That is very interesting, Dr. Poole." She turned to her cameraman and said, "That should give all of our viewers something to think about." She then turned back to Dr. Poole and Rebecca. "I'd like to thank you very much for your time and expertise."

Dr. Poole replied with a nod, "You're quite welcome."

The reporter motioned to her cameraman who lowered his camera and began checking the equipment. She then turned to Dr. Poole once again. In a much more normal voice than the one she used for her on-air performance, she asked, "Dr. Poole, do you honestly believe everything that you said here today?"

"The part about Mr. Connelly being incapable of committing such a violent act against his mother? Absolutely. The rest was conjecture in an attempt to get people to understand the lengths that those in our justice system will go to just to assure a conviction. The guilt or innocence of the suspect is meaningless; the conviction is all that matters to them."

"I will admit that you certainly made me rethink my stance on this case. It was truly a pleasure meeting you, Dr. Poole. I thank you."

"You're welcome. I'm sorry, I don't normally watch the news and didn't catch your name."

"Oh, I'm sorry. My name is Courtney Bancroft."

"Ms. Bancroft, thank you for allowing me to use your news report to hopefully open some eyes to what may be a serious injustice."

*****

While on their way back to the station, Cassidy was still fuming. "Rabbits and vultures and missing meat. What a line of total crap."

"I don't know. What she said actually made quite a bit of sense to me. We did blast through this investigation. It's only been one week and now a man is going to prison."

Cassidy glared at his partner. "Are you serious right now? Can you honestly sit there and tell me that you think Dean Connelly is innocent and was framed for the murder of his mother?"

Kidd sat silently for several seconds as he drove. Eventually, he shook his head. "The odds that Dean was framed for this are incredibly low. Everything points to his being guilty."

"But? You ended that, yet it sounded like you meant to say 'but.'"

"But … she does have a valid point. Just because the evidence points in a certain direction doesn't mean that's the only direction there is. Remember, both of us believed he was innocent until we found that bra."

"Oh, hell. She got to you! You got all hot and bothered because of how attractive she is, and now your brain's stopped functioning and Little Willy is in command."

"Actually, the more I think about it, the more attracted I am to Rebecca. Dr. Poole is gorgeous; don't get me wrong. I just don't think I could keep up with someone who is that damned intelligent. I'd feel like a moron most of the time."

"You're acting like a moron right now! Dean Connelly is guilty as hell. He admitted so in a court of law. Now he's going to sit in a jail cell until he can be transferred to the state pen."

"Cassidy, I'm just saying that if the higher ups in our government weren't pushing for this to be solved, we normally would have taken a little more time. That might have led to other suspects. At least it wouldn't look like we locked onto one person and pushed him into confessing."

As they pulled into the parking lot of the police station, Cassidy was laughing. "I don't care if we had a hundred suspects and took a year to narrow the field. In the end, we'd still have arrested Dean Connelly and still gotten our conviction."

Before Kidd could respond, Cassidy's phone buzzed. "Cassidy here."

"Where the hell are you?"

"Captain? We just pulled into the station parking lot. You sound pissed, what's going on?"

"That bitch just butchered us in front of the entire city!"

"Whoa, Captain. What the hell are you talking about?"

"That bitch, Poole! Get in here. It's recorded … I think. Hold on a second." The voice became muffled but could still be heard. "Billings! Are you sure that damn thing was recorded? OK." Captain Bordeaux's voice became clear once again. "Get your ass in here. She singled you out specifically."

"We're on our way up." As he put his phone away he told Kidd, "She apparently threw us under the bus. Come on."

After watching the playback of Courtney Bancroft's impromptu interview with Dr. Poole, Cassidy looked as though he was going to have a stroke. "I can't believe she said that shit!"

Captain Bordeaux said, "You go talk to her. If possible, get her to give a full retraction! When Harrison sees that, he's going to shit a whole building full of bricks. She made it look like we were only out to throw people in jail and to hell with whether or not they actually did anything to deserve it."

Cassidy stormed out of the office. Kidd sighed then rushed to catch up to him.

Kidd was behind the wheel again. Not just because he was the one who had the keys to the unmarked car in the first place, but because he would have been terrified to ride with Cassidy while he was this pissed off.

"That bitch! Where the hell does she get off? She basically accused the entire legal system of being corrupt."

Kidd shook his head and said, "Calm down, she did not. She stated what everyone already knows. She's actually right about a lot of that. It's our job to determine who's guilty. Then we send it to the courts. The prosecuting attorney's job is to get a conviction. The defense attorney's job is to do what's best for his client. There are times when innocent people go to jail. It happens."

"I can't believe you're on her side on this!"

"Cassidy, I'm not on any side on this. I'm just saying that you and I both know innocent people who are serving time just because their lawyer sucked or because they couldn't afford to properly fight the charges against them. I'm just saying, sometimes it happens."

"I'm going to give that bitch a piece of my mind. She's going to beg to give a full retraction when I'm done with her."

Kidd glanced over and saw Cassidy's face. It was very nearly purple. "Proceed with caution here. Remember what Harrison told us. She's a full on genius. You're not going to win an argument with a genius who's highly educated. None of this can possibly turn out well for you, especially if you go in there with that attitude."

"You just keep me from killing her. That's your only job here."

*****

"Detectives? How can I help you?" Rebecca was quite surprised to see them.

Cassidy replied, "I'm here to speak with Dr. Poole."

Rebecca raised her eyebrows and looked at Kidd.

Kidd said, "Don't look at me, I'm just here to laugh at him when she verbally tap dances him into the ground."

Cassidy snapped his head around and glared at Kidd.

Kidd cleared his throat and said, "I mean, I'm just here for moral support for my partner."

Rebecca responded with a smile, "Hold on a moment, please."

She picked up her phone and hit a button. "Dr. Poole? There are two gentlemen here to see you. Yes, that's correct."

After a few moments of silence, she asked, "Are you sure? You want me to do what? Alright."

She hit a button on her phone then set the handset back in its cradle and directed, "Please follow me."

Cassidy smiled while Kidd shook his head.

When they were let into Dr. Poole's office, she was standing in front of her desk leaning against it with her arms folded in front of her. "Thank you, Rebecca. I'll buzz you when they're ready to leave."

"You mean I can't stay?"

"No, you have a job to do, and there are still clients downstairs."

Rebecca sighed and closed the door.

Dr. Poole looked back and forth between the two of them and finally said, "It appears by your expressions that this is your idea, Detective Cassidy. You have my full attention. What would you like to say?"

Kidd leaned back against the closed door and laced his fingers together in front of him.

Dr. Poole saw the expression on his face and mentally prepared herself. It appeared to her that he was very concerned about how Cassidy would act.

Cassidy took a deep breath and asked, "Do you have any idea how much damage those statements that you made to that reporter did to the integrity of our legal system and our police department?"

"I was simply being honest. The integrity of the legal system should be able to stand up under the scrutiny of honesty."

He began to get more tense, and his face was once again flushed. "No! You essentially said that I failed to properly do my job and because of that, the entire legal system just followed my lead."

"As I just said, I was being honest."

Cassidy was beginning to visibly shake now, and Dr. Poole noticed Kidd's attention sharpen at this. He appeared to be ready to tackle Cassidy to the ground at a moment's notice. He was no longer leaning against the closed door, and his hands were no longer clasped in front of him. Dr. Poole was careful to maintain her physically casual stance. Provoking Cassidy right now would most likely end in a very embarrassing way for Dr. Jacobs' practice. And she'd only been running it for two weeks.

Cassidy took a few seconds to regain some measure of control before speaking again. "It was his golf club with only his prints on it. He was seen leaving the crime scene shortly after the crime was known to have been committed. His mother's bra, with his mother's blood on it, was found in his closet in his house. He had motive, means and opportunity. The son of a bitch is guilty, and I put the cuffs on him myself. I was actually happy when I did, too."

"I'm going to say something, and I hope you don't take this the wrong way. I don't deal with evidence. I don't deal with crime scenes. What I deal with are people. More accurately, the way they walk and carry themselves. The way they talk and not only what they say but how they say it. I deal with human psyches, traits and tendencies. What I saw from Dean Connelly was a twenty-three year old who had been coddled and supported by his mother for his entire life. She paid his way through college, where he undoubtedly attended more parties than classes, yet he was still given a degree. Not because he earned it, but because his father was a senator and his mother threw money at the university. He never earned a single thing in his entire life and lacks any ambition to try to earn anything for himself. He's weak and quite childish in many ways.

"There are dozens of other characteristics that I could bring up but, in short, if you were to put the weapon in his hand and tell him that if he killed his mother he'd be financially set for the rest of his life and never spend a day in jail for it, he still wouldn't be able to swing the damn thing, let alone cave in his mother's skull."

"Alright, doctor, since you're so much smarter than us, in spite of the evidence against him, let's say he didn't do it. If, as you're convinced, that's the case … then who the hell did?"

Now her carefully maintained expression faltered. A look of surprise took over her entire being. "How am I supposed to know? Finding out who actually killed his mother is supposed to be your job."

Kidd raised his eyebrows and smiled but said nothing.

Cassidy was now red in the face again and his fists were clenched. "We did our job, and everything led to him!"

"Then you didn't do your job well enough now, did you?"

"My God, you're a pain in the ass."

"I have news for you detective; if you don't unclench your fists and calm down, you're going to find out where else I can be a pain." She knew this wasn't the wisest course of action to take at that particular moment, but he was actually getting under her skin and she couldn't help herself.

"Are you serious? Now you're physically threatening me?"

Dr. Poole slowly shook her head and said, "That wasn't a threat; it was a response to yours."

"What threat? I never threatened you! Kidd, did you hear me threaten her?" He was breathing heavily now and the veins in his neck were visibly pulsing from the increased blood pressure.

"Not verbally. Physically you're telling me that you'd like nothing better right now than to smash my face in. It's the second time today that you issued that very same threat toward me. Your entire body is screaming that fact more clearly than if you declared it verbally. You see, my job is to read all of those signs and interpret their meanings. And I am quite good at my job. However, since your physical stance and posture indicate that you're either blatantly threatening me, or at the very least attempting to intimidate me, you are currently a potential danger. I'm simply responding in a way you can understand. If you attack me, I'll be forced to injure you so severely that a stay in the hospital wouldn't be outside the realm of possibility."

Cassidy took a step back and tilted his head toward the ceiling. He stayed that way for a few moments then burst out laughing. Kidd had been carefully studying her body language while she and Cassidy had been speaking, and a shiver went down his spine. She wasn't joking, and he knew it. Whether or not she was physically capable of what she said was of little consequence. She believed that she was capable of carrying out what she stated, and that made him very nervous. But since he felt the possibility that Cassidy might really physically assault her had passed, he relaxed again and leaned back against the closed door.

Cassidy was now shaking his head and laughing so hard that tears were beginning to stream down his cheeks. Dr. Poole was still leaning against her desk in a completely relaxed pose. Eventually Cassidy composed himself enough to speak. "Alright, doc, you've got balls. I'll give you that much. But there is no way that Dean Connelly is innocent, just like there is no way that someone else killed Sarah Connelly in order to frame him. Come on, Kidd. Let's let the doctor get back to her work."

Cassidy stepped forward and reached out his hand, "I don't like the things you said to that reporter, and I think you overstepped your bounds. But I will admit that you earned my admiration and respect. It definitely takes big brass balls to do what you did, and I have to respect that."

She casually unfolded her arms and shook his hand. "I know that you and Detective Kidd have a very difficult job. I wasn't trying to downplay that. But, I stand by my statements and hope that someday they'll be proven correct."

Cassidy released her hand and stepped back. He then stared into her eyes for a moment before asking, "Have we met before today? You look very familiar to me."

"I'm sure I would remember had I met you before."

Cassidy stared for a bit longer then nodded. "You're probably right. There's just something I can't quite put my finger on."

Kidd finally stepped away from the door and reached for the handle. "Come on, Cassidy, you said what you came to say. It's time for us to get back to work. Let's go."

Cassidy nodded. "Maybe we'll meet again."

Dr. Poole replied, "Maybe we shall."

With that, Kidd opened the door and let Cassidy walk out. Once Cassidy was outside the office, Kidd looked straight into Dr. Poole's eyes and simply nodded. Then he turned and followed Cassidy down the hall toward the stairs.

That simple look and nod told Dr. Poole that Detective Kidd knew she wasn't just running her mouth. He was either smarter than Cassidy, or he was paying closer attention than Cassidy was.

Not thirty seconds after the detectives left the office building, there was a knock on the door. "Come in, Rebecca."

Rebecca entered with a wide grin on her face. "You're terrible, do you know that?"

Dr. Poole smiled. "I wanted a witness who wasn't on their side. Just in case Cassidy was unable to control his temper. Should it have become violent, I couldn't trust his partner to have been honest about the events and how they unfolded. You understand."

"I have to admit I was quite surprised when you asked me to keep the line open to your office phone. You must have had your end muted so they couldn't hear me."

"Yes, I had the volume turned all the way down. If they had known someone else was listening, I wouldn't have gotten a sincere reaction from Cassidy. I also didn't want them to hear you if you started laughing!"

"I was laughing! I can't believe you said half of that stuff to him. A couple of clients waiting to see the therapists were looking at me like I was the one that needed help. By the way, you are aware that he carries a gun, right? Why would you threaten a police officer?"

"He was standing far too close to have actually used it effectively. The other detective, however, could have protected his partner had it gotten that far."

Rebecca's expression changed as she asked, "You were serious when you told him that you were going to hospitalize him, weren't you?"

"Very."

"He was right, hon. You got balls. Big, shiny, brass balls!"

Stacey ran her hand down the front of her skirt and said, "You know … maybe I do." Both of them began to laugh wildly. "Now get out of here and go back to work. I have a lot to do and don't want to be stuck here all evening again."

As Rebecca was getting ready to go back down to her station at the reception desk, there was a very gentle knock on Dr. Poole's door. Rebecca opened the door with a puzzled look on her face. When she saw who was standing there, she was genuinely surprised. Not so much because of who it was, but because of the look of absolute fear that she saw on his face.

"Dr. Poole, what was Cassidy doing here? What'd he say about me?"

Dr. Poole was completely taken off guard. "Quinn? Why would Detective Cassidy have anything to say about you?"

Quinn visibly relaxed, but not completely. "This was a one-time visit, right? He won't be coming here often, will he?"

Rebecca asked, "Quinn, what the hell is wrong with you? Why does Detective Cassidy make you so nervous?"

"Never mind. It's not important. I just needed to make sure he wasn't here for me."

Dr. Poole was still recovering from her initial surprise at Quinn's reaction to Cassidy's visit, but her curiosity was overwhelming. "Quinn, relax. Take a breath. Come all the way into the office and close the door."

Quinn nodded and did as she instructed.

"Alright. Now, what is your issue with Detective Cassidy?"

"He wants me dead! That's my issue with Detective Cassidy. When a man who carries a gun threatens to kill you, you tend to get a little nervous."

Dr. Poole and Rebecca looked quickly at each other then returned their focus to Quinn. Rebecca had never seen Quinn like this. In fact, she'd rarely seen Quinn be serious at all. "Why did Detective Cassidy threaten your life?"

Quinn thought about it for a moment and shook his head. "I probably shouldn't say anything. Just tell me that his visit was a one-time deal."

Dr. Poole said, "I don't know if I can do that. I made him very upset with the interview I gave earlier about Dean Connelly."

Instead of asking what she'd said to upset Cassidy, Quinn simply stood there, clearly in deep thought about something.

Dr. Poole prompted, "Quinn, what is your issue? If you're serious about the threat against your life, I think we need to know. There are five other therapists who work here and their safety, as well as yours, is my responsibility inside this building."

Quinn nodded quickly and took a deep breath. "I've been having an affair with his wife for just over a year, and he found out about it a couple of weeks ago. I was supposed to be meeting Kathy on a recent Saturday while he was out of town on a fishing trip or something, but he showed up instead of Kathy. He was so pissed, he was shaking. He told me that if I ever lay eyes on his wife again, he'll kill me and bury me in the mountains. Dr. Poole, he was deadly serious when he threatened me. I'm absolutely certain that if we hadn't been in a public restaurant, he'd have pulled out his gun and shot me right then and there."

Rebecca quietly asked, "An affair with his wife? Quinn, what the hell were you thinking?"

Quinn snapped his head toward her and exclaimed, "It wasn't like I knew she was married! At least, not at first. When Kathy and I first met, she claimed her husband had died. It wasn't until we'd been together for a few weeks and I asked why she never invited me to her place that she told me the truth. By then, it was too late. I was head over heels in love."

Rebecca exclaimed, "Surely you haven't seen her since Cassidy threatened you? Please tell me that you weren't stupid enough to do that!"

Quinn was shaking his head and tears were beginning to well up in his eyes. "No. I haven't seen her, but God, I miss her. I had been trying to get her to leave him for months. Both of them are Catholic; divorce wasn't something she was willing to do. At least not yet. Then, somehow, he found out. He probably threatened her life, too."

Dr. Poole calmly directed, "Slow down, Quinn. Aside from today, have you seen Cassidy since he threatened you?"

"No."

"Then as long as you stay away from his wife, I don't think he'll come after you. I do have to ask though. The day I arrived here and introduced myself, you'd just slept with someone the night before. If you were so head over heels in love with Mrs. Cassidy, what were you doing out with someone else?"

"Hell, I don't know. I went out for a couple of drinks to try to take my mind off Kathy. This tall blonde was sitting by herself at the bar, so we started talking. Next thing I know, we're pawing at each other. You probably don't need many details about the rest of that night. It helped a little though. It was the first time I'd gone that long without thinking about Kathy."

Rebecca asked, "What about all of those times you came in wearing wrinkled clothes and smelling of perfume?"

"For the last year, that was probably Kathy's perfume. Anytime he'd get a call to investigate something during the middle of the night, she'd come over. I just never bothered telling anyone that I'd been sleeping with one woman, and you all just assumed that I was being a male whore."

"Of course we did! It wasn't an assumption. You *are* a male whore. That's why it's so surprising to me that you claim you fell in love."

"Hey, I have feelings just like anyone else!"

Rebecca took a deep breath and said, "I'm sure you do. I'm sorry I said that. But the front you put up didn't do anything to back up what you're telling us now."

He looked back and forth. "You guys aren't going to say anything to anyone, right?"

"No, Quinn. You're secret is safe here. I wouldn't want any of the other therapists to know you actually have a heart or anything."

"Good, thank you. I appreciate that."

Dr. Poole was smiling and seemingly off in her own world at the moment. Rebecca noticed and asked, "What are you smiling about?"

Dr. Poole snapped herself out of whatever it was she had been thinking and looked directly at Quinn. "I was thinking about our threesome."

Quinn relaxed a bit and started to quietly laugh. Rebecca was staring at Stacey with her mouth wide open and her eyes the size of silver dollars.

Dr. Poole said, "Seriously, though, if Cassidy gives you any shit, I need to know about it immediately. If a case of harassment begins to develop, it needs to be documented and reported without hesitation."

Quinn was still laughing at Dr. Poole's reply—but he was actually laughing more at Rebecca's reaction. But he still nodded and thanked both of them as he left the office.

Rebecca stood quite still for several seconds after Quinn left, just staring at Stacey. Finally, she asked, "Why would you encourage him like that?"

"He's been dealing with a broken heart and fear over a homicide detective threatening his life. Yet he managed to hide that from all of you. I was just letting him know that he could still be himself around us. It appeared to work. Why are you so shocked?"

"I just can't believe you'd feed into him like that. I've spent years trying to get him to stop hitting on me like he's a dog in heat, and here you are egging him on like it's alright."

"Aw, Rebecca. We're all adults here. He does that stuff to see the reactions. If you want him to back off, don't give him the reactions he wants. That's all I was doing. Relax. It's not like you're going to wake up completely worn out and entirely sexually satisfied lying in bed with the two of us one morning."

"Oh, my God! You might be worse than he is. Thanks. It's going to take me days to get that image out of my head now."

Dr. Poole was laughing as she went back to her seat behind the desk and said, "Get out of here; I have a lot of work to do."

Rebecca was still staring in disbelief as she slipped out of her office.

*****

That evening all of the news reports—local, state and national— were announcing that Dr. Stacey Poole stood alone as the only person who believed Dean Connelly was innocent of killing his mother in cold blood in her own home. As a side story for most of the networks, they began to run analyses from so-called experts. Everyone was talking about the state and federal legal systems and whether or not Dr. Poole's evaluation of that system was valid in any way. The general tone of most of the news agencies that were broadcasting Courtney Bancroft's interview with Dr. Poole was that, while there was validity to her criticism of the legal system, Detective Cassidy was completely justified in his investigation and arrest of Dean Connelly.

CHAPTER 7

Monday, August 3

Cassidy answered his cell phone. "This is Cassidy. What? Wait a minute, you received what? When? By mail? We're on our way!"

Kidd remained silent but looked questioningly at Cassidy.

Cassidy hit his flashers and did a high speed U-turn. "I don't believe it. I can't believe it. I'm not even going to tell you what they said. If it's true, you'll have to see it for yourself. Hell, I won't believe it until I see it for myself."

Kidd nodded slowly as he made sure his safety belt was snug. "Where are we going?"

"Back to the station."

Kidd glanced over at the speedometer as it passed seventy miles per hour. He watched out the windshield as cars rushed to get out of their way. During the entire five minutes that it took to get back to the station, he didn't bother to say a word.

Once in the station they went straight to the captain's office. The blinds were pulled, which was always a bad sign. The only time either of them ever saw the blinds closed was when the captain was chewing out one of the officers for screwing up. Cassidy banged on the door; a few moments later, they saw the blinds shift and a set of eyes peering back at them. Then the eyes vanished behind the blinds, and they heard the click of the door being unlocked.

When they entered the room, they saw that Assistant District Attorney Harrison was also present. They also saw that he was as pale as a ghost.

There were no greetings, no welcomes, not even a nod of acknowledgement. The captain, William Bordeaux, hurried back behind his desk and picked up the padded manila envelope. He and Harrison were both wearing latex gloves, which was extremely odd. Captain Bordeaux waved the envelope back and forth a couple of times before he spoke.

"Alright, guys, we really screwed the pooch on this one. We need to proceed cautiously and develop a plan to limit the fallout. Maybe we can still come out of this with our jobs if we're able to manage the situation."

Kidd, who still didn't know what any of this was about, stepped forward and asked as he stared at the envelope, "Would someone mind telling me what the hell is going on and why you're all so paranoid?"

Captain Bordeaux set the envelope on his desk. He gently slid out the paper and set it so that Kidd and Cassidy could read it.

It was great fun watching the lawyers convince a man to plead guilty to a crime he didn't commit. It makes me proud to be an American. Make no mistake; I will kill again. King Midas is too damned dumb to catch me. But there is a way to stop me. King Midas must die. When his heart stops beating, I will stop killing. What do you say, King Midas? Are you the type of man who will choose to end his own life to spare the lives of the innocent? Or are you a coward who will let others die so you can keep on breathing?

Cassidy and Kidd read the message over and over again. Not because they were studying it for clues and certainly not because they were trying to gain a better understanding of the message. They were both in shock, and their minds couldn't keep up with what they were seeing.

Finally, Kidd said, "Maybe this is just some asshole that's trying to get attention."

"I'm afraid that's not the case," Captain Bordeaux stated glumly. He then carefully slid out a Ziploc sandwich bag and placed it next to the letter.

Cassidy quietly asked, "Is that … ?"

Captain Bordeaux nodded in confirmation. "We think that's one of Mrs. Connelly's missing toes."

Kidd said, "We need to get that to forensics. They need to go over every inch of all of this with the most powerful microscope they have. There has to be something that tells us who sent it."

The captain continued, "We already called Robin. She's on her way over right now. We need to contain this. Not a word about this gets out to anybody until we get some answers as to who this toe belongs to."

Cassidy speculated, "Maybe Dean has an accomplice. The doc said it herself; he wasn't capable of committing the crime. Maybe he had someone do it for him and that's who's responsible for this."

For the first time since the detectives arrived at the office, ADA Harrison cleared his throat and began to talk. "We already thought about that. The problem is, if someone was working with Connelly, why wouldn't he have sent this before Connelly confessed? Why wait until Connelly was already convicted? It doesn't make any sense."

"Where was this mailed from?"

"It just has a Denver post mark. It could have been dropped into any public mailbox downtown."

Kidd looked at each of them in turn then asked, "So where's the other toe?"

They heard a knock and, as before, Captain Bordeaux peeked through the blinds to see who it was before unlocking the door. He cracked it and looked around before opening it so that Robin could enter.

"Thank you for coming so quickly. We need you to tell us anything you can find out about this." He motioned to his desk.

Robin looked over the envelope and Ziploc bag then read the note. The color drained from her face and she pulled a pair of latex gloves from her kit and snapped them on without a word. She then produced three evidence bags and carefully bagged each item separately. Once they were sealed, she wrote on the evidence bags the time, date and location where the contents were collected; then she pulled out a notebook and wrote down who was in the room.

Once she finished and the evidence bags were tucked out of sight in her collection kit, she looked at Captain Bordeaux. "Who touched what?"

Bordeaux said, "The envelope? Who can tell? I know I did because I opened it. Ross was the one who brought it to my office. Before that, I have no idea. As for the contents, I touched the letter and the Ziploc bag. Once I saw what they were, I put these on and nobody else touched them besides me."

"What time did this arrive here?"

"Ross brought it to me with the morning mail. That would have been just after 9:00 a.m."

She finished and put her notebook away then said, "I'll call you the instant we're done processing these. It just became our highest priority. I'd also like one of your men to escort me back to the lab. I don't want any of this to be transported by just one person. I want no opportunity for anyone to claim we acted in any fashion except with the utmost professionalism."

Cassidy offered, "I'll escort you."

Captain Bordeaux exploded, "Like hell you will! You're benched. I want you nowhere near any of this shit. In fact, go home. Take the rest of the day. Shit, take the rest of the week off. Dr. Poole may as well have told the world that you set up Connelly to take the fall for his mother's murder. I want you under the biggest rock you can find."

"Captain! Are you suspending me?"

"No, I'm strongly suggesting that you put in for personal leave. Eventually the media is going to have to be let in on this, and I want you nowhere near any of it when we tell them. As of right now, you're done here until this all gets sorted out."

"What about me, Captain?"

"Jeremy, the note was directed at Cassidy. I don't see any reason why you can't continue to dig into this. Just do so quietly. I'll have Brandon escort the evidence back to the lab though. Since you're his partner, I don't want you near those items while they're in transit."

Kidd nodded then said, "Maybe we should bring in Dr. Brandt and get him up to speed. We could have him work up a profile."

"Good idea. I'll call him once those are safely in the lab. I made a handwritten copy of the letter. He should be able to work with that until Robin's done with the original."

Cassidy looked as though he were about to say something when the captain raised his hand to cut him off. "I don't want to hear a word out of you. Get the paperwork filled out. As of today I expect you to be on vacation or personal leave. Hell! I don't care if you write down that it's for maternity leave. Just turn in the paper to human resources and get the hell out of here!"

Cassidy clamped his jaw tight and left the office without a word.

"Kidd, go have Brandon escort Robin back to the lab; but I want nobody telling him a damn thing about why. Lie to him if you have to. We need to keep this contained."

Kidd said, "I'll call Brandt and bring him in, too. You and Harrison need to spend your time trying to figure out how to deal with this."

"Fine. One more thing, Kidd. Cassidy is a damn good cop, but he's as stubborn as all of my ex-wives combined. If that jackass even thinks about sticking his nose into any of this, I want you to arrest him and put him in solitary downstairs."

Kidd nodded and offered as he left the office, "Come on, Robin. I'll take you to Brandon so you can get to work on those."

Once out in the bullpen, Kidd spotted Brandon pouring a cup of coffee. "Hey, Brandon. I have a little chore for you."

Brandon set down his cup and walked over to Kidd and Robin. "Hi, Robin, it's been a long time. What brings you over here?"

Robin cheerfully lifted her evidence collection bag and said, "ADA Harrison had some stuff for a case he's handling and wanted it processed. Would you mind walking me back to the lab, please? He suggested that I have an escort since it's sensitive."

"Of course. I'd be happy to. How are the kids doing?"

They began to walk toward the exit as Robin kept up the small talk. Once they were out of the bullpen, Kidd hurried over to his desk to call Dr. Brandt.

"This is bullshit," Cassidy whispered as he continued to fill out the request for leave papers.

"For now, just do as the captain ordered. I was told to arrest you if I catch you snooping into any of this, and I think he was serious this time. Go home; take your wife shopping or something."

"Christ, this sucks!"

"Keep your voice down, dumb ass. Get out of here."

Cassidy snatched the request for leave forms and stormed off, presumably headed to HR to turn them in.

Kidd watched him leave then looked around the bullpen. Nobody had paid any attention to Cassidy. He was hotheaded, and they were all so used to him that they didn't even notice as he stomped out of the room. Kidd sighed and collected his thoughts before he punched some keys on his computer and found the number for Dr. Brandt.

"Hello, Renee, this is Detective Kidd. Is Dr. Brandt in? Great, can you patch me through to him please? Hello, Dr. Brandt, Jeremy here. Would you mind coming down to the station please? We have something that requires your expertise. No, I'm afraid it can't wait. Yes, as soon as humanly possible; it's quite important. Yes, that may be an understatement. Okay, I'll inform the captain and we'll see you in twenty minutes. Thank you."

He went back and softly knocked on the captain's door. This time, the door opened for him immediately.

"Well?"

"Cassidy filled out the forms and stormed out of the bullpen … I assume he's on his way to HR with them. Brandon is escorting Robin back to the lab, and I just hung up with Dr. Brandt. He'll be here in twenty."

"Alright, Harrison, do you have any ideas right now?"

"Just one. Through all of this, the only one who steadfastly claimed that Dean was innocent was Dr. Poole. She didn't just *think* he was innocent, she was *convinced*. If she's that damned good, I'd like to have her work with Dr. Brandt on this profile. We need to know more about the type of person that's doing this."

"Are you sure?"

"Captain, you didn't see her at the courthouse Thursday, although you did see her interview after Connelly pled guilty. Anyway, after a two-hour evaluation with Connelly, there wasn't a doubt in her mind that he was innocent. Even after he took the plea agreement, she was adamant. I want her brought into the loop. We need all the help we can get." He then paused for a few seconds before continuing. "She gave the legal system a black eye with that interview. In the eyes of the media, it would go a long way toward repairing that damage by having her work with us on this."

"Damage control. Good idea. You got it. Kidd, can you make that happen?"

"I'll see if she can come in."

"When you're done with that, go talk to Connelly again. He hasn't been transported yet. Be subtle, but try to figure out if there's still any way he could be involved. Maybe this is someone that's working with him. It isn't like he wouldn't have access to the funds to pay someone."

Kidd nodded and said, "I'll go see if Dr. Poole's at her office. It'd be better than trying to explain things over a phone. I'll get to Dean this afternoon. When's he slated to be transferred?"

Harrison jumped in, "Actually, I'm canceling the transfer. In light of the new developments, it may be best to keep him close for now."

Captain Bordeaux asked, "In light of the developments? Who the fuck do you think you're talking to here? We're not some damned reporter that you can buffalo with a smile and a wink. You're in this up to your pearly whites just like we are. But you're right about postponing the transfer. If it turns out that Connelly isn't involved, what's it going to take to get him released?"

"A hell of a lot. Once someone confesses and accepts a plea agreement, reversing that isn't going to happen overnight."

"Great, so if it turns out that Connelly actually is innocent, every day that he spends behind bars is going to mean another day of persecution from the media. Kidd … why are you still here?"

"I'm not, captain." With that he left the office.

*****

"Hi, Rebecca, remember me?"

"Of course I do; it's nice to see you again, detective." She looked around behind him then back to his face.

"He's not with me this time. In fact, he's taking some personal leave. I think he's going to spend some quality time with his wife."

Rebecca raised her eyebrows. "Oh?"

Kidd smiled and said, "Alright, maybe Dr. Poole rattled him a bit."

"Yes, I can see how she might have that effect on someone. What can I do for you?"

"I was wondering if Dr. Poole might be in. I need to speak with her, and it's actually kind of time sensitive."

"She's in her office; hold on a moment." Rebecca flipped open the calendar of Dr. Poole's appointments then said, "Actually, it looks like she's just doing reviews today. I'll give her a call."

"Dr. Poole, Detective Kidd is here and says he needs to speak with you. No, I guess he's on personal leave or something. I don't know, but the detective says it's time sensitive. Okay, I will."

She hung up the phone and motioned to the door. "She asked me to have you go on up. You remember the way?"

Kidd smiled and nodded then said, "Thank you very much. I'm sorry, I don't mean to be a pest or anything, but do you happen to be currently unattached? I was wondering if you'd like to have coffee with me sometime, or maybe lunch?"

Rebecca smiled and replied, "Coffee would be good. Let me know when, and I'll see what I can do."

Kidd's smile grew wider as he nodded and disappeared through the door into the hallway.

The smile was still on his face as he knocked on Dr. Poole's door.

"Come in, detective."

He entered the room and motioned to the seat across the desk from Dr. Poole. "May I?"

Dr. Poole tilted her head and squinted slightly as she nodded. "Alright, something happened that I'm not yet aware of. You have an expression and a bounce in your step that tells me you're happy about something. Yet, after the way things were left last week, I'm having difficulty figuring out just what that might be and why it brings you to me."

Kidd shook his head and replied, "No … well, yes. I mean, I'm happy but not because I'm here to see you."

Dr. Poole raised her eyebrows and said, "I'm sorry to disappoint you, but I didn't force you to come see me."

"No, that's not it. I mean, I'm happy to be here but … shit. I'm here to ask you something on behalf of the department. I'm not happy about having to do that. But downstairs, I asked Rebecca if she'd like to go have coffee with me sometime and she seemed quite receptive to the idea. I am happy about that."

Dr. Poole nodded slowly then continued, "We'll get back to Rebecca and your expectations of where that may lead in a bit. What's this department business that you need me for?"

Kidd felt for a moment as though he were confronting a parent about going on a date with her teenage daughter before realizing that Stacey was most likely messing with him. "Alright, forget about Rebecca, that's completely unrelated to why I'm actually here."

"So should I let her know that she's an afterthought and probably wouldn't have been asked out if it weren't for department business bringing you here?"

"Stop it! No. Can we please start over and this time proceed without you screwing with my head?"

Dr. Poole smiled in apology. "I'm sorry. Sometimes I just amuse myself at the expense of others. I should really put forth the effort to stop doing that, but I get such little entertainment elsewhere. What's this about department business, and where's your volatile partner?"

"He's been asked to take the rest of the week off. I hope like hell he's on his way home to spend that time relaxing with his wife. The reason I'm here is because we received a letter this morning. It looks like you might have been right in your assessment of Dean Connelly. The letter that we received sheds serious doubt on his guilt. The captain wants you to … no, scratch that. The captain would like to know if you'd be willing to assist our department psychologist, Dr. Brandt, in building a profile. Have you had any training as a profiler?"

"Actually, I have. One of my degrees is in criminal psychology. Yet I find it hard to believe that the captain would ask to have me help build a profile. That sounds more like something Harrison would come up with."

"Yes, he is the one that suggested you help us. What led you to him being the one that asked for you?"

"Because he's the one that believes he has the most to lose if it's found out that Dean is innocent. Harrison is the type of man who does whatever's necessary to cover his ass if he thinks there's a chance it could get bitten. He wants to bring me in because I've been vocal about Dean's innocence since my assessment. He's setting things up so that, when the media gets involved, he doesn't take as much heat from them."

Kidd seemed impressed. "That just about covers how it went down, actually."

"Now, about this letter. It must be something pretty serious if you're here in person to ask for my help."

"You've no idea. On second thought, maybe you do have an idea. You seem to be on top of everything else so far. I was asked to see if you'd be willing to come to the station with me. The letter is in forensics right now, but the captain made a handwritten copy word for word."

"Hmm. This sounds intriguing. Yes, I think I'd like to see what the letter says and work with Dr. Brandt on a profile of the author. I'd need access to the full evidence roster from the case and transcripts of all the interviews you and Detective Cassidy had with Mr. Connelly. I don't suppose you videotaped the interviews, did you?"

"The interview at the station we did, and you can have access to my notes of all other interactions with him. Cassidy didn't have much to do with Dean though. He was playing the asshole. I was the one who was supposed to form a link with him."

"You mean you two actually played good cop/bad cop with Mr. Connelly? I thought that only happened in movies."

"It's an effective tool sometimes, in the right circumstances."

"When is Dr. Brandt supposed to be at the station?"

Kidd glanced at his watch and said, "He should be there any minute now."

She grabbed her purse and stood. "Then what are we waiting for?"

On the way through the reception area, she stopped at Rebecca's desk. "I'm going to the station with Detective Kidd. I'll probably be gone for the rest of the day. Do you need me for anything before I go?"

Rebecca shook her head and muttered, "I've been babysitting these fools for years without Dr. Jacobs' assistance. I can handle them for the rest of today."

"Alright, and I expect you to be on your best behavior when you go on your date with Detective Kidd."

Rebecca flushed a little as she questioned, "Oh, you do?"

"Yes, you've been on your own far too long, and I don't want you scaring him off right away. You can be somewhat overbearing from time to time."

Kidd said, "Hello, I'm standing right here."

Both of them ignored him as Rebecca responded. "Hey, I've been on my own for so long because men are generally good-for-nothing asses. Also, if he can't handle me as I am then he isn't going to be man enough for me to consider a second date."

Dr. Poole nodded and said, "You present a valid point. Perhaps subtlety may not be the best way to go for your first personal interaction. That does make some tactical sense. Hmm, hit him with the full on brunt of your personality right up front and see if he's truly man enough to handle it. That is an interesting approach. Okay then, just be yourself and it'll take no time at all before you figure out if he's actually worthy of further consideration."

Kidd spoke up, "Again, I can hear all of this."

Rebecca said, "I am going to insist on paying for what I order though. I certainly wouldn't want him to get the idea that I owe him anything. Also, that chauvinistic male chivalry thing gets very old very fast."

"It sounds like you have a solid game plan for this. You'll have to fill me in on the details after your evaluation's complete."

"Should that be written, or do you think an oral review would be sufficient since it's only a coffee date?"

"If it remains just a coffee date, I see no issue with an oral review. But if the coffee date turns into a long weekend, I'll definitely want more details."

"Alright, I'll make a note of that." Rebecca then began jotting something down on a pad behind the counter.

"Oh, you two are hilarious. Can we please go now?"

"Lead on, oh manly one."

They could hear Rebecca chuckling as they made their way out to the street.

*****

Dr. Poole was led toward the bullpen and met by the captain in the hallway. "He's gone to the lab. The handwritten copy wasn't good enough for him, but he still took it with him anyway."

Kidd sighed and said, "Okay. Doctor, if you wouldn't mind following me please?"

They checked themselves into the lab and found Dr. Brandt standing in front of a large monitor. On the screen was the image of the original note.

"Dr. Brandt, I'd like to introduce you to Dr. Stacey Poole. Dr. Poole, this is Dr. Brandt."

"Dr. Poole, I must say I am honored to make your acquaintance. I've heard wonderful things about you over the past few years. I wish we'd have gotten the opportunity to meet in a more casual setting though. Will we be collaborating on this project?"

"Dr. Brandt, it's a pleasure. If you don't mind, I'd like to offer my assistance." She motioned to the screen. "What kind of paper was this sent on?"

"Ah, yes, excellent! On to business then. It looked as though it were standard copy paper. The kind purchased in any office supply store."

From several feet away Robin said, "Yep, nothing special at all about the paper. It also looks as though it was done using an inkjet printer."

"So it wasn't written on a typewriter of any sort?"

"Nope, there are no impressions of keys striking the sheet. You can also rule out a laser printer, too. It was just a standard inkjet that can be purchased pretty much anywhere."

"Alright, so it was low budget and homemade as opposed to being printed at a public workstation."

Kidd asked, "Is that important?"

Brandt chimed in, "Very astute. I hadn't thought about that. Yes, it means the author of this note probably used a personal computer and printer and produced it at home."

Robin said, "Already covered that. There are no pet hairs or foreign fibers on the paper. If the person who wrote this used personal equipment, a lot of care was taken not to let any contaminants from the home get on the sheet. They must have one of the cleanest printers I've ever seen, too."

Dr. Poole said, "So we're looking for someone meticulous and very clean with a good understanding of how forensics works."

Dr. Brandt responded, "Unfortunately, with the advent of television shows and even entire channels dedicated to the inner workings of forensics, that doesn't narrow down the field a whole lot."

"You're right, so let's focus on the wording. Bold print. That suggests that this person is dedicated to carrying out the threat. The intention is to remove any doubt about it being written halfheartedly."

Dr. Brandt nodded and said, "Also note the use of punctuation and sentence structure. It shows at least some degree of education. Most likely at least a high school graduate. The sentences are short, concise and direct. The author left no room for interpretation. That indicates a preformed plan. Perhaps the author has already chosen the next victim."

Dr. Poole added, "Since there's no timeframe given, we don't know when that might happen. Next week, next month—no limit is given as to when he expects King Midas to expire."

"No, but the implication is that he wants King Midas to kill himself. Note the two-part structure of the note. The author understood that someone other than Cassidy would first read the note. The first few sentences appear to be written to a different person, and then it switches to the last few sentences being directed solely to Cassidy."

"You're right, Dr. Brandt. 'When his heart stops beating, I will stop killing.' is where the note switches to speak directly to Cassidy. The first part of the note being directed at the media makes perfect sense. But the killer can't possibly expect that the police would allow the media to see something like this. If the first part of the note isn't directed at the news outlets, then who do you suppose it is meant for?"

"Also Dr. Poole, notice how the author never actually names Cassidy. Instead he refers to him as King Midas throughout. There's a derogatory nature to the use of that nickname. The author of this note must have had some personal interaction with Cassidy in the past and is clearly indicating that the nickname wasn't warranted."

Robin spoke up, "But he's solved every case he's had since he became a detective. None of those convictions were questioned. This is the first case where the person behind bars may not be the correct one."

Dr. Brandt thought about this for a moment and said, "What if he arrested the wrong man some time before he became a detective?"

Dr. Poole shook her head, "I don't know; how long has Cassidy been a detective?"

Kidd replied, "For fourteen years. He became a detective when he was twenty nine."

Dr. Brandt said with a sigh, "That is a long time to remain silent if the author was convinced that Cassidy sent an innocent man to prison before becoming a detective."

Kidd asked, "Why do you believe the author thinks Cassidy arrested the wrong person some time in the past? It looks like this note was written about only the most recent conviction."

Dr. Poole replied, "If you read the tone of the note instead of just the words, the inference is that this has happened before."

Dr. Brandt was nodding. "There is long-standing hatred associated with this message. So, let us assume that the author of this note actually was the one who killed Mrs. Connelly. That means this whole case was set up to have you and Cassidy arrest and convict the wrong man. That would entail a great deal of planning … selecting just the right victim and just the right potential suspect and then carrying out the murder at just the right time. And we can't forget that the killer also would have needed to plant that bloodied bra at Dean's house and do so in a way that would make it very unlikely that he'd stumble across it before the search was carried out. Very methodical and quite intricate."

Dr. Poole said, "Hence the correct spelling and punctuation. This person must have some level of education and, at the very least, above average intelligence."

She turned to Dr. Brandt and said, "Maybe the person who wrote this was the wrongly convicted man. It could have taken this long before he acted because he was physically unable to act before now."

Dr. Brandt became a bit more excited, "Yes, had this individual been in prison all these years and recently released, that would have given more than ample time to plan all of this. It also explains the obvious hatred more clearly than if the author was enraged about someone else being wrongfully convicted."

Kidd was writing in his notepad this whole time and remarked as he finished scribbling, "Let me make a phone call." With that he moved away to an unpopulated corner of the lab.

Robin said, "The only prints on this paper belong to Captain Bordeaux. Larry, have you come up with anything from the envelope?"

"My name's Arthur, not Larry. There are four sets of prints on the envelope, one of them belonging to Bordeaux. I'll have to run the others through the database, but I have a feeling that they're going to belong to postal employees or someone from the department mail room. The address was written using a simple plastic stencil and Sharpie, the kind you'd find in any grade school classroom."

Dr. Brandt nodded and said, "I suspect you're correct. From what I've seen so far, this person carried this out far too meticulously to then be careless enough to leave a print on the envelope."

Robin called over to another table, "Darryl, do you have anything from that Ziploc bag?"

Dr. Poole raised her eyebrows, "Ziploc bag?"

The other tech guy said, "I looked up Larry, Darryl and Darryl on the Internet. I have to say, the reference is certainly not flattering."

"Just tell me what you got."

"Nothing. The only set of prints belongs to Bordeaux and, other than that, it is factory clean. I mean just like it was still in the box it left the factory in. Not a single hair, no fibers, no particulates. It is absolutely clean. The inside of the bag contains only what one would expect if it held a severed digit. The cells from the blood that was inside the bag tell us that it spent some time in a freezer. The cells show definite signs of having been frozen."

Robin turned to the doctors and continued, "We can run DNA tests, but this guy was far too careful. We already took the sample from the toe though. We won't have the results for some time, but I can tell you that the blood type matched the victim."

Dr. Poole asked, "The toe?"

Dr. Brandt nodded as he explained, "That little bit of information was withheld during this whole thing. The killer took the time to not only cut off the victim's bra but also the pinky toe from each foot."

Dr. Poole cocked her head slightly and asked, "If the killer cut off a toe from each foot, how many are here?"

Robin replied, "Only one was sent … from the left foot."

Dr. Brandt was staring at the note on the monitor again as he quietly asked, "So where's the other toe, and what does the killer plan to do with it?"

"Son of a bitch!" Kidd slammed his phone back into his pocket. "I'm afraid I can answer that one for you, doc. It was sent to the local news station. They just got done interrupting their regularly scheduled programming to air an identical note, and they stated it was accompanied by a human toe. I can't believe they aired that without calling the department first!"

After a few seconds of pacing back and forth, Kidd finally added, "It looks like you called it, Dr. Poole. Now that the whole city, and probably the whole nation, knows about this, any ideas on what we can do next?"

Dr. Poole looked at the note on the monitor again, then looked to Dr. Brandt.

His face held no answers, and all he could do was stare back.

After a moment she said, "The only thing I can think of right now is to free Dean Connelly. Maybe that'll calm the author of this note long enough for you to figure out a way to find him."

"I'm sure after seeing that on the news, Dean's lawyer is drafting papers to file with the courts as we speak."

"Dr. Brandt, let's get to work on this profile. The sooner we get that into the hands of the police, the better."

"Yes Dr. Poole, I believe you're right. Robin do you have anywhere here that we may use as a work station for a short while?"

"Grab that table in the corner. What do you need as far as materials go?"

Dr. Poole replied, "Paper, a lot of it. Legal pads would work. Some ink pens, preferably red and black, and time. Detective, we'll need access to your notes about Mr. Connelly and the video of your interview."

Kidd nodded and said on his way out of the lab, "I'll be back as soon as I can."

Dr. Brandt added, "Maybe some caffeine. Perhaps a fair amount of that."

"Darryl, you heard the doctors. Get on it!"

One of the lab techs turned to the other and said, "Apparently I'm the second Darryl; she had to have been speaking to you."

*****

All the rest of that day, every news agency was broadcasting Dr. Poole's interview with Ms. Bancroft from the courthouse. The tone of their reports suggested that the police either rushed or botched the investigation and that the courts coerced Dean Connelly into falsely confessing. Some media outlets were calling for sweeping reforms to the way our nation's legal system functions. All of them were making Detective Cassidy look like he was everything from a bumbling fool to an active conspirator on the case. And all of them were treating Dr. Stacey Poole as though she were now "America's Darling." Almost as an afterthought, they reported on the lengthy process of reversing a conviction and just how much time Dean Connelly would have to sit behind bars before he could eventually be released.

CHAPTER 8

————•——

Friday, August 8

"Good morning, detective. Any word about Cassidy yet?"

"I spoke with him yesterday. He's anxious to get back to work. Hopefully we'll get some resolution soon. What do you have for me?"

"Aaron Matthews, 47. According to the initial findings of the medical examiner, he was killed late last night. The ME put the approximate time of death between 11:00 p.m. and 1:00 a.m. The cause of death was strangulation. We have his wife in custody. She's in the back of one of the patrol cars outside, but she swears she didn't do it. She's the one that called 911 at 5:37 a.m. She said she woke up and he wasn't in bed, so she got up to see if he fell asleep in front of the television again. According to her, she was getting ready to cover him with a blanket when she noticed the marks on his neck. She tried to wake him up, but he was cold and stiff. That's when she called 911. When we got here, we found a broken table lamp and blood on the lamp cord. The lamp was lying on the floor behind his chair."

Chills went through Detective Kidd. "Has he been moved?"

"No, we were waiting for you and forensics to get here."

Kidd went to the living room and scanned the entire scene. "Where's the ME?"

"I'm in here; is that you, Kidd?"

Kidd followed the voice to the kitchen where he found the medical examiner sitting at the kitchen table eating a fried egg sandwich.

"Why are you looking at me like that? I made it before I came to the scene. It's cold, but not bad, and I didn't get a chance to have breakfast before rushing over here."

Kidd shook his head. "Did you already get the photos you needed?"

"Yes, Jeff has the camera. Why?"

"He's still wearing his work boots. Have you checked yet?"

The ME looked puzzled for a moment before an expression of understanding touched his features. "You don't think ... Oh, my word. No, I didn't. Let's go."

He wrapped up the fried egg sandwich and stuffed it back into his bag. He and Detective Kidd went to the living room and moved to stand between Aaron Matthews and the television. The ME gave a quick glance toward Detective Kidd before he knelt down and began carefully unlacing one of the work boots. After a bit of effort, he managed to free the boot from the victim's foot and saw a blood stain on the outside of the white crew sock. He carefully rolled the sock down, removed it, and placed it in the evidence bag Kidd had already opened for him.

"Just like Mrs. Connelly," the ME muttered.

"I need to talk to the wife. Everybody clear the house until forensics gets here. I want nothing else touched anywhere."

Once everyone was out of the house and the exits were secured, Kidd went over to the officer who responded to the 911 call. After reading his name tag, he directed, "Ross, I need you to gather as many officers as you can. I want this yard scoured. Any gum wrapper, any footprint—I don't care how insignificant it seems—I want it measured and photographed, and I want its location documented. I want every square inch covered. I need a few men to start canvassing the area. Go door to door. I need to know if anyone saw anything at all between 10:00 p.m. and 2:00 a.m. Again, no detail can be considered trivial. If someone was walking a dog, I want a description of that person. Do you understand?"

"Yes, sir." As he turned to walk away, he keyed up his radio and Kidd could hear him requesting manpower at the scene as his voice trailed off into the distance.

"Doc, do you need any assistance with the body? I can have men here to help you. Whatever you need, just let me know."

"All I need is for forensics to collect everything they need so I can get the body down to autopsy."

"Alright, can someone tell me where the wife is, please?"

One of the uniformed officers pointed toward a patrol car parked across the street.

"Are you Mrs. Matthews?"

The handcuffed lady in the back of the cruiser nodded quickly while tears streamed down her face.

"Alright, this is extremely important. Can you tell me exactly what happened last night? I don't want speculation; I don't want supposition. I want only what you can verify as having actually happened. Can you do that?"

Again she nodded.

"What time did your husband come home last night?"

"He works afternoon shift down at the plant. He got home at 11:15 p.m. I was already in bed but still awake. I looked at the alarm clock on the nightstand when I heard him come in. He came to the bedroom, but I pretended to be asleep. He went to the kitchen and opened the fridge. I heard him open a bottle of beer, then I heard the TV come on. I closed my eyes and fell asleep not long after that. I woke up just after 5:30 a.m. and realized he'd never come to bed. I assumed he'd fallen asleep watching TV. I went to the bathroom then went to the living room to check on him. I grabbed a blanket and got ready to cover him with it when the TV screen switched to something that was brighter. In the extra light, I noticed a little blood on the corner of his mouth. I turned on the living room light and saw the marks around his neck and the lamp lying behind the chair. When I touched him, he was cold. I dropped the blanket and ran back to the bedroom and called 911. I didn't leave the bedroom until the officers came banging on the door."

Kidd finished jotting down his notes and said, "Thank you. Can I get an officer over here to take these cuffs off Mrs. Matthews, please?"

One of the uniformed officers trotted over and helped her out of the car. After removing the handcuffs, he went back to join his fellow officers searching the yard.

"I'll need an official statement from you, so you're going to have to come down to the station with us; but I don't see any reason to keep you handcuffed until then."

"You believe me? The other officer looked at me like I was making everything up. I think he believed I did this."

"It's alright. Right now I need you to have a seat right here. I won't lock you in, but I need your word that you won't leave this car, okay?"

"Yes, thank you for taking the cuffs off. I'll stay right here. I promise."

Robin had a hard time finding Kidd amongst the flashers and dim morning light emanating from the overcast sky. "Kidd! My team's here, and they're ready."

"Great. I'll be back in a minute, Mrs. Matthews. Robin, bring your team and follow me."

Once inside the house, he pointed to the living room. "The victim is in there, but I want this entire house gone over. It looks like our killer has struck again."

Robin grimaced. "Are you sure?"

"Not positive, but the ME and I checked one of his feet … the little toe was removed."

Robin sighed as she directed, "Okay, boys. You know what to do. We'll go room by room. Larry, go get the extra evidence bags from the van and bring the UV light. We're doing a full workup on this residence."

She turned back to Kidd and said, "By the time we're done here and get everything back to the lab, I don't know how much time we'll have to go over what we collect."

"Just give me a call, Robin."

"Alright, you got it. Darryl and Darryl, you two with me, we need to collect what we can from the body so the ME can get it out of here pronto! Let's move."

Kidd watched for a few minutes while the forensic team went into action. Finally, Robin noticed him standing there and said, "Don't you have a jaywalker to arrest or something?"

Kidd got the hint and went back outside. The uniformed officers were disbanding their search of the yard as the responding officer came up to him. "We got nothing. No footprints, and nothing that looked like it hadn't been there for some time."

"This guy can't be a damned ghost. There must be something. How did he get into the house? Where'd he go when he left the house? How many people do you have banging on doors?"

"It's 7:00 a.m. A lot of people are still sleeping. My men are doing what they can."

Kidd took a deep breath and said, "I know. I'm sorry. Report back to me when you find something. Have someone take Mrs. Matthews to the station. Keep her comfortable and, if she's hungry, get her something eat and drink. Tell her I'll be there as soon as I can."

He pulled out his phone and cursed as he hit the button. "Captain, it's Kidd. Yeah, I know what time it is. Yes, I know you're not at the office yet. Of course I know this is your damned personal phone; I'm the one that called you. I think he struck again. No, not positive yet, but the victim is missing his pinky toe on at least one foot. The ME will check the other one when he gets to autopsy. Yes, Robin's team is going over every inch of the house, and I had the uniforms do a search of the yard. No, nothing so far. I'm sending the victim's wife to the station. If you don't want to wait for me, then have one of the guys at the station question her and take her statement.

"Hell, yes, I expect her to stay there until we know for certain; but, Captain … if we don't find his toes, we can't be expected to arrest her. Yes, Captain, I'm aware … oh, shit. How the hell do they know already? I have to go; the media is rolling in."

He hung up on his captain and grabbed the nearest uniformed officer. By now, three more squad cars had arrived and those officers were helping bang on doors. "Hey, I need you to head off that news van. Get your men to set up a barrier and keep them well away from this yard. Christ, I wish Cassidy were here to help me with this shit."

As Kidd turned to check with an officer who had been going door to door, one of the bystanders that was watching the coordinated chaos of the crime scene investigation turned to the guy who had just walked up next to him. "Can you believe this shit? Dude, are you alright? You look all sweaty, and it must only be in the sixties right now."

With a big grin on his face, he responded. "Yeah, I'm freaking great! I just busted my ass pedaling my mountain bike over here. It was at least two miles. I made great time. Did you overhear anything from any of the cops?"

The first gentleman reached out his hand. "My name's Alex, Alex Tanner. You rode your bike here from two miles away? How'd you find out about this?"

As he shook Alex's hand he offered, "Travis Parker. I have a police scanner. I heard the call and hauled ass. Well? Did you hear any details from any of the cops?"

"No, as I was walking up, they were just moving the crime scene tape to include the entire yard. I've been too far away to hear anything."

Behind them and off to their left they heard a reporter asking her cameraman about the lighting. "It's not even seven yet. I know it's overcast, but you have me looking straight into the morning sun. Can't we turn a bit and do this at an angle?"

Travis turned and watched them as they were setting up to film and nudged his new friend Alex. "Hey, they're getting ready to film a report. We need to move over there so we're not in frame."

"Are you kidding? We might be on TV. Why would you want to move?"

"I really don't want to be on TV. You can stay here if you want, but I'm going over there so they don't catch me on film by accident."

"Alright, I'll move with you."

"Do you know the victim?"

"Yeah, I live over there. The guy is a complete douche bag. I've heard him yelling at his wife some. I never heard her yell back though. I'm pretty sure he'd hit her sometimes, too."

"Where's his wife? Did they already arrest her and take her away?"

"No, she's right over there. See that cruiser? That's her leaning against the trunk."

Travis squinted to get a better view of her through the strobes and flashers of the cruiser. "She doesn't even look like she's cuffed."

Alex pointed at Detective Kidd and explained, "Just before you got here, that dude went over and let her out of the cruiser. They had her cuffed, then he called to one of the uniforms to take the cuffs off her. She's just been hanging out around that cruiser since then."

Travis frowned a bit and said, "I wonder why they took the cuffs off her. That doesn't make sense." He then noticed a police officer banging on the door of one of the houses down the block. As he turned, he saw two more cruisers roll up and join the other three that were already there. He then began doing a head count and came up with twelve officers he could see. There had to be more though. He could see four scattered around at the different houses on the block. They were canvassing the neighborhood. He could still see four more who appeared to be scanning different areas of the small yard. Two were talking with Detective Kidd, and he'd just seen two others enter the house where the crime had been committed.

"If she's not in cuffs and they're talking to the neighbors, they must think the guy who sent that note is the one who did this."

Alex glanced at him and asked, "Huh? What are you talking about?"

"From the Connelly murder. They broadcast the note on Monday."

"Oh, yeah. That King Midas crap, right?"

Travis nodded, then recited the note word for word. He then pulled out a small notebook and pen from his back pocket and began scribbling down notes.

"Dude. Are you some kind of reporter or something? Oh, wait! Are you writing a book?"

Travis shook his head as he answered, "I'm a college student studying law. I came down here because seeing actual police investigations helps me with the classes I'll be taking this semester."

Alex seemed to be let down by the news that he wasn't a reporter or an author gathering information for an upcoming book.

Travis turned to listened more closely to the reporter. Apparently she noticed that the victim's wife wasn't under arrest, too. Her speculation as she gabbed with her cameraman followed his same assumption. Just then, the medical examiner wheeled a gurney through the front door and out to the road where they hefted it into the back of a van.

"Hey, look," he said as he nudged Alex. "The guy's wife is just staring at the gurney. She isn't even crying."

"Why would she? I already told you that the guy was a douche bag. She's probably happy as hell he's dead."

"I see Sundance; I wonder where Butch is?"

"Who?"

"Detective Cassidy. He and Detective Kidd are partners. That's Detective Kidd over there. I haven't seen Detective Cassidy yet though."

"You mean he's the other half of the whole Butch and Sundance thing? I heard about them on the news before. Hey, isn't Cassidy the guy you're talking about—the one they call King Midas?"

"Yeah, that's why I'm wondering why he isn't here. You'd think if this was done by the same person who killed Sarah Connelly, he'd be right in the middle of it trying to figure out who was responsible."

"Well, he isn't here. I've been here since the first patrol car pulled up, and that's the only cop that isn't in a uniform."

"Strange." He noticed more reporters setting up to film their reports and reached out his hand toward Alex. "I need to get going. It was very nice meeting you though."

Alex shook his hand and said, "You too, dude. Travis, right?"

Travis nodded and called back over his shoulder as he headed off toward his mountain bike, "Later!"

Alex watched as he pulled the hood from his sweat jacket up to cover his head then carefully avoided the camera crews as he worked his way back to where he had parked his bike. He glanced back only once before riding away quickly.

*****

Rebecca looked up to see Detective Kidd and an older gentleman entering the front door to the office building. She adjusted her blouse and, as they came into the reception area, smiled and asked, "What can I do for you today?"

The look on Kidd's face made her smile fade away. "You need to talk with Dr. Poole. Hold on, I'll call her."

Once in Dr. Poole's office Dr. Brandt said, "We need to adjust the profile."

"Alright, what new information did you get?"

Kidd replied, "The full picture isn't very clear yet, and it'll be a while before we can go over the forensic team's findings. But I can tell you that there's been another murder, and it's our guy."

Dr. Poole nodded and grabbed a pad and pen. "I'm ready. Hit me with what you have so far."

After fifteen minutes, Kidd finally stopped to take a drink of water from the cooler. Dr. Brandt had pulled out a legal pad from his briefcase and was sitting in the chair in front of Dr. Poole's desk.

Dr. Poole began to summarize their information. "So, different type of murder. Male this time, not female. This time there was a potential witness in the other room who was left unharmed. Again, the murder weapon was not only left at the scene but also originated from the house, like before. So aside from the missing toes, nobody would have known this was our guy. Yet he took the time to not only cut off the toes but also replace the socks and work boots. Do we have any common factors between the two victims? Is there anything linking them except for the toes?"

Kidd shook his head. "I have people in several departments checking into everything, but so far—different income brackets, different social circles—we can't find anything that the victims have in common."

Both Dr. Poole and Dr. Brandt spent some time scratching down notes on their respective pads before Dr. Brandt finally spoke. "This confirms our theory about the state of mind of the killer. He obviously wasn't concerned about being caught by the sleeping wife. That shows a complete lack of self-preservation which is in stark contrast to the fact that he managed to enter and leave without a single witness and, at least as far as we know, without leaving any physical evidence behind."

Dr. Poole said, "Unless he was fully prepared to kill the wife had she interrupted him."

"True. For all of the planning that's obviously involved in these crimes, it's strange that he doesn't bring a murder weapon to the scene with him."

"What if he does? He might carry a gun or knife and just hasn't been forced to use it yet. It appears as though he finds something in the house to commit the murders with, but what if he can't find something quickly once he's inside? He must have a backup plan. There's too much thought put into this to run the risk of failure."

Dr. Brandt thought for a moment before asking, "Detective, how large would you say the victim was?"

Kidd closed his eyes and pictured the victim. "Well, he was sitting when I saw him so I'm not sure about the height, but he had to have been close to six feet tall. He probably weighed about two hundred pounds. Once we get the autopsy findings from Doc Brown, we'll have more exact information. Why?"

"Both victims were taken by surprise from behind. Perhaps our killer isn't very large in stature. It doesn't take a strong person to fracture a skull with a five iron, just as it doesn't take a large person to use a lamp cord to strangle someone. I know it sounds like that should require a fair amount of force, especially against a victim so large, but hear me out for a moment."

"You said the victim had two empty beer bottles next to him and a third that was nearly empty. What if the victim had fallen asleep or was nearly asleep when the attack began? The shock of having a cord wrapped around one's neck and being unable to breathe would cause panic. The killer was behind the chair and had leverage. So even if the victim tried to stand, the full weight of the killer would be at the other end of the electric cord, not to mention the back of the chair that could be used to brace against. Our killer may be below average in height and weight. At least I've seen nothing so far that would indicate that he couldn't be smaller."

Dr. Poole was nodding emphatically. "That would also correspond to the psychological profile. Sneaking in and out without being seen. It could also be the reason he's not going directly after Cassidy. Perhaps he doesn't think he can win a direct confrontation with Cassidy. I'll add the small stature theory to the overall profile. These are all tactics more consistent with smaller, less powerful individuals."

Dr. Brandt added, "The change to the MO is disturbing to me. Most killers who strike more than once tend to have a favored style. If they get away with it, they stick with it. In their minds it offers a greater chance of success and less chance of getting caught. Yet this killer used blunt force trauma, then strangulation. Two very different forms of murder. That is puzzling."

Kidd was dialing his phone, "I'll have the guys at the station go back over Cassidy's arrests and pay particular attention to those who are below average height or weight."

Poole asked, "Doctor, what about the lamp? Do we know where the killer got it? I don't have that in my notes."

Dr. Brandt flipped a couple of pages back and forth and finally hit his finger against the pad. "It was from a spare bedroom."

"So the killer had to walk past the bedroom where Mrs. Matthews was sleeping to get the lamp, then walk past it again to commit the murder? That's very brazen."

Dr. Brandt nodded and said, "Yes, well, we've already determined that our subject is suffering from some level of at least one mental disorder. Most likely he's a very high functioning sociopath with a superiority complex. The fearlessness of passing a room with a sleeping person in it to find an electronic appliance with a suitable cord lends credence to this train of thought. The kitchen was right next to the living room, after all. So if he was bent on strangulation by electrical cord for this victim, I'm quite certain there were items in there that would have sufficed."

Kidd said, "Hold on a second." He then put his hand over the phone. "The lamp was from a spare bedroom. The five iron was from a set of clubs that was in a spare bedroom. I'm sorry, it probably means nothing but I tend to take notice when patterns emerge."

Dr. Poole nodded quickly, "He may be onto something there. In both instances the killer chose a weapon from the furthest room away from the victim. It's almost like he was familiarizing himself with the house before committing the murder and choosing something from a largely unused room as the means."

Dr. Brandt started scribbling notes then said, "People who have spent long periods in jail cells or confined to small quarters tend to exhibit similar behavior when entering unfamiliar places. They like to learn the layout and don't feel comfortable until they've explored their surroundings. As for choosing weapons from unused rooms, that could be a subconscious metaphor for how he feels toward Cassidy. Insignificant and relatively unnoticed in the grand scheme of things, yet in possession of enough power to make sweeping changes in many people's lives. Very good, Dr. Poole."

Kidd put his phone away and remarked, "Unfortunately, that doesn't get us any closer to stopping this maniac."

Dr. Brandt said, "Forgive me for my bluntness, but our killer has already told us how to stop him. It would cost the life of your partner. We're just choosing not to take that course of action."

Kidd became agitated. "We're not choosing that course of action because it's simply wrong!"

Dr. Brandt held up his hand and said, "Don't misunderstand me, here. I'm not stating that we should end Detective Cassidy's life just to stop this particular killer. But I am stating that doing so is only wrong because of our modern society and the way we view the world. Many cultures throughout the millennia would have not only viewed this type of threat very differently than we do, but also acted very differently. In some cultures it would have been expected that if Cassidy were an honorable man, he would have instantly volunteered to end his life before any of his fellow citizens were forced to suffer."

Kidd exclaimed, "That's sick! How can you compare ancient civilizations with ours like that?"

Dr. Poole shook her head and replied, "Some of those civilizations aren't very far removed from our own in terms of time. It was only a century or so ago that the Japanese would have looked at a situation like this in much the same way as Dr. Brandt described."

Dr. Brandt held up a finger and his eyes widened. "That's it. It would explain a great many parts of the profile that we're developing."

Kidd nodded and said, "So, go on. I'm listening."

Dr. Poole was also nodding as she agreed, "Yes, I see. Very good, doctor. Go ahead and explain."

Dr. Brandt cleared his throat and continued, "The typical stereotype of an oriental man is one who is short and thin, yet muscular and in possession of power beyond his size. There are reasons stereotypes exist and, while in today's society they're frowned upon, they all have some basis in fact. The average height of citizens from many Asian nations is below the worldwide average. The same goes for the average weight. We may be looking for someone of Asian ancestry."

Kidd said, "Alright, it can't hurt. I'll add that to the list we already have."

Kidd's phone buzzed again and he held up a finger while he answered it. "Yes? And she corroborated that? Okay, thank you."

"That was the guy at the station who just finished questioning Mrs. Matthews. It seems our victim was a wife beater. They got information about her medical file from the local hospital, and she's apparently a regular there. A few months ago it was a broken wrist. Last year it was a concussion and scalp laceration requiring twenty-three stitches. The reports go back years. The staff suspected she was being abused, but when she was confronted, she denied any wrongdoing. Now that her husband is deceased, she finally feels secure enough to confirm the reports."

Dr. Brandt was deep in thought when Kidd asked, "What? Did that trigger an idea?"

"I was just considering the choice in victims. An overbearing mother, a spouse abusing husband. You don't suppose the killer is choosing these people because of the power that they represent over the one's closest to them in their lives, do you? It may just be coincidence, but it may also be something to look at."

Kidd said, "Where would the killer get the information that these people are overbearing or controlling?"

"I couldn't even hazard a guess at that," Brandt replied.

"I might be able to offer a guess," Dr. Poole raised a finger as she spoke. "Proximity of the crime scenes indicates that they would have shared the same hospital. It's probably nothing and most likely won't lead to anything, but at least it's one point in common between the two cases."

"Alright, if you two come up with anything else, you know how to reach me. I need to get to the coroner's office and see what they have. The autopsy should be done by now. I'll also have the department look into hospital employees and volunteers."

Dr. Poole said, "By the way, detective, you've been out with our Rebecca a couple of times this week. How are things going?"

Kidd smiled and thought about it for a moment before saying, "You're her boss and from the way you two act around each other, you're also friends. You tell me, doc. How does she think things are going?"

Dr. Poole smiled and said, "Very good, detective. You're a quick study."

Kidd's smile broadened, and he nodded to the two doctors as he left the office.

*****

"Hey, doc, what'd the corpse tell you?"

"Nothing more than we already knew from our preliminary findings. Cause of death was, of course, strangulation. Both pinky toes were removed post mortem with a very sharp instrument of some sort. He was a heavy drinker, as attested to by his liver. I can tell you that our killer had at least studied how to properly garrote someone prior to performing this act or was familiar with the practice through previous application."

"You think he killed like this sometime before?"

"As I said, either that or he studied how to. It's amazing what one can find on the Internet. Most people who consider the act of strangulation picture it like they show it in most movies. You take a piece of wire with one end in each hand and swing it over the head, catching the person under the chin. Then you simply apply pressure. That isn't a very effective way of actually killing someone, however.

"The proper way is to loop the cord first, then drop the loop over someone's head and apply pressure by spreading the hands outward. In this way, far less physical force is required to close the air and blood supply to the brain. It's also far more effective in controlling the victim's movements as he struggles. This is how our killer did it. He created the loop first then strangled him."

"What's the smallest someone could most likely be and still be able to strangle our victim in that manner?"

Doctor Brown raised his eyebrows and said, "Not very large at all, actually, if the killer used a knee in the back of the chair for leverage and looped the cord so that it took very little pressure to shut off the air supply through the windpipe. I'd say an average sized teen would be sufficient."

"So it could be a woman?"

Brown nodded and said, "Sure, I suppose so. Keep in mind I'm not the expert on this, but I recall reading somewhere that females tend not to murder in such violent ways as bludgeoning or strangulation. But physically speaking, certainly a female could have carried out these murders. Why? Do you have someone in mind?"

"Not yet, but if you had told me that a woman wasn't capable, that would have cut my suspect pool down from nearly the entire population of the city to only about half."

"Sorry I couldn't have been of more help. On a grimmer note, how long would you say before the packages arrive?"

"I'd say early next week now that the killer isn't waiting for someone else to be convicted of the crime. I'm actually hoping to gain some clue as to who this person is from the next note. Now how sick is that?"

"You're just doing your job, detective. I cut open dead people for a living. Care to compare notes on which may be considered sicker by the general population?"

Kidd laughed and shook his head. "Alright, doc. I concede that one."

Just then Kidd's phone rang. "Talk with you later, doc. This is Kidd."

On the other end of the line he heard Cassidy's voice. "Is it true? Was this another of the killer's victims?"

"How the hell did you hear about it?"

"So it is true then."

"I didn't say that."

"You didn't have to. The fact that you didn't instantly deny it was confirmation enough."

"Mike, you can't be part of this and you know it. How are you getting your information?"

"A good officer never reveals his confidential informants. That's why they put the word confidential in front of informant."

"It's good to know your ability to be a complete smartass hasn't vanished in the last four days. How are you holding up?"

"How do you think I'm holding up? People are dying because of me, and I'm not allowed to do anything about it. This is pure torture. I'm driving my wife nuts; we're arguing all the time. I can't find anything to do to occupy my mind. I'm going insane."

"When did the captain say you could come back?"

"I'm coming back Monday."

"Alright, but when did the captain say you could come back?"

"Officially, I'm on vacation; and I'm ending my vacation when I come back Monday. If the captain doesn't want me there, he can take my badge and gun."

"Wonderful attitude, partner. I've got everyone working on this, including Dr. Poole. She's helping Dr. Brandt with a profile. Speaking of which, have you ever arrested anyone of Asian descent?"

"Wait a minute. You mean Dr. Poole is actually helping me?"

"I don't think she's helping you as much as she's helping us try to catch what appears to be turning into a serial killer."

"Asian, huh? I'm sure I have, why? Is our killer Asian?"

"I don't know; it was just something the doctors were saying. I'm heading back to the station right now. I'll get with the guys going over your arrest history to see if anything catches my eye."

"Okay, if the wife doesn't kill me before then, I'll see you Monday."

"Good luck, Mike."

"Thanks, I'll need it."

*****

On the televised evening news report, the murder was one of the main stories. "This appears to be the second victim for the killer that some people have begun calling 'The Denver City Specter.' The moniker's been issued due to the killer's ability to sneak in and out of his victims' homes without leaving behind any physical evidence. There also appear to be no witnesses who have seen anyone near either home around the time of each murder. One of our sources near the police department did state that, as with the first murder, each baby toe had been severed after the victim was dead. It wasn't until after Dean Connelly had confessed to the first murder that we received the envelope containing the severed toe along with the note demanding Detective Cassidy's death. We believe that it's just a matter of time before we receive a similar envelope again. The police have asked us not to air the note, should we receive one. According to police, the wording of the notes may be used to eliminate suspects, so having them broadcast by our station could be detrimental to their investigation.

"Police are urging us to remind our viewers to keep their doors locked. The more difficult it is to enter your home, the better chance you have of avoiding becoming one of the Specter's victims.

"The reporter on the scene at this morning's murder also told us that Detective Cassidy was mysteriously missing from the group of officers there conducting the investigation. We confirmed this through our source at the Denver City Police Department and were also told that he'd been on vacation during this last week. I have to admit, it seems quite strange to me that a homicide detective would choose this particular time to go on vacation. One has to wonder if it was due to the killer singling him out after the first murder.

"On a side note to this story, it has been confirmed that Dr. Stacey Poole has been working closely with the police trying to produce a profile of the killer. As all of you know, Dr. Poole was the only one who steadfastly maintained that Dean Connelly was innocent of Sarah Connelly's murder. Mr. Connelly continues to languish in jail awaiting a judge's decision on the motion to overturn his conviction. Our legal experts have stated that overturning a conviction such as his is a lengthy and complicated matter, however. But this latest murder can only be considered as confirmation that Dean Connelly is innocent and should have never been pushed by police into making a false confession. We hope to see a speedy release for Mr. Connelly now, especially in light of this new development."

"In the national spotlight this week, it looks like … "

CHAPTER 9

Monday, August 11

"I still don't want you out in the field, Cassidy. If you want to work, sit your ass behind that desk. You can coordinate on investigations and run down leads by phone. But this department simply can't afford to have you out on the streets."

"I'm a detective! If I'm not out there, I'm not doing my job."

"You're options are simple. I suspend you until this shit is cleared up, or you ride a desk."

"This is bullshit, captain. What would you do if our situation was reversed?"

"Don't try to spin it that way; you know damn well what I'd do. That's why I don't want you to force me to suspend you."

As he finished that sentence his phone rang. "Bordeaux. Are you serious? Fuck me!" He slammed the phone. "Cassidy, desk now or get the hell out of this station."

Bordeaux picked up the phone and punched a few buttons. "Bordeaux here … yeah, I know you have caller ID and I don't have to announce myself! Technology's fucking wonderful. Get your team over here. No, in the mail room. I'll meet you there." He slammed the phone and glared at Cassidy. "Desk! Now!"

Cassidy went to his desk and threw himself into his chair as he turned on his computer.

Kidd quietly asked, "The envelope?"

Bordeaux nodded and commanded, "Go guard the damn thing before someone in the mail room screws with it." He then sat back behind his desk and pulled a bottle of antacid tablets from his desk drawer and poured a handful of them into his mouth. While he was crunching on those, he pointed toward the door.

Kidd left the bullpen and pulled out his phone on his way to the mail room. "Yes, Dr. Brandt. The envelope is here and forensics is coming to collect it. No, it's still sealed. Good idea; have her meet us in the lab."

Robin arrived ten minutes later in the police station's mail room. "Where is it?"

There was a pile of mail spread out across a long wooden table. The manila envelope was sitting on top of the pile. Had someone with no prior information witnessed this scene, it would have seemed that there was an unexploded bomb where the envelope was. There were four officers plus Detective Kidd and Robin. Everyone was staring at the envelope, but all of them were at least fifteen feet away.

Robin was already wearing latex gloves as she pulled the evidence bag from her kit. She slowly approached the manila envelope and carefully picked it up by one corner using only her index finger and thumb. Once she slid the envelope into the evidence bag, she followed procedure and documented the pertinent information then turned to Kidd.

Kidd nodded. "The docs are supposed to be meeting us in your lab. You ready?"

Robin nodded as she replied, "I already have my minions setting up the table for them. Let's go."

Once in the lab it was back to business as usual. Arthur, otherwise referred to as Larry, was working on the envelope. Robin had the note. Spencer, a.k.a. Darryl, had just returned from dropping off the toe to Doc Brown in autopsy and was pulling the generic Ziploc bag from its own evidence bag. Bill, who was the second Darryl according to Robin, had the sample taken from the toe under the microscope for examination.

Kidd was wandering back and forth impatiently while Doctors Poole and Brandt were quietly discussing theories and quickly filling up their second legal pad with hastily jotted notes over at the corner table. Kidd stopped and looked back at the monitor where an image of the second note was displayed.

> **King Midas still breathes so another had to die in his place. At least this time the wrong person isn't sitting in prison. Could it be because King Midas wasn't leading this investigation? I think so. You can stop this, King Midas. All you have to do is end your life. I won't wait long. What will it be? Your life or the life of another?**

Robin was shaking her head. "Minions! Anything?"

The room remained silent except for the quiet voices of the doctors from the corner. After a few moments she muttered on a sigh, "Me neither."

"Come on, Robin. I've seen you do magic with far less. Are you telling me that with four pieces of evidence we're still no closer to figuring this out than we were last week?" asked Kidd.

"That's what I'm telling you. Standard copy paper that could have been purchased, well, quite literally anywhere and at any time," Robin exclaimed in frustration.

Arthur nodded and said, "A common padded manila envelope with a string enclosure. Millions of them are in the hands of the postal service on any given day. The address was done with that same, cheap as hell, plastic stencil and black Sharpie. There's absolutely nothing here."

"This Ziploc bag is identical to the last one. No prints, no particulates, except for the toe that was in it. It's as if it just came straight out of the box," Spencer added.

Bill finished up with, "Don't look at me; other than the blood type from this toe sample matching the blood type of the victim, there isn't much I can tell you."

Kidd sighed and turned toward the doctors. "Do you two have anything new?"

Dr. Brandt stopped and sighed. "I'm afraid we do. It was actually Dr. Poole with her studies in anthropology who brought it up."

Kidd looked questioningly at Dr. Poole. She looked him straight in the eye and said, "You're not going to like it."

Kidd remained motionless while mentally steeling himself for whatever he was about to be told.

Dr. Poole nodded and continued, "There are most likely going to be a lot more murders. Probably very soon and most likely from all over the city."

Kidd furrowed his brow and asked, "What are you talking about?"

With every eye in the lab trained on her, Stacey raised her voice slightly so everyone could hear and began to speak. "Before you say anything, hear me out completely. At the first crime, our killer went out of his way to frame someone for the murder. Including planting evidence at another location. The killer then waited patiently for the full result of the crime to be played out. The instant the conviction was in place, the killer released proof that the wrong man was accused then set about killing the second victim. This time the wrong person wasn't accused, and the proof that it was our killer was sent nearly immediately. Our killer made certain to inform the media just as he informed the police.

"Look at the setup. All over this city, anyone who has a grudge against anyone else now has free reign to kill that person and make it look like our killer is responsible. With no consistent MO, a murderer can choose any method he wants and we can't say it isn't our guy. Also, there's no foreign physical evidence left behind at either crime scene. The envelopes sent to the media and police are generic. The only thing that might separate a copycat from our killer could be the toes. Our killer uses something that is razor sharp and cuts cleanly. Obviously, that tool is the only thing that we know for certain the killer actually brought with him to each crime scene. If a copycat killer uses some other instrument to remove the toes of his victim, that might be the only way to separate our killer from others using this as a cover to get rid of people they hate."

There was deafening silence in the lab for a full ten seconds before Kidd finally spoke. "If we get a barrage of killings over the next few weeks, we won't know which is our killer and which was actually done by the person that the evidence suggests. My God."

Brandt cleared his throat and encouraged, "Tell them the rest, my dear."

Kidd looked up sharply and asked, "There's more wonderful news?"

Dr. Poole lowered her head a bit and sighed again. "Those people in this city who don't use this as a cover to commit their own murder … "

Kidd waited a moment then commanded, "Spill it!"

"Well, they might try to end the killing spree by going after Cassidy directly. Our killer made it very clear that if we want the killings to stop, Cassidy must die."

Robin gasped and said, "Son of a bitch."

Kidd stood frozen for a bit then pulled out his phone. "Captain, get Cassidy out of the city. Out of the state if possible. Hell, make him go to Europe or something. Dr. Poole just suggested … you know what, we'll be there in a few minutes. Is Cassidy still there? He what? That stubborn ass. Alright, I'm bringing Dr. Poole, and we'll be there in a few minutes. Try to track him down. We'll explain when we get there."

Dr. Brandt directed, "You go on ahead, Dr. Poole. It was your idea anyway. I'll remain here and continue to refine what we have so far on our killer."

Kidd then motioned to the door. "Doctor?"

As they were leaving the lab Dr. Poole suggested, "You might want to get in touch with the ME to see if the cuts on the amputated toes match the ones from the first crime."

Kidd was raising the phone to his ear as he replied, "Already on it."

As they were leaving the building and making their way toward the station, Kidd hung up. "They match. This one was done by our killer."

Once in Captain Bordeaux's office, they explained everything that Dr. Poole had said in the lab. The color drained from the captain's face as he picked up his phone. After a few moments he slammed it down in the cradle. "Straight to voice mail! The son of a bitch must have it turned off."

Kidd asked, "What all happened before he stormed out?"

"He was sitting at his desk when he suddenly stood and blurted out, 'This is bullshit' and stormed out of the station. One of the uniforms saw him speeding away in his car, but since he's always so hotheaded, the uniform didn't think anything of it until he spoke with some other officers."

"So we have no idea where he went or what he's doing. He has a bull's-eye painted on his chest and doesn't even realize it."

Dr. Poole quietly offered, "I'm sorry, I should have worked out all this earlier. I have no excuse."

Captain Bordeaux said, "Nonsense! You were working on trying to figure out what type of person we're hunting, not what the future ramifications might be for what they started. But we need to find that idiot before he gets himself killed."

Kidd asked, "The media? Were they instructed not to air anything that they receive concerning this case?"

"They were. My guess is that they won't put up the note on every television station in the city, but they'll still say they received it and turned it over to us. It doesn't take a goddamned genius to pretty much figure out what the second note says."

"I certainly hope I'm wrong, sir."

"I do, too. Unfortunately, every city has its crackpots, and I'm sure you're right. It'll just be a matter of time."

CHAPTER 10

Tuesday, August 12

Kidd rushed into the emergency room trauma center and stopped to look around for a moment. An orderly approached and asked, "May I help you with something?"

Kidd shook his head and told him he couldn't. He then started going from bed to bed. Everywhere the dividing sheet had been closed, he slid it open to see who was lying behind it.

The orderly exclaimed, "Hey, you can't do that! I'm going to call the police."

Kidd said, "Go right ahead! I could use their help in my search."

As the orderly ran to the intake desk and grabbed a phone, Kidd heard a voice call out. It was weak and faint, but he recognized it.

"I'm here, Mike, where are you?"

"Kidd, I'm here." Again it was weak but unmistakable.

Kidd threw open the dividing sheet that hung around the bed and saw Cassidy lying there with an oxygen tube running to his nose and an IV line in his arm.

"Cassidy! You dumb son of a bitch! Tell me what happened."

Just then the emergency room doctor on duty came rushing up. "You can't be here! Get away from him!"

Kidd spun and pulled his service pistol. "Doc, you either go on about your business and leave me alone or find your own weapon and shoot me. I'm not going anywhere until I'm damn good and ready."

The doctor raised his hands and slowly backed away.

Kidd turned back to Cassidy and said, "I need everything you can remember."

Cassidy coughed a few times and covered his abdomen with one hand. "I was with Kathy. I got your messages and was getting ready to take her to a hotel where she would be safe. We stopped at the corner of our street, and this guy stepped off the curb and opened fire. I pulled my weapon and shot back, but I don't know if I hit him. Then the lights went out. Kathy. She must be here somewhere. Find her; tell me if she's alright."

Kidd lowered his head and slowly began to shake it back and forth. "Mike, she's gone. She was reported as dead at the scene. I'm so sorry."

Cassidy began to cough again and tears started streaming from his eyes.

"Mike, I know this won't mean much to you right now, but you got him. He was also reported as dead at the scene. By the time I got there, you had already been loaded into the ambulance."

Cassidy focused on Kidd and reached up to grab his shirt. "Was that the rotten son of a bitch who started all of this?"

Kidd did nothing to remove Cassidy's clenched fist. "We have no idea yet. Doc Brown has him in autopsy. The instant they tell me something, I'll let you know. Right now, I'm going to have a guard—actually, two guards—posted with you at all times … one outside the room and one inside. Nobody will get to you in here."

Just then he heard a voice yell, "Freeze! Let me see your hands, asshole."

Kidd slowly raised his hands where they could be seen while Cassidy let go of his shirt. As Kidd turned to face the voice he asked, "Which asshole are you referring to, me or him?"

The officer lowered his weapon and exclaimed, "My God. Butch! You look like hell."

Kidd lowered his hands and said, "I want you to find two officers. Good men. I want them here immediately. I'm not going to leave until I know he has protection."

The uniformed officer holstered his pistol and nodded, "On it!"

Kidd turned back to Cassidy and promised, "When I know something, you'll know. Until then, rest and try to get better."

Cassidy whispered, "Kathy's family ... you do it. I don't want it coming from a stranger. Which uniform is that?"

Kidd said, "Turner."

Cassidy nodded. "I'll be fine with him here. Get out of here and let her family know. Then find out if that was the son of a bitch or not. If it wasn't, you hunt him down for me. As soon as I get out of here, I'll join you. We'll get him ... we'll get him."

A nurse and a doctor approached the bed. "We need to get him into surgery now. I'm sorry, I didn't realize who you were, but you'll have to leave now. The longer we wait to get him opened up, the worse his odds are for surviving this."

Kidd never took his eyes off Cassidy while he slowly backed away. "Doc, if anyone on that surgical team lets him die, I will be the last thing they see."

Kidd turned to face Officer Turner with a questioning look on his face.

"I have two men from my squad on their way. I trust them with my life. We'll set up a rotation. He'll be guarded around the clock."

Kidd lowered his head and nodded. "Thank you." As he took off down the hallway, he pulled his phone from his pocket.

"Hi, Rebecca. I don't suppose Dr. Poole is available. Thank you. Yes, Dr. Poole? Can you meet me at autopsy? Right. I have one stop to make first, then I'll see you there."

As he exited the hospital, a patrol car came screaming into the parking lot with lights flashing. Two uniformed officers jumped out and hurriedly approached the building. One of them spotted Kidd and called out, "Go get that bastard; we'll make sure Cassidy stays alive."

Kidd thanked them and climbed behind the wheel of his unmarked car.

The stop at Kathy's parents' house took only a few minutes. He left them standing on their porch, crying in each other's arms.

Dr. Poole's Outback was already in the lot when he arrived at the morgue. He found her and Dr. Brown in the autopsy room. One table held a body with a thin sheet pulled up to cover the face, but the feet protruding at the bottom were a woman's. He quickly looked away and approached the other table where Dr. Poole and Dr. Brown were standing.

"Detective!" Dr. Brown exclaimed when he noticed him. "How's Cassidy?"

"They were getting ready to take him into surgery when I left. Two uniforms will be with him at all times though. Have you had a chance to find anything out about our shooter yet?"

"Dr. Poole and I were just discussing that."

Dr. Poole went on, "We probably won't be able to figure out anything here. Your people will have to gather information about him first. Since our killer didn't leave anything behind at either of the crime scenes, we'll only be able to determine whether this is him from his background."

Kidd looked at Dr. Poole and said, "I thank you for being subtle, but now's not the time. Right now, I want the blunt truth. Do you believe this is our killer?"

Dr. Poole shook her head as she replied, "No, I don't. It makes no sense for our killer to go through all the trouble of taunting Cassidy just to turn around and try to kill him from a street corner."

Kidd nodded before saying, "That's what I thought. Doc, did she suffer?"

Dr. Brown glanced over at the other table and then back to Detective Kidd. "No, I believe the first wound she received was the fatal one, and she wouldn't have even known what hit her. The only reason detective Cassidy is still alive is because the shooter approached from the passenger side of the car and had to go through her to get to him. She didn't suffer, Jeremy."

"At least there's that. Dr. Poole, what do we do now? I'm lost. How do we hunt down a ghost? We have no DNA, no hair samples, no footprints, no description … we have absolutely nothing. Please tell me that you have an idea."

Dr. Poole lowered her eyes and shook her head. "I'm sorry, a profile is only worth the information that created it, and we don't have a lot of information to go on. I have no idea how to proceed based solely on what we have right now. Did your men find anything while going through Cassidy's arrest records?"

"They're chasing down a couple of leads, but those are pretty thin. They've expanded their search to include friends and relatives of those that Cassidy put behind bars. Maybe they'll come up with something from that."

Kidd's cell phone rang, and he lifted it to his ear. "You can't be serious. Where? Alright, I'm on my way."

Kidd put the phone away. "Doc, you should be getting a call any minute … "

Just then Dr. Brown's phone rang. He walked over and picked it up and listened. After a few moments, he confirmed, "Yes, I'm aware. Find Jeff and tell him to get the van ready."

"Dr. Poole, we'll keep you informed."

"You go find out if this was our killer or not. I have to go back to the office anyway. I need to deliver the news before he finds out from someone else," she said.

Kidd, who was getting ready to leave autopsy and go to the newest crime scene, suddenly stopped and looked at Dr. Poole with a puzzled look on his face. "Deliver what news?"

Dr. Poole motioned to the table that held the body of Kathy Cassidy. "That she was killed this morning."

"You said 'he.' Who needs this news delivered to them before they find out some other way?"

"Quinn, of course. I know, you probably hate him as much as Cassidy does right now. But he's still one of my therapists and, whether you like it or not, he was in love."

"Quinn? The one that Rebecca complained about? She told me that he sleeps with any woman who has a heartbeat. Why would you … did you say in love? Are you telling me that Quinn was in love with Kathy?"

"Oh, I thought you already knew. I'm so sorry, Jeremy. I just figured that since you and Cassidy were partners, he'd have told you already."

Kidd went silent and walked over to the table where Kathy Cassidy rested beneath a sheet. After a few seconds he turned and asked, "Kathy? And Quinn? And Mike knew about it?"

Dr. Poole nodded slowly. "Again, I'm so sorry. I probably shouldn't have mentioned it, but I honestly thought Mike would have told you. You two are so close."

"How long?"

"According to Quinn, the affair started over a year ago. If you meant to ask how long Mike knew, I guess he found out three or four weeks ago."

Kidd stood there for another ten seconds without saying a word. Then his expression changed in a flash. "Three or four weeks ago? You mean just before the first murder? Holy shit. You don't think … oh, I need to talk to this guy."

"Hold on. Quinn is a self-absorbed, egotistic asshole, but he's definitely no killer."

"No? He fell in love with Kathy. My partner's wife. Now there's someone running around killing people and sending notes saying he won't stop until Cassidy is dead. Right now, he's the best lead we have."

"Detective, you're way off base here. When Cassidy found out about the affair, he threatened Quinn's life. Quinn and Kathy haven't seen each other since."

"That's even more reason I need to talk with him. You're not doing him any favors right now. Go back to your office and make sure he doesn't leave until I get there. I need to go button up this crime scene, but I'll be there before your office closes for the day."

"Alright, but I'm telling you, Quinn isn't any more capable of doing any of this than Dean Connelly was of killing his mother."

"Duly noted. Make sure he doesn't leave until I've talked with him."

Dr. Poole sighed and said, "I'll make sure he talks to you."

*****

Kidd looked over the crime scene and made some notes then left the room to Dr. Brown. He walked out to the responding officer and asked, "Where is he?"

The uniformed officer motioned toward one of the squad cars, and Kidd trudged over. The rear window was down a few inches, so Kidd made no move to open the door. "Tell me what happened, sir."

The man began talking fast, running his sentences together. "I just ran down to the hardware store. I needed a new hinge to fix the cabinet door. I couldn't have been gone more than half an hour. When I got back, there she was. She was covered in blood. There was so much blood." He then began to sob, but Kidd noticed that there were no actual tears.

Kidd asked, "Which store did you go to for the hinge?"

The man kept his head down and maintained the sounds of heavy sobbing. But between the sobs he managed to say, "The one over on 12th."

"Then you have the receipt?"

"I don't keep those things. I threw it away when I left the store."

"I see, then where's the hinge you bought?"

"I must have dropped it when I found her." He began wailing loudly.

Kidd sighed. "Alright, you see if you can calm down a bit, and I'll be back shortly."

As Kidd started to walk away, the man in the back of the squad car yelled after him, "Hey, aren't you going to take off these cuffs? It wasn't me. I didn't do this. It was the Denver City Specter."

Kidd spun around and asked, "Who?"

"You know, the Denver City Specter. The same one that has that hard on for King Midas. In fact, one of the other channels called him The King Midas Killer. Damn, man, it's all over the news."

Kidd turned back toward the house and shook his head, "Didn't take long for them to give him a name."

Dr. Brown met him at the door. "Doc, that was quick. What's the word?"

Dr. Brown shook his head, "This wasn't done by our guy. The toes were cut off, but the cuts are jagged and you can see where the soft tissue was crushed. If you look, you'll probably find them in the garbage disposal or someplace like that. Also, I'd check the shed out back for a pair of bolt cutters in need of sharpening."

Kidd sighed and said, "It's already beginning. Just one day after Dr. Poole predicted it would. What the hell are we going to do, doc?"

Dr. Brown shook his head and motioned toward the squad car. "I suppose the first order of business for you is to get him put behind bars and make sure the evidence is properly collected."

Kidd began barking out orders to the uniformed officers just as Robin and her team approached the house. "Not to interrupt while you're bossing people around here, but the media is right behind us."

"Son of a bitch! Gary, go contain those assholes. Sorry, hi, Robin. Hi, minions. This isn't our guy. It's a copycat, and the moron's in the back of the squad car over there. The doc here told us we should be looking for dull bolt cutters or something similar. Also, her throat was cut. Try to find the knife that was used. I want enough to bury this idiot. Maybe we can make an example of him so that others won't try the same shit. Oh, and check the disposal unit and trash bins. The doc seems to think he probably just threw away the toes."

Robin tossed back over her shoulder, "You're going to have to deal with the media pretty soon. If you tell them this is a copycat, maybe they'll cooperate and broadcast a plea so that others won't try the same thing."

Arthur nodded, "Instead of treating them like they're the enemy, how about using them? Suggest they have their viewers set up neighborhood watches. If the killer strikes in homes and there are civilian patrols out on the streets, maybe they can spot someone lurking around outside a residence and get a description."

Bill added, "Yeah, instead of letting the city's population tear itself apart in fear, use them. This could galvanize them."

Robin said, "Larry, Darryl, very impressive. Just for that, you two don't have to go dumpster diving." She turned toward the other lab tech. "You get that honor now."

He punched Arthur in the shoulder and exclaimed, "Thanks, you two assholes! You just stole my ideas, and now I'm getting punished for it."

"Think nothing of it. No thanks necessary!"

Kidd said, "I'll have to think about that for a while. I need to go talk to someone right now. Do you guys have this under control?"

Robin cocked her head slightly and asked sarcastically, "Did you forget who you're talking to?"

"That isn't what I meant. If I take off, will you guys be okay?"

Robin folded her arms and adopted a stance that told him she was seriously considering kicking his ass.

Kidd backed up a step and rephrased, "I mean, you guys will be alright if I take off. I'm gonna leave Perry in charge here. He can wrap things up once you've collected all the evidence you need. I'm just going to … " Kidd turned and started hunting down Officer Perry.

*****

148

It was just after four in the afternoon when Kidd arrived at the Jacobs Psychiatric Center. "Hi, Rebecca."

"Jeremy! What brings you down here? Did you stop by just to say hi?"

He shuffled his feet a bit and slowly shook his head. "Seeing you happens to be an incredibly fortunate perk. I have to speak with one of the therapists."

Rebecca looked a little surprised then lowered her head to look at the appointment book in front of her. "I don't think you have the right day, sir. I can't find your name in here anywhere. Which therapist is it that you think you have an appointment with?"

"Very funny. I need to speak with Quinn."

"Why? What'd he do this time?"

"I wish I could discuss it with you. Maybe after I talk with Quinn, I can. When will he be available?"

Rebecca eyed him suspiciously for a moment but decided not to press the issue. She scanned her appointment book and answered, "Actually, he's probably just finishing up with his notes for the day. He didn't have a four o'clock appointment. I'll call his office."

She let the phone ring several times before hanging up. "He's not answering; let's go see if he left yet."

She and Cassidy left the reception area and went to the hallway that contained the offices. When she got to Quinn's, she tried the handle then opened the door. "He's not in here. Let's see if his car's still in the lot."

They then went to the employee entrance and found that his bright red Porsche was still parked where he'd left it when he came in that morning.

Kidd asked, "Maybe the bathroom?"

"I'm not going in if that's where he is. You're on your own there."

She led him to the employee restrooms and he headed into the men's. After a few seconds he came out shaking his head.

"The only other place I can imagine he might be is … "

"Dr. Poole's office," Kidd interrupted.

They headed upstairs and Rebecca gently knocked when they reached the doctor's door. From the other side of the door, she heard Dr. Poole's muffled voice ask, "Who is it?"

This caught Rebecca by surprise. Every other time she'd knocked in the past, the response was always to come in. "It's Rebecca."

"Hold on a moment."

Rebecca glanced at Jeremy with an expression of suspicion on her face then stared at the door once again.

Twenty seconds later, Dr. Poole opened the door. Sitting in the chair across from her desk with his back to them was Quinn.

Rebecca raised her eyebrows and looked as though she were about to ask a question when Kidd brushed past her and entered the office. "Quinton Foster? My name's Detective Kidd. I need to ask you a few questions."

Quinn didn't respond; he only lowered his head a bit more than it already was. As Jeremy walked around the chair to look Quinn in the face, Rebecca followed him into the office before Dr. Poole had a chance to stop her. When Quinn looked up, it was obvious that he'd been crying.

Rebecca moved forward and asked, "Oh, my God, what's the matter, Quinn?"

As soon as she got close to him, Jeremy gently caught her by the arm and moved her back. He positioned himself directly in front of Quinn's chair and began, "I'm Detective Cassidy's partner. It appears that Dr. Poole already delivered the news about his wife. Did she tell you that I'd be coming to speak with you as well?"

Quinn didn't speak. He simply nodded his head in the affirmative.

"Good, where were you on the night of Thursday, August 7, between the hours of 11:00 p.m. and 1:00 a.m.?"

Quinn looked somewhat surprised when he answered. "I was probably at home asleep."

"Can anyone verify that?"

Quinn slowly shook his head no then asked, "What's this about?"

Kidd ignored him and asked, "How about the evening of Wednesday, July 22, around 6:00 p.m.?"

Quinn shook his head and answered, "I don't know. I may have been at a restaurant, I guess. Are you asking me about alibis for the dates of the murders? You think I'm the one killing these people?"

"It's recently come to my attention that, up until this morning, you had plenty of reason to want Detective Cassidy dead. I need to know if you have any way of confirming that you weren't at either of the crime scenes at the times of those murders."

Rebecca looked at Jeremy then Quinn before she finally turned to Dr. Poole. Her mouth was hanging open, but before she could ask anything, Dr. Poole raised her hand and shook her head.

Quinn was also shaking his head. "I don't know. Maybe. July 22? Wednesday … I probably had pizza. I'm not sure, that was a couple of weeks ago. No wait … the day of the murder. I think I met up with Allison. That would have been around seven." He looked over at Dr. Poole and clarified, "You know, the blonde." He then motioned to the lapel of his jacket.

"I'll need her contact information."

Quinn pulled his phone from his breast pocket and scrolled through a list of names. "Here's her number. Call her."

Kidd wrote down her number then asked, "Her address, please?"

Quinn hit another button on his phone to display her full name and address.

After Kidd finished jotting down the information, he directed, "If I were you, I wouldn't think about leaving town anytime soon. I'd also start making sure I hung around quite a few people. That way, if another murder occurs, you might have a better alibi for your whereabouts."

Quinn slumped back in the chair, and tears began to roll down his cheeks again. "I can't believe she's dead."

Kidd studied his face and body language for several seconds then relaxed his own body a bit. "Look, I'll check out your alibi with this Allison. Right now, however, you have more reason to want Detective Cassidy dead than anybody else we've come up with so far."

Quinn nodded and said, "I understand. I know you're just doing your job, but he's the one who threatened my life. I couldn't kill anyone. I just wanted her to divorce him so we could be together. Now … it doesn't matter anymore."

Kidd sighed and walked out of Dr. Poole's office with Rebecca following close behind.

Dr. Poole went back to her seat behind her desk and asked, "Are you going to be alright? Do you want to take a few days? I can have Rebecca rearrange your appointments for you."

Quinn looked at her for a few moments before lowering his head. "No, you don't need to do that. I'll be okay. I just need to be alone for a while."

"Go home then. I'll get your notes from today's sessions another time."

Quinn slowly stood and headed out of the office. Just before he went through the door, he paused without looking back. "I really did love her, you know." Without waiting for any kind of response, he left and closed the door behind himself.

CHAPTER 11

---·---

Wednesday, August 13

"Jeremy!" Then, sounding just slightly disappointed, she muttered, "Oh, you're probably here to see Dr. Poole again, right? Or ... are you here to accuse Quinn of murder again?"

Detective Kidd smiled and replied, "Actually, I'm here to see both you and Dr. Poole. As for Quinn, he was telling the truth about Allison. She confirmed that they met for dinner at 7:00 p.m. It's highly unlikely that he could have cleaned up after the murder and made it to the restaurant in time to meet with her."

"Good. He's an immature asshole, but I knew damn well he was no murderer. So then, whom do you need to see first? Me or Dr. Poole?"

"Well, I'm here to see you because I'd like to know if you might be free for dinner after work this evening."

Rebecca's eyes lit up as she nodded quickly. "Absolutely. Do you have anything in mind or would you like to just see where our empty bellies take us?"

"I was actually thinking Italian."

Rebecca closed her eyes and moved her hand to her stomach. "Rigatoni with garlic bread and a nice red wine. That sounds wonderful. Oh, you said you needed to talk with Dr. Poole, too. Would you like me to ring her?"

"If you don't mind."

As Rebecca was lifting the handset, Dr. Poole came through the door into the reception area.

"Well, what do you know? What timing!" remarked Rebecca as she replaced the handset.

Dr. Poole looked back and forth between Jeremy and Rebecca and asked, "Timing? Why? Did you want to tell me that you two are going on another date? Believe me, that isn't the biggest news flash in the city at the moment. Or maybe you're here to tell me that Quinn is in the clear?"

"Alright, Dr. Poole," Jeremy said with a hint of sarcasm. "You're right. Quinn is in the clear. Now, if you're so damned good at reading people, where are we going tonight?"

Dr. Poole pulled a file from her briefcase and speculated as she was setting it down for Rebecca, "Probably someplace like the Odyssey. Italian this time."

Jeremy and Rebecca stared at each other in open-mouthed surprise. Finally, Rebecca recovered enough to inquire, "How'd you figure that out?"

Dr. Poole closed her briefcase then glanced back and forth between them as she explained, "Process of elimination. First couple of dates were lunch. Sandwiches and fries or chips. Casual with no strings or expectations. Sort of 'let's get to know each other' dates. Then the dinner date. But that was oriental food. Thai, if I remember correctly. Still casual with no romantic atmosphere. A kind of 'lunch was nice, but let's see if there's a reason to continue this' date. This one is the standard third stage date. You two obviously determined that you like each other from your previous dates. So this date is the 'nice romantic dinner with just the right mood and ambiance to see if we like each other enough to have sex' date. Italian was the obvious choice, and the Odyssey has the right setting and atmosphere."

Both of them had been stunned even before Dr. Poole offered her explanation, but now they both looked absolutely stupefied. Jeremy exclaimed, "You don't pull any punches, do you, doctor?"

Dr. Poole had been obviously slightly distracted when she rattled off how she figured out they were going to have Italian food, but after Jeremy's question, she snapped her full attention to both of them. "What? Was I incorrect?"

Jeremy started to laugh a little nervously and looked down at the floor. Rebecca blushed a bit and said, "Well, not exactly. We had decided on Italian food."

Dr. Poole shook her head and asked, "Then what did I do that's got you two so flustered right now?"

Rebecca retorted, "Subtlety was never one of your strengths as you were growing up, was it?"

For as brilliant as Dr. Poole actually was, right now she appeared lost. She quickly ran the conversation back through her head and then stared blankly at them. "Apparently I missed something. You asked how I guessed that you were going to have Italian, and I told you. I'm sorry, but my mind was elsewhere. Did I miss something?"

Jeremy replied, "No, it's alright, doctor."

Dr. Poole cocked her head slightly and squinted her eyes as she looked back and forth between them. She eventually gave up trying to figure out what their problem was. It most likely didn't have anything to do with her anyway. "Rebecca, I don't have any appointments this afternoon, do I?"

Rebecca flipped open a book and ran her finger down a sheet. "Nope, nothing remaining for you today."

"I finished reviewing the therapists' notes from yesterday's sessions. There are only a few minor changes to dosages for a few of the clients. Those are in that folder I just gave you. Would you make sure they get the information for me? Also, please let poor Quinn know that he's no longer a suspect in these murders."

"Sure. Are you leaving early today?"

"I am. I spoke with the landlord last night and asked if I could do some painting. I'd like to brighten up the apartment a little. She gave her consent and offered to reduce my rent by a hundred dollars this month, plus the costs of any paint as long as I submit a receipt to her. So I'm going to pick out some colors. I think I'll start with the kitchen cabinets. That old faded yellow is starting to get to me. Also, I was thinking about going with a dark red for the living room. What do you think?"

"Oh, that would go well with the light gray carpet. What about the trim?"

"I'm torn between a charcoal gray or simply painting the trim white."

Rebecca was shaking her head, "Charcoal gray would offset the walls from that light colored carpet beautifully."

Dr. Poole smiled and said, "Then it's settled. I'll start with those and when I'm done, I'll figure out something for my bedroom. I hope you two have a great night."

As Dr. Poole turned to leave, Rebecca exclaimed, "Oh, wait! Didn't you want to talk to her about something, Jeremy?"

"Oh, yes. Dr. Poole, do you have a few minutes?"

"Of course, what is it?"

"At the crime scene yesterday, Robin's minions mentioned that I should stop treating the media like they're the enemy. They suggested I use the media to my advantage and have them broadcast a plea to have the city's population band together to form neighborhood watches. My only issue with that is that our killer is extremely dangerous. I'd like your professional opinion on this. Do you think asking the citizens to start patrolling the neighborhoods would be a good idea or do you think it would only be putting them in harm's way?"

Dr. Poole's eyes lit up. "I think it's a fantastic idea. Our killer is essentially a classic home invader. He kills inside someone else's residence where he has the time to set the scene as he sees fit without prying eyes around to give away his identity. Citizens on the street would act as a shield against him choosing a residence there. He's shown no sign of intention to attack out in the open so far, and I see no reason why he'd change that now. In fact, I think I'd like to get involved with this. Maybe I could speak with some of my neighbors, and we could be the first to set up patrols."

Rebecca offered, "I live only a couple of blocks from where your apartment is. I know quite a few of our neighbors. I could help with that, too. I think it's a great idea. Maybe we could get enough people to volunteer so that we could have three or four pairs out patrolling each night."

Jeremy said, "That settles it, then. As long as you're fairly certain that our guy won't start killing people on the street, I'll try to make that happen."

Dr. Poole was shaking her head. "No. Our killer has been successful because he doesn't stand out. He doesn't want to be noticed. He's got some vendetta against Cassidy, and he's using this city as a game board; but he knows if he's actually seen, he'll lose the game. So the more eyes we have on the streets, the tougher it'll be for him to remain unseen. There is one more thing though. Each neighborhood watch group should submit lists of their members to the police. It might also be a good idea to include the times and areas they intend to patrol as well."

Dr. Poole paused for several seconds and, just as Jeremy was getting ready to speak to her, Rebecca shook her head no, causing Jeremy to stop and simply wait.

Finally, Dr. Poole looked at Jeremy and asked, "Do you know of any officers that would be willing to come to the first meeting for each group? It'd be nice to have them explain what the civilians should and shouldn't do while out on patrol. Maybe the officers could institute a protocol for any of the watch members who spot something suspicious, too."

"Excellent idea. Safety protocols and who to contact for suspicious behavior ... got it. Yes, I know officers who could stop by these meetings once they're scheduled. When I go into the station tomorrow I'll get some of them together and we'll set up a standardized training sheet."

"Glad I could help. Is there anything else you need from me right now?"

"I don't think so; thank you, doctor. Rebecca, shall I pick you up around eight o'clock?"

Rebecca smiled broadly. "That would be wonderful."

Dr. Poole shook her head and laughed as she once more turned to leave.

Rebecca couldn't help herself. "What's so funny, doctor?"

As Stacey reached the door she glanced around to make sure there were no clients waiting to be seen. Since none were in the waiting room, she turned back toward them and said, "This antiquated courtship thing is cute, but in today's society, it's really quite old-fashioned. Why don't you two just grab a pizza to go? That way you'll have plenty of time to find out if you're compatible in bed and still get a full night's rest before you have to get up for work in the morning? The only choice then would be his place or yours."

Rebecca raised her eyebrows again and said, "That way of thinking might be why you're still single, doctor."

Dr. Poole shook her head. "No. I'm still single because I choose to be. I don't want someone around all the time that I have to report to about where I've been and what I've been doing." She actually physically shuddered and added, "Or worse, have them expect me to ask permission to do something." In a mocking voice she said, "Honey, do you mind if I go visit with Rebecca this evening? I should be back no later than nine."

After shivering yet again she stated unequivocally, "Not a chance in hell I'm ever going to be in that situation. Nope, when the urge hits to have sex, I find a suitable partner and sate that urge. It's called being practical." And with that, she left the two of them staring at the door she exited through.

After a few moments, Rebecca looked up at Jeremy and said, "Alright then, well ... I suppose pizza is still technically Italian food."

He quickly nodded and asked, "Your place or mine?"

"Mine. Seven o'clock instead of eight. And ... Jeremy?"

"Yes?"

"You might want to bring with you what you'll need to get ready for work in the morning."

Jeremy smiled and left through the main entrance.

*****

Around five thirty that afternoon as Dr. Poole was preparing to make her second trip from her Outback to her apartment, she heard the rumble of a V-8 engine and looked over her shoulder in time to see Rebecca pulling into the visitor's parking space.

"Hey, do you need a hand?"

"That would be great! Can you grab the rollers and brushes and close the back of the car?"

Once they were both inside Stacey's apartment and the painting supplies had been stowed in a corner, Rebecca said, "I'd like to thank you for the advice on ordering takeout. You're right. The need for old-fashioned dating rituals is long since passed. Besides, with his schedule, setting up expensive dates would be impractical. Who knows, we might be out sometime when he gets a call and has to leave. Then we'd have just wasted a lot of money for a disappointing evening."

"Glad I could help. Oh, and welcome to the twenty-first century of dating. So what'd you decide to go with for takeout?"

Rebecca blushed and answered, "He's just going to bring over pizza."

Dr. Poole nodded and said, "Very sensible of you. If I come in tomorrow and find you in a great mood, then I'll know you two were compatible in bed. If you seem disappointed, I'll know there probably will be no more dates."

Rebecca laughed. "He also wants both of us to watch the six o'clock news."

"Aw, you know I hate watching the news. It's a bunch of depressing stuff followed by one feel-good piece. What are we supposed to be watching for?"

"I don't know. He just told us to watch the evening news. It probably won't take long since he's planning on getting to my place at seven."

"Alright, fine. Here's the remote; you find the channel."

*****

It didn't take very long at all before they moved to the big story across Denver. "Our sources confirmed that the murder that occurred yesterday was a copycat killing. James Bartlett has been in custody since he reported finding his wife dead after returning home from the hardware store. He even went so far as to cut off each of her baby toes. Crime scene investigators found both of those toes in the trash bin outside the back door of their home."

"In a related story, Dr. Stacey Poole and receptionist Rebecca Mann from the Jacobs Psychiatric Center spoke with one of the lead investigators on the Denver City Specter killings today. Detective Jeremy Kidd informed us that they'd like citizens in the Denver area to band together and begin forming neighborhood watch programs. You should see contact information at the bottom of your screen. If you'd like to begin a neighborhood watch program in your area or are interested in joining one of these groups, please contact the city police department using this contact information. They'll help you get organized and instruct you on what you should and shouldn't do while patrolling the streets of your neighborhood. Police are urging as many citizens as possible to become involved with this. I quote Detective Jeremy Kidd in saying, 'It's my hope that together we can put an end to the murders perpetrated by this killer.'

"The police department as well as those of us here at this station would like to thank Dr. Poole and Rebecca Mann for pushing for the neighborhood watch program. It sounds like a fantastic way to bring the citizens of Denver closer together and galvanize us as a city. Remember though that trying to form a patrol without notifying the city's police department by using the contact number at the bottom of your screen could cause confusion and make a dangerous situation even more so. Please call the number that you see on your screen now.

"Also related to the Denver City Specter, Detective Michael Cassidy is still in intensive care from a shooting yesterday morning that resulted in the death of his wife, Katherine Cassidy. He was rushed into surgery shortly after the incident, and a full day after the fact he remains in critical but stable condition. During his recovery, he is being guarded around the clock by uniformed police officers who are volunteering their off-duty hours to protect the detective from any future threats to his life.

"And finally, the group calling themselves the F.D.C., short for Free Dean Connelly, began camping outside the courthouse and county jail last night. Their numbers have been steadily growing since our station received confirmation that the Denver City Specter still roams our streets. They now claim that they number in the hundreds and have been applying pressure to both our courts and our state legislators. They want long-standing practices, like those that wrongfully imprisoned Mr. Connelly, abolished. They're also getting very vocal about how much time Mr. Connelly is spending behind bars when everyone knows that he's innocent of the crime that his lawyer urged him to plead guilty to."

*****

Robin's lab tech, Spencer, had just sat down on his sofa with a plateful of reheated lasagna when the news broadcaster announced all of this.

"Seriously? Now, instead of Bill and Arthur stealing my ideas, Dr. Poole and Rebecca Mann are getting the credit? Life just isn't fair."

As he lifted the forkful of lasagna to his mouth, a large drop of sauce fell onto his chest. He looked down at the stain soaking into his shirt and sighed.

CHAPTER 12

Wednesday, August 20

"Detective Kidd, I'm surprised to see you here. I thought they were releasing Cassidy today. I figured you'd want to be there to pick him up."

"They want to run a few more tests before they release him, so I have a couple of hours to kill. I just stopped by to see how your neighborhood watch program is going."

Dr. Poole shook her head and contradicted, "No, you stopped by to see Rebecca. You're using the neighborhood watch as a reason to speak with me." She eyed him closely and after a few seconds added, "He'll be fine, but it's going to take some time. In the last thirty days, he's been singled out by a sociopath who has a serious vendetta against him but won't let him know why. He lost his wife and suffered a severe physical trauma simultaneously. Also, half the city wants him dead just so the killings will stop, and the other half is demanding that he does what he's always done in the past … catch the son of a bitch. It's been a very rough month for him. The best advice I know of doesn't take a laundry list of college degrees to figure out. Be his friend. Listen and be supportive, but don't push him either. If he says he's ready to come back to work and the department psychologist clears him, don't fight him on it. The alternative would mean sitting in an empty house looking at everything around him that reminds him of his recently deceased wife. It would also mean that someone else is being forced to fight his battle with this killer for him. Above all else, don't treat him any differently than you used to. If you two called each other names, keep calling each other names. Pity can be a very powerful emotion for both the one giving it as well as the one receiving it."

"Dr. Poole, I finally figured out why you're really single. It isn't because you choose to be, as you said last week. It's really because there's no mystery involved for you with someone that might be your boyfriend. You spend so much of your time figuring out people that you might be missing out on the greatest gift a relationship has to offer."

Dr. Poole appeared puzzled and asked, "What's that?"

"Being surprised by them sometimes. Anyway, thank you for saving me the embarrassment of having to ask you how I should handle Cassidy. I appreciate the advice and plan to follow it. I know it won't be easy, and he'll be a miserable bastard to deal with. But thank you."

Dr. Poole sighed. "You're welcome. I suppose you may have a point with the whole relationship thing, as well. I simply can't turn off my training though. When I look at someone, I interpret everything about that person. It's a huge part of my job and invades my personal life, too. Maybe someday I'll consider finding someone to be exclusive with, but it isn't going to happen anytime soon."

"I'll let you get back to whatever it is that you were doing before I interrupted you. Thanks again for the talk. I'll see you later."

"Hold on, detective. I've never been good at keeping up with the local news. How have things been this week? Since nobody contacted me for official business, I assume there haven't been any additional murders?"

"Actually, there have been three murders in the last week. None of them have been our killer though. So far, everything's been very quiet where he's concerned. We went through Cassidy's arrest history completely and can't find anyone there that we can consider for this either. It's frustrating as hell. For all I know, this could be an old high school classmate that's been holding a grudge for decades and is just now acting out."

Dr. Poole was shaking her head as she said, "No, this is no high school classmate of his with a grudge. This is far more serious, and I'd bet my reputation that it does have something to do with someone he's arrested. Or … "

"I really hate it when you do that, doctor. Alright, I'll play along. Or what?"

"Have there been any officer involved shootings in his past where he's had to kill a suspect?"

"Good thought, doctor, but we already looked into that. He's had five officer involved shooting incidents in his career. The most recent was last week when his wife died. The other four were thoroughly gone over by our guys. We can't find anyone associated with any of them that would be capable of going to this extreme for payback."

"Just a thought. Look, I know he isn't my biggest fan. Tell him I'm sorry about his wife though."

"I'll pass that along. Are you going out on patrol with your neighborhood watch tonight?"

"No, not tonight. I finished painting the kitchen cabinets a few days ago, and tonight I start on the living room."

Detective Kidd tossed back with a smile as he left her office, "You have fun with that, doctor."

*****

"Cassidy, quit being such an ass! You have to see the psychologist before they'll let you go back to active duty. Not only that, but even if the psychologist clears you, there's still the captain to deal with. We're not even three blocks from the hospital, and you already want to respond to the latest call. It isn't even a homicide, for Christ's sake."

"Yes, Mother, I know I have to talk to the shrink. As for the captain, he'll either take me off desk duty or he'll have to suspend me. In fact, that might not be a bad idea. If he suspends me, I'll have the freedom to pursue this without concern for how my actions affect the department. Yeah, that's actually a damn good idea, in fact."

"Shut the hell up. I'm taking you back to your house so you can get some appropriate clothes and then to the department to set up an appointment with our shrink. As for active duty, your left arm is in a sling. You just got released from the hospital after receiving three gunshot wounds to your torso. You couldn't even come close to passing the physical for active duty right now."

"I can run circles around your slow ass, and it's my left arm that's in a sling. I'm right-handed if you hadn't already noticed that, *detective*. So that means I can still shoot. As for my clothes, screw going back to the house to change. Just take me to the station."

"Right because the tee shirt and jeans your mother-in-law brought to the hospital for you is so appropriate."

"What's wrong with what I'm wearing? They're my clothes. She just grabbed the first shirt and pants she found."

"I don't think setting up an appointment with the department shrink while wearing a shirt that says 'I'm fluent in three languages … English, Sarcasm and Profanity' is the best way to convince him that you're mentally ready to wear a badge and carry a gun."

"You became far more stubborn over the last week than you used to be. Where's the sympathy? Aren't you supposed to be kissing my ass because I nearly died?"

"Ha, that's a good one. Now if you'd *actually* died, that would be worthy of a little bit of sympathy."

"Just take me to the station."

"Alright, fine. The station it is."

After a full minute of silence, Cassidy said, "The funeral was postponed until I was released so that I could attend. It's tomorrow at three. They couldn't do a viewing because of … "

"Yeah, I know. I'll make sure you're there for it. You will be changing clothes for that, right?"

Cassidy actually laughed a little then looked down at his shirt. "Yeah, this wouldn't do at all for something like that. I have another one that says 'I'm not bragging, I'm just being honest.' I was thinking about wearing that one instead."

As they pulled into the station parking lot, Kidd was shaking his head. "Are you sure the doctor said you didn't have a concussion?"

"No concussion, this is who I am. I wouldn't even be in this sling if my foot hadn't slipped off the brake when I went unconscious. You'd think traffic would have stopped when they heard the gunfire. I can't believe that flake in the minivan slammed into my driver's side door. You know, she totaled my car."

As they were walking into the station Kidd said, "Yeah, and the responding officer put her in for a commendation instead of writing her a ticket."

As they entered the bullpen, everyone rose and slowly began to clap. The captain came out of his office and extended his hand to Cassidy.

"What's all this about?" Cassidy asked while shaking his hand.

"The men are just showing their respect for a fellow officer who took down a gunman while simultaneously catching three bullets in the chest. I'm terribly sorry about your wife, Mike. She was a damn good woman and very fine cook."

"Thank you, captain … and I thank all of you. Now stop the applause, damn it. There's a killer out there that needs to be caught. Go back to work. As soon as I get the okay from the shrink, I'll be right here helping you catch the son of a bitch, too. So, captain? When can I talk to the shrink and get cleared to return to duty?"

"Slow down, Cassidy. We'll set up something for next week."

"It's Wednesday! What the hell do you expect me to do between now and Monday?"

The captain lowered his voice and said, "I expect you to at least bury your lovely wife before you start talking about joining the hunt for that psychopath."

Cassidy fell silent and lowered his head a bit. He finally admitted, "You're right."

"Well of course I am, you idiot. They didn't make me captain just because I'm the best-looking guy in the department. Now go home. Put your feet up. Have a cold beer. Hell, masturbate to Internet porn for all I care. You just can't be here. Not right now."

Cassidy looked around at the guys he worked with. "Alright. I'll leave. But the hand that I masturbate with is currently in a sling."

With that, the tension was broken and the guys in the bullpen started laughing and wishing him a swift recovery and quick return. Kidd led him back down to the car and couldn't help himself when he slid behind the wheel. "I would think all you'd need is a thumb and index finger. Seems like either hand would work for such a small job."

"Go screw yourself!" He then started to chuckle a little. That started Kidd laughing. By the time they were halfway back to Cassidy's house, both of them were full on belly laughing.

Finally, after they both calmed down a bit, Cassidy said, "Thank you."

"For what?"

"For not treating me like I'm made of glass. I loved her to death, and I'm going to miss her terribly. I just can't sit around. I'll end up going nuts."

"Nah, you've already been nuts for years. And you're welcome."

Just as he was pulling into Cassidy's driveway, a report of a body being found came across the police band.

Both of them said at the same time, "Son of a bitch."

Cassidy jumped out of the car and commanded tersely, "Go bust the prick. Let me know if it was our guy or another moron pissed off at their significant other."

Kidd nodded and hit the flashers as he backed out onto the road.

*****

"Today there was another homicide in the city of Denver." The camera angle changed and a close-up of the attractive brunette on the evening news replaced the wider shot. "It was quickly proven to be completely unrelated to those that were committed by the Denver City Specter, however. Police are reminding the citizens of our city that there are commonalities between the killings known to have been committed by the Specter that clearly distinguish them from the recent rash of copycats. We have been asked to read this statement issued by Captain Bordeaux. 'If you're unhappy with your spouse, get a divorce. If you're mad at your boyfriend or girlfriend, break up with them and move out. If your brother or sister has done something that made you angry, go see a shrink. Just stop killing each other.' We directly quoted Captain Bordeaux, so those of you who are offended by his politically incorrect use of the word *shrink*, please send your comments to the Denver City Police Department instead of to our station.

"On a brighter note, many of you have joined a neighborhood watch program, thanks to Dr. Stacey Poole's recommendations. During this last week, all crimes except the copycat homicides have diminished to the point of being nearly nonexistent. The city of Denver, as well as this station, would like to offer our gratitude to Dr. Stacey Poole, who is very quickly becoming one of this city's favored residents.

"Homicide Detective Michael Cassidy was released from the hospital this afternoon after spending much of the week in intensive care. The fatal shooting that took the life of his wife of fifteen years also left Detective Cassidy with three bullet wounds in his torso.

He suffered a collapsed lung and extensive blood loss as well as a dislocated shoulder when his car rolled into the intersection and was broadsided by a minivan. Despite losing his wife and having bullets slam into him and his car, he managed to get off three shots of his own, ending the life of his assailant. We have been asked not to release the name of Detective Cassidy's late wife out of respect and not to release the name of the gunman who ended her life out of consideration for his family that still resides locally."

CHAPTER 13

Thursday, August 21

The priest had just finished a dialogue about what a good Catholic Kathy Cassidy was and how she would be welcomed into the kingdom of heaven with open arms. There was only a small gathering at the grave site but throngs of people were milling about outside the cemetery gates. Intermingled among them were news reporters taking statements about why they were there showing their support and getting back stories from anyone who claimed to have any kind of personal involvement with the deceased or her husband, Michael Cassidy.

As the ceremony concluded, a line of people formed to offer condolences to Cassidy. He patiently offered his thanks to all of them. At the end of that line was Jeremy Kidd followed closely by Rebecca Mann and Dr. Stacey Poole.

Kidd leaned close and whispered, "It doesn't look like you're wearing your vest."

Cassidy sighed and gently patted his stomach. "I lost some weight in the hospital. I'm wearing it."

Kidd nodded and stood back to allow Rebecca and Dr. Poole to approach.

Cassidy smiled and said, "Rebecca. I've been told that you're trying to make an honest man out of my partner."

Rebecca glanced over at Kidd then back to Cassidy. "He's a wonderful man, but we're just dating right now. We'll have to see where things lead."

Cassidy continued, "I hope you're as patient a woman as my Kathy was. Dating a homicide detective is a damned difficult thing to deal with. I wish you two the very best though. It's nice to see him happy."

"Thank you, detective."

As she moved aside, Dr. Poole extended her hand. "I'd like to offer my condolences. I'm very sorry for your loss."

Cassidy shook her hand and remarked, "I was told that you weren't sure about attending because of the way we met."

Dr. Poole nodded as she spoke. "We didn't exactly hit it off, that's for sure."

"Well, you were right about Connelly. Maybe we can start over. I'm Detective Michael Cassidy, and it's a pleasure to meet you."

Dr. Poole smiled and responded, "Please call me Stacey. It's very nice to meet you as well."

Cassidy looked around the cemetery and said, "You and Rebecca have a lot of guts showing up to this. It means a lot to me though."

Stacey replied, "No guts were needed. I noticed that your department has people scattered all around the grounds. I doubt a shooter would be able to get close enough to try anything here."

"Still, it means a lot that so many people would risk their lives being near me right now. I appreciate the support."

Kidd cleared his throat and whispered once he got their attention, "They want us to pack up and head back to the SUV's. Rebecca, Stacey, I'll be over there in a minute, if you don't mind."

Once the girls were gone, Kidd looked Cassidy in the eye a moment before saying, "I'll leave you alone for a few minutes, but don't take too much time. Security is getting very nervous now that the group has dispersed and you no longer have them for cover."

Cassidy nodded and knelt at the casket. After thirty seconds, he struggled back to his feet and without a word—and without looking back—he trudged slowly to the black SUV's.

There were four identical black vehicles, all with their windows heavily tinted. When they left the cemetery, nobody could be certain which one Cassidy was in. All were accompanied by marked patrol cars with their flashers on. To the general public, it appeared to be a stately official convoy meant to honor the fallen wife of a law enforcement officer. To those in charge of security, it was a shell game with flashers and strobes meant to distract any potential shooters from getting off a clean shot at any of the vehicles that might contain Cassidy.

As they opened the gates to the cemetery, many in the crowd stood silently and watched as the convoy began to exit the grounds. There were a few people shouting for Cassidy to end the reign of terror the city was under by killing himself.

Naturally, uniformed officers were on hand forming a human barricade between the people and the transport vehicles. The few fights that broke out between those showing their respect and those calling for Cassidy's death were swiftly dealt with by the uniformed officers. As always, the media had their cameras rolling, recording it all.

"Vultures," Kidd muttered.

Cassidy remained silent but watched the chaos as they rolled past.

Rebecca asked, "You don't suppose the killer is actually here, do you?"

Dr. Poole responded, "If he is, it might be his first mistake. With that many cameras around, he'd be certain to have been caught on film. I would think the department will be doing background checks on every person that showed up."

Kidd nodded in confirmation. "As well as the FBI."

Rebecca appeared somewhat surprised. "I had no idea they were involved."

Kidd squeezed her hand a little tighter. "Officially, they're not. Unofficially, since this is getting very close to the territory of a serial killer, as well as the other murders that all of this has spawned, they decided it'd be in their interest to have a presence here."

Dr. Poole said, "Speaking of other murders, what happened last night?"

Kidd shook his head. "A fourteen-year-old girl killed both of her parents. She hadn't cut off any toes or anything and didn't try to blame this on our killer. Her parents apparently forbade her from going to see a movie with some boy. She got pissed and stormed off to her room. Fifteen minutes later, she came out with a large shard of broken glass that she'd wrapped one of her shirts around as a handle. She then proceeded to slash her parents to death. A neighbor heard the screams and called 911. Police arrived while she was in the shower washing off their blood. When the officers took her into custody, she became enraged. Not because she was being arrested for the murder of her parents, but because she still wasn't going to be able to meet that boy at the theater."

Rebecca was shaking her head. "That's horrifying."

Dr. Poole nodded and said, "Things like that are why I chose the profession that I did."

After they were all silent for several seconds, Cassidy asked, "Dr. Poole … "

"Please, outside the office if it's for unofficial business, call me Stacey."

Cassidy thought about it for a second then continued, "Dr. Poole, would you be available to speak with me for a little while this afternoon?"

She raised one eyebrow slightly and nodded, "Rebecca, can you clear some time for me?"

Rebecca answered, "You have no appointments. You were just going to review the notes from the therapists. Your schedule is open."

"Would my office be good or would you prefer some other setting?"

"Your office would be fine. Just give me a chance to get out of this suit. Say, four?"

Dr. Poole nodded in agreement. "I'll be there."

After another several seconds of silence, Cassidy said, "Hey, Kidd?"

"Yeah … yeah. I know. Jeremy's taxi service, at your disposal. After you have your little meeting, I'm taking you to the used car lot."

Cassidy smiled for the first time that morning. "You mean you don't like driving me all over the city?"

"No. You don't tip for shit, you cheap bastard."

They were now pulling into the secure parking garage of the city lab. This was where they all parked their personal vehicles before the funeral. As they dispersed and Cassidy was moving to where Kathy's parents were, he looked over his shoulder to Rebecca, Stacey and Jeremy. "Not a word about this, alright?"

Dr. Poole nodded as she pulled herself up into Rebecca's lifted blazer.

*****

At exactly four o'clock, Dr. Poole's phone buzzed. "Yes?"

Rebecca's voice was on the other end of the line. "Doctor, your four o'clock appointment is here."

"Thank you. Send him up, please." She then went and opened the door to her office.

"Dr. Poole, thank you for seeing me. Do you mind if Jeremy sits in on this? I'd like him to be here as well."

Dr. Poole shook her head and said, "You asked for this meeting. Since I don't know what it's going to entail, you may have anyone here that you'd like."

Kidd smiled and shook his head as he plopped down on the overstuffed sofa.

"Is something funny, Detective Kidd?"

"Yeah, the fact that you're trying to pass this off like you have no idea what it's going to be about."

"Does that mean you know why Detective Cassidy requested this meeting?"

"Nope. He wouldn't say a word to me about it no matter how much I bugged him. But from what I've learned about you over the last few weeks, I seriously doubt that you don't know why we're here."

Cassidy moved the chair that sat across the desk from Dr. Poole so they could all see each other, then sat down. "Do you know why I asked to meet with you?"

Dr. Poole nodded and answered, "I believe it has to do with your upcoming evaluation for the department and whether or not you're ready to return to duty. I also think you're hesitant about returning to duty because you know the killer, who has remained silent while you were in the hospital, might start killing again once you do. Why you chose me to speak with, especially after our little run-in over the first murder, remains a matter for conjecture."

Cassidy turned to Kidd and stared at him.

Kidd smiled and said, "I told you."

"You are good at what you do. Why I chose you should be obvious, I would think. While Kidd and I were convinced that Connelly had played us, we were just as convinced he was guilty. You were the only one that was adamant that he wasn't. As for the rest of it, let's have at it. Should I try to return to duty or would it be better for this city if I just left?"

Dr. Poole took a few seconds before responding. When she did, she chose her words carefully. "We don't have much to go on when it comes to motivation for why this individual has singled you out. We do have a fair amount to go on as to how the killer plans to proceed. You have two options as far as I can tell right now. You can leave the city, either temporarily or permanently … or you can try to return to duty. Let us first consider option one. Based on what I know of the two murders attributed to this person, along with the notes he sent to the media and police, I would say that leaving the city won't solve anything. I believe that the killer will simply ramp up his activity and then blame the additional murders on you for not staying and seeing this to its conclusion."

Cassidy said, "When I ran this through my head while in the hospital, that's what I came up with as well."

Kidd countered, "But while you were in the hospital, our guy stopped killing."

Cassidy nodded. "I had given that some thought as well. I had been injured on the field. As in football, play is suspended until the injured player is taken off the field. Now I'm facing the possibility of going back into the game or leaving the stadium. Play is no longer suspended no matter which way I go."

Dr. Poole was nodding in affirmation. "A very rough analogy, but not inconsistent with what we know right now. While Cassidy was in the hospital, what purpose would be served by killing more citizens? Obviously, Cassidy wasn't in a position to respond. Now that he's been released from the hospital, he is. Even if he's no longer on duty with the department, he is able to respond."

"Great!" Kidd exclaimed in disgust. "So you're telling me that I should expect our guy to start back up again?"

Cassidy turned back to Dr. Poole. "Alright, so if I leave the city I should expect a rash of murders in an attempt to draw me back. If I'm returned to active duty again, shouldn't I expect the same?"

Again Dr. Poole nodded. "Yes, but not to the extent that would happen if you abandon the city. From the onset, this had the flavor of a game of sorts. A murder was committed and carefully designed to get you to arrest the wrong person. Once the plea was in place, essentially the same thing as a guilty verdict, our guy killed again and quickly informed the police and media that the wrong man was behind bars. It was obviously set up to make you and the justice system appear inept. Now, the media and police are looking only at the short term, but our killer is looking at the end game."

Cassidy leaned forward and said, "I don't get it; what do you mean?"

Kidd was also leaning forward now and nodded. "Right, what end game?"

Dr. Poole continued, "The notes pretty much explained it all. The end game is that our guy is either captured or killed or Cassidy dies. Everything that's currently happening is leading to that finale. There is no other way that this can be stopped."

Cassidy lowered his head and muttered, "If killing myself to save the people of this city from what's happening were an option, I'd have already done it."

"You're Catholic," Dr. Poole stated, as opposed to asked.

"I'm Catholic."

Kidd shook his head. "Killing yourself isn't an option whether you're Catholic or not. This is bullshit. Do you even think the killer knows you're Catholic?"

As Cassidy began to nod, Dr. Poole said, "Absolutely. In fact, I'm quite sure the killer knows very much more about you than you'd even guess."

"Dr. Poole, why would he kill strangers? If the end game is either my death or his, why hasn't he directly come after me? He could have picked me off anytime."

"The killer perceives some sort of injustice that you committed against him at some point. The King Midas reference leads me to believe that it has to do with your time as a law enforcement officer. It's because of your job that you received that nickname by the media. This is also why the killer is directly involving the media. Perhaps had the media been involved during whatever injustice he believes happened to him, that injustice would have been corrected."

Kidd shook his head and said, "Now that you bring it up in that light, from my perspective at least, I think the media was involved during that injustice and did nothing to help."

Dr. Poole shrugged as she went on, "That could very well be the case. The media built your reputation though. Now the media is being used in an attempt to destroy it. Killing you would be too quick and final. This guy wants you to suffer. Apparently, much in the same way that you made him suffer at some point."

"Alright, so I go through with the evaluation and get back on active duty. What then? We wait for another murder? How do we get ahead of this guy before others die?"

Dr. Poole shrugged again. "Until a mistake is made, there'll be no way to do that."

"This evaluation … it's scheduled for Monday. Do you think I can pass?"

"I haven't performed the evaluation so I couldn't answer that with certainty. Based on what I see right now, your biggest hurdle to overcome is that you haven't properly grieved yet."

"I have."

"Not by the standards of expectations that the psychologist will have. Your wife died a week ago. You spent the majority of that week in a hospital bed fighting for your life. It's only been a short while since you were released, and grieving takes time. Convincing him that you're psychologically ready to return to active duty is going to be a challenge."

Cassidy smiled and said, "My wife is in a better place. My only grief is that I'll have to wait to join her there. If there's nothing special I should know about this evaluation, I should have no problem passing."

"Just be honest, detective. If you don't pass the evaluation on the first try, take a bit of time then give it another shot. You should be alright. In the meantime, much of the city has established neighborhood watches. Should our killer try to commit another murder, doing so without being spotted will be very difficult."

"Oh, yeah," Kidd chimed in, "Rebecca said your own little neighborhood watch is very active."

"We have over sixty volunteers. We're running three sets of two people per four-hour shift. Since both of the murders happened in the evening, we've set up our shifts to run from 6:00 p.m. to 2:00

a.m. If our killer strikes at some other time of the day, we'll adjust our patrols to match."

Cassidy sighed and said, "I just hope they don't get hurt trying to help the police."

"Thanks to Detective Kidd, all of our members have been briefed on exactly what they should do if they see anything out of the ordinary. As long as no one tries to be a hero, they should be just fine. All they were instructed to do was get as good a description as possible and stay out of the way. Our teams actually carry flash cameras. They were instructed to start snapping pictures should they see anyone suspicious. Since our guy is using stealth to enter and commit these crimes, the flashbulbs alone should drive him away if he's spotted."

Cassidy stood and extended his hand. "I'm sorry for the way I acted last month. I thank you for being so helpful in all of this."

As Dr. Poole shook his hand she offered, "I'm glad I can help and, again, I'm very sorry for your loss."

Just then there was a loud, insistent banging at her office door. "It's not locked."

Rebecca poked her head in and said, "I tried to buzz you several times. Didn't you see the light on your phone?"

"I have the ringer turned off, and we were in pretty deep discussion. What's the problem?"

"Line 2, someone from the Christian Cable Channel wants you on an open panel to discuss the murders and what people in this city should do."

Dr. Poole bit her lower lip and quietly responded, "Please turn them down. That wouldn't be a good idea."

Cassidy remarked, "Actually, I think you should do it. You can tell people how to protect themselves, set up makeshift noisemakers at the entrances of their homes and things like that. Imagine the population you could reach."

Dr. Poole was shaking her head. "No, it would be a very bad idea."

Kidd questioned, "Why? You want to help the people of this city. This would be a great medium to accomplish that."

"You don't understand; I'm an atheist."

All three of them paused for a moment. Eventually, Cassidy asked, "How can you not believe in God?"

"See? That's exactly why I should turn this down. It won't end well."

Cassidy said, "I'm sorry. I shouldn't have said that. This is still an excellent opportunity for you to speak to the city. Maybe tell people what kind of behavior they should be looking for in someone. Or as Kidd said, simply tell people how to set up their homes to be more resistant to being invaded. I think you should do it."

Dr. Poole looked from face to face and finally asked, "All of you feel this strongly?"

All three of them nodded emphatically.

Dr. Poole sighed and picked up her phone. "This is Dr. Poole." After thirty seconds of listening she asked, "Who else is going to be on this panel? Alright, and what time would you need me there? Okay, I'll see you tomorrow."

Kidd promised, "You won't regret this. You can go a long way toward calming the population. Who knows, maybe the killer will be watching and you can affect him in some way as well."

Dr. Poole was still unhappy. "You're right, I probably won't regret this. A whole lot of others might though."

CHAPTER 14

———•———

Friday, August 22

"Dr. Poole. You'll sit here between Reverend Murray and Dr. Virgil Carson. Dr. Phyllis Ayers will be next to Dr. Carson, and our panel host will be at the desk there. Is your microphone working? Let's see." The young woman who was directing the panelists tapped the clip-on microphone a few times then listened to a disembodied voice in her headset.

"Excuse me, what was your name?"

"Jessica. Jessica Frye. You're microphone is working great. Now if you wouldn't mind having a seat, please. Oh, and please remember that this is being broadcast live so mind your language."

"Yes, of course. But what are Dr. Ayers and Dr. Carson actually doctors of?"

"Oh, Dr. Ayers is a regular on these panels. She's a doctor of religious philosophy. Dr. Carson is a neurosurgeon at Saint Mary's Hospital for Advanced Medicine."

"I'm sorry, just one more thing. I thought live broadcasts weren't done anymore."

"It's actually on a fifteen-second delay. That way if someone slips and says a bad word, our guys in the booth can cut it out of the aired broadcast."

Dr. Poole sighed heavily and sat down.

The auditorium was filled nearly to capacity and people were still steadily streaming in. After fifteen minutes, the other panelists were in place, and the host of this broadcast was taking her seat behind her desk.

Everyone introduced themselves to those they didn't already know and, as they were settling down, a man near one of the cameras called for a countdown to begin the show—3 ... 2 ... 1 ...

"I'd like to thank you for tuning in for today's program. We have with us Dr. Phyllis Ayers. As most of our regular viewers know, she gives wonderful insight into how current events shape our world and affect our beliefs. Next we have Dr. Virgil Carson—a neurosurgeon who can offer explanations regarding the physical nature of our brains and how we perceive the world. Seated beside him is Dr. Stacey Poole. She's one of the few people who stood by poor Mr. Connelly when the majority of this city was ready to crucify him. She's a psychiatrist working in Dr. Jacobs' absence at the Jacobs Psychiatric Center and will be sharing information regarding the mindset and motivations of the Denver City Specter. Finally, we have Reverend Phillip Murray who will offer spiritual guidance and recommendations to our viewers during these terrifying and troubling times. I'm Sheila Raines, the host of *His Glorious World*.

"Since we have two panelists who haven't been on our program before, may we please have a warm welcome for Doctors Stacey Poole and Virgil Carson?"

After the audience stopped clapping, Sheila Raines continued, "Now, the topic for our panel today will be the murderer dubbed as the Denver City Specter or the King Midas Killer. I'd like to start with someone who personally knows King Midas, also known as Detective Michael Cassidy. Dr. Poole, how is Detective Cassidy handling not only the loss of his dear wife but also having to deal with a madman who wants him dead?"

"Detective Cassidy is a strong man and seems to be dealing with the death of his wife as well as can be expected given the circumstances. He's dedicated himself to stopping these murders."

Sheila nodded and said, "I know that he's Catholic, so it would be a mortal sin in the eyes of the Lord for him to commit suicide. He must be suffering greatly, knowing he can put a stop to these killings by ending his own life. Yet his inability to do that due to his religion has to be affecting him terribly."

"Yes, he mentioned that to me just yesterday. As I said, he's trying to recover from his physical injuries and emotional loss so he can continue the hunt for this killer."

Dr. Phyllis Ayers jumped in. "Situations like this truly test one's faith in what the Lord has planned for us all. I, for one, applaud his convictions. I hope he's able to end this abomination who was obviously sent forth by Satan to sway us in our faith."

The crowd responded in unison, "Amen."

Dr. Poole bit her lip but remained silent.

Reverend Murray asked, "Dr. Carson, are there physical defects in the brain which could account for someone behaving in such an irrational manner as this Denver City Specter?"

Dr. Carson replied, "There have been cases where defects in the brain or injuries sustained by the brain have dramatically affected one's behavior. Without an MRI I couldn't say if this individual suffers from such a malady. I do have to address the use of the word *irrational*, however. The actions taken by this killer have been cold and calculated with an extreme amount of forethought and planning. Considering his actions irrational might not be the best description."

Sheila Raines questioned, "But, doctor, surely you don't consider murdering people in their homes to be a rational act?"

"There are many definitions for the word *rational*. If you're looking at it as meaning *sensible*, then I would agree. Murdering strangers in their homes to torment Detective Cassidy into killing himself would not be sensible. But if you look at the rest of the definitions, if the acts are designed to exact some form of revenge against the detective, this is a very well-planned way to do just that."

Reverend Murray said, "Rational or not, we have to figure out a way to foil Satan's plans. After all, let's remember that this killer is acting under the influence of a very powerful evil entity. Whether it's due to a birth defect or a later change in the brain, Satan is the cause."

"Dr. Poole," Sheila continued, "being a psychiatrist, do you have any insight into how Satan's influence would affect the overall mental health of not only our killer, but also any of our viewers?"

Dr. Poole looked back and forth for a moment then replied simply, "No."

Sheila laughed a little and said, "Being nervous is understandable, dear, but could you try to elaborate for us just a bit?"

Dr. Poole thought carefully about how to respond. "Without knowing the religious convictions of the killer, I couldn't offer any insight concerning what he may or may not think of Satan."

Dr. Carson was nodding, though it was nearly imperceptible.

The reverend asked, "So do you think it could be possible that this killer actually welcomed Satan into his life?"

Dr. Poole appeared physically uncomfortable. "I couldn't offer any opinion at all about that."

Dr. Ayers leaned forward a bit and remarked, "It appears you don't believe Satan is playing a role in all of this. If that's true and these killings aren't the result of Satan's influence, what could cause someone to behave in such an evil way?"

Finally, Dr. Poole had a question she could respond to. "Actually, there are several conditions that have nothing to do with God or Satan that cause people to act out in this fashion. Paranoid schizophrenia matches some of the actions that we know this killer has taken. If one were a sociopath, for example, that would explain nearly all of his actions. Killing without remorse, casually ending the lives of strangers to cause Detective Cassidy to suffer—these are traits of someone afflicted with that or a similar mental disorder. The means wouldn't matter to him as long as the end turned out like he wanted."

Sheila said, "If being a sociopath is causing this person to kill our citizens, it certainly sounds to me like that would be the very definition of Satan's work."

The crowd again said, "Amen," this time a little more enthusiastically.

"No. It's much like Dr. Carson said of the physical nature of the brain. Some people are born with these types of mental disorders while others suffer traumatic events which force them to ignore or completely destroy their own conscience."

The reverend sat back and remarked, "Yet again, to me at least, that sounds exactly like the work of Satan."

Dr. Poole bit her lower lip again and replied, "I'm sorry, perhaps it was a mistake for me to agree to be part of this panel." She began to reach up to remove her microphone from her collar.

Dr. Ayers asked, "Dr. Poole, you appear to be saying to us that this evil wasn't caused by Satan?"

Dr. Poole closed her eyes briefly then repeated, "This was a mistake; I'll leave you to your discussions."

Sheila jumped in and seemed to exude pity as she asked, "Please, Dr. Poole. Are you one of those atheists? If so, perhaps we can help educate you. I can have my producer bring you some literature that I'm sure will enlighten you once you've had the opportunity to read it."

Dr. Poole stopped before removing her microphone. "I'm sorry. Are you suggesting that if my education were sufficient, then I'd believe in God?"

"Don't be embarrassed, dear. Some people are just raised by apathetic parents who don't properly educate their children. That's why atheism is becoming so widespread in our society. It's also why we're dedicated to wiping it out wherever we encounter it."

The audience yelled, "Amen!"

Dr. Poole calmly sat back and placed her hands in her lap. "Since the topic has now shifted away from the murderer that's terrorizing this city to my personal belief and education, I think I will stay a bit longer. I'd like you and all of your viewers to know something. I am educated. I studied the various versions of the Bible and the writings that they contain. It's because I did this that I chose to disregard the existence of an invisible magic guy sitting in the clouds watching every single individual and every single action that we take. According to that book, your God sat back for thousands of years and did nothing while every civilization on this planet worshiped a plethora of other deities. Then, all of a sudden, he decided to become jealous of not getting the credit he believed he deserved. So this supposedly all-powerful being, instead of just waving a hand and making everyone believe in him, chose to scour the globe for a married woman who allegedly hadn't yet consummated her marriage with her husband. He then committed an adulterous act by impregnating her. Of all of the women available for this, he happened to choose one that was married with the intent being to make her raise a son who would eventually pass along his wishes to those around him. Let's go back even further. Citizens in a couple of cities were misbehaving in his eyes. Instead of this all-powerful being waving a hand and correcting their behavior, he decided to kill every man, woman and child in each of these cities except for Lot and his family. Actually, let's forget about that for now. The great flood. Again, being all powerful, instead of just changing the behavior of the people on this planet, he allegedly caused a great flood that killed every man, woman and child on earth except for Noah and his family. I will apologize to all of you if you're offended by this. If that's God, even if he does exist, I would rather end my life than worship someone who's made those kinds of piss poor decisions. If you want to know why I don't believe in God, I'll tell you. I choose to believe that God doesn't exist because the alternative would be unthinkable for me. Your God, at least according to the Bible, is the most prolific mass murderer that humanity has ever known."

"One last thing before I excuse myself from this panel. I am an atheist. I am also an American. As an American who is an atheist, I recognize your right to believe in whatever you choose. I also don't seek to change those beliefs. So, regardless of your religious convictions, I am greatly offended that you feel completely justified in trying to force your beliefs onto me. According to the tenets set forth when this nation was born, you are not within your rights to do so. I hope you all have a wonderful day. I'm going to go back to work so I can help those who are seeking it."

As she pulled the microphone from her blouse and stood, she looked at Dr. Carson.

He nodded and smiled as he stood. "I couldn't have put that any better than you did, Dr. Poole." He then removed his microphone and followed her off the stage.

They both ignored everyone who tried to speak with them as they were exiting the auditorium. Once they were alone in the parking lot, he spoke again. "I was misinformed as to the nature of this panel before accepting. Once I found out what it was going to be like, the hospital wouldn't allow me to back out. But your bravery in admitting that you're an atheist gave me the courage to leave. I thank you."

"I try to stay out of discussions of that nature. I think it's shameful that people who are religious proudly proclaim their beliefs to anyone who'll listen while those of us who don't believe in God are shunned into silence … especially in this nation. A big reason for declaring independence from Great Britain was so that the people of this country could escape religious persecution. Now we find ourselves being persecuted by the religious for not being religious. As I said, I find it shameful."

Dr. Carson nodded and said, "Again, I thank you, doctor. I wish you the best in helping the police with the hunt for this killer."

*****

"What the hell were you thinking?"

"Calm down, Rebecca."

"Rebecca's right, you couldn't have just gone along with them until you had the chance to inform the viewers how to protect themselves from a home invader?"

"Detective, if I remember correctly, I said I shouldn't accept the invitation to the show. Both of you, along with Cassidy, disagreed with me. I knew there was a high potential that things would go badly."

"But to announce to the world that you're an atheist. What were you thinking?"

Dr. Poole looked at Rebecca with an expression of surprise. "I hardly announced it to the world. It was a local cable station. Besides, would you have any issue with going on TV and announcing whatever your religion is?"

"Of course not, but it's because I believe in God."

Dr. Poole shook her head and retorted, "That is exactly what I was talking about. Let's say that you got invited to sit on a panel made up of nonbelievers. If the situation were reversed, you'd have no issue stating that you believed in God. Why? Because in today's society, believing in God is expected and accepted. But to the religious, not believing in God is absolutely unacceptable."

There was silence for several seconds before Rebecca looked at Jeremy and said, "Alright, I get it."

Jeremy nodded. "Yeah. As long as we believe in God, whether we're Methodist, Catholic or some other religion, we're not looked down upon like an atheist is. But did you have to be so harsh toward them? I mean, you claimed that God made piss poor decisions. That we worship the most prolific mass murderer in history. That is quite extreme."

"I was treated like I was the one with a mental disorder. I was told that I was uneducated when, in all actuality, I most likely know more about their Bible than they do. Those people acted like I was broken and they would fix me. Would it be any more extreme if I treated all of you like you're idiots for not only believing in God but worshiping him after the Bible tells you just how many people he single-handedly killed?"

"It wasn't like that; you don't understand … "

Dr. Poole cut him off. "See? Once again it comes down to my education on the topic. Because I disagree with the existence of God, I obviously lack enough education to know that he exists. I'm expected to shut up and take it when people bash me for being an atheist. Yet, the instant someone questions what you believe, a heated reaction and defense is mounted. You don't need to defend your belief in God to me. What you believe is your choice as an American citizen and is protected by the Constitution. I'm not going to judge you because of it. All I'm asking is the same courtesy from you in return."

Again Jeremy and Rebecca looked at each other before they both lowered their gazes. Jeremy said, "Understood. I won't bring it up again."

"Me either."

"Thank you. Now, instead of coming here and harassing my receptionist all day long, why don't you put together something for the media to broadcast about how people can set up their homes to prevent the killer from sneaking in like he did in the first two murders?"

"Oh, that's a good idea. I'll run that past my captain when I get back to the station. He can set up a news conference."

"Good, now if you don't mind letting me get back to work, perhaps you two can do the same."

Rebecca looked up and said, "I'm sorry."

"Forget about it. I'm used to being treated like that by the religious."

"But I know you. I shouldn't have treated you any differently than I had before."

"Correct. And as long as you go back to the way you treated me over the last month, we won't have any problems."

"Deal."

Jeremy turned to Rebecca and asked, "If you don't have any plans this weekend, would you like to come over?"

"Oh, I'm so sorry. Stacey and I had set up a weekend of off-road exploration outside the city. We've actually had the plans in place for weeks."

Jeremy nodded and said, "A girl's weekend." He raised his hands and backed away a step. "I know better than to get in the way of that. You two have fun and be safe. I don't want to hear any reports about an ancient Blazer rolling down the side of a mountain or anything."

Rebecca turned to face Stacey. "Did he really just insult my baby and my driving in one breath?"

Stacey was nodding. "Yes, he did."

"No ... wait. That wasn't what ... "

Rebecca stood and started to walk around her counter in the reception area as Stacey began to move so that he'd have to go past her to get out the back entrance of the building.

He recognized the maneuver and rushed to the front doors before Rebecca could cut him off. "I didn't mean that your driving was bad. Hon, come on. You know I was just trying to show you that I care."

"Ancient? Rolling down the side of a mountain? That's how you show that you care?"

"Stacey, help me here. You know I didn't mean anything by it. Stacey?"

"I don't know, Jeremy. You put your foot in your own mouth this time. I think you're on your own."

As he was backing out onto the sidewalk, he yelled back, "You two have a great weekend! I'll call you when ... you know what? I'll wait to hear from you when you're done. Okay, Hon?"

"I'll 'Hon' you!"

Before she could say anything else, he turned and started running down the sidewalk.

Rebecca turned toward Stacey and both of them burst out laughing. It was at that moment that Quinn walked into the reception area from the offices and stopped to look at both of them.

"Did I just miss something?"

Both of them looked at him and started laughing even harder.

"I'll just … " He motioned back to where he'd come from and slowly backed through the door he'd just entered.

*****

On the evening news, the perky brunette shifted some papers that were in front of her and looked directly into the camera. "It would appear that Dr. Stacey Poole may have lost some appeal to many in this city today. She was sitting in as a panelist on the Christian Cable Network's discussion program called *His Glorious World*. The topic of the program was supposed to be The Denver City Specter. However, once the religious nature of the program became evident, Dr. Poole attempted to leave the panel. When the host of the program implied that she was an atheist because she lacked proper education on the topic, Dr. Poole calmly and rationally explained to all those in attendance, as well as home viewers, exactly what she thought of God."

The broadcast of Stacey's little monologue was then replayed by the news station. When it ended, the camera cut back to the attractive brunette. With a broad smile on her face she began to speak again. "In offending the beliefs of the religious, Dr. Poole may have bitten off a bit more than she can handle this time. Good luck, doctor. You'll probably need it."

CHAPTER 15

Monday, August 25

As Stacey arrived at work the next morning, she noticed that the employee parking lot was filled nearly to capacity. To her left she saw the news vans. At the employee entrance there were a dozen or more people carrying signs and walking in circles. She let out an exasperated sigh as she grabbed her briefcase and moved toward the door. The scene was just like watching a school of fish react to something else in the water. As soon as one of them noticed her approach, they all turned and moved as one.

The shouts were just what she expected. One yelled that she was going to burn in hell for eternity. Another shouted something about her soul being damned forever. On and on it went as she cut her own path down the center of the sign-carrying group. Finally, one of the news reporters got in front of her and shouted into the microphone, "Dr. Poole, did you expect this type of reaction to the statements you made on Friday's program?" The reporter then thrust the microphone directly into Dr. Poole's face.

Dr. Poole stopped and looked at the reporter, as well as the handful of others who all had microphones held up to catch her response. When she spoke, she did so deliberately and loud enough for all to hear her over what they were saying. "There is a killer somewhere in this city—one who's murdered two people in cold blood in their own homes. Are you people seriously trying to tell me that a few comments I made on a local cable program made me the biggest news story in the city at this time? You should all be ashamed of yourselves … especially the media. Giving this idiocy attention and coverage when this city faces real issues is unconscionable. All of you, grow the hell up, people! You disgust me."

She made it only one step closer to the building's entrance before someone yelled out, "Aren't you even going to apologize for the horrible things you said about our Lord?"

Dr. Poole spun on her heels and glared at the entire crowd. The immediate silence was impressive. "No. I will not apologize for being an atheist and having my own beliefs any more than I would ask you to apologize for believing in God and being religious. If you have so much time on your hands, why aren't you at the jail? There's an innocent man still sitting behind bars from the first murder. Go tell your local justice system that you won't tolerate him being held in a cage when he's done nothing to deserve it. Go carry signs in front of their offices. Go stick your microphones in their faces. Go ask them why they can't release a man that everyone in this country knows is innocent. Most of all, stop trying to bully me into being more like you!"

She turned and entered the building expecting to hear shouts and taunts, but the silence was all that remained. After a few minutes, those who were carrying signs and walking in circles outside the front of the building also quieted. Within half an hour, they had all left.

Rebecca was shaking her head as she entered Stacey's office an hour and a half later. Dr. Poole looked up and asked, "What is it? Why are you looking at me like that?"

"You got them to leave. I can't believe you actually got them to leave. That's quite a feat."

Dr. Poole smiled and looked back down at the document she had been reading and asked, "Was there something you wanted to speak with me about?"

"Yes, you told me to give you a reminder at ten. You never told me what I was supposed to remind you of, but when you came in this morning, that's what you said. In the mood you were in, I just said I would and left it at that."

"Oh, yes. Detective Cassidy should just be finishing up with his psych evaluation. I wanted to go down and speak with him. I'm sure he'll have some questions and anxiety until the psychologist issues his results to the department. Thank you."

Rebecca walked with her down to the employee entrance. "If you see Jeremy, tell him it's safe to call me. I think we might have really scared him Friday. I haven't gotten so much as a text from him."

"I will, but I'm quite sure it's only because his focus is on Cassidy at the moment."

*****

"That was bullshit!"

"It was just an evaluation. It isn't like you haven't had to go through the process before."

"How does the death of my wife make me feel? What kind of moron expects an answer to a question like that?"

Kidd quietly asked, "Oh, shit, what did you tell him?"

"What the hell do you think I told him? I told him that it made me feel like turning into a puddle on the ground and getting walked on by a thousand stomping feet."

Dr. Poole smiled and said, "You took my advice and were honest. Good."

"You think that was honest? Like hell it was. Honest would have been if I told him that it made me feel like pulling my service pistol and emptying the clip into his expressionless face for having the balls to ask me such a stupid ass question."

Both Stacey and Jeremy started laughing, slowly at first, then building up to a full blown fit of laughter.

Cassidy stared at them for a few moments before starting to laugh, too.

Finally, they all calmed enough for Cassidy to ask, "How long do I have to wait for the shrink to turn in his findings?"

Dr. Poole checked the time before offering, "I would think that he should be done writing up the results any time now."

Just as she finished saying that, a uniformed officer walked into the hallway and said, "There you are. Cassidy, the captain wants to see you. You too, Kidd."

"At least I didn't have to wait days for this. Let's go, partner."

Dr. Poole spoke. "I'll wait down here; please let me know how it went." Five minutes later, her phone buzzed and she smiled as she read the following text: *He's back, but riding a desk until his wounds heal.*

She punched some buttons on the phone and passed along the message to Rebecca with an additional text to say she was taking the afternoon off. She then sent a message to all three of them saying, "Dinner at my house, 6:00 p.m. Bring only your appetites."

On the midday news broadcasts on all of the local networks, Detective Michael Cassidy was one of the main stories. "Only days after being released from the hospital and attending the funeral of his wife, Detective Michael Cassidy rejoins the active duty roster for the city police department. A source at the police station said that he's still wearing a sling for his left arm and he's moving a bit slowly due to the healing gunshot wounds in his chest, but confirmed that he is back on the job. The only restriction is that he's limited to desk duty until his wounds heal properly and he can get a doctor to sign off on a physical release. Once those conditions have been met, the word around the station is that Detective Cassidy expects to return to full duty once again."

***** *

As they arrived at Stacey's apartment later that evening, Rebecca used her key to open the security door. When the three of them reached the actual apartment door, it swung open before they could knock.

"Congratulations, Detective Cassidy. I'm glad you're reinstated. Please come in."

The smell as they filed in was extraordinary. Rebecca sniffed the air and asked, "What are we having?"

"Mexican lasagna, refried beans and fried rice. I wanted something spicy and upbeat. Have a seat; it should be ready in about ten minutes." She then turned and went into the kitchen.

The walls of the living room were only partially painted with the new dark red. Clear plastic covered one of the end tables and part of the floor where she was going to paint next.

The table had already been set for four, and they engaged in small talk as they were seated. Finally, Stacey came out with a lasagna pan and set it down on some hot pads in the center of the table. "I'll be right out with the rice and beans."

As she was setting down the bowls and preparing to take her seat, Jeremy's phone buzzed. "Excuse me for a moment," he said as he put the phone to his ear. After only a few seconds he muttered, "I got it."

Everyone looked at him expectantly, but none more intently than Cassidy. Kidd stood and sighed. "I'm sorry, I have to go."

Cassidy asked, "Is it our guy?"

Kidd said, "I don't know yet. I won't know until the ME can examine the body. I'm sorry, save me some. It smells wonderful."

"I'm coming with you!"

"You can't. You're handcuffed to a desk."

"I'll stay with the car. I won't say anything to anyone. Just tell them that we were on our way to a movie when you got the call and you didn't have time to drop me off."

"I'm not telling those assholes that you and I were on a date with each other. Are you out of your damn mind? I should submit you for another psych evaluation, you moron."

Cassidy stood and said, "I'm sorry, Stacey. It smells wonderful, and I'm sure it tastes fantastic. But I have to go."

"It's alright. This is obviously more important than a dinner. I'll have plenty left over. When you get done at the crime scene, give me a buzz if you're still hungry."

Cassidy turned to Kidd, "If you don't want me to come with you, shoot me."

Kidd thought about that for a moment and actually reached for his shoulder holster before lowering his hand. "You promise you'll stay with the car and not speak to anyone?"

"Scout's honor."

"Weren't you kicked out of the scouts?"

"What difference does that make? Yes, I promise."

Both of them disappeared through the door of Stacey's apartment, leaving the two ladies alone.

Rebecca smiled and grabbed the spatula. "Piss on them; I haven't eaten in hours."

Stacey laughed and began scooping rice onto her plate. "You want to hang out here until we find out what's going on?"

"Sounds good to me. Want help painting after dinner?"

"Nah, let's just relax. Maybe watch a movie or something. How long do you think they'll be?"

"Who knows? I guess it depends on whether this is our guy or not. Shall I say grace?"

Stacey stopped scooping food onto her plate and grinned. "Very funny."

*****

"Stay!"

"Kidd, quit treating me like a dog."

"Start acting smarter than one, and I'll consider it. Let me put this in terms that you can understand. You've been reinstated for less than eight hours. If you don't stay with the car, you'll set a record for the shortest period of reinstatement in history. Not only will the captain suspend you, but he'll boot my ass out for being the idiot that let myself get talked into bringing you to a crime scene."

"Relax! I'll be right here. I'll even snarl if someone gets too close the car. Go do your damned job."

"Seriously, stay away from the scene."

"Go!"

Kidd was stopped by the ME before he could get a report from the responding officer. They looked each other in the eyes, but neither uttered a word. Eventually, Kidd lowered his head and sighed as he continued on into the house.

Robin and her minions were scouring the room. The victim was a teenage boy. He was seated in front of a computer monitor in his bedroom with his headset still covering his ears. Kidd asked, "Where can I step?"

Robin pointed to a section of floor next to the boy. "We already got the desk, his clothes and the floor around him. Don't touch anything else though."

As Kidd turned, he saw a corkboard hanging on the wall. In the middle of the corkboard was a standard sheet of printer paper held in place with a pushpin. In bold print were the words, "Welcome back, King Midas."

Kidd turned back to Robin, but before he could say anything she nodded and ordered, "Yeah, don't touch that either."

"Son of a bitch." After jotting some notes and doing a visual inspection, he stormed past Robin and her crew and went to track down the ME. Not surprisingly, Cassidy was talking with him.

"You dumb bastard! Did I not make myself clear about staying with the car?"

Cassidy asked, "This medical quack won't tell me a damn thing. Is it our guy or not?"

"Sorry, doctor. I'm done in there if you want to take the body."

The ME called out, "Jeff! Get the stretcher. I'll waddle inside and wait for you." He then turned to Cassidy and made a quacking sound like a duck before walking away with an exaggerated waddle.

Cassidy glared at Kidd.

Finally, Kidd called to one of the uniformed officers that was near and directed, "Take this idiot back to his house. If he refuses, shoot him in the knee. If you have even the slightest hint that he won't stay at his house, handcuff him to his bed."

Cassidy grabbed Kidd by his shoulder and quietly asked again. "Is it our guy?"

Kidd hesitated for a moment then replied, "It looks like it. Now go home. Once you get the sling off, you can get cleared to work in the field again. Right now, you're a liability and you need to leave."

Both of them turned to see the first news reporters jogging up the road with their cameramen struggling to keep up.

Cassidy gritted out, "Oh, shit," and turned to follow the officer to his car before they could get any footage of him being at the scene.

Kidd put his hands to his face and shook his head. "I need a shot."

*****

"King Midas is at the crime scene."

Another of the onlookers standing just outside the yellow crime scene tape turned and asked, "What'd you say? I'm sorry, I couldn't hear you."

"I said he's back. That's him right there."

The other man turned and followed where he was pointing. "Oh, shit, that's Detective Cassidy. I thought he was restricted to desk duty."

"Apparently Detective Kidd decided to let him tag along to this one."

"Wow, good catch spotting King Midas at the crime scene, man. What's your name?"

"Travis, what's yours?"

"Willie. Nice to meet you."

"Yeah, you too. Uh oh, here come the news guys."

Willie glanced over to see the first few reporters come trotting up the sidewalk. He then nudged Travis and pointed. "And there goes King Midas. I thought the news said he was moving slowly due to his injuries. Looks to me like he's moving pretty damned fast right now."

"Since he's restricted and can't be in the field, I'm sure he's just trying to get away before he's caught on camera at the scene."

"Hey, you live around here or something? How'd you find out about this?"

"Police scanner. I'm just getting ready to move into my dorm room, so I'm back and forth between the university and where I've been staying for the summer."

Willie motioned with his head before saying, "I'm from the next block over. I saw the flashers and wandered this way to see what all the fuss was about. So? Do you think this is the work of that Specter that the news has been going on about or do you think this is just another copycat?"

"This is the Specter."

Willie looked somewhat surprised. "What makes you so sure it isn't just a copycat killing?"

Travis looked Willie straight in his eyes and said, "Just a feeling. That's all. Just a gut feeling."

Two hours later, Kidd was following Dr. Brown in circles around a stainless steel table jotting notes as the doctor continued his visual inspection of the body. "Jeff, help me get him turned over, please."

Once the body was face up, the doctor continued, "The only wound I can find is this puncture beneath the chin. The blade was inserted up through the back of the mouth and into the brain cavity. Without opening him up to verify, I'd say that his brain would have suffered trauma very near where the spinal cord attaches. Death would have been almost instantaneous. I put his time of death somewhere near 2:00 p.m. Robin confirmed that the instant messages he was exchanging with his girlfriend abruptly stopped a few minutes after two."

"The knife we found in the sink?"

"Very likely the murder weapon. Of course, you'd need Robin and her minions to verify that."

"The killer didn't waste any time, did he?"

"No. I caught the midday news and heard of Cassidy's reinstatement then. It took less than two hours for our killer to strike after the media reported it."

Kidd looked down at the body and said, "He was going to be heading to college in another couple of weeks."

"Did his mother tell you that?"

Kidd nodded. "She found the body when she got home from work at 5:30."

The doctor said, "It's a shame that he wasn't on video cam with his girlfriend or we'd have a witness to the murder."

Kidd looked down at the victim's feet and asked, "Doc, why the hell would the killer still remove the baby toes?"

Dr. Brown responded, "It has become somewhat of a signature. Perhaps that's all it is anymore. Did anyone see anybody coming or going from the house at about the time of the murder?"

"No. Our guys went through the entire block. Nobody could remember seeing anyone near the residence this afternoon."

"Then it appears as though our killer is quickly earning his moniker. Specter is an apt description. How long before Robin can give you any information?"

"Probably not until tomorrow afternoon. They logged all of the evidence they collected and called it a night. The FBI spoke with Captain Bordeaux and told him that they'd offer whatever resources we needed, but that they'd leave the investigation in our hands for now. They're on board and joining the hunt, but they're not taking lead."

Kidd's phone buzzed, and he checked the caller ID then sighed. "Yeah, Cassidy, what is it?"

"They torched my house!"

"What?"

"My house! Are you freaking deaf? Someone torched my house."

"Are you alright?"

"Yeah, I heard a few noises but didn't see anything. Then I smelled the smoke. By the time I figured out that they'd set it on fire, both the front and back doors were engulfed. I made it out a window and called the fire department. I don't think they're going to be able to do much. It looks like it's going to be a total loss."

"I'll be right there."

The doctor was looking quizzically at Kidd as he put his phone away. "I have to go, doc. Someone torched Cassidy's house while he was in it. He's fine, but I have to go get him. He'll need a place to stay."

Before he could leave, Doc Brown dug in his bag and dumped a couple of pills into a small plastic cup. "Here, aspirin. You look like you could use 'em."

"You don't happen to have any scotch to chase these down with, do you?"

"Only rubbing alcohol. Sorry."

*****

"Today's report is going to be accompanied by a public apology." The face of the attractive news broadcaster was instantly replaced with the scene of a parking lot. The image showed Dr. Stacey Poole getting out of her Outback and surveying the protesters before approaching the employee entrance of the Jacobs Psychiatric Center. "This morning Dr. Stacey Poole was filmed as she arrived at work. Protesters had gathered outside both entrances to the Jacobs Psychiatric Center where she's been working in place of Dr. Jacobs. They were rallying against the comments that Dr. Poole made about God and religion on Friday's broadcast of *His Glorious World*. After her statements about God making poor decisions and God being the most prolific mass murderer known to humanity, the religious community was up in arms. Showing no signs of fear or intimidation, Dr. Poole courageously approached the protesters who blocked the entrance to the office building. After making her way through the heart of the crowd and silently enduring the taunts they threw her way, our own Jennifer Goodwin asked for her comments about the statements she'd made and the resulting protest. Here is that exchange."

They brought up the sound on the footage that was being aired as the news broadcaster was speaking. After they replayed the entire scene up to the point where Dr. Poole entered the building, the image cut back to the broadcaster in the studio.

"In her usual straightforward and no nonsense manner, Dr. Poole managed to let us, as well as this city, know exactly where she stood. After careful consideration by the producers at this station, it was determined that she was absolutely correct in what she stated. The Denver City Specter is still at large and killing indiscriminately. Dean Connelly still sits in a jail cell awaiting a decision concerning his plea agreement and confession of murdering his mother, Mrs. Sarah Connelly. With all of this happening, the fact that religious demonstrators were picketing the office building where Dr. Poole works does have the appearance of being quite petty in the grand scheme of things. On top of that, our news agency's coverage of that demonstration only added validity to a situation that has been blown out of proportion. This agency and those of us who are employed by it are officially offering our most sincere apology to Dr. Stacey Poole. In this nation, one's religious beliefs or lack thereof are protected by the law. For our news agency to become complicit in the condemnation of an individual's personal beliefs oversteps our purview. Dr. Poole, if you're watching this broadcast, we are terribly sorry for both the harassment you were forced to endure as well as our coverage of it.

"While still on the topic of the Specter, there was another murder this afternoon involving a young man who was preparing to begin his first year at college. Sources say his death has been confirmed as the third murder by the killer known as the Specter, and it occurred within hours of the announcement that Detective Michael Cassidy was cleared to return to duty with the city police department. As with the other two murders, nobody saw anything out of the ordinary at or near the residence during the timeframe given for the homicide. Police are asking for your help in remaining vigilant and reporting any behavior that may be considered suspicious.

"Finally, it appears to authorities that another attempt has been made on the life of Detective Cassidy. While he occupied his home this evening, someone set fire to both exits in an attempt to burn the detective alive. After escaping the burning structure through a bedroom window, Detective Cassidy called the fire department. How much tragedy can one man endure in such a short span of time? Chris, what's the weather supposed to look like over the next few days?"

CHAPTER 16

Tuesday, August 26

Rebecca rubbed her eyes and looked around. Stacey was on the couch next to her, sound asleep. She glanced at the digital readout on the cable box near the television and jumped to her feet. "Stacey! We're late. We have to get to the office. Wake up."

Stacey opened her eyes and looked around quickly. "It's only 7:30. We're not late yet."

Rebecca was scurrying around the apartment. "I won't even have time for a shower. I have to get the place unlocked for the therapists. They'll be getting there any minute. Where the hell are my shoes?"

Stacey pointed toward the entertainment center and said, "They're right there. Calm down. It isn't like anything terrible is going to happen if you're five minutes late. It won't be the end of the world."

After slipping on her shoes, she checked her phone and found no messages waiting for her. "I can't believe he didn't let us know what happened at the crime scene."

"Rebecca, take a deep breath. Go unlock the building and get the therapists set up. Have Regina man your counter for a couple of hours while you go home and get cleaned up and change clothes."

Rebecca slowed down a moment and took three deep breaths. "Alright. I'm alright. I'm going to go unlock the building. Thanks. I'll see you later."

After Rebecca left, Stacey looked around for a minute. To herself she said, "I don't have to be there right now." She then picked up the popcorn bowl and blankets they'd used while watching movies the night before and slowly began straightening up the apartment.

Two hours later she arrived at the Center to find Rebecca calmly sitting in her usual spot at the reception counter. Three people sat in the lobby reading magazines. Rebecca was wearing a fresh set of clothes, and when she saw Stacey she led her through the heavy wooden door to the hallway without saying a word.

As they entered the break room, Rebecca said, "Someone burned down Cassidy's house last night."

Before Dr. Poole could respond, they both heard a male voice say, "Too bad he wasn't caught inside."

They turned to look and saw Quinn sitting at one of the empty tables with a cup of coffee in front of him.

Dr. Poole asked Rebecca, "Was he home when it happened?"

Rebecca was nodding. "He made it out a window and he's okay. Also, that murder that they responded to was the Specter. The victim was a teenage boy. I recognized the name. His uncle used to be one of our clients."

"What was the name? I'll go pull the file from the archives."

"Stanton. The former client was Clyde Stanton. I remember him talking about his sister and nephew once when he was waiting for his appointment."

"I'll call you once I get the file pulled. We should probably let the police know, too."

"I already told Jeremy that his uncle had been a client here. He wants you to contact him."

"Let me review the file, then I'll give him a call." She then turned to Quinn. "As for you, that isn't very nice."

Quinn set down his coffee and stared back with empty eyes. "Getting Kathy killed wasn't very nice either. I hope he suffers greatly before somebody finally kills that son of a bitch."

Rebecca was shocked. "Quinn, even coming from you, that's pretty rough. The poor guy's lost everything. Couldn't you show a little bit of sympathy? Put yourself in his place for a moment."

"Not a chance in hell that'll ever happen."

After a few seconds Dr. Poole turned back to Rebecca. "Oh, I almost forgot, you left your phone charger at my place this morning." She then pulled the charger from her purse and handed it to Rebecca.

"Oh, thank you, I don't know what I'd have done without this."

Quinn raised his eyebrows and asked, "So tell me, what were you doing at Dr. Poole's place this morning, Rebecca?"

"Don't worry about it, Quinn."

"Come on," Quinn was smiling now. "Let's imagine how this played out then."

Dr. Poole was standing back with a very slight smile watching this interaction.

Rebecca was glaring at Quinn. "Knock it off. What are you, twelve?"

Quinn completely ignored her and closed his eyes. "So we go back to last night. The two of you share an evening together. Some wine, dim lights, maybe a romantic movie while you snuggle with each other. Then comes the passion ignited by the alcohol and fueled by the close contact as you caress each other. Finally, covered in sweat from the physical exertion, you climax together. Slowly, as your heart rates return to normal, you gently fall asleep in each other's arms. When you wake in the morning you feel the shame of giving in to your carnal desires and in your rush to leave Dr. Poole's apartment, you forget to grab your phone charger." He opened his eyes with a wide smile on his lips.

Before Rebecca could respond, Dr. Poole stepped up next to her and began rubbing her shoulder with the back of her hand. In a sexy voice she slowly said, "It's time to come clean, Rebecca. He really wasn't that far off. If he can guess, how long do you expect us to hide it from the other therapists?"

Rebecca snapped her head around and looked at Dr. Poole for a moment. She then dropped her shoulders in defeat and sighed. "Fine. Alright, Quinn, you caught us. I just have one question though. How did you know that we climaxed together? Were you spying on us last night?"

Quinn looked shocked. His eyes widened, and he sat bolt upright from his formerly stooped position. "Oh, my God! No, but I sure as hell wish I had been." He then leaned forward and asked, "I don't suppose it occurred to either of you to video it?"

Dr. Poole started laughing while Rebecca took a step toward Quinn. "Nothing happened, you pervert. We fell asleep while watching movies last night. We woke up late and, in my rush to get here, I left my charger."

Quinn appeared to be staring past the two of them as he dreamily intoned, "I can see it in my mind. A thin layer of sweat as your naked bodies slowly writhe together … "

Rebecca slammed both hands down on the table he was sitting at. "We were just screwing with you, you sick bastard. Nothing happened."

While Stacey was still laughing, Quinn muttered, "Screwing with me. If only that were true." His vision cleared and he looked directly into her eyes. "I'll pay you! Hell, I'll give you my Porsche. Even if I'm not directly included, just let me watch."

Rebecca spun and exclaimed, "Stacey! You are *not* helping here. Look what you started."

Dr. Poole stopped laughing and said, "Really? You'll sign over the Porsche? Rebecca? What do you say?"

"Oh, my God! So not helping." She was red in the face but you couldn't tell if it was from anger or embarrassment. Finally, after looking back and forth at the two of them a couple of times, she threw up her hands and shook her head as she walked out of the break room past Dr. Poole.

Stacey turned to follow her, "Rebecca! It's a Porsche … "

"You two are terrible. Leave me alone."

*****

Clyde Stanton's file was on the desk in front of Dr. Poole as she reached for her phone. "Hey, Jeremy, how's Cassidy holding up? Oh, that isn't a good idea. You should probably put him in a hotel somewhere instead of letting him stay with you. No, it just wouldn't be safe to have him living there. Right, the insurance … they'll cover a place for him to stay while the claim is being processed. Yes, I have the file right here. Other than mentioning his sister and her family during a few sessions, it doesn't tell us very much at all. No, his issues weren't family related. I can't go into that level of detail; you know that. No, I doubt it'd be worth getting a court order. There really isn't anything here that would help you. Oh, hold on, I'll check. No, he had been seeing Regina. Okay, where? Let me make sure my schedule is open. Yes, I'll see you there."

She disconnected the call with Detective Kidd and hit the button for Rebecca. "I think I have two appointments today. Is there any way you can reschedule them for me? Yes, Jeremy wants to test out a new tactic with me; he wants me to go with him to the crime scene. I don't know, maybe. It'd be nice to actually see the scene as the killer did. Who knows? Maybe it'll give me some insight into his personality. Okay, thanks. Please apologize to them for me. Hey, if they're willing, see if they'll allow one of the other therapists to take their sessions today instead of rescheduling. Yeah, since I'm getting wrapped up with the police on this, my time might not be as open for the clients as it should be. Good idea, there aren't many that have been seeing me directly, anyway. Maybe they'll all allow the therapists to work with them temporarily. No, I'll get in touch with you when Jeremy's done with me. Bye."

In the parking lot of the police department, Jeremy was waiting for her by his unmarked car. Cassidy was sitting in the passenger seat with the window rolled down.

"I heard you two slept in this morning."

"Neither of us expected to fall asleep while watching a movie, so we didn't have an alarm set. Hey, Cassidy. How are you doing?"

"Why the hell does everyone ask me that? I've been shot, my car was destroyed, my arm's been dislocated, my wife's been killed, my house burned down and the captain wants me to push papers around on my desk for the next week until the sling comes off my arm. I'm doing just freaking wonderful."

Jeremy looked at Dr. Poole with an apologetic expression on his face. Dr. Poole looked back at him and smiled. "Cassidy?"

"What?"

"I don't need you to sugar coat it for me. How do you really feel?"

Cassidy looked up at her through the open window of the car and instantly burst out laughing. "Get your ass in here before Jeremy revokes my field trip pass and drags me back to my desk."

At the crime scene they ducked under the yellow crime tape and opened the garage door. After finding the light switch and closing the door again, Cassidy started snooping around in the boxes along the back wall.

"Alright," Jeremy said to Dr. Poole. "I wanted to bring you here to do a walk-through of the place and get your insight as to how the killer may have acted once inside. Anything would be helpful, no matter how trivial you think it might be. Cassidy and I find it useful to just talk the entire time we're at a crime scene. Whether it's to ourselves or to each other makes no difference. Any thought you have, if you just say it out loud, might trigger something that one of us could use."

"I understand. What do you expect to find in those boxes?"

Cassidy looked up and replied, "I was just wondering if they had some old clothes stashed out here that might fit me so I didn't have to wear Jeremy's outdated shit anymore."

Jeremy retorted, "Don't listen to him. The more we see, the more we get a feel for how the victim and his family lived. That's all."

"You think the killer spent time in the garage?"

"You and Dr. Brandt said the killer might familiarize himself with the house. It's very possible."

Dr. Poole nodded and asked, "Do you know how the killer keeps getting into these places?"

Cassidy was looking at one of the bikes that was hanging by a peg along the side wall of the garage as he speculated, "At Connelly's house, we think the killer actually entered while Sarah and Dean were arguing with each other. They probably didn't bother locking the door since Dean wasn't going to be staying very long. For all we know, the killer might have actually followed them home from the golf course."

Jeremy added, "It's far more likely that the killer was already near the residence waiting for them to get home though."

Cassidy nodded and turned his attention to her. "At the second crime scene, it appears that the killer found an open window and snuck in that way. Jeremy said that one of the screens looked like it had been bent and then straightened again. Here, it looks like the killer could have just strolled in. Either the front or back door would have worked. Both of them were unlocked."

Dr. Poole looked around the garage and said, "Did the murder weapon originate from in here?"

Jeremy shook his head. "From the kitchen."

"Interesting."

Cassidy asked, "What do you mean?"

"For the first two crimes the killer chose an item from an unused bedroom. Here, the killer chose something from the kitchen. It's a deviation."

Kidd said, "This time, there really wasn't an unused bedroom to choose from."

"Oh. Well then, maybe getting the weapon from the kitchen wasn't so much a deviation as a matter of convenience. Alright, the first murder was blunt force trauma. The second murder was strangulation. What was the method for this murder?"

Jeremy said, "Stabbing. Apparently with great precision. After we leave here, you can go talk with Dr. Brown if you'd like. He'll be able to give you a more medically accurate description of the wound."

She started walking toward the door that led into the house then stopped short. "Is it alright to enter?"

"Yeah. The entire house has been processed already."

"What time did the murder happen?"

"About 2:00 p.m."

"We'll have to adjust our neighborhood watch schedules then. This one wasn't in the evening."

The door from the garage led directly into the kitchen. Other than the dishes needing to be washed, it was tidy and clean. The only blood she could see was a little bit in the side of the sink that didn't contain the dirty dishes and silverware. "Did the killer try to clean up here?"

"No, that was where the murder weapon was placed after Jessie was killed."

She looked over the kitchen floor very closely. "I don't see any blood drops. There's no trail."

"Very good; you're right. The knife was used and then set down on the carpet near the victim for a little while. When you get in there, you'll see where it rested. The carpet absorbed enough blood from the knife that there wasn't enough left on it to drip off when it was brought in here. What little is in the sink is from the direct contact as the blade was dropped."

"Dropped? Not placed?"

Jeremy pointed to the stain and noted, "See here where there's just that little bit that looks like a splatter?"

Dr. Poole nodded. "I see. If the knife had been gently placed in the sink, the stain would have been only where the bloody blade touched the surface. Because it was dropped into the sink, this little bit was shaken off the blade. I get it now. I'm sorry, it's been a long time since I completed my forensic classes. Since I haven't been using those skills, I guess they're a little rusty."

Cassidy said, "It's alright, doc. The forensic team already covered this place. We didn't bring you here for your expertise in crime reconstruction. We want you to try to get into the head of this killer."

As she gazed into the sink, she remarked, "This is a deviation from the first two murders. I can't figure out any significance though."

Kidd and Cassidy looked back and forth at each other before Cassidy asked, "What deviation are you talking about?"

Dr. Poole appeared to be deep in thought when the question was asked and offhandedly answered with a question of her own. "Why would the murderer remove the weapon from the room where the crime occurred this time?"

Kidd started jotting notes as he explained, "You're right. The murder weapon was left near the victim for the first two crimes. This time he brought it to the sink. Could that mean something?"

"I don't know," Dr. Poole said. "It's just a fact that's unlike the first two murders. It might mean nothing at all. It could just be force of habit from the way the killer was raised. In most homes, when the utensils are done being used, it becomes habit to return them to the kitchen sink for washing later. It could just be a subconscious action on the part of our killer to return the knife to the kitchen."

She nodded and moved toward the back door then turned around quickly. "Wait. Does your captain know that you brought me here?"

Cassidy started laughing and said, "Hell, the captain doesn't know that he brought me here. He thinks I'm at some doctor appointment."

"Good. Then I guess you won't have to lie to the captain when you see him."

Cassidy asked, "How do you mean?"

Stacey motioned to herself. "You made an appointment with a doctor then kept that appointment. Here we are."

She turned to the back door and tested the knob. "I thought you said this was unlocked."

"Our guys locked it when they sealed the scene, but go ahead. You can open it."

She unlocked it and turned the knob. There was an audible click when the bolt slid free from the jam and a moderate squeak from the hinges as the door swung open. "The killer wouldn't have come in here. Too noisy. Even if that was the original plan, the instant the killer heard the noise from the door, he'd have sought entrance another way."

She poked her head out back and looked around. There was one tree in the middle of the backyard and an eight-foot privacy fence enclosing the entire area. "Also, climbing over that fence would be too obvious in the afternoon. The risk of being noticed would have been too great. Jumping a fence isn't exactly something you'd do if you were trying to blend into the neighborhood."

She closed the back door and walked through to the living room. After unlocking that door, she turned the knob and opened it. "No squeak. The killer must have come through the front door." She looked outside at the houses across the street then back and forth to the neighboring properties. "The killer had to have been dressed casually enough not to have stood out, because there are a lot of places with a direct line of sight to this spot."

Cassidy glanced over at Kidd as he made a few notes in his notepad.

She surveyed the living room for a minute before moving to the hallway. After looking down the dark hallway for a few seconds she asked, "Which room?"

Jeremy pointed toward a closed door.

She nodded and purposely avoided it. Across the hall from the closed door was the bathroom. She flipped on the light and looked inside but didn't enter. "Was any evidence found in this room?"

Jeremy shook his head. "No, as far as we can tell, if the killer entered this room, he didn't do anything while in here."

She flipped off the light and moved further down the hall.

At the end of the hall she opened a door that led to a linen closet. Without paying much attention to the contents, she closed that door and chose the room to the left. It was a large bedroom with a half bath off of it. She entered and walked around the bed then peeked into the smaller bathroom. "The parents' room?"

Jeremy said, "It was only the mother. She'd divorced some time ago."

She left that bedroom and opened the door directly across the hall. "This room belongs to a girl."

"The daughter was away visiting her father for the last time before fall classes start. She's a senior in high school this year."

"How would the killer know that?"

Cassidy said, "The killer could have been casing this place for days just waiting for me to be released."

Dr. Poole nodded and said, "I suppose so. Why wasn't the son away as well?"

"Different fathers. His father and mother were never married."

She closed the door to the girl's room and moved to stand in front of the boy's door. "Do you know if the door was closed when the killer was here or not?"

"We assume the door was open. It would have been a risk to just open the door while the son was inside. The element of surprise would have still existed, but a confrontation would have resulted."

Dr. Poole was nodding again, "Right, and our killer doesn't do direct confrontation."

She opened the door but didn't enter right away. She remained standing in the doorway studying the room for a couple of minutes. The bloodstain could still be seen plainly under the computer chair where the victim was killed but other than that, the room seemed relatively undisturbed.

"Robin is certainly good at her job. You'd never be able to tell that she and her team collected evidence in here. It looks like nothing was even moved from where the victim kept things."

The computer desk was small and cheap without much legroom beneath. There was a hard plastic mat for the computer chair to roll on, but it was quite small; the imprint where the chair would sometimes roll off the back of it onto the carpet was clearly visible. She moved to stand directly behind the computer chair and looked out the window in front of the desk. Then she looked at the monitor, followed by the chair.

Cassidy and Kidd were in the bedroom with her but were standing beside the bed, well out of the way. They were intently staring at her as she made her observations.

After several seconds, she moved back to the doorway and looked at the room again. This time when she entered, she stayed close to the left wall of the room and moved like she was sneaking up behind someone. She then asked, "How was the wound inflicted?"

Jeremy said, "According to Doc Brown, it was an upward thrust from beneath the chin through the back of the mouth into the brain cavity."

"Delivered right- or left-handed?"

Jeremy responded, "Right-handed."

"So our killer was only pretending to be left-handed at the first murder because it worked better to set up his intended patsy." She then made a thrusting motion as though someone were sitting in the chair in front of her. She repositioned the chair and repeated the motion. After three more adjustments to the chair, each followed by a mock stab, she stood back and nodded.

Cassidy said, "Remember, talking is a good thing. What do you have?"

"Sorry, I was just imagining the position of the killer and victim as the killing blow was struck. How large was the victim?"

Cassidy replied, "Now that I lost some weight from my stint in the hospital, I'm almost exactly the same size the victim was."

"Would you mind sitting here, please?"

Cassidy went to the bathroom and grabbed a bath towel off the rack then draped it so it covered the seat and back of the computer chair and sat down.

"No, that isn't right. Rebecca told me that the victim was a teenage boy preparing for college. He'd be more relaxed here in his bedroom. Lean back."

Cassidy did as he was told.

She looked over the desk and position of the chair and then slid it closer to the desk. "I know your left arm is in a sling, but act like you're typing with your right hand."

He reached up and placed his fingers on the keyboard.

"That still isn't quite right. The monitor is sitting at an angle on the desk. The killer would have been seen as a reflection on the screen before he could act." She adjusted the chair and again studied his position at the desk. "Yes. That looks better. Now can you see my reflection in the monitor?"

Cassidy shook his head.

"How about in the window?"

Cassidy turned slightly to look at the window and said, "No, from this angle there'd be no reflection of the killer."

She returned to the door. "See if any reflections catch your eye." She then entered the room acting as though she were holding a knife in her right hand. She crept up behind Cassidy, staying close to the side wall of the bedroom then with her left hand she quickly placed her palm on his forehead and pulled back as she brought her right hand up under his chin near where his neck and head met.

The movement was blinding fast and, even though Cassidy was expecting her to do something, he was still startled when it happened.

She released him and stood back for a moment looking at the floor, chair and desk. "Could you see any reflections at all in the monitor or window?"

"No, and I was looking for them."

"Alright, stay there for a moment." She returned to the door and repeated the process three more times.

Kidd asked, "Is something bothering you?"

After a few moments she bit her lip then asked, "The floor squeaks. How could he not know the killer was behind him? Even taking an angle that doesn't show a reflection in the window or computer monitor, he should have heard someone entering his room. He should have reacted."

Cassidy slowly turned to look at Jeremy.

Jeremy finally said, "The victim was listening to music while wearing headphones."

"Well, how convenient for our killer. I guess that explains that then."

Cassidy asked, "Can I get up now?"

"No, you're dead. Let your arms and head go limp."

Cassidy faced the monitor then laid his head back and allowed his right arm to go limp.

Dr. Poole pulled the chair back until it hit the carpet and then moved it a few more inches. "Now I can reach the feet."

She moved to where she'd have to be in order to cut off the toes and looked around. "Yep. Here's where the knife was set down."

After a minute she stood back and asked, "Was this how the victim was discovered?"

"No, the computer chair was closer to the desk. The killer had pushed it forward again after cutting off the toes."

She stood and got back behind the chair to move it forward but when it caught on the edge of the plastic mat, she had to struggle to move Cassidy's weight. After lifting up on the arms of the chair, she managed to roll it back to where it was when the police arrived.

"Robin's team didn't find anything on the back of the chair or under the armrests?"

"Nothing in the way of useful evidence but yes, the killer brushed up against the blood from the stab wound that was on the back of the chair. Also, there was smeared blood under the right armrest."

"So the killer left with blood on his clothing."

Cassidy asked, "Can I get out of this chair now?"

"Sorry, yes. That doesn't make any sense. It was a bright, clear afternoon yesterday. There had to be a fair amount of blood on the right sleeve of the killer as well as the contact stain on the front of his shirt after moving the chair back in place. It would have been conspicuous had anyone gotten anywhere near him."

Dr. Poole paced back and forth a few times and finally continued, "A backpack or something close to that. It's the only explanation that makes sense. After the killer was finished, he'd need to strip off his shirt and gloves and put them somewhere. Our killer has to be wearing something like a backpack."

Jeremy was writing down notes in his pad as Cassidy asked, "Wouldn't it look strange for someone to be wearing a backpack around?"

"Your killer must be young enough so that if someone saw him with a backpack on, it wouldn't arouse suspicion. Look at any high school campus. Most of the kids are wearing backpacks. Even at the mall a few weeks ago, I saw plenty sporting packs. It was summer and no classes were in session. They use them to carry their electronic devices, snacks, bottled water or other beverages. Backpacks have become a standard for today's youth."

"You mean our killer might be a high school kid?"

Dr. Poole shrugged and offered, "Maybe college. Or just out of high school and still dressing like he's a college or high school student. Think about it. How threatening would a small guy in his late teens or early twenties actually seem if you saw him walking down the sidewalk?"

Cassidy quietly added, "Or a petite girl."

Dr. Poole nodded quickly then said, "Yes, I'm sorry. I just fell into that natural pattern of labeling. When someone says murderer, the first thought is always male. The murderer is nearly always referred to as 'he' unless it's specifically determined that it's a female. But you're quite correct. All three murders could easily have been committed by a female instead of a male."

She then turned to look Cassidy directly in his eyes and in a playful voice asked, "Detective Cassidy, could there be a woman out there that might be holding a grudge against you? Say, one that might have shared some bed time with a good Catholic detective who's upset that you spurned her to stay with your wife?"

Cassidy lowered his head and said, "That really isn't funny, doctor."

Dr. Poole agreed, "No, it isn't. But you specifically adding that it could be a woman does bring up former lovers from a time before you were married. All joking aside, is that a possibility?"

Cassidy quickly answered, "No, it isn't."

Dr. Poole smiled and said, "Okay, forget I mentioned it then."

Jeremy finished jotting down some notes and checked his watch. "Do you think you'd be able to get anything more out of being here? Take a good look around and let me know if there's anything else that catches your eye."

Dr. Poole looked around a bit then shook her head. "I don't think so."

"I need to get you back to your desk, Cassidy. I also have to check in with the FBI. This information might help. Dr. Poole, I would like to thank you for your time and expertise. This has been very enlightening."

Cassidy was gently running his finger beneath his chin where she'd pretended to thrust a knife blade as he muttered, "Not to mention somewhat disconcerting."

"Oh, relax, you were perfectly safe. I didn't harm you."

"Alright, class," Jeremy said, "time to get back on the bus. Field trip over."

*****

Once back at the station parking lot, they waved goodbye to Dr. Poole and then turned to face each other.

"Now don't you feel like a jackass?"

"I admit it didn't go like I expected. But you also have to admit, the coincidences are astounding."

"No, Cassidy. They really aren't. The only reason you think they're astounding is because she made you feel stupid when you went to her office to try to put her in her place."

"Jeremy, I'm telling you. I know I met her someplace before. I just have no idea where or when. Do I need to remind you of those coincidences? They actually are astounding."

"Some of those coincidences are there because she was the one who came up with the ideas for the profile that she and Brandt have been working on."

"Look, she came to Denver and less than a week later, our first killing happened. I don't know how she did it, but she got ADA Harrison to hire her to do the psych evaluation on Dean Connelly. She never once showed any sign of wavering in her proclamations that he was innocent. She even went so far as to say that evidence would surface exonerating Connelly. Next thing you know, she's proven right again. Another murder was then committed, and evidence sent to the police and media specifically to prove that Connelly was, in fact, innocent."

"Yeah, and all of that could be because she's really that damned good at her job. You weren't there, Mike. With just a single look at Rebecca and me, she figured out that we'd set up a date and planned on Italian food. Even though I'd never mentioned to Rebecca where I was going to take her, Stacey managed to name the restaurant that I had in mind. Face it. She has deductive reasoning skills that are incredible."

"Rebecca said that this kid's uncle was a patient at that center. I bet if we check, we'll find someone associated with each of the victims that was a patient there."

"Two problems with that, Mike. You and I are associated with someone who's being seen at that center. Remember when Jefferson said his wife goes there? I'd lay odds that most of the people in this city know someone who's been seen at that center at some point in the past. It's been there for decades. Also, this victim's uncle was a former client at the Center and stopped being seen years ago. That was long before Dr. Poole ever even heard of the place, let alone took it over from Dr. Jacobs. Good luck getting a judge to sign off on a court order to open up those records based on that. Hell, every judge in this city has probably either used that place or known someone who has at some point. You may as well be accusing Rebecca of being the murderer. She's petite and was at least there when the uncle was a client."

"Yeah, petite or small. Alright, forget about the Center; explain the profile. Someone small and inconspicuous that blends in and wouldn't be suspected if someone saw them."

"Mike, she helped write the damn profile. If she were the one doing all of this, why wouldn't she steer the profile away from someone with her body size?"

"Maybe because she was working with Brandt and couldn't. Maybe because if she was the one that came up with the idea of someone small in stature, then people like you would think she couldn't possibly be guilty."

"Now you're just starting to sound insane. Alright, what about at the crime scene? Not once. Not one single time did she give that corkboard even one look. You said it yourself; if she was guilty, she'd at least glance at it to see where the note was pinned. She not only didn't ask about it; she didn't pay it any attention at all. While we're at it, she asked all of the right questions. Was it right-handed or left? Where was the chair? Why wouldn't he hear the killer? You'd think that if she were the one who'd killed the kid, she'd have slipped up at least once. Yet she didn't. Not a single time."

Cassidy was rubbing his throat. "I know. Like you said, she's damn good. How about the re-creation of the attack though? That was identical to how Doc Brown and Robin said it had to have happened."

"I told her about the wound because she asked. And, she's a medical doctor. If you tell a medical doctor that a wound exists, they damn well better be able to figure out how it was inflicted. Mike, she even seemed surprised that this was a stabbing."

"I know, I know. But damn it, I'm telling you, something isn't right with her. I feel it."

Cassidy pulled out his phone and remarked as he hit a few buttons, "I followed you on this so far. I'm calling the FBI. If their information doesn't play out, will you please drop this?"

Cassidy said suspiciously, "I'll stop bugging you, but I'm going to be keeping my eye on her. Very closely."

"Yes, hello. This is Detective Kidd. I'm trying to reach Fred Stockwell. Yes, that's right. Thank you, I'll hold."

"Cassidy, I'm telling you, you're off base about her. She's done nothing but try to help us ... "

"Yes, Agent Stockwell? Right, this is Kidd. Yes, I'm calling about the results for the cell phone track as well as the GPS log. Right, Dr. Stacey Poole. That's right, those are the dates and times in question. Are you certain? There's no way that information could have been altered? Great, thank you. If we come up with anyone else, I'll get ahold of you."

Cassidy questioned, "Well?"

"According to the FBI, neither her car's nor her cell phone's GPS unit places her near any of the crime scenes on the dates or at the times when the crimes were being committed. Are you done now?"

Cassidy looked down at the ground and nodded. "I know I've met her before."

"We went through your entire professional career, Mike. If you met her, she's not in any of the records."

Cassidy sighed and said, "Alright. You win. I'll drop it."

"Good. Because I feel like shit for dragging her to the crime scene just so we could have the FBI get to her car's navigation unit. Just so you know, I'm still leaning toward Quinn."

"I thought you told me Quinn had an alibi for one of the murders."

"A lady named Allison that he'd slept with a few times. Not very bright and not a convincing alibi."

"You told Stacey and Rebecca that Quinn had been cleared."

"I told them that so they wouldn't act weird around him at work. I'm still looking into a few things with him though."

Just then Kidd's phone buzzed. "This is Kidd. Really? Yes, e-mail me the list. Thanks."

As he put his phone away he explained, "That was Stockwell again. He said we gave him an idea when we had him check Dr. Poole's cell phone and car GPS. He did a search to crosscheck the times and dates of the murders against cell phone locations and came up with four matches."

Cassidy lit up a little and asked, "You mean that there were four cell phones in this city that were in the area of each of the crimes at the times they were being committed?"

"Yeah, let's go check that list."

In the station's bullpen, Kidd logged onto his computer and brought up his e-mail. "Here it is."

Cassidy stood over his shoulder as they both read the e-mail. "Detective, I ran a general search for any cell phone numbers that pinged the towers which service the location of each crime scene. I then cross-referenced the lists of numbers against each other looking for matches. Four numbers were in the area of each cell phone tower at the same time that each murder was being committed. One of those numbers belongs to a burner phone. I'm having my guys see if they can figure out who bought it right now. If they can find the owner, I'll pass along that information. The other three were phones on registered plans. The attachment has their information. I hope this helps. Good luck."

Kidd opened the PDF attachment and saw a map of Denver and the surrounding suburbs. There were black dots with corresponding black circles around them covering the entire city. There were three red dots indicating the locations of each of the murders with a label below that said, "Cell phone grid for Denver and surrounding area."

Typed beneath this was another message from Agent Stockwell. "Here are the names of the individuals that hold the plans for these phones. Remember, just because someone owns the plan for the phone, it doesn't necessarily mean that individual is the one who carries the phone. One more disclaimer needs to be added before you act. These are just the towers that the phone pinged, so it doesn't mean that any of these people were actually at each residence—only that they were within the circle of coverage for the cell towers at the times of the murders."

Below this was a list of names, addresses and the cell phone numbers that had been tracked. One of the names listed was "unknown." That one had to indicate the prepaid phone. The second name listed was Erin Hennessy. The third name listed was Randolph Cates. The final name was Rebecca Mann.

Kidd's face went pale as he turned to look over his shoulder at Cassidy.

Cassidy's mouth was hanging open as he returned the stare. "Print the attachment," he finally directed.

Kidd was shaking his head, "It can't be her. There's no way. She was at work yesterday at two. She couldn't have been in the range of the cell tower for the third murder. Look, that tower doesn't cover the psychiatric center. It has to be a mistake."

Cassidy repeated, "Print the attachment."

Kidd stared blankly at the monitor as he commanded the computer to print.

Cassidy hurried over to the printer and retrieved the sheet. He just stood there staring at it for a moment.

Kidd repeated, "It can't be her."

Cassidy brought the sheet over and set it down in front of Kidd. "Then clear her. Give her a call and have her come in. It shouldn't take long to clear her."

Kidd shook his head no. "I can't do that. Do you have any idea how she'd react?"

Cassidy replied, "Just call her in. Show her this list if you want so that she knows you're just doing your job. We can't just ignore her name."

Kidd reached for the phone then pulled back his hand. "You do it. I'll check the other two names we have."

Cassidy nodded and said, "That might be better, anyway. You're too close to her. If she lies to you, you'd be too willing to believe it."

Kidd slowly stood from his chair and threatened, "Tread lightly, Mike. You're walking on dangerous ground here."

Cassidy calmed him. "Slow down. I'm just saying that I'd be more objective when speaking with her than you would. I'm not saying I think she's guilty. After all, she's been living in this city for nearly her entire life. Had she wanted to come after me for some reason, she didn't have to wait this long to do it."

Kidd glared at him for a moment before reaching for the phone to call Erin Hennessy.

Cassidy pulled his cell phone from his pocket and hit the number for Rebecca Mann as he moved to the other side of the bullpen so Kidd wouldn't be able to hear as easily.

"Hi, Detective Cassidy. Is Dr. Poole on her way back to the Center?"

"Hi, Rebecca. Yes, she left here about ten minutes ago. She should be there shortly. I'm not calling for her though."

"Oh? What is it that I can help you with? Wait, did something happen to Jeremy? Is he alright?"

"Yeah, he's still the same asshole we all know and love. Nothing's happened to him. I do have to ask a favor of you though. I'm not sure just how to ask this so that you don't take it the wrong way."

"Well, after spending the last month hanging around Dr. Poole, I've figured out that the best way to do things might just be the straightforward way. I'll tell you what. You ask for the favor, and I'll reserve judgment and not take it the wrong way instantly."

"That sounds fair. Is there any way that you could make some time to come down to the station this afternoon?"

"Hold on a second; let me see what the schedule looks like."

After a few seconds, she replied, "Tony's last appointment for the day ends at three. I could have him watch the counter for me. Why do you need me at the station?"

"It's something I'd rather not go into over the phone if that's alright with you. Do you think he'd be able to handle the counter until the end of the business day?"

"I'll have to ask him, but I don't see why he wouldn't. Do you want me to see if Dr. Poole can come with me?"

"No. She was a big help this morning; we shouldn't need to bother her anymore."

"This sounds rather ominous, but as I told you, I'll reserve judgment. See you between 3:00 and 3:30."

"Thank you for taking the time. I'll see you then."

Kidd was hanging up his phone as Cassidy approached. "How'd she react?"

"I only asked her to come to the station. I didn't explain why, and she handled it very well."

Kidd was still pissed but was making an effort to control his temper. "I know how this works, and I've seen you question people before. I want you to know something. I care about this woman a great deal. You will treat her with respect, or you'll have to deal with me."

Cassidy thought about the healing bullet wounds in his abdomen as well as his aching left shoulder and nodded. He was in no shape to defend himself if Kidd became hostile, so he'd have to be very careful of what he said and did. "Duly noted. I will treat her with the utmost respect and dignity. What about the other two on the list?"

"I'm going to go talk with Erin right now. She leaves for her sophomore year of college in a week, so I'm going to get this out of the way for her as soon as possible. I left a message for Mr. Cates."

"Alright, I'll keep bugging the FBI until I get something on this prepaid phone then." He returned to his desk and pretended not to notice as Kidd continued to glare after him. After a few seconds, Kidd picked up the keys to the department's unmarked car and stormed out of the bullpen.

Kidd's interview with Erin lasted only half an hour and part of that was just the two of them making small talk. She wasn't completely cleared just yet, but she gave him more than enough information that could be verified so that once he'd finished following up, he was certain she'd no longer be a person of interest.

It was just after three when Kidd returned to the station.

Cassidy asked, "How'd it go with the girl?"

"Her story checks out fine. I have to run down her statements and do verification, but she's not our killer."

Cassidy nodded. "Mr. Cates called back. He works for the electric company. He's all over this city all of the time. I spoke with his superior who confirmed that he had been on calls that put him in the area of the first and third crime scenes while they were being committed. His home is in the cell tower radius for the second murder. That explains why his phone was there during the second murder. I'm going to follow up on his calls to make sure he actually was doing what his boss told us he was doing, but he doesn't look good for this either."

Kidd tensed. "So we're down to two then. Is that what you're trying to tell me? Just what are you getting at?"

Cassidy put his good hand up in a gesture to back off. "I'm not trying to tell you anything except exactly what I just said. We're just clearing names on a list. It's something we've done hundreds of times over the years. Take a tranquilizer or something."

Kidd relaxed slightly, but the stern expression on his face remained. "I wasn't kidding earlier, Cassidy. I know what you're like. You go easy on her, or you'll be dealing with me."

Cassidy took note of the other officers in the room. They were all acting like they were busy, but he knew damn well that they were all paying close attention to his interaction with Kidd. They had seen the two of them argue with each other countless times. This time was different, and everyone knew it.

As he lowered his hand he said soothingly, "Just clearing names on a list, man. Everything's gonna be fine."

A few minutes later a uniformed officer brought Rebecca into the bullpen. "Cassidy! Ms. Mann says you wanted her to come speak with you."

"Thanks, Turner, I got it. Oh, by the way, if I didn't mention it before, I'd like to thank you for your protection detail while I was at the hospital. I know it couldn't have been easy for you guys volunteering your personal time to babysit me."

"Don't mention it. If it were me lying in that hospital, I'd like to think these guys would have done the same."

Rebecca smiled and said, "Hi, Jeremy. What's going on?"

Detective Kidd handed the printed sheet to Cassidy as he answered her. "Mike's going to ask you a few simple questions. Just answer them honestly, and this'll be over within a few minutes."

Rebecca's expression changed, and she tensed. "Jeremy? What's really going on here? What's this about?"

He went over to her. After looking into her eyes for a moment, he hugged her and whispered into her ear as he did so. "Hon, your name came up on a list, and we just have to ask you a few questions so we can take your name off that list. It's no big deal, and I don't want you to get mad at me over it. Cassidy is going to be talking to you because it wouldn't look right if I were the one who did it. Alright?"

As he released her and stood back, she looked up at him and nodded. The expression on her face was still not the usual pleasant one that he'd come to expect from her—but under the circumstances, he completely understood.

Cassidy spoke. "I'm sorry, Rebecca. This shouldn't take very long at all. Would you mind coming over here, please?"

Jeremy moved aside and told her, "I'll be downstairs. When you get done, come find me."

Rebecca nodded and went over to Cassidy's desk.

Before he said anything, he took the paper that Kidd had handed him and placed it in front of Rebecca. He looked up in time to see Jeremy leaving the room.

"Rebecca, do you know what this is?"

She looked over the paper and an expression of surprise appeared on her face. "That's the cell tower coverage for the city, and my name is listed at the bottom."

"These red dots indicate the locations of the three murders that were committed by our killer. The black dots and circles around them are the cell towers and coverage zones. This is a list of cell phones that were in the coverage zones of the cell towers that serviced the areas where the crimes were committed. These phones were in these zones at the time that each murder happened. Your cell phone was one of the ones on this list. Now, all we're doing is eliminating the names on this list as potential suspects. That's why we need to speak with you."

Rebecca nodded and said, "I understand."

"Good. Now I know which apartment building you live in, so that explains the match for the second murder. On July 22—that would have been a Wednesday—can you tell me why your phone would have been in this circle of coverage around 6:00 p.m.?"

Rebecca looked at the map and nodded. "I was probably shopping. When I get produce, it's from the farmer's market on this corner." She pointed to a spot on the map with her finger.

Cassidy jotted down the information and asked, "Do you keep your receipts?"

Rebecca's mouth hung open slightly in surprise.

Cassidy quickly continued, "I'm really just doing my job. If we catch someone and it goes to trial, if I haven't completely cleared you, the defense could use you to create reasonable doubt. Seriously, I'm not accusing you of anything; I'm just making sure that you're properly cleared of suspicion."

Rebecca sighed and said, "No, when I decide to make a salad, I don't bother keeping the receipt for the ingredients."

"It's not a problem. Very few people keep all of their receipts. We'll be able to check the receipts from the farmer's market. Someone there must know you if you're a regular. We'll be able to verify what you say."

Rebecca looked dubious but nodded.

"Now, can you explain why your cell phone was pinging this tower here yesterday at about 2:00 p.m.?" He pointed to the tower that covered the most recent murder victim's home.

"I had a lull in the afternoon clients and used the time to sneak out of the office. Let me rephrase that. I left the office because we didn't have any clients scheduled to come in. Wait, that didn't come out right either."

Cassidy encouraged, "Relax. If you get flustered, Kidd is going to bust my nose. Right now that's one of the few places on my body that isn't damaged. Take a deep breath, then just tell me why you went to this area."

Rebecca relaxed a bit and reached into her purse. "I knew we were all meeting at Stacey's last night. I wanted to get Jeremy a present so I could give it to him after dinner."

She pulled out a small black box and put it on Cassidy's desk. As he opened it, she continued to speak. "I went over to Williamson's, the jewelry store, and bought him this tie clasp. We had spoken earlier about him using those tie pins that he always wears and how he should switch to clasps so they don't leave holes in his nice ties.

I just thought that after dinner would be a good time to give him this. Then he got the call, and I never had the chance."

Cassidy finished writing his notes and smiled. "Now, see, that wasn't so bad. Please make sure to let Kidd know that I wasn't mean or accusatory, okay?"

Rebecca slid the tie clasp back into her purse and asked, "Was he really going to punch you if you treated me like a suspect?"

Cassidy leaned back and maintained his smile. "He was going to punch me when I told him we needed to talk to you. If I'd have treated you like a suspect, who the hell knows what he'd have done to me then."

She appeared to be happy over the news, "Really?" Then she looked back at the sheet and asked, "Have these names been cleared yet?"

Cassidy nodded and replied, "We may not be able to track down who this 'unknown' is. It was a prepaid phone. But we're looking into it. Other than that, yes. The other two look like they're in the clear. Now remember, as I told you earlier, we have to follow up on these so that if this goes to trial later nobody can claim that we didn't do our job here and try to raise reasonable doubt."

"I'll go tell Jeremy he can relax. I don't think you'll have to worry about getting punched in the nose."

"Thank you, and I'm sorry that we had to go through this with you. I hope you understand."

Rebecca nodded and stood. "No problem. I don't envy you two for the job you have to do. This can't be easy."

Cassidy stood and reached to shake her hand. "No. None of this is easy. Especially with what I've gone through in the last month. But as long as I have Jeremy to lean on, I can endure."

Jeremy was waiting at the bottom of the stairs for her to come down. Before she even reached the bottom step, he began, "I am so sorry, Rebecca. I never once thought for an instant that you might have anything to do with any of this."

"It's alright, Jeremy. Mike explained why he had to ask me those questions."

Jeremy instantly became tense again. "That asshole didn't make you feel like a suspect, did he?"

Rebecca put a hand on his chest and said, "Relax. He was fine. He just asked why my phone was where it was on those dates at those times. Once I explained, he thanked me and that was it. By the way, I have something for you that I was going to give you last night. You got called away before I could."

She reached into her purse and pulled out the small black box. "This was why my phone was in range of that cell tower yesterday when the third murder was being committed."

Jeremy opened the box and said, "It's fantastic. I'll put it on right away." He leaned down and kissed her gently on the lips.

Before she turned to leave the station, she asked, "Care to come over tonight?"

Jeremy grinned and asked, "Should I bring pizza?"

Rebecca offered a flirty shake of her hips and quipped, "Meat Eater's Special this time."

*****

"Locally, the police are still no closer to determining the identity of the killer who's been dubbed The Denver City Specter. We have received unofficial confirmation that yesterday's murder was the handiwork of the Specter. By committing the murder in the middle of the afternoon, the Specter managed to avoid dealing with the neighborhood watch programs. This killing took place only hours after the announcement that Detective Michael Cassidy had been cleared to return to duty. As with the other two murders, if and when we receive the envelope from the Specter, we will pass that information along to our viewers, though the police have requested we not show the note on the air as the contents may be sensitive to their investigation."

"On a related note, thanks to statements made yesterday morning by Dr. Stacey Poole, the protesters that had been targeting psychiatric center where she works moved on to the courthouse and jail today. They joined several that had been holding vigil there since it became obvious that Dean Connelly couldn't have been guilty of murdering his mother. With the added energy of the new protesters, the group has become much more vocal about Dean Connelly being released from custody now that he has been exonerated. So far, things have remained peaceful. Let us hope they remain that way and that a decision is reached soon concerning Connelly's freedom."

CHAPTER 17

Wednesday, August 27

Cassidy poked his head into Bordeaux's office, "Hey, have you seen Kidd anywhere?"

Bordeaux replied, "He's in the mail room. He's expecting another envelope."

"Oh, yeah." Cassidy made his way down to the mail room to find Kidd and two uniformed officers sifting through the mail bag.

Billings responded, "Yep, here it is."

Kidd pulled the manila envelope from the bag, holding it gently by one corner. "You got the evidence bag ready?"

"Here you go."

Kidd slowly slid the envelope into the evidence bag then pulled out a pen and scribbled on it. "Alright, thanks. You can tell them they can have the mail room back now."

He turned and saw Cassidy. "I just can't wait to see what this one says." Sarcasm dripped from every word as he tucked the evidence bag under one arm and began to trudge up the stairs.

"I'm coming with you this time." Cassidy said.

"Yeah, by now I don't think it makes any difference. Call Stacey and let her know it arrived."

Cassidy grunted as he pulled out his phone.

"Minions, you know the routine well enough by now," Robin barked out. "Let's hope our guy made a mistake this time."

Larry, Darryl and Darryl—as Robin affectionately called them—went to work immediately. Their movements were methodical but efficient, and within a matter of fifteen minutes they were studying every inch of the envelope as well as the contents for any trace evidence.

"When do you think the envelope from the news station will arrive? It would be nice to get that processed this morning as well."

Kidd checked his watch as he replied, "It should be here within the hour. I have two guys over there waiting for it to arrive."

One of the minions bagged the toe and left the lab. "I'll be back in fifteen."

Robin sighed as she adjusted her microscope, "How sad is it that this is becoming routine for us?"

Cassidy was pacing back and forth while Kidd stood in front of the blank monitor waiting patiently.

After another two minutes, an out-of-focus image appeared on the monitor. Kidd stared as the tech adjusted a knob on his machine. "How's that?"

Kidd nodded and replied, "Good, thanks."

> *People, your King Midas is failing you. This time he allowed a teenager to die. When are you going to see that he cares more about his own skin than about all of you? When are you going to rise up and put an end to him? I think the time is coming soon, King Midas. Are you looking over your shoulder yet? You should be. All Kings fall in time. The revolution is coming.*

Cassidy whispered under his breath, "You can't go on forever. You'll make a mistake."

Kidd glanced over at him quickly and added, "How many have to die before that mistake is made?"

Cassidy glared back at him but said nothing. Finally, he moved up behind Robin, but before he had a chance to say anything she reached back with one hand in a halting motion. She never once moved her eyes away from the microscope.

"Cassidy, this takes time. Either leave or go sit down somewhere."

Cassidy sighed and went to sit on a stool.

Kidd's phone buzzed. "Yes? Alright, thanks."

Robin pulled back from the microscope and asked, "The other envelope?"

Kidd simply responded, "Yes."

"How long?"

Kidd looked at his watch. "Ten minutes, tops."

This time Cassidy's phone buzzed. "What? What? Oh, shit."

Kidd snapped his attention to Cassidy as he was putting away his phone. "What bad news is that?"

"The judge declined to overturn the conviction. Connelly will have to go through a trial."

"This city is going to tear itself to shreds."

He had no sooner uttered those words than his phone buzzed again. Before he had a chance to answer it, Cassidy's went off as well.

They both answered then sat in silence as the color visibly drained from their faces.

Robin was watching them intently. When they both pocketed their phones without saying a word, she quickly demanded, "What the hell's going on?"

Kidd looked over at Cassidy then back to Robin. "The Free Connelly protesters in front of the courthouse got the news that he isn't going to be freed. They're rioting. Cars are being smashed and set on fire. The judge that made the ruling is locked in his chambers, and police have barricaded the courthouse."

She looked over at Cassidy. "Did you get the same news on your call?"

Cassidy nodded dumbly and added, "I'm supposed to wait here for the FBI. They're placing me in protective custody."

One of the lab techs clicked a remote, and the image of the killer's note vanished only to be replaced by a scene of total chaos. At the tech raised the volume, they heard a female reporter's frantic voice saying, "Three of the protesters are down. We don't know if they were killed or if the police used non-lethal force. As you can see, their motionless bodies are lying on the steps of the courthouse."

A male voice broke in and, as it did, the screen split to show a middle-aged man wearing a suit and tie sitting behind a curved counter. The left half of the screen still showed the protesters destroying everything they could get near. "Angela, can you say for certain that you and your crew are out of harm's way?"

The reporter's voice responded as the cameraman continued to pan the crowd, showing people abandoning their cars and running from the scene while others began smashing the windows. "They seem to want us to film this. I don't think we're in danger, but nobody should come near the courthouse right now. Oh, God! Over there."

The camera swung over to the right. As the reporter began to speak again, the screen showed a uniformed officer being pulled from his police car while protesters pummeled him to the ground. "He never got a chance to defend himself. They just yanked him out as the cruiser pulled up and began beating him."

Just then, gunshots rang out. The four people beating the officer instantly moved away from him. Three began to run behind other vehicles that were stopped in the middle of the street while the fourth crawled for a couple of feet before collapsing. The cameraman shifted his angle to show another uniformed officer rushing around the front of the patrol car, service pistol drawn. When he got to the beaten officer, he opened the back door of the cruiser and lifted his motionless body to shove him inside. From outside of the view of the camera, an object flew toward the police car and struck the assisting officer as he helped his partner into the backseat. It glanced off of him then struck the roof of the car and shattered, sending shards of broken glass raining down on both officers. As the officer closed the back door, he spun and fired three more shots at someone who couldn't be seen on the monitor. With blood streaming from his head as he got behind the wheel, the officer slammed the car into reverse and drove away.

The camera panned back to the courthouse steps as more gunfire erupted. Cassidy commanded, "Turn it off."

Nobody moved and the scene continued to unfold on the monitor. In frustration he yelled, "Turn it off!"

The screen went black.

Cassidy quietly said, "That's it; I'm done." With that he turned to leave the lab.

Kidd snapped out of the fog he was in and demanded, "What? Where do you think you're going?"

Cassidy continued to walk toward the exit as he stated unequivocally, "I can't sit here waiting to be taken into custody while good cops are out there fighting a war."

Kidd hurried to get between him and the door. "Are you nuts? If you go out there, someone will kill you!"

"Good. Then this nightmare will finally end!"

Kidd put his hand on Cassidy's good shoulder to block his exit. "You're going to stay right here until the FBI shows up."

Without hesitation, Cassidy swung his right fist and caught Kidd squarely on his jaw, rocking his head back and knocking him against the lab door. Before Kidd could recover, Cassidy swung again with a roundhouse punch that caught Kidd on the left temple. He crumpled and fell away from the door. Cassidy didn't even look down at him; he just stepped over the groaning figure on the floor and left the lab.

Robin rushed over and began tending to Kidd. "Let the dumb ass go get himself killed, Kidd."

It took a few seconds, but Kidd finally dragged himself to his feet. He was wobbly as Robin helped him to a stool. As he was rubbing the side of his head, he spat, "If they don't kill him, I just might. Contact Grant and have that idiot stopped at the door."

Robin called out, "Larry!"

The tech responded instantly. He hit a button on the phone and spoke rapidly. "Cassidy just assaulted Kidd. Detain him and don't let him leave."

Kidd pulled his phone and punched a number. "Who is this? Billings? Cassidy lost it. He just assaulted me and left the lab. Go make sure that dumb son of a bitch doesn't get his hands on a car."

Cassidy was smart enough not to try the front entrance. Instead, he took the stairs down to the garage beneath the building. While Grant was tracing the path toward the lab trying to find him, Cassidy simply strolled out of the garage.

He looked up and down the street, which was serene compared to the scene he'd just witnessed on the monitor. After patting his pockets, he pulled out a set of keys and made his way to the police station parking lot. As he was getting behind the wheel of the unmarked car, a uniformed officer spotted him and ran over.

With his arm in a sling, he didn't have time to close the car door before Billings reached him. "Butch, what are you doing? You can't take that. The FBI is on their way."

Cassidy drew his service pistol and aimed it at Billings. "I need to go help. Back away."

Billings paused for only an instant before deciding that the threat was hollow. He moved forward and grabbed Cassidy by the collar of his shirt and yanked hard, pulling him out of the car and down to the asphalt.

Cassidy yelled in agony as pain shot through his shoulder and chest and his gun fell from his hand.

Officer Billings kicked the gun under the car then keyed the microphone that was strapped to his shoulder. "Officer needs assistance in the police station parking lot."

Within fifteen seconds a handful of uniformed cops were dragging Cassidy into the station.

Kidd's phone rang. "Yeah," he mumbled. "Good, lock that son of a bitch in a holding cell. Let the FBI know where they can collect his sorry ass. Yes, I'm serious."

Robin was waiting for one of her machines to do its magic when the call ended. "At least he didn't find a car and go to the courthouse."

Kidd looked at the floor and said dully, "Maybe I should have let him."

Robin spun on Kidd but then her expression changed and she calmly responded, "Maybe you're right. I don't know if the killings would stop or not, but they definitely won't while he's alive."

Kidd felt like hell for thinking exactly what Robin had said. Then he felt shame for being relieved that he wasn't the only one to have the thought.

The doors to the lab opened and a uniformed officer handed an evidence bag to Robin. While she was signing for it, he looked at Kidd. "I heard already. Did Cassidy get away?"

"No, I told Billings to lock him in a holding cell until the FBI can pick him up."

"Are you going to press assault charges?"

Kidd glared at Officer Tanner. "What the hell's the matter with you? He's still a cop. Of course not!"

Tanner calmly nodded and said, "Just thought I'd ask. I also got the news over the radio on the way over here that the governor has granted clemency for Dean Connelly. They're announcing it over the public address at the courthouse as we speak. Hopefully that'll put an end to the riot."

Kidd nodded and asked, "Is this a full pardon then? Will Connelly finally be set free?"

Tanner said, "That's what it sounded like. I have no idea if the judge that refused to overturn the conviction will face any kind of repercussions."

Kidd sighed and said, "Have someone keep me informed of what's going on. I'm going to stay here and see if these guys find anything."

As Tanner was leaving, he nearly ran over Dr. Poole. "I'm so sorry, officer."

"I wasn't looking where I was going. It's my fault. You look absolutely wonderful today, doctor."

"Oh, you think so? Thanks, I actually got this blouse on sale a few weeks ago."

"Well, you do it justice."

Dr. Poole was smiling broadly as she entered the lab. Once she saw the expressions of those before her, her smile slowly disappeared. "I'm guessing something happened that I'm unaware of."

"Where do I start?" Kidd's swollen eye was beginning to darken into a bruise.

"How about with that shiner you're getting ready to sport?"

Robin said, "Cassidy punched him."

Dr. Poole raised her eyebrows. "Why would he do that?"

"Because he's a goddamned stubborn asshole, that's why." Kidd touched his cheek and winced slightly.

Dr. Poole walked over and inspected the bruise that was beginning to show on his chin as well. "Yeah, but that wasn't breaking news to you. What happened to cause him to punch you?"

"The FBI said he needed to wait here so they could send someone to take him into protective custody. With the riot and tempers flaring all over the city, they determined that his life was in more danger than ever."

"Riot? What are you talking about?"

"How is it that you have no idea what's happening? Sit down. I'll explain it all."

As Kidd was bringing Dr. Poole up to speed on current events, Robin sighed. "Same as before. No particulates, no hair, no nothing. Barren as the moon. Actually, the moon has dust." Just then she looked up and saw everyone staring at her. "I suppose you get the point."

"May I see the message, please?"

Robin nodded. "Put it back up on the screen for her."

The image of the note was back in place on the monitor, and it took only ten seconds before Dr. Poole shook her head and said, "Not very imaginative. Alright, thanks. You can pull the image again. Nothing new there."

"Yeah, this is all getting really old, really fast."

"Hey, you need to keep your spirits up, Sundance."

Kidd spun on Dr. Poole and opened his mouth. He then saw the mischievous grin on her face and started to shake his head. "I get it. Keep my head in the game. It's bad enough Cassidy is losing his mind. I need to stay sharp. Thanks, doc."

"No charge."

Kidd's phone buzzed and he lowered his head and sighed. "What now?" he asked no one in particular as he lifted the phone to his ear. "What?"

"Yeah, that's a perfectly reasonable way to answer my phone right now." He listened for twenty seconds without saying a word. Finally, he said, "How do we know this is worth a shit?" He then listened for another thirty seconds or so without speaking. "If you say so," he offered doubtfully before hanging up and shoving the phone in his pocket.

"You look like you just got news that's too good to be true. What was that about?" questioned Stacey.

Kidd laughed as he replied, "You are damn good. I was actually just thinking that this is too good to be true. That call was from the station. They received a tip on the hotline that we need to take a look at a student at Denver University. The caller spent the summer in Europe and just returned a couple of days ago and got caught up with the news of the murders. When the riot broke out, he decided to call the hotline. Apparently, this informant had a roommate last year named Travis Dean Parker. He said the kid was obsessed with

Cassidy and me. Parker supposedly has entire notebooks filled with newspaper clippings and photos covering our careers, going all the way back to the time before we became partners."

"What courses of study is Parker currently pursuing in college?"

"I don't know. I was just told that he's probably on campus right now since fall classes will be starting soon. Hey, are you free today? With Cassidy sitting in a holding cell, I could use someone to tag along with me."

Dr. Poole looked surprised. "I'm not a cop. What could I possibly do?"

"For initial interviews, it's always good to have someone to compare observations with. Usually one of us will engage with the subject while the other observes. Then when the interview is over, we compare notes, so to speak. Impressions, observations thoughts, ideas."

"So you want to take me along as an observer?" Dr. Poole thought about this for a moment then asked, "You don't think he's dangerous?"

"I have no idea. That's one of the things I plan on figuring out."

"Do I get a gun?" Dr. Poole's eyes lit up.

"Hell, no!"

She was obviously disappointment as she responded flatly, "Oh."

"If there's the slightest hint that he may become dangerous, I'll make sure you're safe."

"Sure, I'll go along and offer my observations."

*****

In the police station Cassidy's voice could be heard ringing out through the concrete and steel cell area. "Hey, I've been down here for an hour. This shit isn't funny anymore!"

Out of sight of his cell he heard, "Shut the fuck up down there, dickhead." Another voice yelled out, "You whine like a bitch with fleas." The handful of others currently locked up were becoming restless.

Cassidy sighed and went back to the bunk and sat down. As he did so, Billings appeared in front of his cell. "Finally! Are you here to let me out? What the hell are you smiling about anyway?"

Billings said, "I have to admit, I do find this amusing. Butch Cassidy behind bars. It kind of rewrites history, don't you think?"

"Did you come down here to complete the process of making my life a living hell?"

"I came down here to let you know the FBI is here. They'll be down in a minute to pick you up."

"Yeah? Tell them they're wasting their time. I don't want to be put in protective custody."

As he finished this statement, a man and woman stepped into view. They were both wearing FBI jackets. The female agent looked into the cell and turned to her partner. "And here's a classic case of what I was talking about in the car."

Cassidy shook his head and asked, "Alright, what am I a classic case of?"

She rejoined, "A cop who thinks he's smarter than the world. You already got shot once, and it's a miracle that you were able to even make it to the station today without getting shot again. Half of this city wants you dead."

"I don't need to take your shit, Fed. I lost my wife, I lost my house, I lost my car. The only thing I have left in this world is this job. You guys are going to take me some place and lock me up in some safe house. Then what will I have?"

"Your life, dumb ass."

Billings was grinning from ear to ear during this exchange.

Cassidy stood up and walked to the bars. "What good is having my life if everything that was in it has been taken away from me?"

The female fed shot back, "So, you're giving up then? The killer has won. Why don't you just hang yourself in the cell? Do what that murderer wants and kill yourself!"

Billings retorted, "He can't. We took away his shoelaces and belt. It's standard procedure."

"Yeah, laugh it up, Billings. And you two can go back to spying on Americans' cell phone conversations. I don't want your protective custody."

The male agent reached into his pocket and pulled out his wallet as the female agent held out her hand, palm up. "Thank you, Cassidy. Your stubborn ass just earned me twenty bucks."

"First Robin, now you. Why is it that everyone seems to be making money off me?"

The male agent said, "You should be asking why everyone is losing money because of you. Here, she told me to have this ready for you."

"What is it?"

The female agent said, "It's a waiver stating you voluntarily decline our protection. Essentially, it covers our ass when someone eventually manages to kill you."

Cassidy took the paper and stood for a second before saying, "I need a pen."

Billings shook his head and smiled. "It's against regulations to give prisoners ink pens as they could potentially use one to harm themselves or the staff."

The federal agents began to snicker.

"Oh, you're hilarious. Shut the hell up and give me a damn pen!"

The female agent said, "It's alright, officer. I'll take responsibility for this one. If he stabs himself in the eye or something, I'll deal with the paperwork." She produced a pen and handed it through the bars to Cassidy.

He was grumbling as he signed the paper, but none of them could make out what he was saying.

"Here, take your waiver. Now go away. Billings, open this cage and let me go back to work."

The female agent held up her hand to the bar and requested, "My pen, please?"

"Oh, yeah, here."

"Alright, let's go call this in and see if we can land a real assignment this time. Have a nice day, Officer Billings." She then looked at Cassidy and offered seriously, "Detective ... I sincerely hope you make it through this in one piece."

Both of the agents turned and left the holding cell area.

Billings was turning to leave when Cassidy bit out, "Where the hell do you think you're going? Open up and let me out!"

Billings stopped and said, "Can't do that, Butch. They're still deciding whether or not to press charges against you. As you know, we can hold you up to seventy-two hours without arresting you. It may be the only way to keep you alive for the next three days."

"Are you serious? Hey, don't walk away from me. Get back here!"

From somewhere down the hall, one of the other inmates yelled out, "Hey! Having to listen to his whiny ass should be considered cruel and unusual punishment! Isn't that a violation of my Constitutional rights? Someone please take him out of here!"

Cassidy sighed and plopped back down on his bunk.

*****

At the university, Kidd found the office and was asking about Travis Dean Parker. The young woman behind the counter punched some keys on a computer and said, "Yep, he checked in already. Would you like his room number? I have no idea if he'd be there or somewhere else on campus, but at least it'd be a start for you."

In the dorm, Kidd checked the room number against the one he'd scribbled in his notepad and knocked gently on the door. In response he heard, "It's open."

Kidd turned the knob and eased the door open to a room in the process of being decorated. Cardboard boxes were scattered across the floor. Standing on a chair along the far wall was a short, skinny guy that appeared to be in his mid-teens, though they already knew that he was actually twenty. Kidd queried, "Are you Travis Dean Parker?"

The young man was taping a poster to the wall and didn't turn to see who had entered his room. "Yep, that's me. Who might you be?"

Detective Kidd came on into the room and made a space for Dr. Poole to stand next to him. They closed the dorm room door and Kidd was just about to identify himself when Parker finally glanced over his shoulder. When he did, he nearly fell off the chair. "Oh, my God! You're Jeremy Kidd. Sundance, in the flesh. What happened to your face? Did a suspect attack you? Oh, were you at that riot at the courthouse this morning busting skulls?" Then his eyes shifted to Dr. Poole and his jaw hung open as his eyes widened. He whispered, "Dr. Stacey Poole. The only one who stood by Dean Connelly when everyone else condemned him. This is truly an honor. I am a huge fan. Where's Butch?"

"Would you mind stepping down off that chair, please? I'd like to ask you a few questions."

Parker's eyes lit up. "Questioned by Sundance? You bet!" He climbed down from the chair and looked around the small dorm room. "Would you like to have a seat? I bet you would, Dr. Poole. Here." He turned the chair that he had just been standing on and offered it to her.

"No, thank you, Mr. Parker. I'm fine."

His eyes were locked onto hers. "Yes … yes, you are, Dr. Poole."

Kidd sighed and snapped his fingers a few times in front of Parker's face. "Travis … do you mind if I call you Travis?"

"Sundance, you can call me anything you'd like. This is better than Christmas."

He was becoming frustrated with this kid, and he'd been in the room less than a minute. Dr. Poole obviously found the entire exchange quite amusing.

"Travis, our department received an anonymous call concerning some records that you've been keeping about Detective Cassidy and me. Do you happen to have those notebooks here?"

"Of course I do! They're the first thing I unpacked when I got here. Would you like to see them? In fact, would you do me a huge favor and sign one for me? That would be awesome!"

Kidd patiently said, "First, I'd like to take a look at what you've collected about us. We'll discuss autographs later, okay?"

"Oh, got it." He went to the small two-drawer filing cabinet that stood next to the desk and opened the top drawer. "Do you want to see what I have just about your career? Or maybe you'd like to see what I've collected since you and Detective Butch Cassidy became partners? Better yet, let's start from the beginning."

He pulled six overstuffed files from the top drawer and set them down on the bed. "Those are just on Butch from before you two partnered up." He pulled three more from the top drawer and set them in another stack on his bed. "Those are about you before you teamed up with Butch." He then closed the top drawer and opened the bottom one. "These are all about the pair of you since you became Butch and Sundance!"

He stood proudly and beamed at Kidd and Dr. Poole.

Jeremy turned to look at Stacey and raised his eyebrows. Stacey began, "Mr. Parker … "

"Oh, no. The two of you can call me Travis. Please, I feel like I know both of you so well. It's like we're old friends."

"Travis, what are you studying here at the university?"

"This year, criminal law. I hope to be an attorney someday. Hey, maybe one day I'll be able to prosecute a case that you and Butch worked on!"

Kidd walked over to the two stacks of files on the bed and flipped open the top folder. It was filled with newspaper articles, photos and notebooks. Some of the photos were Polaroid shots of crime scenes that had already been taped off. He flipped open one of the notebooks and saw small, neat handwriting covering every inch of the page. As he flipped through it, page after page was filled with the same handwriting.

"You appear to have been quite thorough in documenting our careers. There's a lot of information here."

"Oh, thank you! Yes, it took quite a bit of effort. I did try to gather all of the information I could get my hands on. It means so much to me that you approve!"

Kidd glanced at him briefly then closed the file. "I don't suppose you'd consider coming down to the station with us and bringing all of this so we can have some time to properly go through it, would you?"

"Really? In the same car with Sundance? Absolutely. Oh, I do need to be back by eight though. There's supposed to be a party in the next dorm, and I've been invited."

Kidd nodded and promised, "I'll do my best to make sure you're back by then."

"Excellent! I'll grab these." He loaded his arms with the files from the bottom drawer. "If you two wouldn't mind getting those two stacks, we can be on our way. Dr. Poole, if you don't mind me saying so, you are much more beautiful in person than your photos indicate."

She smiled graciously as she replied, "Thank you very much, Travis. I appreciate the compliment."

He was struggling with the weight of the files as he asked, "Will Butch be there? I'd like to get his autograph, too."

Kidd nodded. "Actually, he is at the station, but right now he's kind of locked into something. I don't know if he'll get the chance to talk to you."

Obvious disappointment covered Travis's entire being. After a few seconds he brightened slightly and said, "That's not a problem; I understand. He's probably really busy trying to solve the Specter murders. Maybe he can find just a few moments to say hi. It would be great if he could."

As Kidd hefted the larger of the two remaining stacks he responded, "I'll see what I can do, but no promises."

"Excellent! Where'd you park?"

*****

Once they were back at the station, they had Travis wait in the conference room with all of his files. "I'll be back as soon as I can."

"Don't forget to see if Butch can spare a minute please!"

"I won't," Kidd smiled as he closed the door.

He looked at Dr. Poole and rolled his eyes. He whispered, "That kid is absolutely bonkers."

"That wouldn't be considered a valid clinical diagnosis. But yes, he's definitely displaying obsessive behavior where you and Cassidy are concerned. Such behavior is generally accompanied by some form of stalking—either an attempt at personal interaction with the two of you or, more likely in his case, simply going to the places where the two of you go. He'd probably visit crime scenes after the two of you left them. Maybe recreate entire cases based on your arrests and analyze the processes that you used to find your suspects. So far, it appears to be solely based on your professional lives though. I haven't seen anything in his actions that indicates he's delved into either of your personal lives … yet."

"How comforting. I did see snapshots of crime scenes that had already been taped off in that folder I looked through."

"I don't know what you expect to gain by questioning him. He's obviously not your killer."

"Really? How can you be so certain?"

"He simply adores you and Cassidy. He's like a puppy that's attached himself to his owner. Total and unconditional adoration. In fact, fanatical adoration would be a more apt description. He doesn't hate Cassidy, and he's definitely not trying to destroy his career or his life."

"So this is another dead end. I'd still like to have our guys go through his files. Maybe make copies of what he has so that we can take our time analyzing everything. Especially those notebooks. They must have taken hundreds of hours to write."

"You're not going to just leave him there while your guys make copies of all his work, are you?"

"What the hell do you want me to do with him?"

"At least give him the autograph he craves. If Cassidy is here somewhere, it'd be nice to have him sign a paper, too."

"Won't that feed into this guy's … I don't know … insanity?"

"He's obsessed and fanatical, but I'd hardly call him insane. Do you have a favorite sports team?"

"What does that have to do with anything?"

"Do you?"

"Of course I do."

"How would it make you feel if you managed to get the autograph of your favorite player from your favorite team?"

Kidd thought about that for a moment then nodded. "I'll see if someone can get Cassidy's signature."

"I don't think I'm needed here anymore. This isn't a very deep subject we're dealing with. What you see is pretty much what you get with him."

"Okay, doctor. Thanks for coming along though. I'll let you know if anything in those files is worth a closer look."

"You know how to reach me. Good luck with him."

"Yeah, thanks."

*****

That evening's news reports were dominated by footage of the riots that broke out near the courthouse and jail. Reports included the number of people killed and injured as well as interviews with those who suffered property damage or minor personal injury. Almost as an afterthought, the media presented footage of Dean Connelly as he walked out of the county jail and triumphantly raised his hands into the air.

CHAPTER 18

---·---

Thursday, August 28

"Well, are you going to start acting like you have an IQ higher than a mosquito's?"

"Knock it off. There were cops under attack, and I was going to help. That isn't a slam against my intelligence."

"Punching me in the face to go out there is."

Cassidy lowered his eyes and said, "Yeah. I'm sorry about that. That wasn't one of my prouder moments."

"So, here we stand. You locked up so you can't go get yourself killed and me trying to figure out if pressing charges will be the only way to keep you alive."

From a couple of cells down they heard, "Let him out! He'll be fine. If I have to spend another night listening to him whine about how bad his life sucks, I'll snap."

Cassidy and Kidd ignored the intrusion into their conversation as best they could. Cassidy asked, "Aside from keeping me alive, what good does it do to have me locked up?"

"For one, it gives me a bit of satisfaction."

Cassidy walked away from the bars and sat down on his bunk. He sighed heavily but remained silent.

After a few moments Kidd offered, "Thanks for signing that paper last night, by the way."

Cassidy grunted but didn't offer much of a response for a second. Eventually, he asked, "What was that all about anyway? The paper was blank."

"I'd followed up on a tip that led me to this kid. It isn't important. Anyway, this Parker kid was really pushing for your autograph. At least when he got it, he stopped being a complete pain in the ass."

Cassidy slowly looked up and said, "Travis Parker?"

"Yeah. The kid's a little bit obsessive when it comes to us. He seems harmless though. When did you learn about him?"

Cassidy answered slowly, "A couple of years ago. He was standing out at the end of my driveway one morning. It was kind of creepy. I'd had several run-ins with him for about a year, but to make a long story short, I finally threatened to shoot him if I found him anywhere near my wife or my house again. I haven't heard anything from him since then, and that must have been a year ago or maybe more now."

"You never said anything about him to me."

"He was a creepy stalker. What was I going to say?" He adjusted his voice to a mocking tone. "Hey, guess what, Kidd. I have a groupie. Oh yeah, it's very flattering. He shows up at my house sometimes and just stands outside staring. Sometimes he shows up at the station and stares as we drive out of the parking lot. It's great having that kind of attention from a complete lunatic!"

"Yeah, alright. I get it. You still should have told me. If for nothing else, then as a warning in case he got weird with me, too."

"To be honest, I forgot about him until you just mentioned him. Are we looking into him for these murders?"

Kidd laughed and said, "We copied all of the stuff he's collected on us, but I don't think he's good for these murders. Neither does Dr. Poole."

Cassidy grunted as he turned his head at the mention of Dr. Poole's name.

"What the hell's your problem with her?"

Cassidy shook his head for a moment then stood up and began pacing.

"Come on," Kidd prodded. "What is it with her?"

"I don't know, alright! There's just something that … leaves a bad taste in my mouth when I'm around her. I don't know how to explain it any better than that. I do know that you should keep your eye on the Parker kid though. He's a total nut job, and I don't care what your precious Dr. Poole says. That creepy bastard is capable of doing something like this, if for no other reason than to actually become part of one of our cases. That's how nuts he is."

Kidd stood there for a few moments before finally saying, "Maybe I should go pay him another visit."

"I wouldn't. I'd have one of the other guys follow up with him. The more attention you give him, the worse he's going to get. It's bad enough that you tricked me into giving him my signature."

Kidd nodded and agreed, "You may be right. Alright I'll have one of the other guys go talk to him again."

"Good. Now, about getting me out of here."

"No problem, someone will be down to open the door in about forty-eight hours. I suggest you get some rest during the next couple of days. You look like shit."

Cassidy moved up to the bars and shouted angrily, "That's not funny! There's a psychopath out there using me as an excuse to kill people in this city. I can't just sit here."

"Actually, you can, Mike. Until you get your head screwed on right, this is the safest place for you."

Billings came running down the stairs just as Kidd finished his sentence, then paused as he stood breathing heavily from the exertion.

Both of them stared at him for a moment before Kidd finally asked, "Was there something you wanted to tell us or were you just exercising?"

Billings said, "The captain needs you upstairs."

"Tell him I'll be there in a minute."

Billings shook his head as he glanced at Cassidy then back to Kidd. "Now."

Cassidy said, "There's been another murder. Kidd, let me out of here. I want to help."

Kidd shook his head and promised as he followed Billings out of the holding cell area, "I'll keep you informed, but you're staying right there for now."

"Kidd! Let me help!"

They got upstairs but Captain Bordeaux met them before they reached the bullpen and handed Kidd a scrap of paper. "Go. Find out if this is our guy or another crackpot using these murders to off someone that spit in his cereal or something."

One of the vice detectives was passing by, and Kidd reached out to stop him. He pulled his notepad from his pocket and flipped it open. After finding the page he needed, he held it up. "Hey, can you do me a favor and follow up on Travis Parker? If I show up again, I don't think I'll get anything useful out of him."

"What am I looking for?"

"I don't know. There's something off with this kid. Just talk to him, look around his room if he'll let you. See if he's worth pursuing or not."

"I'll head over there in an hour or so." He wrote down the information that Kidd had in his notes. "I'll call if I come up with anything."

"Thanks, I appreciate this." Kidd looked again at the scrap of paper Bordeaux had given him and bolted out the door.

*****

"What have we got, Turner?"

"This one's bad. You'll have to see for yourself."

"Who's the victim?"

Officer Turner replied, "Her name's Jessica Halsey. Twenty-three. She was a dancer at that club over on Evans."

"Is the ME already here?"

Turner nodded, "With the body. He's actually been here since about 7:00 a.m."

Kidd noted that it was now just after 8:00 a.m. as he made his way from the entrance of the small house toward the bathroom down the hall on his right. Inside, he saw Dr. Brown and Jeff. As Dr. Brown would point, Jeff would snap pictures. Kidd cleared his throat but didn't enter the small room.

Dr. Brown glanced over his shoulder. "Jeremy, what the hell? I thought you were on vacation or something. How come it took you so long to respond? Actually, forget it. I don't need to know. This one's rough. It also has me baffled a bit. Come take a look."

Kidd waited as Jeff exited the lavatory to make room for him to enter. Kidd could see that the shower curtain had been pulled from its rod and was bunched up in the tub. As he moved up next to Dr. Brown, he saw that blood covered the majority of the curtain that was toward the back of the tub, and it had already been pulled down to reveal the upper torso and head of the victim. The scene was absolutely grizzly.

Kidd sighed. "Nobody informed me until half an hour ago. I was explaining to Mike why he can't be released from jail yet. What's the story here?"

Dr. Brown began to point to several visible wounds as he spoke. "The knife that you see there appears to be consistent with these wounds. The killer stabbed out both of the poor girl's eyes as well as nearly taking off her entire right ear. I already counted fourteen separate stab wounds in her head, neck and upper torso. It appears that the killer initially struck her while she was showering. The first blows were delivered straight through the shower curtain. But the wounds to her eyes were far too precise to have been accidental. Our killer deliberately attacked both of her eyes, and the wounds appear to be deep. There was no hesitation and nothing tentative about the nature of this attack."

Kidd couldn't see the feet of the victim since they were covered by the tattered remains of the shower curtain, but he had to ask, "The toes?"

Dr. Brown slowly turned to face Detective Kidd and nodded. "Both removed. That's what has me baffled. In the other three murders, our killer did only what was necessary to end the life of each victim. I can't be certain that this is our killer—but, at least from the visual inspection, it appears that the same instrument was used to remove both of the outer digits of the feet just as in the other murders. I'll be able to verify that during the autopsy. This one has the feel of a hate crime, however."

"Haven't they all been hate crimes, doctor?"

"Oh, no. The other three murders that have been committed by our killer haven't been hate crimes at all. Our killer appears to hate Cassidy, but those murders were simply a means to an end. This one is different –the killer appears to have actually been enraged at our victim."

"Can you give me an estimate on the time of death?"

"The best I can do right now is sometime very late last night or very early this morning. I'd say between 12:00 and 4:00 a.m. I might be able to narrow that slightly, but right now that's my best estimate. I should think Robin and her team won't be too long collecting what they need in here. I should be able to have her on the table by nine. I'll give you a call later this afternoon when I have more information."

Kidd looked around the bathroom and noted how clean the rest of it was. He then left the lavatory and found Turner at the front door directing traffic.

"Hey, Kidd. Pretty nasty, wasn't it? She was found this morning by her roommate, Tamara Vickers. I already took an initial statement from her. Do you want to see my notes?"

Kidd nodded his head up and down, but said nothing.

Turner handed him his notepad and continued, "She's out there with Doris right now. I think they gave her a sedative. She was very upset."

Kidd read the notes of the initial interview that Turner had done then handed back the notepad. As he was getting ready to go find the Emergency Response Team that was tending to Tamara, Robin and her crew showed up.

"Are you ready for us yet?"

Kidd nodded and motioned toward the hall with his thumb as he walked past the tech team without saying a word.

He found Doris in the back of the ambulance, using her gloved fingers to gently brush the hair of a sobbing woman who was wrapped in a blanket. She looked up at Kidd with an expression that told him to proceed with extreme caution.

He nodded and gently asked, "Miss Vickers, my name is Detective Kidd. I already read the responses you gave during your talk with Officer Turner, so I'll keep this very short. Can you answer a few questions for me, please?"

The young woman wiped her eyes and nodded. "I'll try."

"Thank you. Can you tell me if anything seemed out of place in the house when you arrived this morning?"

She tensed and asked, "You mean aside from my girlfriend lying slashed to pieces in the bathtub?"

Kidd sighed and said, "I was talking about when you first approached and entered the house. It's very important if you can remember seeing anything that struck you as odd when you first entered."

Miss Vickers relaxed slightly and appeared to try to think. Eventually she shook her head and said, "I don't think so."

Kidd asked, "Was the front door locked or unlocked when you arrived?"

"It was unlocked, but she was expecting me to be home around five. When she left the club last night she said she'd wait up. She doesn't normally lock the door unless she's going to bed."

"Was the shower still running or had the water been turned off?"

"The shower was still on. I turned the water off since it was freezing cold." She began sobbing again as she continued. "The hot water had run out, and I couldn't just leave her like that. I know. What difference does it make if my dead girlfriend has cold water or warm water, but … I couldn't leave cold water running on her, damn it!"

When he'd begun speaking with her, he was standing and looking down at her as she sat on the back deck of the ambulance. He then recalled his training and squatted down so that he had to look up at her instead. "Miss Vickers, I'm not the enemy here. I'm just trying to get some information so that I can find the person who did this. Now please take a deep breath. Try to relax a little bit and just focus on me. I'm here to help."

She sniffled and fought back tears as she took a deep breath. After a few seconds, she nodded.

"Thank you. Can you tell me why you didn't leave the club when Miss Halsey did?"

"I stayed to help clean up after closing. For extra money, some of the girls volunteer to help wipe down tables and restock coolers or vacuum. The manager gives us an extra fifty, and it usually only takes a couple of hours."

Jeremy was writing in his pad when he said, "This next question is very important, Miss Vickers. Was there anyone at the club last night that was paying unwanted attention to Miss Halsey? Had she singled out any particular patron at any point during the night as being a problem?"

Tamara said, "Detective, we take off our clothes for a living. There's always someone who gets a little too turned on and expects more than he's getting."

Kidd nodded and asked, "Does anyone stand out from last night though?"

"There was a group of college kids that showed up toward the end of the shift. One was very creepy. Most of the time college boys are easy to handle. They're usually drunk and just looking for a good time. Sometimes you have to push their hands away when they get a little too physical. While the others were pretty drunk, this one seemed sober. It wasn't just Jessie that he was getting out of hand with, though he did pay her quite a bit of attention now that I think about it."

"Does the club have security cameras?"

"Yes, but I think only the ones covering the entrance and the cash registers record. The others are just for looks to keep the crowd in line. The owner doesn't want an employee to start posting videos online of us dancing. He wouldn't make any money from that."

"Would the owner be at the club today?"

Tamara nodded. "He usually goes in around ten. He tallies the receipts from the previous night and gets the registers set up for the evening. He stays until noon when the early shift begins to show up then makes his run to the bank. After that, sometimes he's there, sometimes he isn't."

Kidd checked his watch and saw that he had about an hour before he could catch the owner at the club. "Thank you, Miss Vickers. I know this has been difficult, and I appreciate your help."

She looked over his shoulder toward the house and saw the stretcher as it was being rolled out the front door. Her face contorted, and she began to cry again.

Kidd nodded to the EMT and left them to go back toward the house.

"Robin, did you find anything that might be useful?"

"Come on, Kidd. You know how this works. We don't speculate; we deal in hard evidence. We collected a few fingerprints from the bathroom, we bagged the knife and the shower curtain, and we're just getting ready to start going through the rest of the house. It'll probably be a couple of hours before we even get what we collect back to the lab."

"Alright, would you give a call if you come up with anything?"

"You got it."

*****

Kidd watched as a Tahoe pulled into the parking lot of the club. Before the man could unlock the door of the building, he got out of his unmarked car and called out. "Mr. Mills?"

The man turned and looked at him suspiciously for a moment then relaxed and said, "Yeah, that's me. What can I do for you, officer?"

Kidd paused briefly as he was approaching and asked, "How do you know I'm a cop?"

"Are you serious? You and your partner have had your faces plastered all over the news for the last month. Even if they weren't, look at yourself. I run a club that features exotic dancers. I deal with cops on a weekly basis. Even without a uniform, everything about you screams that you're a cop."

"Fair enough. Have you heard anything this morning on the news?"

Mills' demeanor changed, and he tensed a little. "No, what happened?"

"Do you mind if we go inside, sir?"

"Oh, shit, that's never a good sign. Yeah, come on in."

Once inside with the door locked behind them, Mr. Mills asked, "What happened?"

"One of your dancers was attacked in her home last night after her shift."

"Oh, God. Who was it?"

Kidd pulled his notepad and flipped a few pages even though he didn't need to. He was doing this to have a few more seconds to observe Mr. Mills. "Her name is Jessica Halsey."

The color drained from Mills' face as he asked, "How was she killed?"

Kidd cocked his head slightly and asked, "Why would you ask that?"

Mr. Mills retorted, "You're a *homicide* detective. I already told you that you've been all over the news … I think it's logical to assume this is probably one of those Specter killings?"

"We don't know for certain yet."

"Oh, poor Tammy. She'll be devastated. What happened?"

"That's what I'm here trying to figure out. Ms. Vickers told us you have security cameras. I was wondering if you'd allow me access to last night's recordings."

Mr. Mills turned and said, "Damn straight. Follow me."

He brought up the digital recording from the previous night as he explained, "I don't have the cameras on the floor connected to the computer. Those are just for looks. It wouldn't do to have footage leaked of these girls getting pawed by horny drunks. Most of their families don't even know they do this. Some go to college and just dance to help pay their way until they can get their degrees. Here we go. I cover the outside and inside of the entrance as well as the hallway that leads to the toilets. There are also two cameras angled at the register behind the bar. I can bring up all of the images at once if you want."

"That'd be great. What time did Ms. Halsey's shift start?"

"She was scheduled from 9:00 p.m. to 2:00 a.m."

"Ms. Vickers said there was a group of college kids that came in kind of late. Can we fast forward to then?"

The images were brought up on a thirty-two-inch monitor in six blocks, each showing a different camera angle. In the bottom right corner of each block was the time and date. After Mills hit a few buttons on the keyboard, the images began to play at sixteen times the normal playback speed. After a minute of watching, the time indicated they were just passing 10:00 p.m.

"Can you bump it up to midnight?"

Mr. Mills nodded and hit a few keys. The images began running again.

"Can you slow it down for me, please?"

Mr. Mills complied, and the playback slowed to four times the normal speed.

"Stop!"

Mills froze the images in place.

Kidd moved closer to the monitor and said, "Alright, can you find where this man left?"

Mr. Mills ran the footage at a faster playback speed, then after a couple of minutes he stopped and slowly reversed the playback. "It looks like he and his pals were some of the last ones out the door."

The time on the image was 2:12 a.m.

"I don't suppose you have any camera angles that show the parking lot, do you?"

"Of course. That's where any drug deals or fights would happen." He hit a few more buttons and four blocks of images appeared on the monitor. A few more keystrokes and the playback showed four angles of the parking lot being played back at normal speed, beginning at 2:12 a.m.

"There are our college kids. It looks like this one is handing the keys over to this one. He just walks away from them."

As Mills paused the playback, he looked at Kidd. "Do you think this guy is who you're looking for?"

Kidd answered, "I don't know yet. But believe me, I'll follow up with him. Thank you for your time, Mr. Mills. Will you save these recordings in case we need them later?"

Mr. Mills pulled a blank CD from a stack on the desk and said, "I'll burn you a copy of the entire night's recordings."

"I appreciate that, Mr. Mills. Thank you for not making me get a court order."

"One of my girls was murdered. Her girlfriend is probably going through hell right now. I want this solved as much as you do, officer."

Five minutes later, Detective Kidd was leaving the club with a copy of the recording in his hand. He slid behind the wheel of his car and was just getting ready to make a call on his cell phone when it buzzed. After checking the caller ID he answered. "What a coincidence. I was just going to call you."

"Yeah, that's amazing alright. That kid you sent me to check on?"

"Yeah, that's what I was going to call you about."

"Right, good call having me do that. He's in the back of my car right now. He was sleeping when we arrived. After waking him up, he consented to having us look around. We found a box under his bed with manila envelopes that were addressed to the news station and to our station. Kidd? There are twenty of each, and they look like they were addressed using the same stencil as those we received after the murders. I blocked off the room and called for uniforms to guard it until we can get forensics over here."

"Good, I have footage placing him at the club where our latest victim worked last night. Maybe this thing is finally going to break for us. Book him in and get him locked up. I need to make another phone call. I'll be down there in a bit."

"No problem. Once the uniforms show up … actually, they just arrived. He'll be sitting in a cell when you get there, Kidd."

Jeremy disconnected the call and punched a few buttons. "Hey, who's handling the holding cells right now? Have him yank Cassidy out. We have someone coming in to be booked, and I don't want him seeing Cassidy behind bars when he gets there. I don't know, but don't let that stubborn ass leave the station. Just keep him out of sight somewhere. Thanks."

Thirty seconds later, he was on the phone again. "Hi, Rebecca. Is Stacey available? Of course I want to talk with you, but this happens to be official. Thank you. Hello, Dr. Poole? Do you have time to come to the station? Yes. I'm on my way there now. Don't go in until I get there. I'll meet you in the parking lot. Right. Thanks … and please tell Rebecca I'll call her later."

When he got to the station, he saw Dr. Poole's Outback there already. When she saw him, she got out of her car. "What's going on, Jeremy?"

"Parker, that's what's going on."

"Oh? What'd you find?"

"Another body. This time, he's linked with the victim. Let's go inside. I'll fill you in."

Once inside, he led her to the empty conference room. "This morning a woman was murdered in her home. The killing was gruesome. It was a stabbing; and, take my word for it, it was overkill. She worked as a dancer at an exotic club, and Parker was there last night. I have footage of him and his college buddies as they were leaving. He gave one of them the keys and left on foot. The victim's home was eight blocks from the club and within walking distance for Parker."

Dr. Poole said, "That doesn't sound like very much to go on, but it might be something."

"How about this? Cassidy knew who Parker was because he'd had issues with him for about a year. Last year he got fed up with Parker and threatened him. So I sent another detective to talk with him again, and he found a box containing addressed manila envelopes. The exact same kind our killer uses. They were already addressed using the same stencil our killer uses, and the addresses were to the news station and here."

Dr. Poole raised her eyebrow and continued, "That sounds more substantial. Had I known that Parker had already made the leap from fanatical adoration to physically stalking Cassidy, my assessment yesterday would have been quite different."

"So you do think there's a chance he could be our killer now?"

She slowly nodded and said, "If Detective Cassidy already warned him off once, he'd have felt spurned by the object of his obsession. That certainly could have manifested itself into a dichotomy of conflicting desires."

"I'm not entirely sure what that means, doc. I'm a cop, remember?"

"Sorry, while still adoring Cassidy and continuing to follow your careers, Cassidy confronting him and warning him to leave him alone could have caused animosity. You said it was a year ago when Cassidy had his run-in with Parker?"

"According to Cassidy." Kidd was nodding.

"That would be enough time for Parker to warp the encounter in his mind. Over that length of time, it's certainly possible that Parker developed a loathing for the way Cassidy treated him. Of course, I'd need to spend some time with Parker before I could confirm that theory."

Kid rejected that immediately. "I don't think that's a very good idea. We'll have Dr. Brandt handle any direct contact with Parker. I do want you to watch as he's being questioned though. Would that be okay?"

"Certainly. Observing his reactions and hearing the inflection in his voice during his responses would give me a solid basis to formulate some opinions."

"Good. Just relax for a little bit. Once we're ready, I'll have you go into the captain's office where you can observe on the monitor."

*****

Detective Cassidy, Dr. Poole and Captain Bordeaux were in the office with the door locked and the blinds pulled.

"Alright, go ahead," Bordeaux commanded via the phone on his desk.

Dr. Poole asked, "Where's Detective Kidd? Shouldn't he be here, too?"

Cassidy said, "He's talking with Doc Brown about the autopsy results. Phillips and Jennings are conducting the interrogation."

As the two detectives entered the small interrogation room, Parker leaned forward with a smile on his face. "Where are Butch and Sundance? Shouldn't they be the ones talking to me? You know, I spoke with Sundance yesterday. He had my research copied. He probably has a team going over what I've collected so far. I bet it'll help with the investigation."

"They're very busy right now, Mr. Parker. Can you tell us where you were last night?"

"Yeah, there was a party on campus."

"How long were you at the party?"

"It started to get boring, so we left around 11:30 p.m. or so."

"And where did you go after you left the party?"

"We went to a strip club."

"How long were you at the club?"

"Right up until they were getting ready to close."

"After you left the club?"

"I was walking around mostly."

"Walking around where?"

"Oh, Detective Cassidy wouldn't be happy if I told you that."

"And why would he be unhappy with where you were walking around?"

"I probably shouldn't be talking about this."

The detective said, "I suppose that's up to you, but if you want to help with this investigation, answering our questions will go a long way toward doing that."

Parker thought about this for a moment then went on, "Well, I might have gone a little too far with Butch. It was a while ago, but he threatened to shoot me if he ever caught me at his house again."

"And what would that have to do with you walking around this morning?"

"I went over to see how badly his house had gotten burned. I felt sorry for him. He won't know I was there, will he? He'd be very angry if he found out."

"It's okay. This is just between us. So, you're telling me that after you left the club, you walked twelve blocks to go look at Cassidy's burned up house?"

Parker nodded and said, "Yeah, like I said, I felt sorry for him. He's been through so much lately."

"Is there anywhere else that you went while you were walking around?"

"Oh, sure. Like I told you, I was just out walking around. The city is really nice at that time of the morning. It's quiet, and I can think."

"So, where else did you walk to then?"

"Oh, no place in particular. I was just walking around and thinking."

"How did you get back to the university this morning?"

"I jogged."

"So you were out walking around for a few hours then you decided to jog back to the university. That must be three miles or so. How long did it take you to get back?"

"Less than half an hour."

"Alright, then what time did you get back to the university this morning?"

"Probably around six. That's why I was sleeping when you came to visit this morning. It had been a long night."

"How come you didn't call a taxi to come get you this morning?"

"My cell phone was dead. I'd forgotten to charge it before the party."

"How long have you been going to Denver University?"

"Three years. I'm just starting my fourth."

"According to our information, you don't live in Denver. Where were you staying before the dorms opened up for fall classes?"

"This summer a friend was nice enough to let me stay at his place. He was doing some remodeling and had a room over his garage. He let me stay there in exchange for help with painting, replacing carpeting, things like that."

"That's nice, so you actually remained in the city during the entire summer?"

Parker was nodding. "Except for a few trips back home to visit friends for weekends."

"Do you own a vehicle, Mr. Parker?"

"Yeah, but it broke down last year, and I haven't had the money to get it fixed. It's not a problem though. Everything I need is really close to the university. I also got in way better shape since I've been walking and jogging places."

"Let's get back to last night, if you don't mind." He pulled out a photo they'd gotten from the Internet and placed it on the table. "Do you recognize this woman?"

Parker leaned forward and smiled. "Hey, she was dancing at the club last night. She's gorgeous!"

"Did she dance for you last night?"

"Yes, she seemed to like me very much. In fact, I was trying to get her to dance for me again when they were getting ready to close for the night. Too bad. I think I was making headway with her, if you know what I mean."

"Mr. Parker, she was found murdered this morning in her home."

"Oh, that's terrible news. Such a shame. She was beautiful."

"You wouldn't happen to know anything about how she was murdered, would you?"

"No. Wait. You think because she liked me that I might be involved with her murder? Look, she obviously wanted to pursue a physical relationship with me. If I'd have had more time before the club closed, I think that could have happened. But I told you, I was out walking around last night. I wasn't killing her."

"Yes, you told us your alibi already. Out walking around. Near Detective Cassidy's home, correct?"

Parker nodded. "That's right; so since I was there, I couldn't have been at her house killing her."

"Why is that?"

"Because her house is the other direction from Detective Cassidy's."

"How is it that you know where her house is?"

Parker paused, but only for an instant. "As I said, we were getting quite friendly at the club. She told me where she lived. I just didn't get the chance to go visit her."

"Let's talk about the envelopes we found under your bed for a moment."

"I told you when you found them that I was doing research. I was trying to determine how long it took to address each envelope using that stencil."

"Right, I recall that now. Why were you doing that again?"

"I told you, I was trying to figure out if the Specter had them all set up prior to committing each murder or if they were created afterward. Given the time it took for the Postal Service to deliver the last two envelopes, I figured that they must have been mailed right after each murder. Would you like to know my results?"

"Sure, what'd you come up with?"

"The murderer had to have already addressed the envelopes before committing the murders. That way he could have just packed the note and toe inside and put it into a mailbox before the morning pick up. It took me over fifteen minutes to address two envelopes with that stencil and marker. It's very time consuming. So I came to the conclusion that before the Specter committed each murder, the related notes and envelopes were already printed and addressed."

"Very interesting. Do you know what else we found in your dorm room? The same generic Ziploc bags as those sent to us, and a brand new printer that looks like it's only been used a few times. We also found half a box of latex gloves. It looks like you were quite thorough."

"Of course. I got the Ziploc bags to test how well they actually sealed, and I needed the printer for college. My old one stopped working last year. Since the killer obviously wore gloves, when I addressed the envelopes, I wore them also. It helped to get a feel for what was involved in the process."

"Alright, Mr. Parker. Here's where we stand. We believe that you were actually the one who killed this young woman last night when she turned down your advances. If you cooperate with us, things will go much more smoothly for you."

"I didn't kill anyone! I was trying to help Butch and Sundance with their investigation. That's all!"

"Why don't you just write down how you committed the murder for us."

Parker stopped for a few seconds and looked at the legal pad that was sitting in front of him. "I thought you brought me in to let me know how much you appreciated my help with the investigation. I didn't kill anyone. Are you arresting me?"

"That depends on you, Mr. Parker. Are you going to cooperate with us?"

"I have been." Travis leaned back in his chair and sat silently for a few seconds. "I think I should have a lawyer now."

"Are you sure you don't want to continue to cooperate with us?"

"I think you should get me a lawyer."

"Okay, Mr. Parker. Please stand up. We're placing you under arrest for the murder of Jessica Halsey ... "

*****

Captain Bordeaux shut off the monitor and asked, "Well, doctor? What do you think?"

"He certainly slipped up when he admitted that he knew where Ms. Halsey lived. Those preaddressed envelopes are rather damning as well."

Cassidy was nodding. "I'd like to apologize to you, Dr. Poole."

She raised her eyebrows and asked, "Really? What for?"

"Because up until I saw this interrogation, I was convinced that you were the one killing these people."

A.J. SMELTZER

Bordeaux looked shocked. Dr. Poole couldn't hide the surprise on her face either.

"Me? What on earth would lead you to think I was the killer?"

"Several things. You came to town just before the first murder was committed. You were so certain that Connelly was innocent, even after he confessed. You're petite and, according to the profile that you and Dr. Brandt put together, you both said the killer was below average height and weight. There are other things as well. Look, I'm a homicide detective. I'm suspicious by nature. That's all."

"Well I'm very glad you didn't act on your suspicions. It would have been quite embarrassing had you arrested me. Not to mention the damage that it may have caused to Dr. Jacobs' practice. And then there's my reputation. The arrest alone could have ruined my reputation. Even when it would have later been determined that I was innocent, that kind of damage couldn't have been undone."

"I know. Again, I apologize for believing you were the killer. But, it looks like we finally have our guy. We'll have to determine his alibis for the previous three murders, of course. But I'm hopeful."

Bordeaux ordered, "Cassidy, shut up and go sit at your desk."

Cassidy retorted, "I was apologizing!"

Bordeaux pointed to the door then watched as Cassidy left and slammed the door closed behind him.

"I am terribly sorry, Dr. Poole. Had I thought for an instant that he suspected you in any way, I'd have pulled him from the case weeks ago. I think his head's been messed up since this started. Then once he lost his wife … "

"There's no need to apologize on his behalf. He's been through a lot this last month. He's actually handling things far better than many would in his position. It's okay, captain. Congratulations on catching this guy. I hope you can make a case that sticks. I should probably be getting back to the office though. Can you have Detective Kidd contact me later? I'd like to thank him for having me come down here for this. After the time I've put in on this case so far, it was rather rewarding."

274

"Of course, Dr. Poole. And thank you again for all the effort you've put into helping us."

*****

The news report for that evening was filled with the latest murder. "An arrest has been made in the murder of an exotic dancer. A local college student named Travis Dean Parker was taken into custody this morning only hours after the body of the victim was discovered by her roommate. While there has been no official word that this murder was related to those attributed to the Specter, a source close to the department told us that there was evidence collected at Mr. Parker's college dorm that leads investigators to believe that he may be the killer that's been tormenting this city since July. Let's hope Detective Cassidy finally got the right man."

CHAPTER 19

————·————

Friday, August 29

"Rebecca, what's wrong?"
        "I'm still pissed!"
Dr. Poole calmly replied, "You should be happy. It looks like they might actually have the guy that's been killing these people."

"I still can't believe that jackass said he thought you were the one who was doing all of this."

"Rebecca, it's alright. He's a homicide detective. According to what I've been told, he's a very good homicide detective, too. That means he's naturally suspicious. He even had you brought in so he could eliminate you as a suspect. He was just doing his job."

"He had me brought in because of a coincidence that put my name on a list. Why the hell would he think you had anything to do with any of this?"

"He told me that it was because the first murder was committed right after I arrived to fill in for Dr. Jacobs. He also said that my defense of Dean Connelly's innocence, even after he'd confessed, seemed suspicious to him."

"Well, I don't care. I already told Jeremy that I don't want anything to do with Cassidy anymore."

"You should be a little more forgiving. The poor guy lost everything during the last month. His wife, his house, even his car. He almost lost his own life. Can you imagine the stress he's been under? Anyone's judgment would be affected. Just think about cutting him some slack. Especially if things are getting serious between you and Jeremy. They do spend a lot of time working together, you know."

"Stacey, you amaze me sometimes. Even after he admitted that he thought you were a serial killer, you still defend him. But I suppose you do have a point. I couldn't imagine going through what he has this last month. I'm still not happy with him, but I'll try to give him the benefit of the doubt."

"I won't. That son of a bitch scares the hell out of me."

They both turned to see Quinn entering the break room.

Rebecca retorted, "I have no doubt he scares the hell out of you. You were sleeping with his wife, for Christ's sake. He has every right to be pissed at you."

Quinn froze for an instant before finally joining them at their table. He remained silent though.

Rebecca's expression softened. "I'm so sorry. I didn't mean it to sound like that. It's just still sinking in that you could actually care about someone as much as you did for Kathy. That's all."

Quinn nodded. "I know. I didn't do much to make anyone believe that I was anything except a walking erection just looking for the next conquest."

"No, you didn't. Speaking of that, how could you care so much for Kathy while still hitting on me the whole time?"

"I was just hitting on you because I knew you'd never say yes."

Rebecca shook her head. "That makes no sense at all."

"I know. It doesn't make sense because you're a woman."

"What the hell does that mean?"

Quinn finished taking a sip of his steaming hot coffee before continuing. "Are all redheads so hot-tempered?"

Stacey shook her head. "Actually, no, though that does bring up an interesting topic that I looked into back in college. The Scottish and Irish have a higher than average number of redheads. Because of their traditions and lifestyles, they tend to be outspoken and brash. The tendency to believe that all redheads are like that has bled into our own society. To some degree, because redheads are expected to act in that fashion, they tend to actually behave the way they're expected to. That brings up the question of whether stereotypes exist because of the way people behave, or whether people behave the way they do because of the stereotypes?"

Rebecca was sitting there with her mouth hanging open. "This is just lovely! So the two of you are saying that either I'm a bitch because I'm a redhead or because I'm a redhead and expected to be a bitch, I just naturally comply? Either way, you're both saying I'm a bitch."

Both Quinn and Stacey were smiling. Eventually Stacey said, "I think I can speak for everyone here when I say this. It doesn't matter to us why you're a bitch. We love you just the same and wouldn't want you to change a thing."

Rebecca's face flushed for a few moments before she noticed that both Quinn and Stacey were actively trying not to laugh. "Oh, you two are freaking hilarious. But you," she motioned back to Quinn, "and that comment about not understanding because I'm a woman. What kind of sexist shit is that?"

Quinn calmly glanced at Stacey and asked, "Would you like to explain it or should I try?"

Stacey sat back in her chair and motioned for him to go ahead. "I'd like to hear you explain this to her. It should be entertaining, to say the very least."

Rebecca appeared surprised. "You mean you understand the comment? Worse, you agree with it?"

Stacey nodded as she confirmed, "Actually, I do. But I'll let him explain it to you. After he's done putting his foot in his mouth, I'll explain it better, then tell you why I agree with him."

Rebecca folded her arms and glared at Quinn.

Quinn set his coffee down and began. "Alright, I'll see if I can do this without getting kicked in the shin."

Rebecca quipped, "It won't be in the shin."

Quinn winced and slid his chair back a bit to keep out of range. "It goes back to society and expectations, just like Dr. Poole was saying. How many times have you actively hit on a guy?"

Rebecca thought about it and answered, "I've flirted, why?"

Quinn shook his head. "Not flirting. How many times have you actually seen a guy that you thought you might want a physical relationship with and then informed him of it?"

"A few times, I suppose."

Quinn said, "My guess is that you've never done that before. You're a woman. You play the game because society expects you to play the game. If you see someone you're interested in, you stay subtle. You smile a certain way, you blink faster, you adjust your body language. In short, you flirt. But you never actually tell the guy that you're interested. You expect that if you show those subtle signs, he'll respond by hitting on you. Then, as long as the guy plays the game well enough, it progresses from that little back and forth to spending more time around each other. Eventually, maybe a date or two. Finally, after playing the game for days or even weeks, it eventually turns physical. It's nothing sexist. It's just the way society expects people to behave. The women flirt, the men then ask the women out. Now, society has changed a lot over the last several decades; women are becoming much more aggressive than they used to be. You just still exist in that old-school way of thinking."

"Well, I'm not a tramp!"

"Exactly what I was saying. If a woman walks up to a man and says, 'I'd love to have sex with you,' she's considered a tramp. Why?

Because society deems that she is. Let me ask you something. When you first saw Jeremy, were you instantly attracted to him?"

"Sort of. He's handsome and all. It wasn't until I saw how he acted, heard how he spoke, actually went out on a date with him that the real attraction began."

"Now we're getting back to my comment about you not understanding because you're a woman. While there's some physical attraction that a woman instantly feels toward a man, the vast majority of any attraction is still based on personality traits. Level of confidence, sense of humor, intelligence … the list is extensive. Men, however, are much more visual. Physical attraction is instant and occurs purely on sight. That level of attraction can be adjusted by how she acts, but a man can look at a woman and, without a word being said, determine if he wants to have sex with her. No relationship is considered, no future is considered, it's instant and primal. Most of the time, women just don't understand that because they don't think like that."

Rebecca thought about this for a moment then spoke. "So because I'm a redhead, I'm a bitch. And because you're a man, you're a pig."

Quinn laughed and nodded. "Essentially."

Stacey remarked, "Actually, I'm quite impressed, Quinn. I was fully expecting you to revert back to being a twelve year old. Yet you managed to explain that concisely and intelligently. Yes … I am quite impressed."

Quinn raised an eyebrow and adjusted his voice to make it a little sexier and deeper, then said, "Stacey, I'd love to have sex with you."

Rebecca grunted with disgust and shook her head, but Stacey's expression remained neutral. She just continued to look into Quinn's eyes without saying anything.

Rebecca could take it no more, "You're not seriously considering saying yes to him, are you?"

While keeping her gaze locked on Quinn, she answered Rebecca. "Let's just say the answer isn't no. At least not yet."

Quinn perked up instantly. "Really?"

Rebecca was shocked. Stacey, on the other hand, kept that neutral expression on her face. "I didn't say yes. I just didn't say no."

Quinn smiled broadly. "Maybe is always better than no."

With that, he stood and left the break room.

"You can't be serious," Rebecca finally manage to spit out.

Stacey shrugged. "You have to admit, the man is confident. That leads me to believe that he knows what he's doing in bed. Finding a partner who knows the right buttons to push at just the right time? How could anyone be expected to turn that down?"

Before Rebecca could say anything further, Stacey's phone buzzed. She checked the caller ID and furrowed her brow. "Hello?"

After listening to the voice on the other end of the conversation for twenty seconds, she smiled and responded, "That sounds very interesting. You're aware that we've met before and he actually knows who I am, right?"

After another lengthy pause she spoke again, "No, that's true. Set up the appointment with our receptionist, Rebecca. Yes, I'll talk with you again soon." She then disconnected the call.

Rebecca sat awaiting an explanation.

"That was Travis Parker's attorney. She's some big shot from New York City who took on Parker's defense *pro bono*. She wants me to perform Parker's evaluation for the upcoming trial."

Rebecca asked, "You're not going to work for the defense, are you?"

Stacey sighed. "I don't work for anyone. My findings won't be altered by who pays me. But yes, I'm going to do the evaluation."

"Do you realize what that's going to do to this city? They love you. What are they going to think when you do an evaluation for the defense?"

"Again, my findings won't be altered by who pays me. I'll evaluate him and submit my results. It's up to the lawyers to argue over what I submit. Besides, the media determines what the people think. There hasn't been unbiased news reported in this country in decades."

"Who's the lawyer?"

"Ms. Adrienne Welles."

Rebecca raised her eyebrows. "Wow, she's the one who defended that guy in Atlanta a couple of years ago. That trial went on for months before he was finally acquitted. She's supposed to be very good."

Stacey shrugged. "I have no idea who she is or how good she is. All I know is that sometime next week I'm supposed to do a psych evaluation on Travis Parker. It should prove to be very interesting."

*****

"I didn't do it!"

"Calm down, Mr. Parker. I'm not the one you need to convince, remember? I'm your lawyer."

"But how could they arrest me? Since I didn't do it, there can't be any physical evidence at any of the crime scenes. I explained why I had the envelopes, the stencil and the Ziploc bags. I can't believe that Butch and Sundance would think for an instant that I was the killer. I need to speak with them. Once I tell them what a mistake this all is, they'll have to let me go. After all, they're the best there is."

"No, they're people. People make mistakes. And it's exactly because there's no physical evidence tying you to any of these crimes that you'll be acquitted."

"I can't go to trial for this. I have classes starting soon."

"Mr. Parker … "

"Call me Travis. May I call you Adrienne?"

"When it's just the two of us, sure. When we're in the courtroom you have to call me Ms. Welles though. Maintain the appearance of professionalism at all times when in front of the prosecutor or the judge. You said you were studying law; you should know this."

Travis nodded. "You're right. I need to start thinking like a lawyer. Okay, professionalism at all times unless it's just the two of us. Thank you, Adrienne."

"Good, now start from when you left the club. What happened once you handed the keys to your friend."

"He's not actually my friend. In fact, I think the only reason I was invited was because I don't drink. I'm allergic to alcohol."

Ms. Welles sighed and reminded herself to be patient. "Mr. Par ... Sorry, Travis. I need you to focus. After you handed the keys to your friend, where did you go?"

"I just walked around."

"Travis, I don't think you understand your situation. You need to tell me exactly where you went and when you went there."

After a few moments he said, "I only wanted to see what her house looked like. She was so beautiful, I just knew that her house had to be incredible, too."

"How far was it to her house from the club?"

"Only a few blocks. I was walking there when I saw her drive by on her way home."

"How did you find out where she lived? How did you know what she drove?"

Travis looked like he was going to respond, then hesitated. After a moment he said, "I probably shouldn't tell; I'll just end up in more trouble."

"You've been arrested for murder. How much more trouble can you possibly get into? Besides, I'm your attorney and anything you tell me remains confidential."

Travis thought about this for a moment before quietly saying, "I waited until all of the girls were out on the floor, then I snuck back to the dressing room. It didn't take long to find her purse. I just checked her driver's license and proof of insurance. I almost got caught, too. One of the bouncers was walking by just as I was coming back out. I thought he saw me, but he apparently wasn't paying attention."

"Alright, so you were walking to her house after the club closed. Did you pass anyone? Did anyone see you?"

Travis thought about this before shaking his head. "There was some kid on a bike. I saw him a couple of times while I was walking, but I kept my face hidden. A few cars went by, but I doubt any of them would have paid any attention to me, let alone be able to identify me."

Ms. Welles perked up at the idea that there was a person on a bicycle. "What kind of bike was it? Could you identify it? Did you see his face?"

"No, I was trying not to be noticed. I think the bike was one of those mountain bikes. Not a ten speed though. You know, the kind they take through trails and stuff."

"What color was it?"

"I don't know. The street lights aren't great for figuring out what color something is. Besides, I only saw the guy a couple of times. Once right after I left the parking lot of the club and once a few minutes later. After that, I didn't see him anymore. Both times I saw him was way before Jessica passed me on her way home."

"How about clothing? Hair color or style? Think … can you tell me anything more about this person?"

"Sweat pants, tennis shoes and a hooded sweat jacket. All dark colored. The hood was up so I didn't see his face or hair."

"Alright, at least we know that someone else was out that night."

Ms. Welles was writing notes for a few more seconds before she finally asked, "Once you got to her house, what did you do then?"

"I stood outside and took in the property for a minute or two. I could see her moving around inside behind the curtains. When she left the living room and I could no longer see movement, I decided to leave. I wanted to go see how Butch got out of his house while it was on fire. That must have been quite a feat, you know. With his injuries, he's lucky he didn't get stuck in there and die."

"So you were in front of Ms. Halsey's house for only a minute or two before leaving the scene?"

"Right."

"And you never actually went onto the property? You didn't go near her car or the house?"

"Right."

"What time did you arrive at Detective Cassidy's house?"

"I don't know. I don't wear a watch and the battery on my phone was low. I didn't check it for the time, anyway. In fact, I have no idea what time I did anything that night. I only know that my alarm clock said it was just before six in the morning when I arrived back at the dorm."

When Ms. Welles finished writing down her notes she asked, "Do you know what a psychiatric evaluation is?"

Travis instantly became defensive. "I don't need one of those. I'm not nuts."

"Regardless, you're going to have a full evaluation done. I already spoke with Dr. Poole, and she agreed to do the assessment. Once I get those results, I'll sit down with you and explain the strategy that we're going to employ for your upcoming trial."

"Really? Dr. Poole agreed to do my evaluation? She's incredible!"

"Yes, I've been following this in the news for the last month. She's quite good considering how young she is. So you'll have no problem with her administering the evaluation then?"

"Are you kidding? With her doing the evaluation, I'm set. She'll know that I'm innocent. Since she was right about Connelly, the courts will have to let me go once she tells them that I couldn't have done this."

"One thing at a time. Just prepare yourself. This will most likely go to trial, and it could be a long, drawn-out process."

Travis adopted a more serious expression and nodded solemnly.

"Alright, try to relax. I'm going to make sure you don't get convicted of this. If you can remember anything more about the kid you saw on the bike, get ahold of me."

Again, Travis nodded.

"I'll see you soon, and try not to worry."

"Okay."

*****

At the forensic lab Robin and her team were in full swing. "Alright, guys, we've had these envelopes for over an hour now. Do we have anything at all?"

Arthur was the first to speak. "Same as before. We have some prints but ruled them out as being post office employees. The postage revealed nothing. When I managed to get the stamps off, there were no prints on them at all. He must have used tweezers or something similar when he handled the stamps. The stencil used is identical to what was printed on the envelopes we got from that kid's dorm."

Robin asked, "And the envelope itself? Is that the same as what the kid had in his room?"

"Same brand and type."

Robin barked out, "Darryl?"

The picture of the note was displayed on the large monitor. "I got nothing off this note. No prints, no fibers, no hair. It was like it was created in a vacuum. Nothing remarkable about the ink or the paper. Both can be bought from any office supply store."

Robin looked up at the image of the note again.

> *Four dead, and still King Midas lives. If you want me to go away, King Midas must die. Are you feeling the strain yet, Midas? Is the pressure getting to you? How long can you survive like this? How much can you lose before you give up and just end it all?*

Robin shook her head as she read the lines on the note for the hundredth time. "I really hope that the guy they arrested is the sick son of a bitch who sent this. I feel bad for Cassidy. He really has lost a lot."

Arthur looked up from the envelope he was studying and asked, "Where are Cassidy and Kidd, anyway? I expected at least one of them to be here."

Robin shrugged. "I don't know. I just told them that if we found anything new, I'd let them know. Come on, minions, give me the rundown."

"So far, we have nothing new. All of the envelopes from that kid's dorm are clean. We don't have his prints on anything. Not even on the Ziploc bags. His printer is almost new and matches what was printed on the notes to a degree of ninety-eight percent. We can't say for certain that this is the printer nor can we rule out this printer. We have the laptop, and there's nothing on the hard drive that indicates it was used to create the messages. Again, that doesn't mean anything because once the document was created and printed, it could have been deleted. Even the auto save function on the word processing program was turned off. The FBI will be picking it up sometime today. Maybe their techs can find some evidence that we couldn't. They have much more experience with computers and hard drives than we do. Essentially, we don't have anything tangible to give to the ADA stating that this kid actually did any of this."

Robin was still staring at the note on the monitor. "Alright, but we also don't have anything tangible to give the ADA stating that this kid didn't do any of this, either. We can't rule him out. I'll make the call to Harrison."

*****

"Harrison, you can't be serious."

"Look Kidd, I'm just saying that there is no physical evidence. We're still feeling the fallout from the last screw up. If we botch this one, the people in this city might serve up our heads on a platter."

Cassidy was pacing back and forth as he spoke. "Parker has stalked me for at least two years. He has a bunch of envelopes already addressed. He had direct contact with the last victim on the night that she was murdered. His whereabouts can't be confirmed at the time of the murder. This is as close as we can get to saying he's guilty without a confession."

Harrison shook his head. "It's circumstantial. All of it. Welles will shred it all in front of a jury. Yes, he looks good for this. Yes, he's mentally unbalanced. Yes, because of the stalking, I think he's capable of killing. Hell, he even has the education to be able to do all of this without leaving evidence. If it were any other case at any other time, I'd be all over this. But after Connelly, after the riots and after looking like incompetent asses in the eyes of this city … I just want to proceed with caution here. We can't afford to go all in on this and have another body show up next week."

"So what the hell? Are we supposed to just let him go?"

Harrison sat silently for a few moments before shaking his head. "No, we proceed with the prosecution for the murder of Jessica Halsey. Only for the murder of Halsey though. That's the only victim that we have definite evidence of his involvement with. The only way that I can see us tying any of the other murders to Parker is if we find whatever the hell he used to cut off those toes."

Kidd quietly said, "Doc Brown believes it's a cigar cutter."

Harrison quickly retorted, "And nobody's found one of those yet, which seriously hurts our case."

Cassidy said, "For all we know he might have just tossed it down a gutter after he left the scene."

Both Harrison and Kidd looked dubious. Finally, Harrison went on, "If he carried a cigar cutter with him while he committed all four murders, why would he toss the cutter immediately after this one?"

Cassidy grew agitated. "Look, you're supposed to be on our side here. Why are you coming up with all kinds of ways to say this asshole didn't do it?"

"I'm trying to cover your ass as well as mine! Welles isn't some public defender here. She's one of the best. Everything I'm saying here is only a preview of what she'd bring up to a jury. We totally dropped the ball on this shit once. There isn't going to be a single member of that jury that doesn't already know it, too. We need this to be airtight. You want me to be happy about pushing forward with this? Find me that damn cigar cutter."

Cassidy stormed out of Harrison's office without a word. Kidd looked over at Harrison for a moment before slowly standing and turning to leave with a sigh.

"Kidd, rein him in. He's going to snap and, when he does, he's going to hurt any chance we have at putting away this killer."

Kidd nodded and trudged out of the office. He found Cassidy leaning against the passenger door of their unmarked car.

"Cassidy, you have to be able to see things from his perspective. I know you're not an idiot."

"I just want it over."

"I know. We have people ripping Parker's life apart. They're even executing a search warrant on the place he stayed for the summer. Without the device that was used to cut off those toes, there's always going to be someone who says we have the wrong guy."

"I have a headache."

Kidd unlocked the car and replied as they both climbed in, "Me, too, partner. Me, too."

*****

That evening the news broadcast featured a recap of all four murders that had been attributed to the killer known as the Denver City Specter. They also covered the five copycat murders and the people still awaiting trial for committing those crimes.

After broadcasting images of the riot that broke out in front of the courthouse, they cut back to the perky brunette in the studio.

"So after all that's happened over the last five weeks, the question on everyone's mind is still this: have Detective Cassidy and the Denver police force finally caught the Specter? Or are we going to see another murder and receive another toe in the mail? Given their performance over the last month, we all hold our breath and hope that King Midas hasn't made yet another terrible mistake."

CHAPTER 20

---·---

Tuesday, September 1

"We've been housing him in a facility outside the city. We didn't want anyone to know where he was being held. He should be arriving shortly."

Dr. Poole responded, "I can see the reason for keeping his location secret. I'm sure there are people in this city that would like nothing more than to see him dead. Where will we be for the assessment?"

The uniformed officer motioned down the hall. "We have a room set up for you down here."

As they began walking that way, Dr. Poole asked, "He won't be chained up, will he? It's very difficult to read the body language of a man while he's restrained."

"No, we blocked off a cell in solitary. He'll be inside the cell while you'll be in the aisle just outside the bars. But he won't be cuffed or shackled. I don't need to remind you to stay well back from the bars for your own safety, do I?"

Dr. Poole's expression changed to one of disappointment. "Why would you feel the need to insult my intelligence like that?"

The officer paused for a moment then said, "No, I wasn't trying to … "

Dr. Poole cut him off. "Think for a second about what you just asked. 'I don't need to remind you, do I?' That question alone is a reminder. Statements like that might be overlooked by some, but you were obviously thinking, 'Here's a small, weak girl who's going to be confronting a potentially dangerous criminal. I need to treat her like she's an idiot to reinforce the possibility that a careless act might get her hurt.'"

"Really, Dr. Poole. I meant no disrespect by what I … "

She cut him off again. "You absolutely did mean disrespect and most likely just because I'm a woman. Many factors during your life have contributed to your becoming a male chauvinist pig, so I don't necessarily blame you directly for believing that just because I'm a woman, I must not have the sense to know a dangerous situation. I do, however, blame you for opening your mouth and proving it beyond any doubt."

As she glared at him, the officer appeared angry at first, then his expression softened and he lowered his head. "Dr. Poole, I apologize for implying that you might be naïve enough to allow yourself to get within reach of Parker while he's in his cell."

She smiled and said, "Thank you for your apology. In the future, please remember that women are people too. Now, since I see a table and chair set up here, I believe this is where I'll be during our evaluation. There are no cameras or listening devices in this part of the jail, are there?"

"The cameras will be turned off, and there are no listening devices."

"And there will be no guards that can hear anything he may say during this evaluation, correct?"

"That's correct. There's a panic button on your table. If things go beyond your control or you feel threatened, just press that button and guards will pour in here in an instant."

"Thank you. How long before he arrives?"

"I'll find out for you." He keyed the microphone that was strapped to his shoulder and asked, "Where's the prisoner right now?"

Over the radio on his belt they both heard, "Already in the building. He'll be in his cell in a few minutes."

"Again, thank you for showing me to my seat. I'll stand over there while you get him into his cell so that my female naïveté won't put me in harm's way."

The officer bit his lip but remained silent. Within five minutes Parker was in the cell and free from the handcuffs and shackles. The officers all left the area and nothing remained but silence.

Dr. Poole casually took her seat and opened her briefcase. As she removed several papers and writing utensils, she spoke. "Mr. Parker, I'm aware of your courses of study during your time at Denver University, so I'm quite certain you know exactly why we're here. Unfortunately, for legal reasons, I need to ask. Do you understand the purpose of the evaluation that you're about to undergo?"

Travis sat down on the chair that had been provided for him and nodded. "I understand, and may I say that you look absolutely incredible today."

"Thank you. Now please set aside your hormones. This is serious business, and how you respond to these questions can play a large role in how your case is defended."

Travis said, "Yes, ma'am."

Dr. Poole slowly looked up from the papers she was arranging on her table and said, "Please call me Dr. Poole or Doctor. Don't call me ma'am. I'm not old enough to have earned that insult yet."

"Sorry."

"Let's get started."

*****

Once the evaluation was finished, she thanked him for his time and gathered her documents. After stowing them back in her briefcase, she wished him luck and left the area. Cassidy and Kidd were waiting for her in the hallway outside.

"Hi, guys. What warrants this visit? Are you here to escort me back to my car?"

Cassidy asked, "So tell me, what do you think? Do we finally have our guy?"

Dr. Poole gently placed a hand on his arm. "You know I can't tell you anything right now. I have to go type this up, make it all official and submit it to the defense attorney. She'll present it to the prosecutor and the courts. Then they'll determine what to do with the information. I'm sorry, Mike."

Cassidy nodded and said, "Yeah, I know. I was just hoping you could give us some kind of indication on whether or not we screwed the pooch again."

Dr. Poole smiled softly and said, "Again, I'm sorry. I have to follow procedure. I'm sure that Harrison will have my assessment by tomorrow afternoon. He'll probably be willing to share the results with you. Until then, relax, detective."

The three of them began walking down the hallway as they continued talking.

Kidd asked, "Since our last meal was interrupted, I don't suppose you might be available for dinner this evening?"

Dr. Poole responded, "I might be. That depends on the food being served and where it'll be."

Kidd said, "My place. Seven o'clock. Grilled steaks, baked potatoes, corn on the cob and garden salad."

"I haven't had steak in a long time. That sounds wonderful. Thank you for inviting me. Should I bring anything?"

"Rebecca and I have everything covered."

She turned toward Cassidy as they walked. "Does this mean that you'll be joining us, too?"

"I've been invited, but if either you or Rebecca would rather I didn't come, I would definitely understand."

"I can't speak for Rebecca, but I'd love it if you'd be there. I see you got the sling removed. How's your arm doing?"

"Still a bit sore and movement's somewhat restricted, but it's healing well."

As they turned a corner in the hallway, they heard a commotion. Reporters and cameramen lined the walls. They watched as a door opened at the other end of the hallway and two uniformed officers came through. Behind them were two more uniformed officers on either side of Travis Parker, who wore a bulletproof vest over his prison jumpsuit. Behind those three, one last officer followed.

The hallway erupted with noise the instant they saw Parker. Reporters edged closer, holding out microphones and asking for comments or statements. Some were firing questions at Travis. The police appeared annoyed but continued down the hall without making any fuss. The entire time they were walking and dodging reporters, Travis Parker was staring at Michael Cassidy. He had a look on his face that looked a whole lot like the one a kid gets when seeing his favorite sports hero in person.

As the officers who were escorting Parker neared the spot where Cassidy, Kidd and Poole were standing, Parker began talking. "Butch and Sundance! I'm thrilled that you came to see me off. Butch, I am so terribly sorry about your wife. She was such a beautiful woman … "

Cassidy clenched his fists and his face began to flush. At the same time, the officers that were escorting Parker warned him to be quiet, but he continued.

"You were such a lucky man."

Cassidy said, "Shut the hell up, asshole."

Parker ignored him and went on talking as they got closer. "I wish I could have been the one sleeping next to that gorgeous woman for all of those years."

Cassidy yelled, "I said shut the hell up!"

Parker went on as though he never even heard Cassidy. "I bet she was incredible in bed. With that body, she'd have to … "

Cassidy bolted forward, shoved one of the front two officers aside and connected a solid right cross to Travis's jaw, stopping him in mid-sentence. As Parker was crumbling to the ground, Cassidy grabbed the bulletproof vest with his left hand and unleashed four more jackhammer blows with his right.

Kidd hollered at Cassidy, but the resulting pandemonium made it impossible for anyone to hear him. The reporters all began yelling at their cameramen to make sure they were getting the footage. The officers charged with escorting Parker back to the transport began trying to pull Cassidy off Parker. Blood was flying in thick drops with every punch to Parker's face.

Cassidy landed two more solid shots and a third glancing blow as the officers finally dragged him away from the prisoner. Parker was barely moving and appeared to be nearly unconscious as the officer bringing up the rear grabbed him under the arms and dragged him back down the hallway toward the door they'd just entered.

Cassidy was shouting obscenities and still trying to break free from the three officers restraining him as Parker's limp body was hauled through the door and out of sight. Dr. Poole looked over at Detective Kidd just in time to see him lower his head and put his hand up to his forehead. Because of the noise and chaos in the hallway, she couldn't hear him; but she could read his lips as he muttered, "Cassidy, you dumb son of a bitch."

*****

Bordeaux was so angry his face was nearly purple. He looked like he could drop from a stroke at any moment. "You're done!

You'll be lucky if that bastard doesn't have you locked up for the next three months. Forget about being a cop anywhere anymore. You just blasted your career straight to hell!"

Cassidy was wearing handcuffs behind his back as he stood listening to his captain. "That rotten prick deserved every punch. He's lucky I didn't shoot his stupid ass."

"Shut the hell up, Cassidy! Your temper finally did you in. Lock him up!"

The two officers, one on either side of Cassidy, took hold of his elbows. Ironically, they were two of the many officers who had volunteered their time to pull guard duty in the hospital while he was recovering from his wounds.

"Come on, Cassidy. Let's go." One of the officers quietly said as they turned him to walk him out of the captain's office.

"What the hell was I supposed to do? Just let him run his mouth about my dead wife?"

As he was being led out through the bullpen, Bordeaux yelled after him. "You're damn right you should have! The only thing you had left was your job, and now that's over, you hotheaded son of a bitch!"

Kidd watched as Cassidy was taken back to the very same holding cell he had occupied only days before. "Captain, I know he screwed up bad. But remember what he's gone through this last month. Would you have acted any differently?"

Bordeaux was huffing and puffing with rage and stress. "Yes, I would have acted differently! If that little bastard was running his mouth about my dead wife like that, I would have shot that prick in the head!" He then dropped heavily into his chair and tried hard to control his breathing and blood pressure.

Kidd remained silent and looked over at Harrison who had said nothing since Cassidy had been brought into the office.

"Don't look at me. What the hell am I supposed to do? He beat the shit out of Parker in front of every news camera in the city. He's screwed."

Bordeaux was still breathing heavily as he used the remote to turn on the monitor hanging on the wall beside his desk. After finding one of the several stations dedicated to national news, he turned up the volume. As expected, they were talking about Cassidy.

"What I don't understand is, how could a man in that mental state have been released to return to active duty?" A man in his mid to late fifties wearing a suit and tie was sitting next to another man who was dressed almost identically. Next to him was a woman sporting thick-rimmed glasses and wearing a dark red dress.

The woman responded, "That is exactly my point. Obviously the standards that govern the mental state of our police detectives is in need of a complete overhaul."

When the third man chimed in, it became obvious that his role was to play devil's advocate. "Those psychological tests have been in place for decades. For the most part they have proven to be quite effective. Now, because of one incident, you want to call for sweeping changes in the standards that are used to test our police?"

The first man replied. "Do we need to show the clip again? Did you miss the brutality and severity of this attack the first few times you saw it? Roll the clip again."

As he continued speaking, the image on the monitor was replaced with the scene from the hallway where the attack occurred. The clip began the instant Cassidy shoved the officer aside and swung his first punch. It played through the entire attack in slow motion. What the clip omitted was Parker's comments about Cassidy's wife.

"Cassidy launched himself at Mr. Parker, knocking an officer off his feet. He went through one of his own men to get to him. The response by the escorting officers was prompt, and I applaud them for it. Had they hesitated at all, it's quite possible that Mr. Parker could have suffered permanent injury or even brain damage. As it stands now, he'll probably be hospitalized for days. Now get ready to pause it … there."

The image froze on Cassidy's face as two uniformed officers were lifting him off of Parker. The expression captured on his face was one of pure rage.

"Do you see anything on that face to indicate he was remotely in his right mind at that moment?"

The gentleman charged with playing devil's advocate for this little exchange jumped in. "Let us not forget that this detective has just lost his wife, his house, and his car, that he has been critically injured by gunfire, and that half the city of Denver wants him dead."

The woman on the panel cut him off. "Which is exactly why I'm questioning the evaluation that led to him being cleared for active duty. He's obviously completely out of control. How can you justify allowing a man in this condition to carry a weapon and a badge?"

Bordeaux grunted and hit the remote, shutting off the monitor. "We're being crucified on national television. Never mind that the man Cassidy pummeled was being accused of slashing a woman to death in her own shower."

Harrison said, "The politicians are calling for his head. Basically, it's battery. He'll probably have to spend ninety days in jail. I'm more worried about the public perception toward Parker. We only have a circumstantial case to begin with. He's being defended by a pit bull of an attorney and now, with this, the public might actually feel sympathy for a murderer. Imagine trying to put together a jury with that sentiment sweeping the city."

Bordeaux finally said what they were all thinking. "How damned certain are we that this Parker kid actually killed that woman?"

Both Harrison and Kidd looked at him, but neither responded. Bordeaux muttered, "Exactly what I thought."

*****

Dr. Poole entered through the employee entrance and went straight to the lobby. Rebecca was just finishing with a client that had come out of a session with one of the therapists. "So we'll see you next Thursday at one o'clock then."

"Yes, I'll see you then."

Dr. Poole glanced at the seats in the lobby and found them all empty. As soon as the client made it out the front door, she approached Rebecca.

"Hi, Dr. Poole. How'd the evaluation go?"

"The evaluation went fine. Cassidy was the problem."

"I don't understand. What do you mean?"

"Cassidy attacked Parker in front of news cameras and officers. In front of the whole nation, in fact."

"He what?"

"When are your next appointments due to come in?"

Rebecca checked the clock and replied, "Not until this afternoon. It's the midday break."

"Follow me."

They both went up to her office and closed the door. She logged onto the computer and keyed in a quick search. She then turned up the sound and motioned for Rebecca to move so she could see the monitor.

They both sat silently as they watched the news footage of Cassidy's violent and bloody attack on Parker.

Rebecca finally asked, "Why would he do that?"

"Travis was making comments about Kathy. How she was gorgeous and had a great body. About how he wished he could have been the one sleeping with her. Cassidy lost it and, well … you see the results."

"Oh, my. Where's Cassidy now?"

"Sitting behind bars somewhere, I would imagine. It's nationwide news. It's not like the police can downplay it. He'll probably be arrested and convicted and spend quite a bit of time in jail. I don't think he'll ever be a cop again, either."

Rebecca stood there silently for a few moments then finally said, "He's an ass, and I was pissed at him; but he probably didn't deserve all of this. I guess that means the dinner tonight isn't going to happen."

Stacey raised her eyebrows. "You just watched Cassidy beat Parker into unconsciousness, and you're concerned about our get-together tonight?"

Rebecca looked her in the eyes and retorted, "Well? Like I said. He is an ass."

Stacey began to giggle which caused Rebecca to start laughing. After a few seconds Stacey exclaimed, "Oh, I have an idea!"

She picked up her phone and punched a button. "Hey, is your appointment over? Come to my office. I have something you need to see."

As Stacey hung up the phone, Rebecca accused, "You're terrible!"

They both started laughing again. A few minutes later Quinn knocked on the door.

"Come in, it's open."

"Wow, both of you are here. Should I get comfortable on the couch for this? When does the seductive music begin? Just how much is each of you actually going to show me?"

Stacey said, "I'm going to show you something that you've wanted to see for a very long time." As she spoke, she slowly moved her hand to the top button of her blouse.

Quinn grinned broadly and encouraged her with, "Alright!"

Rebecca commanded, "Quit teasing him! There are times I'm not sure you act any more mature than he does. Come here, Quinn; check this out."

They replayed the clip for him on the computer screen and watched his face the whole time. His expression went from surprise to satisfaction to complete elation in a matter of thirty seconds.

Quinn stood there for a few moments after the clip ended, saying nothing.

"Well? Did that brighten your day at all?"

Quinn nodded and started to laugh. "You know, all of this shit going on with the Specter, and all it took to bring down Cassidy was a college kid with a few comments. How ironic is that?"

Rebecca asked, "How is that ironic?"

"This Specter has gone around killing people and setting up others to take the blame for a month now. That's an awful lot of work just to have a college kid run his mouth for a few seconds in front of TV cameras and accomplish the same end. Cassidy is done now. There's no way they'll ever let him wear a badge again." The absolute satisfaction on his face made him look just slightly creepy at that moment.

Rebecca looked at Stacey then back to Quinn. "You sound like you don't think Parker is the Specter."

"Nah, Kathy told me about him months ago. He's just some nut job who had a man crush on Cassidy. It's been going on several years. That kid might have eventually turned into someone who could have killed, but he wasn't even bright enough to be able to stalk without getting caught. He certainly doesn't have the brains to get away with killing four people."

Rebecca looked back at Stacey. "Is this what you came up with during your evaluation?"

Stacey nodded. "He has some mental issues, but Quinn's right. He adored Cassidy. He still adores Cassidy, or did up until this morning. I don't believe he's the killer. He didn't want Cassidy dead. He only wanted his attention and approval."

Rebecca asked, "So if they have the wrong guy again, who really is doing all of this?"

Stacey looked directly at Quinn. After seeing the expression on his face after he watched the video of the attack, she decided this was a good time. "Quinn could be."

Quinn laughed and said, "Well, I definitely had the motive."

Stacey nodded, "Let's not forget the intelligence to have planned all of this. Oh, you had plenty of time, too."

Quinn's laugh faded. "Wait. Are you seriously accusing me of being the Specter?"

Rebecca's jaw was hanging open as she looked back and forth between them.

Stacey shrugged and said, "If Parker isn't the killer, someone is. Was it you, Quinn?"

"Did you forget that I was cleared as having an alibi for one of the murders?"

"Nope, but it was just some blonde you'd been sleeping with. Let's face it, she's not a stellar witness and definitely not one who is beyond coercion."

Quinn's smile vanished. "Yes, I was in love with his wife. Yes, I hated him. I will freely admit that I'd fantasized about his death and the fact that Kathy would then be free to pursue a relationship with me. But a leap to serial killer? There's a lot of ground to cover before reaching that conclusion."

"Maybe not quite as much ground as one might think."

Quinn's smile returned as he made an effort to pass this off as some sort of joke. "If you truly believe I could be the Specter, you're awfully brave to accuse me to my face. Aren't you afraid I'll kill the two of you in an attempt to silence you?"

"No, because in spite of your juvenile behavior, I know how intelligent you actually are. You'd never be dumb enough to attack us in this office."

Quinn's smile was forced, but it remained in place. "You have a hell of a sense of humor, Stacey. I'll give you that much."

Stacey smiled again. "Just thought I'd ask. Glad you got a kick out of Cassidy losing it in front of all those cameras though."

"That did make my day." He now relaxed and returned to his normal glib nature. "I'm off to lunch. Do either of you want me to bring anything back for you?"

Stacy shook her head. "No, thanks. I'm good. Rebecca?"

Rebecca was still standing there with her mouth open. She simply shook her head.

"Okay. Stacey, remember that 'maybe' you mentioned the other day? Should it turn into a yes, I can guarantee that you wouldn't be disappointed."

Stacey's smile broadened as she responded, "I'm sure I wouldn't."

After he left the office, Rebecca said, "You don't seriously think Quinn is the Specter." It was more a statement than a question.

Stacey shrugged and said, "I'm still not positive. I wanted to see his body language as he reacted though."

"You suspected him already, didn't you?"

Stacey nodded. "Think about it. The police had already cleared Cassidy's arrests as not having anything to do with these murders. Who else do we know that has such hatred for the man?"

Rebecca thought about that for a bit before retorting, "But it's Quinn! He has the maturity level of a fourteen year old. He's more interested in getting lucky with some busty bimbo than he is in getting revenge on Cassidy."

"Don't be so certain about that. He's incredibly intelligent and, while he doesn't show it here, he has some very deep wounds because of his affair with Kathy."

"Great! Now I'm not going to be able to look at him without wondering if he's a stone-cold killer." She gasped and grabbed Stacey's arm. "Are you certain he won't come after us to keep us silent?"

Stacey gently pulled Rebecca's hand off her arm. "Quinn knows you're dating Jeremy; he knows you'll tell Jeremy about this conversation. I told you, Quinn is very intelligent. Nothing will happen to us. Besides, he's probably not the killer anyway."

Rebecca looked doubtful, then her expression changed and she began to laugh. "You just did this to mess with me, didn't you? You probably had this set up with Quinn in advance, right?"

Stacey laughed and said, "Go get lunch. Clients are going to start showing up for the afternoon sessions."

Rebecca looked at her suspiciously. "That was all a joke, right?"

"Go grab something to eat, Rebecca."

Rebecca looked uneasy as she left the office. She looked back once, but Stacey was already pulling the papers she needed from her briefcase so she could type up the official evaluation on Parker.

*****

As Jeremy flipped one of the steaks, he tossed over his shoulder, "Just because that moron screwed up what was left of his life this morning doesn't mean we can't still enjoy the evening."

"It sounds like your attitude toward Cassidy has changed since we first met."

Jeremy checked the coals in the grill and moved one of the other steaks to a spot that wasn't quite so hot. There was a lengthy pause as he thought about what Stacey had just said. He finally turned to look at the ladies and nodded. "Yeah, I suppose I see him differently now. When we first partnered up, I was new to homicide. Cassidy took me under his wing, and I learned a lot from him. I looked at him like he was a mentor—someone that I hoped I could emulate. Sure, he was always hotheaded and had a hard time controlling his temper. He was brash and opinionated and absolutely unable to keep his mouth shut when he needed to the most. But when it came to working a case, he was damn good. He taught me how to look at evidence and, from that alone, form a theory as to how a crime was committed. Even a few weeks ago when his world began crashing down around him, I found myself admiring his fortitude. I kept questioning whether or not I would have been able to hold it together if our roles had been reversed. I seriously doubt that I could have handled what he'd been going through with anywhere near the amount of strength he had shown to that point."

Rebecca sipped her wine then pointed out, "Some of what he'd gone through was his own doing. Punching you in the face was when I began to have a problem with him. I didn't say anything before, just because he was your partner and you still had faith in him even after he did that to you."

"It wasn't like he was trying to hurt me; he just wanted me to move so he could leave. I understood that. Hell, it was unbearable to know that police officers were dealing with a riot in the streets while we sat in that lab waiting to find out if there was anything in the evidence that pointed to a specific person. The fact that the riot was, to a great extent, our fault … that was torture. I wanted to rush over to the courthouse to help too."

Stacey said, "But you used your intelligence instead of your emotions. That's the difference between you and Mike. Instead of reacting out of passion, you think."

"In his defense, I wish I had some of his passion sometimes."

Rebecca smiled and rejoined, "I have no issue with your level of passion."

Jeremy actually began to blush as he turned his attention back to the grill.

To break the awkward moment, Rebecca quickly remarked, "Oh, you should have been at the office this afternoon. Stacey accused Quinn of being the Specter. You should have seen it."

Jeremy spun around and questioned, "So you don't think we have the right guy?"

Rebecca stopped and looked at Stacey. "I'm sorry, I probably shouldn't have said anything."

Stacey shook her head. "It's alright. It's not like it's a secret or anything. Once I submit the report tomorrow, everyone will know anyway. No, Jeremy, I don't think Parker killed that Halsey woman. He has an obsessive-compulsive disorder and is focused like a laser on you and Cassidy. Mostly on Cassidy, I suppose. But when I tested him, and believe me when I tell you that I tested him thoroughly, I saw absolutely no signs that led me to believe he was a sociopath or a psychopath. I do believe that, with the right triggers, he could possibly reach the point where he'd kill. However, those triggers haven't happened as of yet. Right now, he's just a guy who looks at Cassidy like he's some kind of superhero. Most likely from the publicity he's received from the media. No, what I initially told you after we left his dorm room that first time I met him still stands. I don't think he'd kill people, cut off their toes and mail them to the police and media, then call for Cassidy's death."

Jeremy turned and stared at the grill for several seconds before quietly saying, "I was afraid of that. To be honest, I wasn't so sure about him either. I mean, I was when I found out about the envelopes. But after I thought about it, I kind of reached the same conclusion. He was obsessed with Mike; why would he want him dead? My problem is this though. If he isn't the Specter, how did the killer know about him? Then, if I disregard that and accept that the killer knew about him, how did the killer happen to pick that victim at that time?"

Stacey said, "If we assume that Parker isn't the killer, the only logical answer to those questions is that the killer is someone close to the case. Close enough to know that Parker had been questioned that day. Then the killer would have had to follow Parker that evening."

Jeremy thought about that for more than a minute. "The only people that knew we were going to interview him were either in the department or in your office."

Rebecca quietly replied, "Quinn knew."

Jeremy turned back around and looked at both of them again. "You accused Quinn. How did he respond?"

Stacey thought a moment before offering, "He reminded me that he had an alibi for one of the murders. When I told him that his alibi was someone he was sleeping with and that she wasn't beyond coercion, he admitted he hated Cassidy. He then said that a leap from hating Cassidy to becoming a serial killer was too big to make."

Jeremy nodded and confirmed, "He's right about that. Without some kind of evidence that points toward him, that's a hell of a leap to make."

Rebecca stated flatly, "The Specter hasn't left any evidence."

Jeremy asked, "Do either of you happen to know his license number?"

Stacey rattled off the number from his license plate and both Rebecca and Jeremy stared at her. She finally said, "Most of the time my memory is a blessing. Sometimes it's a curse."

Jeremy pulled his cell phone from his pocket and punched a few buttons then held the phone to his ear. "Yes, this is Detective Jeremy Kidd. Who do you have on duty assigned to tech for the Specter case? Can you patch me through to her, please?"

While he waited he grabbed one of the napkins and handed it to Stacey. "Please write down the license plate number as well as the make and model of his car."

Just as she handed the napkin back to him, he spoke into the phone again. "Hey, Tina, this is Detective Jeremy Kidd ... yeah, I know we have someone in custody for the Specter case. I need you to check something for me. Can you pull up the satellite navigation for a vehicle if I give you the make, model and license number? Hold on, I'll ask."

He lowered the phone slightly and asked, "She wants to know if he has a built-in navigation unit or if it's a plug-in type."

Rebecca shrugged and looked at Stacey.

"How the hell am I supposed to know? I've never been in his car."

"Tina, we have no idea. Alright, here's the info." After he gave her the car's information, he waited for nearly a minute.

"You can? Can you check for the night that Jessica Halsey was murdered? Was his car anywhere near the college or the crime scene that night? It wasn't. What about his cell phone? Do me a favor, and call me back as soon as you find out. Thank you. Oh, and don't tell anyone that I asked about this, okay? Yeah, I know you have to log the request, just don't tell anyone that I asked. I don't need a leak to get to the media. No, I'm not saying there's a leak in the FBI. I just don't ... never mind. Just don't say anything." With that said, he hung up.

Jeremy looked directly at Stacey. "You must have had some suspicion about him to have accused him. Do you think he could be behind this?"

Stacey thought hard for a few moments before shrugging. "To be honest, I don't know. He's a well-trained psychologist. He knows how to hide tells and signs just as he knows how to look for them. The only reason I thought it might be him is because Cassidy found out about the affair not long before the first murder was committed. He loved Kathy, and I know that he hated Mike after she refused to divorce him. Beyond that, there's really nothing else that raises suspicion."

After a few minutes of silence, Rebecca finally asked, "Isn't Mike in jail? Won't the killer stop while he's behind bars? Kind of like when he was in the hospital, right?"

Both of them looked at Stacey for an answer. "Just because I'm good at my job doesn't mean I'm inside the killer's head. I suppose, based on the last time Cassidy was out of action, the killer might wait until he's released. It's only a guess though. Keep in mind that this time there's a man behind bars accused of being the Specter. He might kill again just to show the police and media that they have the wrong guy. But that's all based on me being correct about Parker's innocence."

Jeremy pulled the steaks off the grill and dropped them onto a platter. After unwrapping the corn from the aluminum foil and setting out the potatoes and salad, they all began dishing up their food.

Once everyone was settled and preparing to eat, Jeremy said, "Mike will probably be released in a couple of days pending sentencing. I guess we'll just have to wait and see what happens."

Rebecca asked, "Can't you have someone keep an eye on Quinn?"

"You mean follow him? We don't have those kinds of resources. That's stuff you see in the movies. Besides, even if we had the manpower to dedicate to around-the-clock surveillance, we already have someone in custody for at least one of the murders. It's not like Bordeaux would sign off on something like that."

Stacey asked, "So Parker will go to trial for this then?"

Jeremy swallowed a bite of steak and nodded. "This afternoon we had witnesses contact us stating that they talked with Parker at the crime scenes. One said that he arrived all out of breath and sweaty. They told us he said he had jumped on his bike and ridden the three miles to the scene after his scanner picked up the report of the murder. Harrison isn't convinced he's guilty, but the circumstantial evidence is strong enough to force him to proceed with the prosecution. Not to mention the politicians breathing down his neck to bring all of this to a swift end. He really doesn't have much choice unless we can come up with someone better than Parker."

Rebecca seemed surprised. "You mean Parker was at every crime scene?"

"After the fact, yes. He'd catch the call on his scanner then show up to watch. Every murder except for Halsey's, that is. He was supposedly asleep when the call went out for that one."

Stacey said, "That just reinforces what I said earlier about his obsession with Cassidy. He'd show up just to watch you guys work a case."

"Right, but in the eyes of the legal system, that's incriminating behavior."

Jeremy's phone interrupted him. He hit a button and held it to his ear. "Yeah? Really? And we have no idea who it belongs to? Why wasn't this looked into the first time it came up? No shit? Alright, have your guys check. If we do it, it'll look like we're still investigating other leads. Great, thanks!"

As he put his phone away, he explained, "Remember the list that caused you to be brought in to answer questions about why your phone was in the cell tower coverage? Well, there was a prepaid phone that was also on that list. We thought since the FBI was the agency that discovered it, they'd also investigate it. After all, they have more resources than we do. But they assumed we'd look into it since they weren't taking lead on the investigation. In other words, that phone never got investigated. As it turns out, it was in the coverage of the tower that handled the Halsey residence at the time of her murder. That means it was the only phone that was in the vicinity of every murder at the time they were committed. The person holding that phone is most likely our killer."

Rebecca smiled and exclaimed, "Then you got him? As soon as they bring you his name, you'll have the killer! That's great news!"

Jeremy shook his head. "It doesn't work like that. They have to find out where the phone was purchased. Then they have to see how it was paid for. If it was cash, we're back at square one. Any video on the date the phone was bought would have probably been recorded over by now. The only way to connect a person with that phone is if it was purchased with a check or credit card. It's a long shot at best. But, if they can find that phone and link it to Parker, it'll be the definitive proof that he's the killer. If they can't find it, Harrison will say that he either hid it very well or threw it away."

Rebecca asked, "Can't they just track where it is right now?"

Since Jeremy was taking another bite of his food, Stacey answered. "Not if it's turned off or if the battery was disconnected. If this killer is as smart as his crimes indicate he is, when he's not carrying it, he'll have it shut off."

Jeremy nodded as he swallowed. "Right, but now that we know that it most likely belongs to the killer, the next time it's turned on again, we'll be able to track it."

"Is it wrong that I hope it turns out not to belong to Quinn? He's a pain in the ass and acts like a teen in heat, but I really hope it isn't him."

Stacey lowered her head slightly before saying, "I might be able to find out."

They both stared at her before Rebecca said, "No! You're not serious. Really?"

Jeremy looked back and forth between them with a puzzled look on his face. "What?"

Rebecca became agitated as she answered. "Stacey's thinking about sleeping with him so she can see if she can find that phone."

Stacey raised her hand and leaned back in her chair. "To be honest, I was considering sleeping with him anyway. Now I'd just have a valid reason."

Rebecca dropped her fork on the table. "A valid reason other than just trying to find out if he's really as good in the sack as you seem to think he might be?"

Stacey smiled and said, "Well, there is that."

Jeremy shook his head. "I can't ask you to do something like that."

"That's the beauty of this. You won't have to."

Rebecca was still shaking her head. "What is it about him? The man is a pig who'll sleep with anyone who has a heartbeat!"

"Oh, I think that's a bit of an overstatement. I'm sure they'd have to be female, too."

Jeremy had been taking a sip of wine when she said this and had to put his hand over his mouth to keep from spraying it across the table.

"I can't believe you think this is funny!"

Jeremy took a moment to compose himself and swallow the wine. "Well? It was kind of funny."

Stacey began to smile. "Rebecca, when it comes to women, the man is oozing with self-confidence. You don't get like that if you're horrible in bed. You also don't carry on a year-long affair with a married woman if you aren't doing something right."

"But it's Quinn! Imagine the talk that will go around the office."

Stacey raised her eyebrows as she swallowed another piece of her steak. "Like the talk that went around the office about his affair with Kathy?"

Rebecca said, "Nobody knew about that."

"My point exactly. He knows how to keep a secret." She then changed her tone of voice. "The big question is, can you?"

Rebecca gasped and put her hand to her chest. "Me? You think I can't keep a secret? Do I need to remind you what my job is?" She then saw the smile that was steadily getting broader on Stacey's face before calming down. "You know full well I'd never say anything."

"Yes, I do. Well, Jeremy? Since I was considering this anyway, want me to see if I can find an extra phone in his apartment or car?"

Jeremy was shaking his head. "Don't involve me in this. I'm not saying anything one way or another about what you do. All I can say is, if a concerned citizen does happen to find a cell phone somewhere, I would certainly hope they'd contact someone at the department about it."

"Jeremy! You're going along with this!"

He shrugged. "I'm just saying, if someone were to stumble upon a hidden phone somewhere, it'd be nice to know about it. Especially before Parker recovers from his injuries enough to actually go on trial."

Rebecca was about to say something when Stacey asked, "How bad are his injuries?"

"Broken nose, broken jaw and two missing teeth. The doctor thinks they'll probably have to wire his jaw shut."

There was silence for several seconds before Stacey said, "Then it's settled. I'll finally get a question answered that I've had for some time now, and should I happen upon a phone that appears to have been hidden somewhere, I'd naturally let that slip during one of our informal conversations."

Rebecca appeared disgusted.

Stacey noticed but continued, "And of course I'd let you know during girl talk just how good he actually is. Shall I rate him on orgasm intensity or frequency?"

"Oh, my God, Stacey!"

"Alright, both it is. I'll even include how long he lasts if I remember to check a clock."

"I don't want to know!"

"Why not? You had no issue sharing the details about you and Jeremy. It's only fair that I return the favor."

Jeremy exploded, "You what?"

Rebecca was shaking her head. "Stacey! Jeremy, I swear I didn't."

Jeremy looked at her accusingly before speaking. "How come? Am I not good enough? Are you ashamed of letting her know how lousy I am in bed?"

"What? No! Oh, my God! Of course not! You're amazing in bed!"

Stacey raised an eyebrow. "Oh? Do tell. Don't leave out anything. I want all the juicy details."

Rebecca looked back and forth between them before lowering her head. "Are you two done having fun at my expense now?"

Stacey shook her head as she reached for her wine glass. "Not even close!"

"Seriously. I have a pretty good sense of humor, but when it's always at my expense, it tends to get a little irritating."

Stacey sighed and promised unenthusiastically, "Fine. I'll try."

"You promise?"

"Yeah, I promise that I'll try."

"Thank you."

CHAPTER 21

Friday, September 4

"Thanks for picking me up and taking me back to my motel room. I really appreciate this."

"What'd your rep say about the charges?"

Cassidy shook his head. "He didn't sound very convincing, but he promised he'd go to bat for me."

"He's supposed to; it's his damn job. Who's your lawyer?"

"Greene. He's handled a lot of stuff for me over the years."

"He's not a criminal attorney. You really should have someone experienced with criminal cases."

"It's a simple battery case. Greene can handle it. Besides, the most time that I'll have to serve is ninety days. I'm hoping to get only thirty."

"You seem to be alright with having to sit in jail. What's gotten into you?"

"Jeremy, I had a few days to think. I tell you, I'm done. I've got no fight left in me. I'm going to take my insurance claim, my savings and my 401k and spend some time alone for a while. I need to get my head straight. What I did was completely uncalled for. That punk ass kid shouldn't have been able to get under my skin so easily."

"You're going to head off to your cabin then?"

"That's the plan. Just me, my fishing pole and the river. I need to take some time to figure out what I'm going to do next. I didn't realize it until I was faced with getting kicked off the force. That job was slowly killing me. The stress was kicking my ass, and I didn't even know it. Hell, that job was probably the reason Kathy felt the need to ... well, you know."

"Yeah, being a cop and being married don't usually go well together."

"It's more than that. I had some time to reflect on how I'd been acting. I mean, I punched you for God's sake. That should have been my wake-up call. I turned into something I don't like. I have no idea how Kathy put up with me, let alone how you did."

"It's water under the bridge, Mike."

"No, it's not. When I'm done with my sentence and get myself settled in at the cabin, I want you to come up for a long weekend. Hell, make a vacation of it and come up for two weeks. Bring Rebecca with you. I need to make it up to you. I feel horrible about how I've acted. Here I claim to be a good Catholic, and I've been treating everyone that's close to me like dirt."

"I'll talk to Rebecca about it, but that actually sounds really nice. It'll be good to get out of the city for a while. I have quite a bit of time built up, too."

"Good, it's a plan. Sentencing should be sometime in the next few weeks. The instant I get out, I'll buy myself a good four-wheel drive and go get the cabin ready for your visit. You know, I haven't been to the cabin since ... wow, I think it's been two years. I may need to have some repairs done when I get there."

"Yeah, it'll be winter by then. Best to make sure the place is up to snuff."

"Hey, tell Stacey I'm sorry, too."

"For what?"

"For everything. I treated her pretty shitty as well. She didn't deserve any of that."

"I'll pass it along." He was pulling into the parking lot of the motel as he said this.

"Thanks again for the ride."

"No problem. Do you need anything? Groceries? Clothes?"

"Nah, aside from liquidating some assets for the fines and court fees, I'm just going to relax. Besides, I'm within walking distance from three restaurants. If I need anything else, I know how to use public transportation."

"You look more relaxed right now than I think I've ever seen you. Stay in touch, and don't hesitate to give me a call if you need anything at all."

As Cassidy was climbing out of the car he said, "Thank you. I don't deserve a friend like you. Again, I'm so sorry."

"Don't worry about it; just take care of yourself. When you find out the sentencing date, let me know. I'll make sure I'm there."

"I'll talk to you later, Jeremy."

As he pulled out of the parking lot he grabbed his phone and put it on speaker before dialing. It rang only once before he heard, "You've reached the Jacobs Psychiatric Center. My name's Rebecca. How may I help you?"

"Hi, Hon. It's me. You're not going to believe this. I just dropped Mike at his motel. He's like a whole new person. He was all apologetic, and he was … nice. Can you believe that? He seems to actually be looking forward to spending some time in jail."

"Wow, that doesn't sound like the guy I met last month. Did they have him on medication while he was in jail?"

"No. Seriously, he seems relaxed and calm. He said when he's done with his sentence … hey!"

"Yes?"

"Are you slamming busy right now or do you have a few minutes?"

"I can make a little time. You planning on stopping in?"

"Yeah, I'm on my way. I'll see you in a few minutes."

When he arrived at the office, he noticed that only two people were waiting in the lobby. Quinn was leaning against Rebecca's counter, and the two of them were talking.

"Hey, speak of the devil and there he is." Quinn smiled and nodded to Jeremy as he walked in.

"Hi, Quinn, how are you doing?"

"We were just talking about you. I was telling her that she's mellowed quite a bit over the last few weeks, and that I attributed it to her relationship with you."

Rebecca spoke quietly enough so that the people in the lobby wouldn't be able to overhear her. "What he actually said is that I haven't been nearly as bitchy as I used to be. He attributed it to my getting laid."

Quinn nodded and remarked, "Yeah, that's what I just told Jeremy."

Rebecca shot him a dirty look.

"Okay, so when I said it to him I didn't use the exact wording that I used with you. The sentiment was still the same."

"Quinn?"

"Yes, Rebecca?"

"Take your client and go act like you're working."

"Yes, Rebecca." He turned to the lobby and said, "Cassie, are you ready?"

Regina led a young man out of the office area and nodded to Rebecca. She then motioned for the only person remaining in the lobby to follow her.

Within two minutes Rebecca and Jeremy were alone. "Okay, what is it that you needed to talk to me about?"

"Several things, but let's start with this. How do you feel about taking a little vacation with me in a few months?"

"A vacation? Where are we going? Wait, let me guess. Jamaica … no, Paris … oh wait, Hawaii!?"

"Wrong, a little cabin in the mountains that runs on a generator and has a river flowing through the backyard."

"Ooh, that sounds very romantic. I'm picturing a fireplace with a soft furry rug in front of it. Very little clothing. A bowl of strawberries and cream. A bottle of wine ... "

"And Cassidy."

Rebecca's dreamy distant gaze focused instantly on Jeremy. "What?"

Jeremy took a deep breath. "He wants to make amends for the way he's been acting lately. When he's done serving his sentence for what he did to Parker, he wants us to join him in his cabin. It's his way of saying he's sorry for being such an ass."

Rebecca's expression went stone cold. "I'll have to think about that for a while."

Jeremy nodded. "I expected as much but it would mean a lot to him. He really seems like he's changed though. He's very sincere about this."

"You want our first trip together to be a therapy session for Cassidy. No matter how you try to spin this, it's going to take me some time to wrap my head around spending days listening to him apologize to us."

"I understand, just please give it some thought. Then, I promise, the next trip will be somewhere for just the two of us."

"Somewhere warm and sunny where the drinks are served with little umbrellas and only a handful of people speak English."

"Deal! Promise to seriously consider it? For me?"

"Okay, I'll let you know. It isn't like we don't have time before this will happen anyway."

Just then the door opened and Stacey entered the lobby.

"Time for what?" She then set down a folder in front of Rebecca.

Rebecca glanced at the folder then tucked it into a drawer. "Jeremy wants to whisk me away on a romantic getaway. Just him, me, a cabin in the wilderness that's powered by a generator ... and Cassidy."

Stacey raised her eyebrows. "Wow, I had no idea that the two of you were so sexually adventurous."

"Very funny," Jeremy said. "After Mike serves his sentence, he invited us to spend a long weekend at his cabin. He wants to atone for the way he's been acting lately; it's his way of apologizing. Oh, he also wanted me to apologize to you for him."

"To me? Why is he apologizing to me? Wait, he isn't expecting me to go with you guys and spend this long weekend with him, is he?"

"No. He wants to apologize for the way he's treated you."

"He was only mean to me the first couple of times we met, and that was because of Connelly. After that, he treated me fine."

Rebecca asked, "Did you already forget that he thought you might be the Specter?"

She shrugged. "He thought Connelly killed his mother. He thinks Parker is the Specter now. It isn't like he hasn't been wrong before. He was still nice to me even when he thought I was the killer. Tell him apology accepted."

"Will do. By the way, I haven't heard anything about how it went with you and Quinn?"

Stacey looked around quickly then lowered her voice. "Quiet! I was going to spring it on him this afternoon when we finish working."

Rebecca still looked disgusted. Jeremy couldn't help but smile at her expression.

Rebecca asked, "What are you grinning about? I think this whole thing is sick. I couldn't imagine letting him put his hands on me. Especially if I thought he was a killer. Gross!"

Stacey lit up a little. "Actually, that's going to add to the excitement. Imagine hands that ended human lives running up and down my naked body. It sends shivers down my spine."

Rebecca eyed her closely then said, "I asked you to stop having fun at my expense, and you promised you'd try."

"You're right, I did. I'm not succeeding very well at that, am I? Sorry."

"You've been flirting with him for weeks now. You had every intention of sleeping with him at some point. You're just using this as an excuse to find out what he's like in bed, aren't you?"

Stacey smiled as she answered, "Hon, I don't need an excuse to find out how good someone is in bed. I give you credit for your level of morality, but I honestly don't share it. Sex is sex. Everyone desires it. I just happen to be a bit more open about it than most."

Jeremy said, "Yes, you surely are." He paused, then went on. "And since you're so open, I just have to ask … I'll understand completely if you don't want to answer, but the curiosity is killing me. Have you ever had sex with another woman before?"

Rebecca instantly gasped, "Jeremy!"

Stacey smiled as she responded, "Relax, Rebecca. Of course I have."

Jeremy looked a bit shocked now. "Which do you prefer?"

"Well, men and women each have their own strengths. I guess it depends on the mood I happen to be in at the time."

Rebecca quietly asked, "The mood you happen to be in? What does that mean?"

Stacey's smile broadened as she said, "If you'd like, I can show you sometime."

Before Rebecca could say anything, Jeremy blurted out, "I'd pay to see that."

Rebecca snapped her head around. "Seriously?"

He started laughing, then Stacey joined in. "Take it easy, Rebecca. I'm still failing at trying not to have fun at your expense. That's all."

Rebecca sighed and was motionless for several seconds. Eventually, she looked up and said, "No, it's not that." She then stood and walked around to the side of the counter that Stacey and Jeremy were on. She slowly ran her hand up Stacey's back until she was seductively twirling her hair between her fingers. "I was just disappointed that you were joking and didn't actually find me attractive enough to hit on."

Jeremy stopped laughing instantly, and it was his turn to say it. "Seriously?"

While Stacey slipped an arm around Rebecca's waist, Rebecca nodded. "Haven't the last few weeks proved to you that I'm not a prude? Look at her, she's gorgeous."

Jeremy's mouth was hanging open.

While Stacey reached across with her other hand to caress Rebecca's arm she asked, "Still want to watch? Or are you thinking about joining in now?"

"Um. Well. Wow. I … "

Stacey started laughing again. "I'm sorry. I can't allow myself to be used to get you into trouble. Before you put your foot in your mouth, here … you can have her back." She then eased Rebecca toward him.

Rebecca was smiling as she said, "Aw, I wanted to see what his reaction would be. It would have let me know if he was going to get laid this weekend or not."

Jeremy took a deep breath and sighed. "I wasn't going to … what I mean is, I didn't … "

"It's alright. As Quinn and Stacey explained to me some time ago, you're a guy. You don't think like we do. I understand."

"Right, I'm a guy." He bit his lip. "I … Okay, I'm going to be honest. That was hot!"

"Jeremy!" Rebecca punched him in the arm while Stacey burst into laughter.

"Well, it was!"

Rebecca moved closer to him and, when she did, he cringed and braced for another punch. Rebecca smiled and asked, "You really think I was hot just then?"

Jeremy relaxed and said, "Hell, yeah."

She nodded as she ran her fingers across his chest. "Then show up at my place this evening." She gently put her other hand on his necktie. "We'll discuss just what hot really is." She then used both hands to tighten the knot of the tie.

He quickly pulled at his collar and backed up a step. "I really need to get back to work now. You ladies have a wonderful afternoon." He was loosening his tie as he backed toward the door.

Rebecca smiled as he was backing up. "See you around seven?"

Jeremy tried to gauge the expression on her face but failed. "Um. I suppose … you want me to come over? I mean, really?"

"Yes, jerk. I'll see you at seven?"

"Do you want me to pick up something?"

Rebecca thought about it for a second. "Strawberries and cream."

Jeremy smiled and relaxed. "See you at seven."

After he left Stacey said, "I know I have some fun at your expense, but there are times when you're just plain cruel to him."

"Yeah, but I more than make up for it later. I actually think he enjoys the abuse."

"Really? Have you ever tried tying him up? Oh, or using his cuffs on him? If he seems to like your verbal abuse, maybe he'd really like being dominated."

Rebecca stopped and asked, "Being dominated?"

"Yeah, you know. Take away his ability to move and have your way with him. Dominated."

Rebecca was obviously running pictures through her mind for a few moments before shaking her head. "No, that would be way weird."

Stacey shrugged. As she was turning to leave the lobby and go back to her office she said, "It's not uncommon for people who hold positions of authority in their professional lives to desire being dominated in their private lives. Consider it like yin and yang."

"The Siamese Twins?"

"No, dork, the Asian philosophy. Balance in all things. If someone spends their time at work telling people what to do and being in charge, then they tend to want people to tell them what to do in their private lives. Balance. Just a thought." She ducked through the door and left Rebecca alone in the lobby.

"Hmm." A smile slowly formed on her lips for a moment before she shook her head. "Work." She then went back to her station and retrieved that folder Stacey had given her.

CHAPTER 22

————•————

Saturday, September 5

Stacey hit the contact on her cell phone and listened to it ring three times. Just as she thought it was going to voice mail, she heard a breathless Rebecca say, "Stacey?"

Stacey paused for only a moment before saying, "I'm sorry, I thought I called Jeremy's phone."

"You did, what's up?"

Stacey smiled and asked, "Well, I was going to tell Jeremy about last night, but now I'm more interested in why you're out of breath and answering his phone. I don't suppose you'd like to tell me about what's happening right now, would you?"

The only response was Rebecca trying to control her breathing. "Rebecca?"

"Yeah, I'm still here. Um. Well, it's like this … "

"Never mind; you don't have to explain. If you'd like I can call back later. Better yet, why don't you have Jeremy call me when you two are done with whatever it is you're doing."

"No, hold on a second." In the background she could hear whispers. She couldn't make out everything that was being said but she definitely caught the words *where* and *the keys*.

After thirty seconds, Jeremy's voice came through the phone. "Hi, Stacey. What's up?"

"Apparently you are at the moment. Would you like me to call back later?"

"No, go ahead. Did you find anything? Actually, hold on a second, I'll put you on speaker. Okay, go ahead."

"Are you done unlocking yourself from your cuffs yet? If not, I can wait."

"How ... never mind. Just don't worry about my cuffs. What'd you figure out?"

Stacey remained silent for a few seconds until she heard a metal click followed by the ratchet sound of handcuffs, then she started to chuckle.

Rebecca said, "Knock it off, and tell us if you found anything."

Stacey replied, "First let me finish with the vision running through my mind."

"Stacey! What'd you find?"

"I found out quite a bit, actually. First, there is definite cause for his arrogance. The man knows what he's doing. Once we got back to his place, while we were kissing, he casually used his thumb and index finger to unhook my bra through my blouse with one hand ... "

"Stacey! About the phone. Did you find a second phone?"

"No, but I didn't have a whole lot of time to look. I did check his car though. Have you ever ridden in a Porsche? The suspension isn't great for handling bumps but, holy shit, it corners well ... "

Jeremy spoke this time. "Stacey?"

"Yes?"

"He doesn't keep an extra phone in his car. That much we got. How well did you get to search his apartment?"

"Oh, well I can state for certainty that there is no prepaid cell phone on or in his couch, on the dining room table, in his shower, nor in his bed. As for the rest of his place, I plan on trying again tonight."

"Stacey!"

"Yes?"

She could tell Jeremy was trying to be quiet as he whispered, "Oh, the table and shower."

She then heard the unmistakable sound of a hand smacking bare flesh. "Jeremy!"

After a bit of a pause Rebecca asked, "You're not seriously going out with him again tonight, are you?"

"Of course not."

"So you were just trying to get a rise out of me again?"

"No. We're really not going out tonight. I'm going back over this evening, then we're going to stay in all night."

"Oh, my God," Rebecca blurted out.

Jeremy said, "So, no phone so far. Then what's the report? Go ahead, right from the top. Let's hear it."

Stacey continued, "Stamina is definitely not an issue. Neither is reload time, for that matter. As far as me, I lost count at six and the intensity was incredible."

Rebecca cut in, "Stacey, he was joking."

Jeremy whispered, "No, I wasn't."

"Yes, you were."

Stacey cut her off. "I'll tell you what. Rebecca, you cuff him to your headboard again and continue whatever it was that you were doing to him. I need to take another shower, anyway. Tonight I'll make a little more time to look around his apartment better. I'll give you a call with another report later."

Jeremy said, "Oh, shit. Hey, hold on a minute. Someone's buzzing in."

Stacey heard a click and the line went silent. She began stripping out of her blouse and skirt and was making her way to the bathroom when Jeremy came back on the line. "You still there?"

"Yep, what's going on?"

"You're not going to believe this. That was the department. They got an envelope. They're calling the news station right now to see if they received one as well."

Stacey froze in the doorway of her bathroom. "You mean another Specter envelope?"

"Looks like it. I'm going to get cleaned up and head in."

"But, you guys haven't had a report of a body, have you?"

"No, we haven't. At least not that I've been made aware of."

"Do you want me at the lab?"

"Yeah, but give me half an hour. I'll meet you there."

"Alright, bye."

*****

When she arrived at the building, she was escorted directly to the lab. Inside she found only Robin and Jeremy.

"Where are your minions?"

"It's Saturday. I left messages for both Darryls but haven't heard back yet. I spoke with Larry. He'll be a no-show. He's visiting his girlfriend's parents in Utah."

Stacey asked, "Larry's dating a girl from Utah? Is it only one girl? Don't they travel in packs in that state?"

"She's not Mormon. At least I don't think she is." Robin looked up from her microscope then continued. "Perhaps I should ask him about that. He might be getting in way over his head."

Jeremy said, "Can we please forget about Larry's potential harem and get back to the reason we're all here on a Saturday?"

"Sorry, you're right. Give me a few more seconds, and I'll put the message up on the monitor."

A few moments later blurred words appeared on the screen before coming into focus. "How's that?"

"Good, thank you."

> *Once again the fools in the police department have the wrong man behind bars. On a topic closer to my heart, oh how the mighty hath fallen! I must say that I was impressed with the pugilistic skills of the fallen hero. I recorded all of the broadcasts I could and put them on a loop on my computer so I can watch them over and over again. I know the man formerly known as King Midas won't personally get to see this, but I hope his sidekick relays the message to him. You've now lost everything in your life that ever meant anything to you. All of it is gone. Now there's only one last thing left to lose. Good-bye, King Midas.*

"Oh, hell," Jeremy grabbed his phone and dialed Cassidy. After a few rings, the call went to voicemail. "Hey, this is Jeremy. We received another letter from the Specter. Watch your ass. It sounds like you're going to be next. Call me when you get this."

Jeremy turned to Stacey. "Any thoughts, Dr. Poole?"

The sound of Jeremy calling her Dr. Poole instead of Stacey snapped her back to reality. "This is the endgame."

Jeremy called the station. "Hey, has anyone heard from the news station yet? Well when you do, we need it brought to the lab as soon as possible. No, the toe is already on its way to Doc Brown. Of course the lab took a sample. They'll be sending it for DNA testing … "

Robin said, "As soon as I get a courier."

Jeremy continued, "As soon as someone gets here to take it over. Do me a favor. Send a unit over to Cassidy's motel. No, I tried to call but it went to voicemail. Right, the letter is the killer's endgame according to Dr. Poole. It essentially threatens Cassidy's life. I need you to babysit him. Let me know when you find him."

Stacey asked, "Robin, when was the envelope sent?"

Robin replied, "Sometime before the mail was picked up Friday morning. That would mean whoever this toe belonged to would have been killed Thursday night or earlier."

Stacey checked her phone and said, "It's 11:20 Saturday morning. The victim's body has gone over twenty-four hours without being discovered."

"Hopefully, whoever this belongs to is in the database so we can get some identification from the DNA results."

Stacey nodded. "I suppose it's too much to hope for that the killer finally left some physical evidence behind, isn't it?"

"I don't know yet. I just went over the envelope and postage. The prints from the envelope should start popping up on our screen any minute. The postage was clean. I haven't gotten to the Ziploc bag or the note yet. Why don't you two go grab lunch or something? This is going to take some time without my minions here to help."

Jeremy shook his head. "I'm staying right here."

Stacey said, "My schedule is open for the day. Besides, I'm not hungry."

Robin retorted, "Fine, just don't touch anything and try to stay out of my way."

One of the monitors flashed through four images, and a speaker near her computer beeped. "Those are the results of the fingerprint search. Will one of you check the images and see if any of them don't work for the police or the postal service?"

Stacey went to the keyboard and brought up each image and its accompanying biographical information. "Cop, postal worker, postal worker and cop. There are only four images, and they all work for the police or the post office."

"As I expected. Same as before."

The phone next to Robin buzzed. She answered it without looking up from her microscope. "What?"

After a brief pause she directed, "Escort them down. I have the sample ready for transport."

A couple of minutes later, the door to the lab opened and two men in business suits entered. One of the men called out, "Hi, Robin. What do you have, and where is it going?"

Robin reached across the lab table and picked up the cardboard box. As she handed it to him she directed, "I need the DNA markers for this sample. Take it to the university's lab. Tell them this is high priority, and I need the results as soon as they have them."

Once the men left the lab with the sample, Jeremy queried, "How long do you think it'll take?"

"The lab at the university is pretty good. I'm hoping to have the information late this afternoon. As for using it to determine who the toe belonged to, that depends on if their markers are in a database or not."

Stacey asked, "Do you know if the toe belonged to a male or a female?"

"Male. Full adult. If you want anything more than that, you'll have to talk to Doc Brown. In fact, why don't you two go over there now? I'll be quite some time before I get done with this."

Jeremy said, "Alright, I know when I'm being thrown out. Call me the instant you're done."

Robin motioned toward the door and said irritably, "Yeah, I know the drill, Sundance. Go away now."

On their way to the parking lot, Jeremy asked, "Do you want to just ride over with me?"

Stacey put her keys back in her purse and said, "Sure."

When they arrived at the morgue, they found Dr. Brown digging through a filing cabinet. He closed the drawer as soon as he saw them. "I was expecting you. I just got off the phone with Robin. She sounds a bit harried, I must say. She was kind enough to tell me that you two were on your way here before she hung up on me."

Jeremy spoke up. "Yeah, she's on her own at the moment. As much as she torments her lab techs, she relies heavily on their help."

"I just received the second toe from the news station. Not that it'll be necessary to spend too much time with it though."

Jeremy asked, "Oh? How come?"

Stacey cut in. "They're toes, Jeremy. All he needs to determine is whether or not they came from the same person. It isn't like one toe will yield different information than the other."

"Correct, Dr. Poole. The man who lost the toe I just finished studying was suffering from an iron deficiency. He was also fighting some form of infection. His white blood cell count was quite high."

Jeremy said, "That doesn't help a whole lot, doc. Can you tell us how tall he was? How much he weighed?"

"From a toe?"

"Don't they do things like that all the time on TV?"

"I'm a pathologist, but my name isn't Quincy."

Stacey raised her eyebrows and asked, "Who's Quincy?"

Dr. Brown shook his head. "I'm afraid he was before your time, my dear."

Jeremy asked, "Is there anything else you can tell us? Why would Robin send us over here?"

Dr. Brown started to laugh. "To get you out of her hair, of course. And you call yourself a detective."

Jeremy's phone buzzed. "If you don't have any information for me, you better just hang up!"

After listening for several seconds longer, he said, "We're on our way."

Stacey asked, "Where are we on our way to now?"

"The motel. That was Turner. He said I needed to get over there."

Stacey saw the expression on his face and asked, "Did they find Cassidy?"

"No, he's not there. Come on."

Fifteen minutes later they arrived at the motel where Cassidy had been staying. They found Turner in the office, and he motioned for them to follow him into a small room behind the counter.

"Play it for him."

The clerk hit a few buttons on the keyboard, and a grainy black and white image appeared on the small monitor. As the image played forward, they noticed the time and date stamp in the bottom right hand corner of the screen read *Saturday, September 5, 01:21 a.m.*

The image showed part of the parking lot and several of the room doors for both the first and second floor of the motel. As they watched, they saw one of the doors open and a man exit the room. He slammed the door behind him and pulled on a jacket as he ran toward the road.

Stacey was squinting. "Was that Cassidy?"

Jeremy directed, "Back it up. Can you slow it down a little?"

The clerk did as he requested.

Jeremy was squinting at the image as well. "It looks like his jacket, but the image isn't clear enough for me to be certain that's Mike."

Turner said, "It's Mike. He received a phone call that was routed through the office. The call came in at 1:17 this morning. That's him leaving his room four minutes later. The call lasted less than a minute. According to the motel's caller ID, the call came from a pay phone only a few blocks from here."

Stacey asked, "You still have pay phones in this city?"

Turner nodded. "There should be a unit there now. They already collected prints. We're trying to obtain an order to get the coin box opened."

"I want to see his room. Have you gone in there yet?"

Turner replied, "I had Kelly open the door. I poked my head in and called for Cassidy, but I never actually went inside."

"Are you Kelly?" Jeremy asked the clerk.

"Yes, sir."

"Will you open it up again for me, please?"

"Here's the key."

Turner said, "I'm going to take this recording over to the lab and see if they can clean it up."

Jeremy was on his way out of the small room with Stacey right on his heels. "Good luck with that. Robin is the only one in right now. It'll probably be a while."

Inside the motel room, they found some of Cassidy's dirty clothes wadded up and stuffed into a garbage bag that he was apparently using as a hamper. His phone charger was plugged into the wall outlet, but the cell phone was missing. The bed was unmade.

Stacey remarked, "Looks just like you'd expect if Cassidy had gotten a phone call in the middle of the night and took off."

Jeremy was poking through a few of the drawers as he said, "He looks like he had every intention of returning though."

Stacey asked aloud, "I wonder what was said to make him jump out of bed and take off like that?"

"I've no idea. Let's go find that pay phone. There's nothing this room is going to be able to tell us that we don't already know."

*****

"Harrison, this is stupid. You're just being stubborn. Release my client already."

"Ms. Welles, be patient. Let me get some more information about what's going on first. All we know right now is that another envelope was sent to the police as well as the news station."

"Exactly! I assume you can do math? They received the envelopes this morning. I already checked with an employee of the postal service and, if the envelopes were mailed from a drop box within the city, that means they had to be sent after the pick up on Thursday and before the pick up on Friday. My client was in jail both Thursday and Friday. That means he couldn't have sent them. I want him released now. Or would you rather I schedule a press conference?"

Harrison looked pale. "Can you at least give me a few hours to check with the police? They haven't even had a chance to go over the contents yet. For all we know, this might be another copycat."

Ms. Welles checked her watch and said, "You have two hours. I'll call you at one this afternoon. By then you should have whatever information you need to know that my client couldn't have sent those envelopes. If you're still going to be a stubborn ass, then my next call will be to the media."

He watched as Ms. Welles left his office. He grabbed his cell phone and punched a contact. "Kidd? This is Harrison. I just got called into my office on a Saturday morning and had a very unpleasant meeting with Parker's lawyer. Tell me this is some copycat just messing with us."

Kidd responded, "I'm kind of in the middle of something right now. All I know is that a toe and note were sent to both the department and the news station. We didn't even know that someone had been killed. They're running the DNA as we speak. We're hoping that'll lead to the identity of the victim."

"Tell me what you think. Is this a copycat or is this the Specter?"

"We just left Doc Brown at the morgue. He's proceeding on the assumption that this is the Specter."

"Son of a bitch! I'm going to have to release Parker."

Jeremy responded, "I would. It doesn't look like he's responsible for the latest envelopes. Now, if you don't mind, as I told you, I'm in the middle of something. Cassidy is missing."

"What? Elaborate. What do you mean, missing?"

"Harrison, I really don't have time for this. He's missing. As in, nobody knows where the hell he is. There isn't anything to elaborate on. The last message from the Specter said 'good-bye,' and I'm trying to figure out if Cassidy is a victim or not. If you want more information, call Doc Brown or Robin."

Jeremy hung up before Harrison had a chance to respond. "There are times I really hate that prick."

Stacey remarked, "I disliked him the instant I saw him."

Jeremy turned to see a cruiser rolling up the street with its flashers on. It squealed to a halt by the curb and a uniformed officer stepped out holding a piece of paper. "We got it. Pull the damn phone!"

Jeremy turned to the cops who were blocking anyone from getting near the pay phone. "You heard him; do it!"

A man wearing a bright yellow vest with a phone company logo stepped past the officers and began to disconnect the phone from its mounting. Five minutes later, the phone was inside a small garbage bag and being taken away by one of the uniformed officers.

Jeremy watched all of this with a look of helplessness on his face.

Finally, Stacey asked, "Can't you ask the FBI to track Cassidy's phone?"

Jeremy nearly dropped his own phone pulling it from his pocket. "I can't believe I forgot about the FBI! Stacey, you're brilliant!"

"Yeah, so I've been told."

"Hello? This is Detective Kidd." There was a long pause before he spoke again. "Hello, this is Detective Kidd. Can you track a cell phone for me? No, it belongs to Detective Michael Cassidy. Yes, it's his personal phone. Here's the number."

After reciting the number to the person on the other end, he motioned for Stacey to follow him and began walking back to his car. Once inside and away from the noise of the traffic he said, "Yeah, I'm still here. What time was that? And where did you say the signal cut out?" He was scratching notes in his little pocket notepad. "Okay. Thanks."

Stacey was staring at him as he sat silently behind the wheel of the parked car. "Well? What the hell? Are you going to tell me anything?"

Jeremy quietly said, "The signal for the phone was last active between one and two this morning. It was either turned off or destroyed sometime during that hour. It hasn't been turned back on yet."

They sat silently for nearly a minute before Jeremy asked, "You were with Quinn all night?"

"I fell asleep around midnight. I woke up about eight, and Quinn was in bed sleeping next to me."

"Are you a sound sleeper, or do you think you'd have noticed had he gotten out of bed once you fell asleep?"

"We drank a little. I don't know if him getting out of bed would have disturbed me or not."

"I think we need to have a talk with Quinn."

"He should be at home. Want me to call him?"

"Yeah, but just find out if he's home. Don't tell him about this."

She punched in a number on her phone and a few seconds later said, "Hi, you home?"

After a pause she said, "Mind if I come over? Alright, I'll see you soon."

She looked at Jeremy and nodded.

*****

Stacey knocked on his door, and a few moments later Quinn opened the door with a smile on his face. Then he looked over her left shoulder and the smile disappeared instantly. "This isn't exactly what I pictured when you asked to come over."

Stacey was about to speak when Jeremy cut her off. "Quinn, I'm sorry to bother you on a Saturday. There's a lot going on right now, and I need to ask you a few questions. Would it be okay if I came inside?"

Quinn looked suspiciously between Stacey and Jeremy. Her expression gave away nothing, as usual. His expression told Quinn that he was anxious and stressed but doing his best to hide it.

Quinn finally stepped back from the door and motioned for them to enter. "I suppose this has something to do with you asking me if I was the Specter earlier this week. I thought we cleared up all that, Stacey."

Again Stacey was about to say something when Jeremy cut him off. "I know you and Stacey shared the evening last night. Can you tell me what time you fell asleep, please?"

Quinn sighed heavily and said, "I'll play along. After a few hours of foreplay and what I can only describe as incredible sex, I was exhausted. I fell asleep around midnight and didn't wake up until Stacey climbed out of bed this morning. I think that was around eight."

Jeremy said, "Normally I wouldn't go this route, but circumstances aren't normal at the moment. I know about your affair with Cassidy's wife, Kathy. I know that Cassidy found out and threatened to kill you. I also know that Kathy told you she wouldn't leave Mike."

Quinn was shaking his head. "Right, so of course you naturally assume that because I have reason to hate the detective, I also have motive to want him dead. I'm not the Specter. Ask Stacey. I'm sure if she thought I was the Specter, last night never would have happened."

Stacey bit her lip and slowly closed her eyes as Jeremy began to speak again. "Actually, the reason last night happened was so that Stacey could gain access to your home and car so she could look for evidence."

Quinn took a step back and through his expression of shock glared directly at Stacey. "Tell me that isn't true," he whispered.

Finally, Stacey was allowed to say something. "Quinn, you have to understand. There's the timing of the end of the affair along with the first murder taking place only a couple of weeks later. The police thoroughly went through Cassidy's professional life and couldn't come up with anyone." Then she shrugged and said, "You were the only one that hated the man enough to want him dead."

Quinn was silent for several seconds. Eventually he raised his gaze back to Stacey. "Get out."

After a few seconds without anyone moving, Quinn raised his voice and repeated, "Get out!"

As Stacey and Jeremy were turning toward the door, Jeremy's phone buzzed. He looked at the screen and hit a button then held it to his ear. "Kidd here, what've you got?" He then froze in place.

After a few seconds he looked out the front window toward the driveway. "Hold on a second."

He rushed out the front door and went straight to the Porsche. He moved so that he could see the front of the car and the color drained from his face. He shifted the phone to his left hand and pulled his pistol with his right as he spun toward the house. Stacey was just outside the front door with a quizzical expression on her face, and Quinn was standing in the open doorway with a look of hatred on his.

Jeremy leveled his pistol directly at Quinn and said, "Quinton Foster, please step out of the house and keep your hands where I can see them."

The look of hatred disappeared instantly from Quinn's face and was replaced by one of shock. He slowly spread his hands away from his torso and stepped out onto the concrete slab just in front of his door. "Detective, what are you doing?"

"Right now, I'm detaining you for questioning. Stacey, hold this please." He handed his phone to Stacey as he pulled a set of cuffs out of a holder on his belt. "Please turn around and put your hands behind your back."

Quinn did as he was told and, once his hands were secured, Jeremy holstered his pistol. He then checked Quinn's pockets and patted him down to verify that he wasn't carrying anything that could be used as a weapon. Once he got his phone back from Stacey, he asked, "Are you still there? Good, get over here with a patrol car. I have someone in custody for questioning in the disappearance of Michael Cassidy."

There was a pause before Jeremy said, "Correct, that's the address. We'll be waiting." He then disconnected the call and put away his phone.

Stacey asked, "What brought this on?"

Jeremy took Quinn by his elbow and led them both to the front of the Porsche. On the front passenger side fender, just in front of the wheel, was a small scrape. There was a little bit of dark green paint at that spot. Jeremy pointed to the damage and explained, "Turner was trying to figure out where Cassidy had run to when he left the area that was covered by the camera. He was walking down the alley behind the motel when he found a dumpster that had been scraped by a car. The paint transfer said it was bright red paint."

Quinn blurted out, "That's not possible!"

Stacey's mouth was hanging open slightly as she looked from the bumper to Quinn. As she stared, she whispered, "Quinn, what did you do with him?"

Quinn looked from her to Jeremy. Then his expression went blank and he muttered, "I want my lawyer."

CHAPTER 23

Saturday, September 5

"Here's the warrant, Kidd."

Jeremy scanned the paper that Billings had just handed him and nodded. "Thank you. How many officers do we have?"

"Only myself and two others right now. I'm sure we can get more though."

Jeremy shook his head. "That'll be fine. We have all day. Let's get to it."

Stacey asked, "What do you need me to do?"

Turning to face her, Jeremy told her, "Rebecca is on her way. She'll pick you up. Go home. I'll let you know if we find anything."

Stacey sighed and leaned against the fender of the patrol car that was parked along the curb. She noticed that several people were lining the sides of the street, staring at the residence as well as at her. She lowered her head and waited for Rebecca. Five minutes later she heard the roar of the Blazer and ran into the street. No sooner did Rebecca come to a stop than Stacey climbed into the passenger seat.

"I can't believe it was Quinn. I mean, I know you accused him, but you said it probably wasn't him. What happened? Jeremy wouldn't tell me anything."

As they pulled away from Quinn's home, Stacey said, "There was a scrape on the Porsche that matches one on a dumpster in the alley behind the motel where Cassidy was staying."

"Oh, my God, you were right. Oh, my God! And you slept with him!"

"Really? That's the biggest issue you can come up with right now?"

"I'm sorry. Where do you want to go?"

"A bar. Any bar. I require copious amounts of alcohol."

Rebecca glanced over at Stacey with a look of concern on her face. "I seem to recall hearing several of our therapists, as well as Dr. Jacobs, inform people that self-medicating is never a good idea."

"Rebecca, this won't be self-medication. This is going to be obliteration. I want to get so drunk that you have to pour me into my bed."

Rebecca nodded silently and said, "I think that might be a good idea. I know just where, too. It's within walking distance of my apartment. We'll have to find someone else to pour us into our beds though."

Stacey smiled and said, "Two intoxicated, as well as intoxicating, women such as ourselves should have no trouble at all finding someone to take us to bed."

*****

"Detective! You have to come out back."

Kidd followed the officer out the back door to a small metal shed in the yard. "What am I looking for?"

The officer slid open the thin metal door and pointed. Inside was a black mountain bike.

Kidd mused aloud, "Parker told us he saw some kid riding a mountain bike the night of the Halsey murder. That would explain why Quinn's GPS never put his car near any of the crime scenes. He rode a bike to them. Cordon this off. I want nothing touched until forensics can get here."

The instant Kidd got back inside, one of the officers called out. "I need the camera over here!"

Kidd took the digital camera from the only other officer on the scene and called out, "Which room?"

"Bedroom closet."

When Kidd got there, he saw a white kitchen trash bag. Through the opening of the trash bag he saw a thick, clear plastic bag. He couldn't see what was inside because the officer who'd found it was still in the way. "Here's the camera. What'd you find?"

"A laptop, wireless printer, paper, envelopes … " As the officer pulled back the white trash bag just a bit further, he continued, "… a box of Sharpies and a plastic stencil. It's all sealed in this clear bag. This is one of those bags that you hook a vacuum to and suck out the air. I saw these advertised on TV. You can put a blanket in it, and once you use the vacuum to draw out the air, it's compressed down to a fraction of its former size."

Kidd was starting to get excited. Then he remembered Parker. "Alright, good job. Document everything … photos, measurements, the works. Remember, our job isn't done here until we find whatever was used to cut off those toes. We've been fooled too many times."

It took two more hours of searching. Finally, beneath the lid on the back of the toilet in the half bath just off Quinn's bedroom, they found what they were looking for. A Velcro strip had been glued to the underside of the lid. Attached to that they found a large freezer bag. Inside was a cell phone with its charger and the one item that could definitively close the case—a cigar cutter.

"Holy shit! We got him. We finally got him." Kidd reached for his cell phone then paused. His expression mirrored his sorrow.

"What's wrong, Kidd? We got him! How come you look like your dog just got run over by a truck?"

"I was reaching for my cell phone to call Mike and let him know we finally got the bastard. He won't be answering though."

The officer lowered his head. "You think he's dead, don't you?"

Kidd nodded slowly. He then lifted his cell phone and brought up the contacts. "Harrison, this is Kidd. We got him dead to rights. It's Quinton Foster. Let Parker's attorney know so he can be released."

He disconnected the call before Harrison could respond then hit another contact as he moved away from the other officers. After two rings he heard, "This is Rebecca's phone. She's currently indecent … " In the background he heard what sounded like Stacey. "You mean indisposed. Indecent probably comes later."

"Oh, yeah, indisposed. At the beep, please leave a message." She then tried to make a beeping sound with her voice but started to laugh.

"Rebecca?"

"Jeremy! Hi!" He then heard her say, "Stacey, it's my boy toy! Maybe you were right about indecent coming later."

"Are you alright? What's going on?"

"We're just having a drink. Maybe two. What's going on with you?"

"Where are you?"

"At that little bar just up the road from my place. Hey! I have an idea! You should drop by. I'll buy you a drink, sailor!"

"I have some things to take care of, but I'll be there as soon as I can. You might want to switch to coffee though."

Her voice got muffled, but he could still make out what she was saying. She had pulled the phone away from her mouth and was talking to Stacey. "He said I should switch to coffee." He heard Stacey respond brightly, "That's a good idea! The caffeine is a stimulant. It'll help counter the depressive properties of the alcohol and make us more awake. Then we can drink more!"

"Thanks, Hon! We'll do that! See you when you get here! Hey, bartender, caffeine all around! Then two more tequila shooters for me and my girlfriend!"

With that, the phone went dead. Kidd pulled it away from his ear and stared at it for a few moments before hitting another contact.

"Robin here."

"Robin, how soon can you be at … "

"Kidd, I'm already on my way. Two of the minions are with me. We should be pulling up in about three minutes."

"Thanks. I'll see you soon."

*****

"Hey, Stacey, look! I think that handsome man in the cheap suit is eyeing me. What do you think? Think he might buy me a drink and take me home?"

"I don't know, Rebecca. Are you sure you can't do better? The guy looks like a civil servant type to me."

"How much have the two of you had so far?"

Stacey and Rebecca looked at each other for a moment before Rebecca turned to the bartender. "Hey, Harry!"

The bartender smiled and shook his head, "Barry, not Harry."

"Harry, Barry, Mary, it's all the same. This officer wants to know how much we've had. Maybe he'll use his cuffs on us!"

Barry looked at Detective Kidd and said, "They've had way too much. I would have cut them off an hour ago, but they aren't causing any trouble and they swore that they were within walking distance of their home."

Kidd looked at the two of them for a moment then turned back to Barry. "You're sure they haven't been causing any trouble?"

"Actually, they've been quite a bit of fun. As you can see, there are only a handful of people in here right now. We don't usually get busy until a few hours from now. Anyway, they've kind of livened up the place. You're not going to arrest them, are you?"

As soon as they heard Barry mention getting arrested, both Rebecca and Stacey held out their arms. Stacey still had a drink in her hand.

Kidd closed his eyes and shook his head. "Nah, I'm not going to arrest them. They seem far too willing for that. Pour me a shot of your best whiskey and whatever beer you have that's too dark to see through."

Barry reached behind the bar and grabbed a bottle. "Want this on their tab or are you paying for your own?"

Stacey said, "Since this fine upstanding officer isn't going to be throwing us in jail, put it on my tab."

As they moved from the barstools to a table, Rebecca asked, "Well? Do you finally have your man?"

Kidd tossed back his shot and followed it with a few gulps of dark ale. "We found it all. His prepaid phone, the cigar cutter, the printer and laptop he used to make the notes. We even found his mountain bike. Parker's lawyer told us that he saw someone on that mountain bike the night that Halsey woman was murdered. Robin and two of her minions are going through all of the evidence as we speak."

Rebecca held up her glass in a toast as she intoned in a solemn voice, "The reign of the Specter is finally over."

After all three of them drank to her version of a toast, Stacey spoke. "It's too bad it was Quinn. I actually liked him. In spite of the fact that he was a pig." She then quickly glanced at Jeremy and explained, "No offense to you or any of the other cops. I didn't mean pig like that."

Rebecca started to giggle. She then held up her glass again and declared, "Here's to pigs, no matter what their jobs!"

Kidd smiled and shook his head then took another swallow of the dark ale. "You two really need to let me catch up. You had a huge head start."

Stacey gently hit the table and said, "Chug." A second later, and a little louder, she did it again. Then Rebecca joined in. After the fifth time, several others in the bar joined their chanting in unison. "Chug ... chug ... chug!"

Jeremy looked at the glass he was holding. He then tipped it and drained it all in a matter of seconds.

Barry was already pouring a replacement when he slammed the empty glass down on the table. Once his fresh glass was delivered, he held it up. "What are we going to toast to next?"

Stacey held up her glass and said, "To Cassidy! King Midas, himself. To Butch and Sundance and the end of an era." She then looked a little sad, and there was a lengthy pause before all three of them tipped their glasses.

Rebecca asked, "Did Quinn say where Cassidy was?"

Jeremy shook his head. "Quinn isn't saying anything. He got a lawyer, and I'm sure the lawyer won't let him speak. Over the next several days, Harrison will offer him some kind of deal in exchange for the information about Cassidy. I'm afraid that we might never find him though."

After a few seconds of silence, Stacey said, "Oh, shit!"

Rebecca appeared concerned as she asked, "What is it?"

"I hope Dr. Jacobs isn't too upset about me having to fire Quinn. Wait. Do I have grounds to fire Quinn without getting sued? Maybe I should just wait until he doesn't show up for three days in a row. Then I can list him as having voluntarily quit."

"What's going to happen to his Porsche?"

Stacey perked up. "Yeah, the Porsche. I wonder how much it'll cost to have that scrape repaired. I really liked that car. Hey, you don't think I can buy it, do you?"

Jeremy said, "It won't be for sale for quite some time, I'm afraid. It's evidence now."

Both of the girls exclaimed in unison, "Damn!"

Stacey then turned to Rebecca. "I thought you didn't like modern cars because they were rolling computers."

"I don't, but then again, it is a Porsche."

Jeremy was silent, seemingly deep in thought.

Rebecca turned to Stacey and said, "Uh oh. I think we lost him. Maybe he just couldn't keep up with us." She then turned to the few others that were in the bar and yelled out. "We just drank a big, strong homicide detective under the table!"

The customers all cheered and raised their glasses, but Jeremy just slowly set down his glass on the table.

Stacey nudged Rebecca and remarked doubtfully, "I don't think this is because of alcohol. It looks like he might be trying to think. See? I'm sure that's steam."

Rebecca looked closely at him then asked, "What's the matter with you?"

"Rolling computers," he muttered. He then pulled his cell phone and scrolled through his contacts. After selecting one, he held it to his ear.

"This is Detective Jeremy Kidd. Can you … "

He paused then replied, "Yep, I'll hold."

Stacey sat down her glass and asked, "What is it?"

Jeremy moved the phone slightly away from his mouth and explained, "Quinn's GPS. If he used his car last night, it might tell us where he went with Cassidy."

After a few more seconds he responded, "Yes, this is Detective Kidd. Remember that Porsche we had you guys check out? Can you check the GPS log again for last night? Yes, I'll hold."

The three of them remained silent while he waited for a response. Finally, he perked up a bit and spoke excitedly. "Really? You do? It did? Can you send me the coordinates? Thanks!"

As he put away his phone, he explained, "According to the GPS in that car, it was about an hour outside Denver at around 2:30 this morning. It stayed there until about 3:30 this morning, then went straight back to his home."

He checked his phone and said, "I have the coordinates. I have to go. Do you want me to drop you off at your place?"

Stacey quickly said, "Just go! We'll be fine!"

Jeremy nearly ran out of the bar.

*****

"Seriously, I am fine. I only had a shot and a beer. You didn't have to drive me out here."

"Jeremy, the media is going to be all over this. We don't need a drunk cop behind the wheel. Besides, your unmarked car might have some trouble with this terrain."

"Really? If a damn Porsche can make it out here, why couldn't my car?"

"That Porsche is all-wheel drive."

Jeremy raised his eyebrows. "It is?"

"You really don't know much about cars, do you, detective?"

"Apparently not. How close are we?"

The state trooper checked a screen in his four-wheel drive police vehicle and said, "We're almost there. Maybe we should go on foot from here. See if we can find the tracks from that Porsche. That should lead us directly to where we need to be."

He stopped his vehicle and the three others that were behind him all pulled off the trail and stopped as well. They exited the cars and started checking the trail ahead for tracks.

It didn't take long before they found what they were looking for. "Here we go. Now we just have to follow these."

Three hundred yards up the trail, the tracks turned and left the dirt. They could still follow its progress through the bent and broken undergrowth. After another twenty yards, the tracks looped around and appeared to follow the incoming path back to the trail.

As the officers began to spread out, they saw signs of disturbance leading away from where the car tracks were. "It looks as though someone was dragged through here. This way." They followed the officer down a slight incline and found a few boulders. As they moved around the boulders, they saw piles of sand and dirt. When they got to the other side of the rocks, they found an opening about three feet by three feet dug into the soft soil next to one of the large rocks.

Jeremy pulled a small flashlight from his jacket pocket and shined it down the opening. "Mike! Are you in there?"

One of the other officers asked, "What do you see?"

"I can't tell. It doesn't look like it goes very deep though. I'm going in."

Followed by the officer that drove him out to the woods, they worked their way into the mouth of the tunnel. It was only about six feet before it opened up into a small cavity.

There, leaning against the back wall of the small cave, they found Detective Michael Cassidy. His hands had been secured behind his back by his own cuffs. He was wearing the same clothes that he had on in the motel video. His jacket was spread open, revealing his chest. There, in the glare from their flashlights, they could see a single bullet hole through his shirt.

His pistol was lying on the ground near his left knee.

"Aw, Mike. I am so sorry I wasn't there for you, partner."

"Jeremy, we need to get out of here and get the ME down here. We'll also need the forensics unit. Try not to disturb the soil; back out slowly."

Once back outside the manmade burrow, Jeremy pulled out his cell phone. "Damn, I don't have a signal."

"Not surprising out here. We'll use the radio in the car."

As the last vestiges of daylight faded, they reached the cars and called for a medical examiner and the forensics team. "You might as well get comfortable, detective. It's going to be at least half an hour before they can get up here."

Jeremy had no desire to shed any tears and was surprised by this. After working with Cassidy for the better part of the last decade, he expected to have more of a reaction. "Is it wrong that other than feeling bad for him, I'm not all torn up inside?"

The state trooper eyed him closely for a moment before shaking his head. "The shock will wear off. I'm sure it'll hit you then."

Jeremy turned to face the state trooper and said, "I don't know. A big part of me is simply relieved that it's finally over."

"I can understand that. You city boys had a hell of a problem to deal with for the last couple of months. Just relax, detective. It's all over now."

*****

On the late news, a bubbly blonde adjusted a few sheets of paper on the desk in front of her and said, "Less than three hours ago, Detective Jeremy Kidd from the Denver Police Department, accompanied by the Colorado State Police, found the lifeless body of Detective Michael Cassidy. GPS coordinates from murder suspect Quinton Foster's car led police to a desolate location in the wooded hills about an hour outside of Denver. After a brief search, they found a small cavity, which had been dug under a boulder. Inside that makeshift grave were the remains of the detective. Reports state that he was secured with his own handcuffs, and that the single gunshot to his chest was inflicted by his personal gun. The suspect lured Detective Cassidy out of his motel room sometime after one this morning. It's still unknown how the suspect subdued Detective Cassidy for the hour-long drive from the city of Denver to that pre-dug hole in the woods as no weapon has been discovered during a search of the suspect's home and property. Our source stated that Foster brazenly left an unidentified woman that he had dated that evening sleeping in his bed while he snuck out to abduct the detective. We have no word yet as to whether a service will be held for Detective Cassidy, and it's expected that no official reports will be issued until Monday morning.

"For the citizens of Denver, it appears that the police finally have the right man behind bars. Travis Parker, a Denver University student, was arrested last week for the murder of an exotic dancer. That murder was attributed to the work of the killer known as the Specter, and police believed Parker was their man until our station and the police department received envelopes, each containing a single toe. Police are still working to identify the individual those toes belonged to. Parker was released from custody this evening after the arrest of Quinton Foster. Sources close to the department tell us that Foster's motive for launching this reign of terror against the citizens of Denver, and specifically against Detective Cassidy, is based on his year-long affair with Detective Cassidy's wife. The detective's wife ended the affair when Cassidy learned about the relationship. Foster was said to have been heartbroken when Mrs. Cassidy was unwilling to leave her marriage of fifteen years. The first killing associated with the Specter occurred only two weeks later.

"The Denver Police Department has asked us to convey their heartfelt condolences to the family members and friends of those targeted by the Specter during the six-week-long killing spree. As an ironic twist in this tragic case, Quinton Foster was working as a therapist at the Jacobs Psychiatric Center where Dr. Stacey Poole recently took over for Dr. Jacobs while he is on sabbatical. As most of you know, Dr. Poole was instrumental in this case as the only person to publicly proclaim the innocence of Dean Connelly, the first suspect arrested for the Specter killings. She worked closely with the detectives affectionately known as 'Butch and Sundance' during the entire time the Specter was on the loose. It's amazing that it turned out to be one of her very own therapists who committed the murders that she was aiding the police in trying to solve. As it stands, the Specter is now behind bars, and the city of Denver will sleep easier tonight."

CHAPTER 24

---•---

Sunday, September 6

Stacey shifted beneath her covers and pain blasted through her head so fiercely that her stomach began to churn. After several minutes of lying completely still and focusing on controlling the urge to vomit, she finally felt comfortable enough to attempt to open her eyes. The light streaming through the window seemed amplified and relentless. It took another full minute before she adjusted to the blinding light enough to take in her surroundings. After realizing that she was in her own bed, she relaxed and sprawled out. It was then that her leg brushed against someone else's. Slowly, she reached her right hand over and gently felt the form that was lying next to her. Moving cautiously so as not to disturb the person, she gently raised up slightly to try to see who was sharing her bed. As she eased the blanket down, she caught a flash of red hair splashed across her pillow.

While she was trying hard to focus on who her bedmate might be, she heard a groan and the blankets were yanked from her grasp and pulled back up over the person's head. Unwilling to ask the person for their identity, she reached under the blanket and ran her hand up a naked back. The person shivered and shifted beneath the blankets.

"What the hell? Leave me alone. My head hurts."

"Rebecca?"

Slowly the form beneath the blanket shifted and a pair of squinting eyes were revealed. "Stacey? Why are we in bed together? Wait. Why am I not wearing any clothes?"

Stacey felt her own torso and realized that she wasn't wearing anything either. "I'm apparently naked as well."

Then both of them heard a noise from somewhere else in the apartment, and they both went silent. After several seconds, they began to sniff the air.

Stacey turned back to Rebecca and whispered, "Is that bacon?"

Rebecca sniffed a few more times and nodded. "I think so. Someone's here with us."

Stacey struggled to look over the edge of her bed toward the floor. "My clothes aren't next to the bed; are yours?"

Rebecca turned to look and had to put her hand over her mouth and hold very still for a few moments. She eventually peeked over her side of the bed and looked back and forth. "I don't see my clothes, either."

Stacey turned to look at Rebecca and quietly asked, "Did you seduce me last night?"

Rebecca was already pale due to the hangover. After hearing Stacey whisper that question, she turned even whiter. "I can't remember anything other than Harry bringing us shots."

"I thought the bartender's name was Barry."

Just then a head peeked around the edge of the bedroom doorjamb. "His name was Barry."

Both of them squinted toward the door to see the grinning face of Jeremy. Neither of them said anything though. They both just continued to squint at him.

"You two were in quite the state last night. I must say it's going to be one of my more interesting memories. I heard you two whispering and started breakfast. How would you like your eggs?"

At the sound of the word *eggs*, Rebecca clamped her hand over her mouth again and fought to control her stomach. Stacey only wrinkled her nose.

Jeremy disappeared from view as he called back, "You two should probably find something to wear and drag your sorry asses out here. I don't know how much you remember, but I need to fill you both in."

Stacey sat up and put her bare feet on the floor, then steadied herself. After two attempts she managed to stand up, but she was quite unsteady on her feet. She finally bent over and used the edge of the bed as a makeshift handrail and worked her way toward a dresser that was against the wall at the foot of her bed. She slid open a drawer and pulled out two oversized tee shirts. After taking a few deep breaths and leaning against the dresser to keep from falling down, she tossed one of the shirts onto the bed while slowly slipping the other over her head.

Rebecca patted around a few times before finally locating the shirt that had been tossed to her. She slipped out of bed and, as she was attempting to stand, she lost her balance and fell backward onto the blankets.

"Need help?"

"I don't know."

From out in the kitchen they both heard, "I'll help if you want."

Rebecca's pale face now flushed. "I got it." She then dragged the shirt over her head and wiggled it down past her waist.

They both shuffled out of the bedroom, and both leaned against a wall and froze in place when the full smell of the sizzling bacon hit them.

Jeremy moved to where he could see them and started laughing loudly.

Rebecca clamped her hands over her ears as Stacey turned and bolted into the bathroom. At the sound of Stacey retching into the toilet, Rebecca doubled over and put her hand over her mouth again. Less than a second later, she was on her knees next to Stacey struggling for a spot in the same toilet.

Jeremy just laughed harder.

Five minutes later, Stacey opened up a brand-new toothbrush and handed it to Rebecca. After splashing cold water onto their faces and trying desperately to brush the horrible taste from their mouths, they both staggered to the living room and plopped down next to each other on the couch.

Jeremy was sitting at the dining room table with a plate in front of him. "Since neither of you answered me when I asked how you wanted your eggs, I decided to make them scrambled." He then shoved a large forkful of the fluffy eggs into his mouth.

Rebecca made the mistake of turning to look at him as he chewed. She didn't head for the bathroom, but she did lean forward and put her head in her hands.

Stacey finally closed her eyes and asked, "Are you going to tell us what the hell happened last night?"

Between bites Jeremy asked, "So neither of you can remember getting back here?"

Rebecca turned to glance at Stacey, then she shrugged.

"I got back to the bar about ten. The two of you were obliterated. Barry had cut you off two hours earlier. Apparently neither of you was happy about that. He told you both that he was giving you the drinks you were ordering, but he wasn't putting any alcohol in them. When I walked in, he simply motioned toward the pair of you and shook his head."

Rebecca explained, "We started drinking just after noon. We drank for eight hours?"

Jeremy crunched into a strip of crispy bacon and nodded. "You didn't just drink for eight hours. You were hammering drinks for eight hours. I was amazed that the two of you weren't passed out in the corner."

Stacey asked, "How did we end up here instead of Rebecca's? Her place was closer."

Jeremy said, "That all happened because Rebecca kept calling you her girlfriend. She wanted to make sure you got home safe. She told us it was the least she could do for her bitch."

Rebecca groaned, "Oh, my God."

Stacey was smiling slightly. "So ... now I'm your bitch, huh?"

Rebecca lifted her head and said, "Please tell me that you didn't take any pictures."

"Already uploaded to the Internet. I didn't post all of them, though I'm pretty sure that I can make some serious money from some of them. I sent out e-mails to a few porn sites. I'm still waiting for responses."

Rebecca groaned again. "If I survive this hangover, I am going to kill you."

Stacey asked, "So you're saying that when Rebecca molested me, you finally got your wish to watch?"

Rebecca turned to look at Jeremy. "Tell me I didn't do that!"

Jeremy smiled broadly but remained silent until Rebecca put her head back into her hands and groaned again.

"Relax. Neither of you molested each other."

Stacey asked, "What happened to our clothes then?"

Jeremy motioned toward the apartment-sized washer and dryer in the small room off the kitchen. "I had to wash your clothes. You both puked all over yourselves."

"And how did we get out of our clothes after that happened?"

"You both did that while you were in the shower together."

Rebecca was shaking her head and groaning again. "I don't think I want to know any more."

Jeremy asked, "Are you sure? It's quite a story. After you'd both thrown up all over your clothes, I told you that you'd have to rinse them before I put them in the wash. Stacey, you promptly went into the bathroom and turned on the shower and stepped inside fully clothed. Rebecca simply followed you in. Once you had them all rinsed off, I was expecting you to both go change and bring out your wet clothes. Instead, you both stripped down while in the shower and tossed the clothes out onto the bathroom floor. I collected the clothes and threw them in the washer. Once you'd both toweled off, you hung up the towels and just walked out of the bathroom butt naked. I suggested that you both go to bed and get some sleep, which you both did without complaint."

Stacey sighed and said, "Thank you for taking care of us last night. I don't normally allow myself to get like that. It's just that the thought of Quinn ... "

Rebecca cut in. "I worked with him for five years! Five years, and I never had a clue that he could be like that."

Jeremy quietly said, "We found Cassidy."

Both of them immediately turned to look at him.

"The navigation unit in the Porsche led us into the woods about an hour outside Denver. Quinn had dug a hole that was at least six feet deep. The cavity at the end of the entrance tunnel was big enough for two people to sit in upright. He apparently dug it in one night though. According to his navigation unit, his car had only been there twice: once in the middle of the night four days ago, and again Friday night when he took Cassidy there."

"He didn't even delete the travel log for the GPS?"

Jeremy had just finished a swallow of orange juice. "Oh, he deleted it. Both trips out there were deleted, but the navigation unit's information is tracked and stored by satellite. The company that manages the unit let us know where it was and how long it stayed there."

Stacey cringed before asking, "How bad was it?"

Jeremy sat down his fork and leaned back. "Surprisingly, Cassidy was killed by a single shot to his heart at point-blank range. There were no signs of torture. I couldn't find any evidence of a beating.

It looks like he drove Mike out there, spent just over an hour with him, then shot him once in the chest."

"So the torment was inflicted psychologically instead of physically. I don't know which I'd consider worse."

"The preliminary assessment was made by an ME that the state police had called to the scene. Mike's remains are being transported to Doc Brown sometime this morning. He'll perform the full autopsy today. But you're right. If there was any torment, it was most likely psychological."

Stacey closed her eyes and leaned her head back against the couch cushion. "You sound skeptical about the psychological torment."

Jeremy went on. "I don't think there was. There was no sign of any struggle in the dirt floor of the little dugout. It looked like Mike was leaned against the back wall while Quinn remained near the tunnel that led out. I worked with Mike for a long time. I think once Mike realized he was trapped and going to die, he simply talked to Quinn. He probably asked questions, got his answers, and when that was done, accepted his fate."

Rebecca said, "That doesn't sound like the Mike Cassidy that was ready to physically assault Stacey when she asserted Connelly was innocent."

"No, you're right. But remember, that was before Mike lost Kathy. Before he was shot. Before his house was burned to the ground. That was before Mike blew his cool and got arrested for attacking Parker. The Mike that I spoke with after all of that happened was calm and apologetic. While he didn't seem to be ready to die, he certainly didn't seem like he had a whole lot to look forward to in life either."

"So you think he peacefully accepted his death then?"

"I think, because he was a good Catholic, he believed that he'd be reunited with Kathy in death. So, yeah. I guess he was at peace with that."

"What happens now?"

"Robin will go over the evidence. She'll present her findings to Harrison. He'll build a case against Quinn, and I think Quinn will never again see the world as a free man."

Rebecca was slowly shaking her head. "I can't see Quinn quietly awaiting his fate. That's not like him at all."

"Oh, according to Billings, he isn't. While he was being transported to holding, he kept saying that the police manufactured evidence against him. He claimed that as soon as we found out about his affair with Kathy, that we were all out to get him. More specifically, that I was out to get him. He accused me of stealing his car while you two were having sex and drove it to that alley to run it into that dumpster. He swore that we'd find nothing at his house. Then he changed that and said if we did find anything at his house, it was because we put it there to frame him. Trust me, he isn't quietly awaiting his fate."

Stacey asked, "How's he explaining the murders then? I mean, if the cops were just out to frame him, does he think the cops staged the murders as well?"

"Billings asked something similar while he was taking him to the station. Quinn's theory is that someone was really out to get Cassidy, but since the police were either too stupid or too inept to figure out who was really killing people, that we set him up to take the fall so the murders would stop."

"I can see how that might be considered a valid theory."

Rebecca turned to Stacey. "I can't believe you just said that!"

"I didn't say I thought he was right. I just said it's a valid theory. Tell me that all police everywhere are above doing something like that to protect their jurisdiction."

Rebecca was silent for a moment before looking over at Jeremy. "Tell her!"

Jeremy swallowed the last of his breakfast and shook his head. "I can't, Hon. In this case, that isn't how things went down. But I've met a lot of cops from a lot of other areas, and I can't state with certainty that they'd never do something like that just to end a killing spree. Cops are people, and people make bad decisions sometimes. Sometimes those decisions are for good reasons, but that doesn't mean they're good decisions. It doesn't matter. With what we found in his house, there's nothing he can say to shake the spotlight that'll be on him. He's done. Now, speaking of done, your breakfast is getting cold."

Stacey leaned forward and struggled to her feet as she held her stomach. "Not for me, thanks. I'm going back to bed."

Rebecca raised her head and watched as Stacey shuffled back toward the bedroom. "Oh, that sounds like a great idea." She then stood and began swaying along behind Stacey.

"Hey! What about me?"

As Rebecca walked past the dining room table, she turned to speak over her shoulder. "Since I'm quite sure you weren't nearly enough of a gentleman to close your eyes as we stumbled naked from the shower to the bed, you can sleep on the couch if you need a nap."

"I slept on the couch all night while you two were passed out all comfortable in Stacey's bed. I was a perfect gentleman."

Rebecca stopped and turned around. "So you didn't look when Stacey and I were naked?"

"Well, I needed to make sure neither of you hurt yourselves. I mean, you were blasted! I made sure that you both made it to bed safely."

Stacey had stopped just before going into her bedroom. "Then you're admitting that you watched us get naked last night."

"It wasn't like that. I wasn't being a pervert. I was making sure that both of you didn't hurt yourselves on the way to bed. I was being a kind and caring gentleman."

Stacey said, "Well then, kind and caring gentleman, here's something for you to think about while we're sleeping through the rest of the morning … all snuggled up next to each other in my warm and comfortable bed." She then peeled off the knee length tee shirt as she stood facing him and tossed it casually into her room.

Once Rebecca saw Stacey strip off her shirt, she turned to face Jeremy then repeated what Stacey had done. Both of them stood there stark naked for a few seconds before walking into the bedroom and closing the door behind them.

"Real mature! You two are really going to make me out to be the bad guy here? That's the last time I go out of my way to take care of your two drunk asses."

There was no sound coming from the bedroom. He moved to the door and questioned in disbelief, "Really? You're not even going to thank me for making sure you got home safe and sound? I made you guys breakfast!"

Rebecca ordered saucily, "Don't forget to do the dishes."

Jeremy sighed and, as he turned to go back to the kitchen to clean up, he had a smile on his face.

Rebecca called out, "You better not be grinning about seeing both of us naked again either ... pervert!"

CHAPTER 25

Saturday, September 5

Cassidy slowly opened his eyes then began to squint. "Where am I? What the hell?" He tried to move his hands and found them cuffed behind his back. There were three bright lights shining directly into his face. He knew someone was behind those lights.

"So this is how it ends?" He looked around and found himself underground in a freshly dug cavity that was just large enough for him and the person he could sense was currently sharing it with him.

"Are you just going to kill me and leave me here without telling me who you are or why you destroyed my life?"

The light on his left went out. Then the light on his right went out. Finally, the third light began to move. After a few seconds, it was sitting on the floor shining straight up, revealing the person who he was certain was about to end his life. "It was you?"

In the glow from the flashlight, he could clearly see the blank and cold expression on the face before him.

"It was me."

"Why?"

"Oh, Mike, we'll get to that. I have about an hour before I have to get back to the city. I had originally envisioned this moment as one where I began to slowly torture you until you begged me to finally end your life. But now, after getting to know what kind of person you really are, I decided to answer all of your questions. Then, if you don't try to become a problem for me, I'll kill you quickly and painlessly."

Cassidy tested the cuffs once more then scanned what he could see of his surroundings. After a few moments he shifted his weight to make himself more comfortable and level his gaze directly at his captor. "I have a lot of questions."

"I'm sure you do. Let's start with how I chose the victims. I'm sure that one's been bugging you."

"Actually, Dr. Poole, you're right. There's nothing that we could find that linked any of the victims with each other."

Stacey shifted her weight and made herself comfortable. "First of all, we're not in my office and this isn't a professional visit. Please, call me Stacey. Now, when I took over for Dr. Jacobs, selecting the victims was my first priority. The ideal place to start looking was in the archives room at the Center."

"But I thought of that already. We checked, and none of the victims were ever clients there."

"I'm disappointed, Mike. After all we've been through, you really think so poorly of my intelligence that I'd choose victims that were clients of the Center? I chose those victims because people they knew had been clients of the Center at some point in the past."

"Please, Stacey, do me the courtesy of being specific."

"Absolutely, Mike. Let's start with our first victim. Sarah Connelly. An overbearing mother who used her money and status to completely spoil an intelligent and promising young man. Her son was never the important thing in her life, you know. Her husband's success was her sole concern. Nannies and babysitters raised Dean. I'm sorry; I'm drifting from the topic, aren't I? I chose Sarah Connelly as my first victim because I read about her relationship with her son in one of the archived files. A few years ago, while Dean was in college, he was dating a lovely young coed named Whitney Sparks. She had issues of her own, which is why she'd started coming to the Center in the first place. But during her sessions, she revealed that her boyfriend had absolutely no backbone when it came to his mother. She really cared for Dean, but no woman wants a man who can't stand up for himself when it comes to his mommy. Anyway, after reading some of the transcripts about Dean's relationship with his mother, along with the fact that she was the widow of a state senator, that made her the easy choice as the first to die. Along with Dean making the perfect patsy. Their weekly golf outing gave me a routine that I could plan around."

"Okay, that makes sense. How did you get in and out of the house without leaving any physical evidence behind? Not only that, but how could you commit that murder so close to the time Dean was seen leaving the residence in order to make him the obvious choice?"

"I'll be honest with you, Mike. You deserve that much, at least. When I'd enter a house with the intent to kill, I didn't have much of a plan as to how it was really going to happen. I just kind of winged it, as it were. But with the Connellys, I entered the house when I heard their raised voices. They were arguing, and the noise masked my entrance. I snuck down the hall to the spare bedroom to hide until Dean left. I wore freshly laundered clothing so that I didn't track in fibers. My shoes had flat soles so nothing could get caught between traction ridges. I kept my hair in a tight bun and always wore a hat. I also carried a backpack with a spare set of clothes in it, just in case the murder got messy. Most importantly, I wore a fanny pack to carry the tools I'd need—including Ziploc bags that contained latex gloves and bleach wipes in case I accidentally touched something. You get the point.

"While in the spare bedroom, listening to that whiny, sniveling candy ass as he begged his mother not to cut off the money she gave him to live on, I saw his golf clubs leaning against the wall and knew

I had found my murder weapon. I selected the five iron, noted that it was a left-handed club and waited patiently until they finished their discussion. Dean went to the kitchen and rinsed a glass that he'd been drinking from then said goodbye to his mother and left the house. I checked the time and found that it was 6:12 p.m., then held my ground and waited for my opportunity. Sarah finally went into the kitchen to heat up the teapot again. I used that time to sneak into the sitting room and have a quick look around. I found the open-faced clock and the rest of my murder fell right into place. I eased the hands of the clock back to one minute after six and snuck back down the hall to the spare bedroom. Once she had her tea and plopped her pompous ass back in that chair, I slipped up behind her and calculated where I'd have to hit her to cause enough blood spray to hit the clock. Once I'd killed her, I set the clock back to the correct time and went about cutting off her toes with a cigar cutter I stole from a guy I used to date. The rest, you pretty much know."

"So that's how we had such an accurate time of death. I'm impressed. What about the envelopes? How did you send those without leaving any evidence on them?"

"Those were already in my pack inside a freezer bag. I prepared those before each murder. Making sure there were no hairs or fibers or anything that could link them back to me was a very time-consuming and meticulous undertaking. That's why, once I knew they were absolutely clean, I sealed them inside the freezer bags. The only thing I had to add were the toes. I was actually going to drop those into a public mailbox that night. Then it hit me. I went to such lengths to make sure that Dean looked guilty, what good would it serve if I sent proof of his innocence right after the murder? I will admit that I didn't like having those toes in my refrigerator for all that time. It wasn't like I had company over or anything; I just didn't like keeping my food in there with the toes. I was quite relieved when I heard that he'd gotten talked into pleading guilty. That saved me months of time."

"I suspected you later. I even had your GPS unit checked. How'd you get to and from the crime scenes?"

"My neighbor has a mountain bike that he never uses. I simply told him I was new to the area and wasn't able to have my own bike shipped here yet. I asked if I could borrow his for some exercise. He was more than willing to lend it to me anytime I needed it. He even gave me a key to his storage shed so I could use it without having to bother him."

"Alright, how about the phone? The FBI did a check of the cell towers and came up with a list of phone numbers. A prepaid phone showed up in the coverage area for every single one of the murders."

"Yeah, I picked up that phone when I was driving to Denver. I had no idea what I might use it for when I got it; it just seemed intelligent to have some form of communication on me at all times. I also downloaded a free app that allowed me to check the police bands for emergency calls. That way, I'd have an alert if I were spotted. The only time I ever turned on that phone was when I was ready to commit a murder."

Cassidy was nodding and actually had a smile on his face. "You have to tell me. How did you manage to get yourself appointed to perform the psychological evaluation on Dean Connelly?"

For the first time since she'd revealed herself to Cassidy, she smiled as well. "Believe it or not, that was just pure bullshit luck. Harrison had called the Center expecting Dr. Jacobs to still be there. Apparently Dr. Jacobs had performed such evaluations in the past for defense attorneys that Harrison went up against. I was chosen because I was acting in place of Jacobs while he was away."

"That explains the first murder and how you chose the Connellys. What about the second murder?"

"He simply deserved to die. He was a wife-beating alcoholic. I chose him because one of his neighbors was a client at the Center. During her sessions, she'd often complain of the stress she felt when she'd hear him beating the hell out of his wife while in one of his drunken stupors."

"And the choice of the lamp cord?"

"I wanted him to suffer and know he was about to die. No husband that horrible should have a quick and easy death. I also sent his toes right after the murder so that if you did arrest her, she wouldn't be in jail very long. That poor lady had suffered enough."

"Did you use your neighbor's bike to get to that crime scene as well?"

"For that one, I just jogged. It was very close to my own apartment. To anyone who passed by, I simply looked like a health nut who was out for a late evening workout."

Cassidy was nodding again. "Makes sense. How about that teenage kid? What could he have possibly done to deserve your wrath?"

The pleasant expression on Stacey's face instantly disappeared only to be replaced by a cold, blank expression. "That little bastard had been molesting his half-sister—not his stepsister, mind you. She was his half-sister; they shared the same mother."

"How could you possibly know he was doing that?"

"His sister confided in a friend who was treated at the Center and spilled it to the therapist. The last session notes that I'd read related that his half-sister was going to be so relieved when he went off to college. No kid should have to go through that kind of hell."

"Why wouldn't she tell her mother what her brother was doing to her?"

"That little bastard had used his phone to secretly record her and her boyfriend having sex. He had threatened to post it online for the world to see if she didn't perform 'sexual favors' for him. She was terrified of what would happen if that video ever got uploaded. When I killed him, I found his phone and deleted that video."

She was gratified by the look of horror on Cassidy's face. It almost made him seem human to her in that moment.

There was silence for several seconds as Cassidy reflected on what he'd just been told, then Stacey checked her watch and motioned for him to ask another question.

"That one I'll give you. Hell, I'd have probably killed the little prick myself had I known what he was doing. By the time that murder occurred, I was convinced you were the one killing these people, by the way. That was why I had Jeremy take both of us there for a walk-through. I was watching you to see if you'd show any sign that you'd been there before or had information about the murder that you shouldn't have had. I must admit, you played that one damn well. I saw nothing to indicate any prior knowledge of the place."

"I thought you might suspect me by then, but I knew for certain when I got back to my car and found that someone had been inside."

"Yeah, I had the FBI check your GPS unit. They can check the installed units remotely, but they had to actually get that particular unit before they could see where you'd been because it's a plug-in type."

Stacey nodded and her expression became pleasant once again. "That was the moment when I began to respect your abilities as a detective, and I'll say this for you too. Seeing how you handled the death of your wife and your own nearly fatal shooting made me respect you as a person. You showed a great deal of strength through that ordeal."

"Thank you. It was the most difficult thing I'd ever faced. I'm talking about Kathy's death, not my own injuries. I can't think of anything else to ask you about that murder, so I guess that brings us to your final murder—Jessica Halsey."

Stacey smiled and replied, "She wasn't my final murder. I killed someone else just before I abducted you tonight. I'll get to that in a minute though. The dancer, Jessica Halsey. Long legs, firm breasts. She was gorgeous. She was also the only victim I chose who was in no way associated with the Center. That was probably also my most difficult murder. If you recall, I killed her after we found out about Travis Parker. That kid showed definite signs of becoming a murderer at some point in his life. You can't be that obsessed with someone without eventually being let down by the object of that obsession. Once you're let down enough, a violent outburst is the next step in the progression."

"So you chose her just because of Parker?"

"Yes, I needed the media to begin hammering the police again. Connelly had been released, and sympathy was the primary tone of the news broadcasts. I couldn't have that, so I had to set up another bad arrest, and Parker was a perfect fit. Once I got back to my place after I killed Jessica, I made my preparations then rode my neighbor's bike to the university. Parker had told Jeremy and me that he'd been invited to a party, so I decided to go blend in. I wore a wig, changed my makeup, and wore glasses instead of my contacts. I succeeded quite well at blending right in with those college kids. I was at that party within feet of Parker, and he had no clue it was me. None of them did. Considering how much face time I'd gotten on TV by that point, not being recognized was quite an accomplishment. I was talking with a group of girls while keeping an eye on Parker and where he went.

"When he and a few other kids looked like they were getting ready to leave the party, I borrowed a phone from one of the girls and sent a text asking where he was going. Once he said he was heading over to that strip club, I had to move fast. Keeping up with a car when all you have is a mountain bike is damn difficult. That was when I lost him for a bit. I had to turn on that prepaid phone and find out where the club actually was. Again, luck must have been on my side because when I turned it on, I was already in the same coverage zone as both Parker and the place where Jessica lived, though I didn't know it at the time. I found a place outside to stash the bike and walked right inside. I handed the bouncer a fifty and strolled past him without even having to show my ID. I went to the bar and lost myself in a crowd there.

"After ordering a soft drink, I watched as Parker turned his obsessive nature toward Jessica. She handled him fairly well while he was inside the club, but when I saw him slip into the dressing room, I figured he was trying to find out more information about her. I quietly slipped back outside and waited until he and his college buddies were getting ready to leave. When I saw him hand the keys to one of them and start walking, I slipped up and got within sight of him. Two blocks later, I thought I had lost him, but while I was trying to find him again, I accidentally passed him on the other side of the street. I knew he noticed me, but I had my hood pulled up over the wig; and the streetlights made it difficult to see facial features at that distance. I managed to get far enough behind him that he wouldn't notice me again, then I just trailed him until he stopped. When he finally began to walk away from where he'd been, I recognized the car in the driveway as one that was parked at the club. I took a chance and left the bike near the sidewalk. I tested the front door and was shocked when I found it unlocked. Believe it or not, had he turned around at that moment, he would have seen me enter the house. He was still that close when I went inside.

Once inside, I heard the shower running and knew I had only a few minutes before she'd be done. I grabbed a knife from the kitchen and a vision of that old black and white shower scene from the movies flashed through my head. So that's exactly what I did. I used the shower curtain to protect myself from any blood spray and stabbed her directly through the curtain. Once she went down, I stabbed out her eyes just because that would fit with Parker's mental issues. Within five minutes, I was done and back outside, riding away."

"How did you avoid the neighborhood watch? You pushed hard to get the watch set up in the first place. Didn't that make it difficult for you?"

"Not at all. Part of the condition of setting up the neighborhood watch was that they'd report their patrol locations to the authorities and to the other groups. Since Rebecca and I were in charge of our group, they told me where they'd be and when."

"Ingenious."

"Coming from you, that actually means quite a bit to me now. Thank you."

"So, what about this murder that I don't know about yet?"

"Ah, you see, that one was the setup for the end game. I chose a victim who was a shut-in. One of the clients at the Center had this uncle who was agoraphobic. He couldn't even step outside his door to pick up the paper. Because of this, he didn't have direct contact with anyone on any kind of regular basis. The perfect victim to obtain my proof of death from before anyone figured out that he'd even been killed. The timing was crucial for this one. I had to make sure that you'd been released from jail after your attack on Parker and that you were back at that motel again. Then I had to set up my date to correspond with sending the envelopes."

"Wait a minute, your date?"

"I'm afraid that we skipped some of the details you weren't made aware of while you were in jail. Perhaps I should back up a bit and catch you up. The first murder, the Connelly murder, was just because of a file that I found in the archives. The therapist who actually handled the sessions for Dean's ex-girlfriend was Quinn—the very same therapist, as it later turned out, to have the absolutely perfect motive for wanting you dead. That was yet another stroke of pure bullshit luck that fell into my lap. After I found out about Quinn and Kathy, all of the other murder victims came out of Quinn's archived sessions. It became part of my ever-evolving plan.

"You see, my original plan was to simply end this with your death. Then when Dr. Jacobs returned, I was going to leave Denver and move on to the next thing. In other words, I was going to leave this as an unsolved mystery. Then Quinn fell into my lap, and I knew that leaving an unsolved mystery meant someone would always be trying to solve it. But … if I had a fall guy sitting in jail when I left Denver, nobody would continue to pick at these murders. Quinn became my fall guy."

The grin on Cassidy's face actually got bigger after thinking about that for a moment. He remained silent, but his smile was firmly in place.

"I'm glad you approve of my choice, Mike."

"I may not live to see another sunrise, but knowing Quinn will be spending the rest of his life behind bars for crimes he had nothing to do with more than makes up for what he put me through."

"As I was saying, I needed to set it up so that one of us was going to be looked at for this." She motioned to the dirt walls that surrounded them. "So, I went to the trouble of stealing his car a few nights ago and bringing it up here when I dug this out. I wanted his navigation unit to have a record of coming to this location twice. And I brought you here in his Porsche."

Cassidy was now snickering. "Go on. I know my faith tells me that I should forgive, but please … tell me more."

"I killed the shut-in. The details don't really matter because it'll be days before they figure out who he is. I used Quinn's laptop to do a search to see if he turned up in any databases, and the searches came back negative. When they run his DNA, he'll remain a John Doe. He probably won't be discovered until one of his relatives checks on him. Anyway, back to the setup. I had carefully planted the idea in Rebecca's mind that Quinn might be the Specter. Naturally, that led Jeremy to take a harder look at him. At the dinner you missed at Jeremy's, I brought up the whole thing and suggested that I sleep with Quinn so I could search his house and car for evidence of his guilt. Rebecca was resistant, but it took surprisingly little effort to get Jeremy on board with the idea."

She checked her watch and said, "I'll condense this so we can get on to your big question. I timed it so that the envelopes containing the shut-in's toes will arrive at the police station and news station later this morning. I also slept with Quinn tonight. I dosed him with the same tranquilizer I used on you. He's sound asleep in his bed, and under the assumption that I'm sleeping right next to him. I used a lower dosage on you because I wanted you awake for this. One of the side effects of the tranquilizer is loss of memory just prior to the administration of the drug. Do you remember receiving a phone call at your motel tonight?"

"No, the last thing I remember is shutting off the lights and going to sleep."

"Well, I called the motel using a voice modulator that I'd installed on my laptop. I recorded Quinn's voice and ran it through the program, which allowed me to speak into the microphone and have the laptop convert my words into his voice pattern. When the clerk at the motel answered the phone, I used the laptop converter to tell the clerk that there was an emergency and that I needed to be connected to your room. She patched the call through to the phone in your room and, when you answered, I used the same program to identify myself as Billings and told you that Jeremy had been in an accident and was in the emergency room. I told you that I was close to the motel and asked you to meet me outside near the alley behind the building. You told me that you'd be outside in five minutes, which gave me enough time to park the Porsche and get into position. As soon as you rounded the corner to the alley, I stabbed you with the syringe. The tranquilizer took effect almost instantly, and you collapsed. I pulled the Porsche into the alley, making sure to scrape it against one of the dumpsters, then loaded you into the passenger seat."

"Before I abducted you, I left all of the evidence in Quinn's house so that any jury in the country will find him guilty of being the Specter. When those envelopes finally get delivered later this morning, I'll act surprised. And if nobody happens to connect the dots, I'll steer things in the right direction. Either way, Quinn will be behind bars by this afternoon, never to see the light of day again. I'll be free of suspicion for the murders, and you will have paid for your crime."

"My crime? What crime did I commit?"

"Your crime … now we come to the reason for all of this. Twenty years ago you were a patrolman in Chicago."

"I was. That was my first job on the force."

"I was an eleven-year-old kid whose father had just come home from work. We were getting ready to go bowling and have burgers when there was a knock on our door. When I answered, there you stood."

Cassidy closed his eyes. "I asked you if your father was home. Brian Banks. My God, you're Stacey Banks. I knew I'd met you before."

"I was Stacey Banks. An eleven year old who had nobody in the whole world except for my father. My mother had died when I was too young to remember her. You showed up at my door and took my father away from me. I only got to see him a few times after that, and never again was I allowed to give him a hug. He was the only person I ever cared about, and you destroyed that."

Cassidy opened his eyes as tears streamed down his cheeks. "I am so sorry."

"You know what? I actually believe you are."

"Your father had been accused of statutory rape. I was executing an arrest warrant. It could have been any cop. It just happened to be me."

"Yes, I know exactly what happened. Because of a twelve-year-old slut who lived in our apartment complex, my father was labeled a child molester. Allow me to fill you in on what actually happened, just in case your captain never bothered to do so.

"Carrie Williamson was almost thirteen. She lived one floor down from us. She had been seeing an eighteen-year-old street hood named Bobby Kolacheski. They used to meet in the building's laundry room and have sex. Eventually, during a trip to the gynecologist, it became apparent that she was no longer a virgin. There were some vaginal abrasions and slight bruising on her thighs. When her mother pressed her for details, she claimed to have been raped and said she kept quiet because she was ashamed. Of course, her mother pushed to find out who it was that defiled her little girl. Carrie certainly wasn't going to throw her boyfriend under the bus, so she came up with someone she'd see from time to time down in the laundry room, Brian Banks. Naturally, the police took her information and, without doing any investigation at all, arrested my father.

"It didn't matter that there was absolutely no physical evidence supporting her claim. It didn't matter that my father steadfastly proclaimed his innocence. It didn't matter that, during his trial, not one witness except for Carrie Williamson testified against my father. It didn't matter that the prosecution completely failed to link my father to any wrongdoing. Nothing mattered except the claim of a twelve-year-old girl who was trying to cover her own ass. My father was convicted and sentenced to prison. Less than a month after his sentence began, other prisoners got together and decided to teach the 'child molester' a lesson. They beat him to death, slowly and painfully.

"Brian Banks was an amazing father and an honest, upstanding citizen. He had a good job and took great care of me. Because of Carrie Williamson, you, and a justice system that completely failed, my father lost his daughter, his freedom and then his life. And I spent the next four years believing that my father had actually molested her."

Tears were steadily trailing down Cassidy's cheeks now. "I was just executing an arrest warrant. I wasn't in charge of the investigation. I know that's no excuse for your tragic loss, nor is it an excuse for the injustice that was committed against your father. But I never testified in that case. I only executed the warrant."

Stacey's expression remained cold and blank. "That was the beginning of your skyrocket ride up the ranks. You arrested a child molester. Shortly after that, you arrested a drug dealer who later confessed to killing a family of four. The media got involved, and within two years you became the golden boy. Everything you touched turned to gold, and every case you were handed, you solved."

"Stacey, if you knew all of this, why didn't you come forth during your father's trial and clear him?"

"Weren't you paying attention? I just told you that I spent the next four years of my life believing he was guilty. I was placed in the system. I never got to speak with Carrie Williamson. I was removed from my home and placed in foster care. Three months after my father was killed in prison, I was adopted by a wonderful couple from Indiana. I was polite and courteous. I followed their rules and did my chores. I genuinely believe they loved me as though I were their own daughter. In fact, I believe they still do. The problem wasn't them; it was me. When you took away my father, something inside me died. I no longer cared. I couldn't love. It was rare when I felt anything at all. But I was smart. I studied and I learned. I not only learned, I excelled.

"It wasn't until I graduated high school at the age of fifteen when I decided to find Carrie Williamson. I was already enrolled at the University of Michigan by that time. That wonderful couple from Indiana dropped me off at college and got me set up in my dorm. I wasn't an adult yet, but I was on my own. I used some of the petty cash they'd given me to buy a bus ticket to Chicago. I had two weeks before classes started, and I used that time to track down Carrie Williamson. I wanted to apologize to her for what my father had done to her. I thought maybe if I atoned for the sins of my father, I'd be able to care about that wonderful couple that had opened their lives to me and taken me into their home. I thought it might fix what was broken inside of me. It didn't take me long to find Carrie, either. She still lived with her mother in that same apartment complex.

"The instant she saw me, she began to shiver. I was just getting ready to say the words that I'd rehearsed over and over again on the bus ride. I was just getting ready to tell her how sorry I was that my father had done those horrible things to her. Instead, she began to cry. She told me that she needed to talk to me in private. She led me out of that apartment complex and down into the basement of an abandoned building down the street. Once we were alone, she looked me in the eyes and blurted out how sorry she was.

"I was confused, so I kept my mouth shut and just listened. I was hoping to find out why she was apologizing to me when the courts said it was my father who'd committed crimes against her. That's when she spilled it all ... having sex with her eighteen-year-old boyfriend, being terrified that he'd go to prison ... how much trouble she'd be in with her mother. She rambled on for fifteen minutes.

"I listened to it all. My mind was reeling but still, I didn't really feel anything. I wasn't angry. I wasn't hurt. I wasn't upset at the injustice that my father had been dealt. I was simply cold. Empty. But I knew that I had to get proof. The system failed, and I needed to clear my father's name. I handed her a piece of paper and an ink pen and asked her to write down what she'd done.

"To my surprise, she actually did. She wrote it all out and even signed it. I read that paper and was just getting ready to walk away from her when she said, 'I don't deserve your forgiveness. I deserve to die for what I did to you and your father', and something clicked in my head. She was right. She did deserve to die for what she'd done. After all, my father had died and he'd done nothing wrong. It was only fair.

"I began to talk to her in a soothing tone. I motioned to an area where we could sit down. As she turned, I reached down and grabbed a broken bottle from the floor. I concealed it in my hand and followed her over to a corner that had a few wooden crates. She sat down and completely lost it. She was bawling her eyes out. I was telling her that it was all going to be okay and brushing her hair back in a comforting motion while she was crying on my shoulder.

"Finally, I had her exactly where I wanted her. I reached up with that broken piece of glass and slammed it into her neck. Then I dragged it as hard as I could all the way across the front of her throat. She reached up and grabbed a hold of the wound and stared at me with those huge eyes. I continued to brush her hair with one hand while I held her hands in place with the other so that she couldn't grab hold of me. We stayed like that for several minutes as she got calmer and calmer. I looked into those huge eyes and watched as they began to dim. I watched as the light that was her life faded from her eyes.

"Once I knew she was dead, I wiped off what blood I could and cleaned myself up. I then took the note she'd written and placed it on a crate next to her. I found a place in Chicago where I could sleep, and I checked the newspapers every day. Finally, after six days, I found a small article in the obituary section:

"Sixteen year old found dead of self-inflicted wound. The deceased had been molested when she was twelve and never recovered from that attack. Her mother had placed her in several types of counseling sessions and believed she was finally beginning to get better. Her name is being withheld out of respect for her family and the torment she suffered. May she finally find the peace in death that eluded her in life."

"I read that article so many times that it's burned into my brain. I'll probably never forget a word of it. I still had questions though. What about her confession? Why was there no mention of the note left next to her that described how she had wrongly accused a single father of a violent crime that eventually led to his death? There was nothing about it at all!

"I returned to the University of Michigan and began my studies. The whole time, I kept digging, trying to find out why there was no mention of the note that was left right next to her body. I also began to analyze myself based on what I was learning at the university. This eventually led to my majoring in psychology. By the time I was sixteen, I had determined that I had a few mental disorders. I won't go into detail about each one, but my primary issue was a complete lack of empathy for others. I remembered what it was like to love my father, to care about how his day went, to want to brighten his mood when he was tired or down. I just couldn't bring back the ability to feel that again. At some point I began to question whether or not I really had those feelings to begin with. Maybe I never really did. Maybe I was just acting the part that was expected of me. To this day, I have no idea if I was born this way or if you, Carrie and the

Chicago justice system made me this way. Either way, I diagnosed myself as a sociopath.

"By the time I turned eighteen, I had earned a couple of degrees. I used that knowledge and the resources of the university and eventually found out that the captain of the Chicago police department, your captain, had been presented with her confession. By that time, you were already a rising star and destined to be King Midas. Through the sources I'd cultivated in the Chicago police department, I learned that your captain buried that confession so it would never see the light of day. He did this just to keep the police department from suffering the persecution of the wrongful arrest and eventual death of an innocent man. I knew then that the world would never know my father was innocent. I also knew that it was up to me to gain retribution for what he'd endured. That path has been a long and winding one. You are only one of the stops along the way. There were others who paid before you, and there are others who have yet to pay.

"And that is the answer to your question. That is why."

Silent tears of empathy continued to roll slowly down Cassidy's cheeks as her story unfolded. He finally managed to choke out the words. "I understand why you came after me … but how can you justify the lives of all the people you murdered here in Denver that had nothing to do with you or your father?"

There was absolutely no hint of anything that could remotely be considered humanity behind her eyes as she offered without any apparent emotion, "Those people were a means to an end. I came here to destroy your life. To take away everything you earned on the back of my father. They were simply tools I needed in order to accomplish my goal."

She then checked her watch and said, "Our time is very nearly up. Because you've earned my respect over the past several weeks, I'll give you a moment if you have anything else you'd like to say?"

Cassidy raised his head and looked directly into her eyes. "Yes. I am truly sorry if I was part of the reason that you became the monster that sits before me. Had I known any of this back then, I swear I would have done everything I could have to prevent the injustice that your father suffered. Stacey, I forgive you."

She nodded and replied calmly, "Thank you. This has been a very enlightening chat." Then Stacey raised his pistol and fired a single shot.

As she climbed out of the hole she'd dug, she removed the latex gloves she had been wearing and packed them into a fresh Ziploc bag. She then pulled out another pair and slid her hands into them. After being sure her hair was tightly secured and her hat in place, Stacey verified that the possibility of leaving any trace evidence was minimal. Then she climbed behind the wheel of Quinn's shiny red Porsche and listened to the purr of the engine as it sprang to life.

"This sure is a nice car. Maybe they'll let me buy it once Quinn's trial is over and they don't need it for evidence anymore," she speculated optimistically.

She was whistling an upbeat tune as she looped the car around and followed her own tracks back out to the trail.